The New Beginning

DAPHANIE CAROL TAYLOR

authorHOUSE®

AuthorHouse™ UK
1663 Liberty Drive
Bloomington, IN 47403 USA
www.authorhouse.co.uk
Phone: 0800.197.4150

Published by AuthorHouse 09/28/2016

ISBN: 978-1-5246-3600-5 (sc)
ISBN: 978-1-5246-3601-2 (hc)
ISBN: 978-1-5246-3599-2 (e)

Library of Congress Control Number: 2016916110

Print information available on the last page.

CHAPTER ONE

In 1937 four friends venture out on an epic eventful journey to Australia, which in those days was considered very daring indeed, each had to be 21 years of age or over and single, two of friends had no prospects whatsoever, a chance meeting in Oldham Market in Lancashire with Cynthia Boardman led to the four of them to apply to go to Australia where new machinery was being installed in a cotton mill, Cynthia, had read an advert in the Oldham Chronicle detailing that women and men with cotton mill experience were wanted to travel to a place called Melbourne in Australia to teach the locals how to use new machinery which hand installed at the mill, all applicants would require interviews as well as birth certificates, and other necessary documents.

Mary one of the friends, was very streetwise, her parents had died at an early age, leaving Mary to tender for herself, she had to work things out, for her reading was a great escape, a bit of a romantic really would read love stories all day long, she also read constantly to glean as much knowledge and information as possible, to help with her education, like all girls at that age she had aspirations, and would imagine and daydream of another world somewhere out there, could this be her big opportunity, to finally realise her burning ambition to escape the humdrum life that she knew.

After various appointments and interviews, they were all accepted along with other girls and boys to teach their skills to the Australian workers, passage and expenses would be met by the owners of the Mill, their wage would be £3.00 a week which was good pay in those days for mill workers, a list of accommodation would be available for them to peruse, it was a three-year contract after that they would be free agents. Mary knew quite a few girls either by sight or even closer by friendship, especially three of them in particular, Cynthia, Kathy, Maggie, then also Jenny, Bridget, Sara, and also Margaret, "How do you know all these other girls?" asked Cynthia, "I went to all the dancing halls in Oldham and Rochdale was Mary's reply, not a wall-flower then, thought Cynthia with a wry smile.

Cynthia was the charismatic one knew her own mind clever, articulate, grammar school educated had high expectations very ambitious. Maggie was the quite one till roused, up till now had lead a normal insular life with her parents well educated in secretarial work, her father wanted her to see the world and open her horizons to the outside world. Kathy was the timid one had an awful upbringing, with very little educational skills, but a caring and a thoughtful person she just wanted to escape from the poverty and her father and brothers.

Finally, the day came to set sail, a coach was waiting to take them down to Tilbury Docks London, everyone was in a buoyant mood, laughing and joking, the lads especially were particular irritating with the girls, for Mary excitement, filled the air as they all boarded the P & O liner Strathaird, everyone in their own thoughts now and expectations. As the ship moved slowly out of Tilbury docks, Mary was struck with a sudden panic and apprehension, what would the future really hold for me, she thought to herself, everyone was already aware of talk of a war with Germany, and here she was sailing to the other side of the world, leaving behind some friends and a boyfriend, in particular, who she was madly in love with, but he had signed up to join the RAF, to her annoyance and it meant she was left high and dry and was feeling very hurt indeed, she thought that he loved her as she did him, that was the reason she made the decision to sail 11.000 miles to Australia, it was just let him know that what he could do, so could she do too, little did she know then, that her decision to leave England would have a profound impact on her life.

The cabins were adequate that's all you could say, everything was in pristine condition, being a brand new ship, Mary, Cynthia, Maggie and Kathy, begged the steward for a cabin for the four of them to stay together, which they managed to do, some girls said.

"How did you manage to stay together we have all been separated." Said one girl.

Cynthia replied, "Mary gave him the biggest kiss you've have ever seen", it wasn't true of course, everyone thought it was funny.

Later on Maggie suggested they look at the information pack that had been provided detailing procedures, information on the dining room/ballroom, times of meals, nearest stairway to their cabins, and instructions in case of a fire etc., blimey that's a lot to think about Mary thought.

The girls chatted for ages between themselves excitement filled the air, they talked about their expectations of what the future might hold, they made a pact to stay friends and to help each other out if any of them needed support, "Like the Four musketeers" chirped Kathy, everyone smiled at each other, suddenly Mary yawned, "I feel so sleepy, I think I will rest now", they all settled down it wasn't too long before everyone was fast asleep.

Mary woke up first and wondered what time is was, she went out to look for a steward, but none could be found, so she then decided to have a look around the ship trying to find her way about their part of the ship but got completely lost, 'Oh! Crumbs! Mary said, and started to panic, suddenly a voice said, "What are you doing here? "I'm lost". Said Mary. Then she looked and saw a very handsome man in an officer's uniform it had stripes on the sleeves, but Mary had no idea who he was.

"You're heading for first class, young lady, what cabin number are you"? "I don't know" was Mary's reply.

Mary blushed, she was usually more organised than this, He'll think I'm stupid, she thought to herself. "Are you with the group from Oldham"? Mary answered, "Yes. "Come I'll show you the way, and pay attention", the officer said.

He spoke to her as though she was three years of age Mary was indignant, pompous git she muttered under her breath. "There you are, straight down the stairs and turn right".

Mary didn't say thank-you, she was furious, she opened the cabin door, "Where have you been"? asked the girls you have been gone for ages, we began to worry about you. Mary told them what had happened and how the officer had treated her, and what, a pompous git he was a right old snob if ever I saw one, Cynthia was bemused.

'Gosh'. Said Maggie, 'What kind of officer was he?

"I don't bloody well know" Mary yelled back, temper, temper now Mary, everyone started to laugh, except Mary of course.

The trip to Australia seemed endless, everyone was so fed up and bored on the ship, there was only so many times you could walk around the deck, or sunbathe, go swimming, read, or play games, there was of course the occasional tea dance to break the monotony, some people were terribly sea-sick and others just wanted get off the ship all together, then suddenly someone shouted.

"I can see land is it Australia"?

"Hooray where here at last." Another said.

"No you are not in Australia just yet," said the steward, he said, it is Ceylon, we will be docking here for a couple of days.

"Will we be able to get off', asked one of the girls.

The steward had a wry smile on his face, "Of course you will".

Thank god for that Mary thought, an anticipation swept through the ship, as they drew closer to shore, the place looked absolutely beautiful it was very exotic, with its Palm trees, lovely white sandy beaches just like you see at the pictures and very humid, the markets stalls were fascinating especially to Mary, everything was so colourful and interesting. The two days went pretty quickly, soon it was full steam ahead for Australia. "How much further steward"? Asked one girl'. We have another three weeks of sailing yet, the steward replied. She groaned, "That long". It had taken her quite some time to walk properly in Ceylon being on the ship for so long it had played havoc with her balance.

Mary decided to make the most of what there was on offer on the ship, and made every effort to enjoy herself, along with her friends, time soon passed, and before they knew it they could see land this time it was Australia, not long now thought Mary, her heart beating faster with enthusiasm the other girls were also eagerly waiting to land in Australia, not long now said of the girls, "Bloody hell girls we'll be at least two more days", said the steward, their hearts sank, so near yet so far one girl said. At last they reached Australia, the ship edged into the docks with the help of tug boats, the ship's crew were busier than ever, everyone was rushing around, then they heard, "This is your Captain speaking, we will be embarking in about twenty minutes first class passengers too de-embark first, then second class I expect everyone to leave in an orderly manner, will all passengers have their passports and documents ready". It seemed ages to get through customs, the custom officers asked lots of questions, some quite silly Mary thought, however the group eventually were allowed into Australia, "What a load of bunkum that was". Said one girl, another one said, "They talk funny don't they".

"Come on everyone we haven't got all day", the chaperone said, the coach had arrived to take them to the Mill, they all clambered onto the coach, everyone feeling exhausted by this time, each in their own thoughts once again, travelling along the roads, the sun catching their eyes through white fluffy clouds, dotted here and there, everything seemed so clean and bright, thought Mary, suddenly the coach stopped "Here we are, follow me", they all scrambled off the coach this time, collecting their suitcases, their cases seemed much heavier than they remembered to some of the girls. "What have you got in there"? The driver asked "A bloody body". Someone yelled, then they entered the mill, everyone was surprised, it didn't look like a mill at all on the outside, well at least, not like the ones in Oldham Mary had always thought the mills looked satanic for some reason in Oldham towering above all the other buildings around, looking down on the poor unfortunates who had to work in them.

They were ushered into a large room, each was given a pack with information about the mill where to find their various work places, such as spinning room, ring room, weaving room etc. The company wished them all a very warm welcome, and hoped they would settle in to their new surroundings quite quickly, each had a list of accommodation for them to go and look at with differing rents to pay depending on which area they choose to live, obviously the nearer the Mill the cheaper the rent, and the name and address of the letting agents. Cynthia obviously took control of the accommodation looking at various properties, she was impressed at the thoroughness of the Mill owners.

"Look girls, I and Maggie would love you to share a house with us",

Mary looked at Kathy.

"We can't afford anything near the rents of these properties your looking at". Said Mary.

"No need to worry about that at the moment we can sort something out later", said Cynthia.

"Well if you are sure you want two lowly paid mill girls to share with you great", was Mary's reply, Kathy just nodded in approval.

"You two stay here while Maggie and I go and sort things out", said Cynthia.

By this time Mary was feeling extremely tired, Kathy too,

"I wish they'd hurry up I'm falling asleep here", said Kathy, it wasn't too long before they returned, Maggie shaking the keys,

"We have chosen a lovey house to rent", said Maggie.

Mary said, "Let's get going",

They soon reached the house it looked lovely with a little veranda at the front facing a park except it wasn't the house Mary thought they were going to live in,

"What about the other house too work", asked Mary?

"This is more suitable for our needs Mary" Cynthia replied, Maggie just shrugged her shoulders,

"I see" said Mary.

They entered so eagerly they nearly fell in, they had a good look around, it had a large kitchen/diner, a large parlour room, upstairs was a bathroom and three bedrooms, the two largest bedrooms being on the front. "Bags this one. "Cynthia said, she would have thought Mary, Maggie had the second largest bedroom which left the other bedroom for Mary and Kathy to share. Cynthia gathered everyone around. "Look girls." Maggie and I have been thinking, we know this house is more expensive to rent, we hope you are not offended, but we have decided that you should only pay half the rent, and Maggie and I will pay the other half,"

Mary looked at them in amazement, and said That's very generous of you both but we couldn't possibly accept your generous offer, we want to pay our way.

Kathy was in agreement, Cynthia was adamant,

"You'll do no such thing, you will pay half between you, Maggie and I are happy to do it". (unknown to Mary and Kathy at the time they were each receiving an allowance from their father's).

Kathy then said, "Well if you are sure", Mary then went along with Kathy.

All too soon the week was over, it was Monday morning, Kathy and Mary were up first, seven o'clock start for them they were scrambling all over the place getting ready, they had no time for breakfast. Cynthia and Maggie had a more civilised time 9.00 am start, which meant they could take their time, no grafting for them, they had acquired office work at the Mill, thanks to Cynthia's father.

It was now nearing the end of 1938, and although Christmas and New Year was approaching, their thoughts were focused on the prospect of war looming in Europe, particular for them in England, Cynthia's letters were full of stories, for preparation of war, Cynthia's two brothers, wanted to enlist, but their father was adamant that they should wait, and not be too eager. Much to the disappointment of her elder Brother Andrew, and her younger brother James, who wanted to join the RAF and thought it would be jolly good fun, Cynthia worries about her father and mother, she writes home on a monthly basis, still hoping that the war is just talk. Cynthia's father has a thriving lorry business in Oldham, and was worried that if the boys left, dad would have to run the business by himself, after all she had a lot to thank her dad for, firstly for allowing his only daughter to travel half way around the world, and secondly securing office work for them at the mill, both her and Maggie had secretarial experience, of course Cynthia was very well educated in the job she would be doing, but it suited her for the time being.

Maggie, was also worried about her Mum and Dad she was an only child and was pampered by her possessive mother, her father was only too pleased to sign the necessary paperwork for Maggie to travel with Cynthia to Australia, Maggie's parents were a well to do family, her father owned a coal merchant business, he was also a freemason, and soon to become Mayor of Oldham. Maggie's mother just cried and cried when she found out her only daughter was leaving to go to the other side of the world, "What will become of her sobbing uncontrollably," A lot better than you", her husband retorted.

Kathy came from a large Irish family, she was the only girl, her mother died in childbirth, Kathy was expected to take over the running of the house, her father was a drunken lout, her brothers were bully's, except for Christopher, who had a kind nature like Kathy, they got on well together, they couldn't wait to get away, as soon as they became twenty-one, Christopher had another year to wait. Reading the Oldham Chronical gave her importance to go for it and apply, Kathy had all her mail sent to Maggie's house as her brothers worked for Maggie's father, he knew her circumstances, Kathy later heard that Christopher had somehow managed to get away, he had joined the Royal Navy.

Mary had no misgivings at all, perhaps just a tinge for the boy she wanted to marry, but she soon moved on, she was completely on her own, with no-one to answer too, of course she kept these thoughts to herself, and showed sympathy to the others.

Christmas was upon them, and thoughts of war were put on hold, the air was full of excitement and cheer, shops where busy selling their wares, the pubs where all decorated out, ready for a bumper few days trading, shops closed on Saturday at 1.00pm pubs closed promptly at 6.00pm no Sunday trading whatsoever. Of course everyone had other ideas, it was no secret that drinking went onto the early hours of the mornings on many occasion, there was always house parties to go to, and if on a Sunday you fancied a drink, you would go out into the suburbs not many miles from town, there was always ways and means to overcome the restrictions. It didn't take long before Christmas came and went, the girls had had a great time their thoughts were on England now, with more doom and gloom, in the newspapers, the movies were a form of escapism for everyone, but even the Pathe News didn't help to take their minds off the deepening threat of war. Eventually the movie started and, soon everyone was engrossed in the film, it was Saratoga, with Clark Gable and Jean Harlow. Cynthia and Mary were avid movie goers.

CHAPTER TWO

Deep down Mary was the romantic, and dreamed of being swept off her feet by a tall handsome stranger, little did she know, that the road was not that far away, with dire consequences, Cynthia, however, was more level headed, she knew exactly what she was looking for in a man, compatibility, and a sense of humour, love would come later. "Come on girls" said one of them," Get a move on we'll miss the Party and fireworks". They were going to Pete's place, for the party he lived in the Brunswick area, not too far away, it was a Jacob's supper, and of course drinks, then later fireworks to celebrate the New Year 1939 little did anyone know how their lives would change that night for ever.

They were all having a great time, when they noticed time was getting on, Kathy was nowhere to be seen, where could she be they asked themselves, Mary suggested they split up to look for her, there were bodies everywhere.

"I'll go upstairs", said Maggie, and ran up the stairs, she soon came down,

"She's not upstairs,"

"Are you sure?", asked Mary,

she is not upstairs", Maggie repeated,

"are you certain? asked Mary. "I thought I saw her go up there with a guy,"

Mary ran up the stairs, a young man brushed passed her, and nearly knocked her down the stairs. "Watch it she yelled",

He didn't even look around, at Mary, "Catch that man! Mary yelled he's up to no good. Mary was becoming frantic by this time, she had a sixth sense that something was wrong, but the other two, where too far gone to notice anything.

"Where are you Kathy" Mary yelled at the top of her voice, a bloke came to a door, "Go home Sheila, we're trying to sleep here", "Have you seen a young girl in her late twenties", Mary asked.

"No I have bloody haven't", then he slammed the door in Mary's face.

By this time Mary was getting very anxious, Mary shouted for Kathy again, "Where are you"? Mary, suddenly heard a voice saying, "Here I am". 'Where?" asked Mary, by now Mary was extremely anxious?

God she sounds so weak, Mary thought, Mary then decided to knock on every door till she found her, the pub only had half a dozen rooms, so Mary tried them all and got load of abuse, one man in particular who was extremely vulgar to her, '" And the same to you, arse-hole". Mary said.

By this time everyone was out on the veranda, "What's going on"? Someone shouted.

"I can't find my friend", said Mary, nearly in tears, she then noticed one of the bedroom doors was still closed, she went to open the door.

'Oh' "my God, get an ambulance, Call the police", Kathy had been brutally beaten up, "Oh! Kathy what has he done to you", Mary cradled her in her arms, 'We'll get him I promise'. Said Mary.

The Police and ambulance arrived, Mary showed them where to go, by this time everyone had sobered up, including Maggie and Cynthia," Oh' Mary, we feel dreadful, you poor thing having to cope with this on your own" Cynthia said," I am sorry too", Maggie said sobbing uncontrollably, Mary was in too much of a daze to speak, the stretcher was carried down the stairs gently, "Where are you taking her", asked Cynthia, Carlton Women's Hospital was the reply.

'Err excuse me Miss", Mary turned around it was a policeman, "My name is Inspector Howard, I need to ask you a few questions",

Oh', can't it wait, I'm exhausted" Mary said, '" Here you are Miss a nice cup of tea", "Thank you officer" Mary replied. The questions seemed endless, would she recognise him, could she describe him, Mary said she would recognise him, in fact she would never forget him. After answering all the questions, Inspector Howard said to Mary," We may need to interview you again, Mary just nodded. Oh', Mary," 'We've been waiting ages", the girls said, to her, they were given a lift by home by the police back to Albert Street, it didn't take long to arrive, nobody said a word they all just went off to bed, Mary looked at the clock it was 5.30am it was New Year's Day, I will never forget, what a night to bring in a New Year she said to herself.

Suddenly, there was a loud knock on the door, Cynthia jumped out of bed, and opened the window there was an elderly man standing there he said. you should all be in work, Cynthia raced down the stairs, the man repeated himself, you should all be in work today, you don't have New Year's Day off, it's a working day, I've come to pick you all up. Cynthia explained to him the circumstances and how they had only got home at 5.30am that morning. you can verify it with police if needs be, I don't think any of us will be back for the next few days.

"I'll pass the message on, sorry for your troubles Miss", then left.

"Who was that about? Asked Maggie,

"A chap from the Mill wanting to know where we are" replied Cynthia,

it was completely alien to Maggie and Cynthia to have to work on New Year's Day,

"The sooner my contracts end I'm off" said Cynthia,

"Me too", chirped Maggie.

It was mid-afternoon before Mary surfaced, her face was ashen, and "Can I get you a cup of tea? Maggie asked, Mary just nodded. "Any news?" asked Mary, no! they both said at once," Do you think we could go and see her" asked Maggie, "I don't see why not", Mary snapped, she had been gravely shocked by what she had seen, "Then we shall all go and visit her, after all we are the only family she has", said Cynthia.

They trundled off to the Women's Hospital for 6.30pm visiting time and went to the information desk, "What room is Kathy O'Brien in?" the girls asked,

"Just a minute", the nurse went away,

"Follow me" the nurse said, a man came through the door dressed in a white coat. Mary groaned, 'Oh please God don't let her die", "I'm sorry ladies' relatives only," the man said, at this Cynthia jumped up, "Excuse me!", we are family, were the only ones she has,

I don't quite understand", said the man, they explained the situation to him, "Well I will see what I can do", then he went away.

It seemed ages, Mary was becoming more pessimistic with each minute suddenly the door opened, "I'm Doctor Reid", the patient is not allowed any visitors at the moment, she has not regained consciousness", said the Doctor," When can we come and visit her they all shouted just get in touch with the hospital, was the reply, desk, they all left in their own thoughts, if only we had kept an eye on her, Mary thought, she felt so guilty knowing how vulnerable and naïve Kathy was days passed with no further news, other than she is improving, we will let you know,

"Well that's it", said Cynthia, we simply have to get back to our own lives, we have done all we can", Mary and Maggie both agreed.

By this time the week was nearly over, they decided to take the Christmas decorations down, and then decided to go out for a meal and indulge themselves, they choose to go to their favourite place on Lyon Street, Maggie wanted to treat Mary, but Mary was adamant and said, "Let's go Dutch". After a super meal it was getting late so they walked back, the trams had stopped, they passed Flinders Street Station, it was beautiful building, one of Melbourne's most iconic Building, it is in fact a Railway Station, noted for its clocks showing time zones from all around the world, they walked soon they were approaching Fitzroy Gardens, not long now we'll soon be home thought Mary. No-one mentioned Kathy for fear of feeling guilty, everyone said, Goodnight.

The next day Maggie suggested they go to St Kilda's, catch the early tram take bathers, have a picnic and go to Lunar Park then rummage around the market stalls, "What a smashing idea" said Mary, "It will take our minds off things",

"We hope" said Cynthia, it took several weeks for Kathy to recover, not only had she been beaten so badly, but also raped repeatedly, Kathy, and would never be able to have children, that came to be a great shock to her, but somehow relieved, she confided in Mary, that she would be alright, and that marriage would probably never be an issue with her.

Kathy told Mary, that in a way she was never really been attracted to men in that way, she enjoyed men's company as long as they were at arm's length, whether it was her upbringing, her father or her brothers, she wasn't sure, watching her mother fade away with all the childbearing she endured, had a great impact on her. Mary had great intuition and noticed from a very early stage that Kathy was happier surrounded by women and girls, and listened intently to the tales the girls got up too on a Monday morning, some of the stories were very eventful.

Like the time when three or four of the workers went out into the outback on the back of a milk float,

Come on girls you'll have it dark, they all set off it took about half an hour to get there, when they arrived the party was in full swing, "What're having darling," "Beer please", said the girl, "blimey! A bloody Pom", "Less of that your Aussie git", He just laughed.

They were having such a great time that no-one noticed the actual time, suddenly, Jake whose milk float it was', 'Come-on we've got to get back, my dad will kill me, I should be delivering milk", "Why what time is it?", asked one of the lads who came with Jake," It's 4.00am", 'Oh, no' we have been at work at seven' said Pete, "Get the girls, where the bloody hell are they?" Jake found Jean half cut in a haystack. Jake threw her on the float, there wasn't a murmur form Suzy, she was well gone, "Give us a lift Jake into town", a couple of lads asked, 'OK', hop on, but no more", they set off like a bat out of hell, Jake was like a madman, everyone was holding onto something for dear life, "Steady on mate" someone shouted, it fell on deaf ears,

"Stop! Stop! yelled somebody's, somebody's fell off", "Any of the girls"? No! "Then he can walk", said Jake.

By this time everyone was sobering up, except Suzy, they reached Carlton, it was 5.00am, "My Pa will skin me alive, hurry up get off", he dumped them all, the other guys helped with Suzy. Where you live love "said one of the lads", not that far, we'll take her from here, said Pete, with that they all went their own way Suzy never made it to work that day.

After Kathy's release from hospital, she was never the quite the same, she never returned to the house, instead she moved in with a woman probably early thirties called Edwina, a striking woman, tall slim and attractive in her own way, was dressed in jeans white T shirt, and casual shoes. The girls were upset to see her go, and didn't have an inkling as to why she had made the decision to leave them, of course Mary had an idea, "Goodbye Mary", Kathy through her arms around Mary, and whispered, thanks for everything, Mary just nodded, "Just keep in touch Kathy", said Cynthia, Mary just knew Kathy wouldn't, they watched her slowly drive away, they were all tinged with a little sadness for they had all very fond of Kathy

By this time, it was getting to the end of August 1939 it seemed war was imminent in England, with Germany marching into Poland, which put great pressure on the then Prime Minister of England, all this was gleaned by Pathe News, and of course, Australian broadcasting, it was very depressing for most of the mill workers, some were relieved that they were in Australia, and others were worried about their families. That night when Cynthia got home, "Fancy the pictures tonight Mary", asked Cynthia, "Can I come too chirped Maggie, I need cheering up what's on?" Mary said, "Well I'm not really in the mood tonight", "That makes a change" Cynthia said, Mary just smiled, she was still worried about Kathy she had her suspicions, about this Edwina there was something about her that Mary didn't like, "We can still go can't we? Asked Maggie, "Of course," Cynthia replied.

After their meal, Mary went upstairs, "I think I'll have a bath and an early night", "Fine we'll see you later", with that the two girls set off to the pictures, it didn't take long to reach the picture house, the film was 'Too Hot to Handle' with Clark Gable and Myrna Loy, 'Great!', Said Cynthia, 'I just love Clark Gable's films'. Maggie just looked at her with a wistful smile. "That was a great film Cynthia, I really enjoyed it", Maggie said, soon they were home, it was 9.30pm by this time, "Cuppa" Maggie" said, "No thanks I'm off to bed", 'Goodnight Maggie', said Cynthia then went upstairs, in a thoughtful mood.

September arrived, by this time the weather was getting that bit warmer, spring was just around the corner, everyone was in an optimistic mood, knowing that summer was not that far off, and the lovely warm weather was something that everyone looked forward too. Although the girls were fully acclimatised to the Australian way of life, one thing they couldn't get their heads around was, it was usually dark by 8.30pm.

Maggie was full of the joys of spring, she had met this lad called Joe, he was visiting Melbourne on business for his father, they were wine growers in the Margret River area of Perth, Maggie listened intently to his waffling on, she had absolutely no idea what he was talking about, all she knew that wine was in a bottle, she agreed to see him on Saturday under the clocks of Flinders St Station at 11.00am.

The week was endless for Maggie, she couldn't wait to see Joe again, and then she could tell him about how she ended up here in Australia Friday night couldn't come soon enough, Maggie was running around like a scolded cock. "Whatever is the matter'? Asked Cynthia in an irritating voice, "I'm seeing Joe tomorrow at eleven, I must look my best", replied Maggie, "My God!! It is only 8.00pm, how much time do you need" Cynthia said, 'Oh' shut up Cynthia, "Leave me alone" said Maggie, with that outburst all went quiet, Mary said, "Blimey you've got it bad Maggie", they all burst out laughing. "Do you fancy window-shopping on Collins Street tomorrow" asked Mary to Cynthia, "Why not we could have something to eat at one of cafes said Cynthia, the night went very peaceful after that, Maggie was humming away to herself, which bemused the other two," I think

I go upstairs", Mary said to Cynthia, "I won't be too long myself Goodnight" Maggie", they both said, Maggie had her head in the clouds and never heard a word.

It was now Saturday morning, they all had breakfast, "What time are you meeting up with this Joe" asked Cynthia, Maggie said in an exasperated voice," I told you last night Cynthia" at 11.00am Finders Street! "Just checking" Cynthia said with a grin, Cynthia liked to wind Maggie up, it bemused her, at times Cynthia had a wrapped sense of humour at times, Mary thought. It was now time to leave they all left together to go into the city, chattering as they usually did, they soon reached Flinders Street, they waved Maggie goodbye" Best of luck, hope he's waiting for you" Mary shouted, Maggie never even looked back. "Let's take a peek at him" and see what he's like" said Mary, which they did.

Maggie was waiting patiently, it was well passed eleven, goodness, I hope he shows up, Maggie was getting more anxious every minute then suddenly from nowhere, a voice said "Here I am, I got lost, sorry I'm late I'm usually a very punctual person", Maggie felt a sigh of relieve, "I knew you would come, that's why I hung around, I just knew you wouldn't let me down", he gently kissed her on her cheek, "What a great girl you are, shall we marry now", said Joe, they strolled off together arm in arm. Cynthia and Mary were taken aback by his gentleness and respect for Maggie, Mary said," I think we are going to lose another housemate", then they strolled arm in arm to window gaze. The day went pretty quickly, soon it was evening, "What shall we do next, fancy a drink", said Mary, "We might catch the last hour", replied Cynthia, "Come on let's hurry", they popped into the Irish bar, everyone was talking about war," I wish they wouldn't keep talking of war, it's beginning to get on my nerves, that's all we hear about," said Cynthia, Mary agreed, soon the bell went for time up.

Everyone piled out, some fell out, one or two put their arms around the girl's waist, take you home darling, "No thank you" Cynthia retorted, "Come on darling I'll show you a good time" said another, suddenly Mary started belting one of the men with her handbag, "Clear off your oaf, who want's you", and with that they hurried back to the house, they clambered into the house laughing and giggling," Buffoons" said Mary," Cuppa, asked Cynthia," Yes please", Mary replied.

Mary then turned on the radio, they both sat down to listen to the music once more in their own thoughts, Mary thinking of Kathy and how she missed her, and Cynthia who knows what she was thinking. Suddenly the door swung open and there stood Maggie, thinking she had met Mr Right, "How did it go?", girls asked, she looked at them, "He is the most handsome man I have ever seen he's lovely, I think I will Marry this one" Mary and Cynthia just looked at one another and smiled.

All of a sudden the radio programme was interrupted, it was an announcement, that England was at war with Germany, the girls just looked at one another in disbelieve, 'Oh' my God' Mary screamed, Cynthia was numbed, she couldn't speak, all she could think of was her mother and father and brothers. Their thoughts were interrupted by Maggie, "Did you hear that" they both nodded, they all just looked at one another," Crumbs I hope Mum and Dad will be alright" cried Maggie, "I'm sure they will be", said Cynthia in a commanding way, Mary in a way felt sorry for them both, as she had no one to worry about, a little later they all retired to bed, no one spoke, when morning came, had they all been dreaming about last night thought Mary, the others were still asleep, she crept downstairs, and opened up the curtains, it was a lovely sunny day. someone in England.

CHAPTER THREE

Cynthia and Maggie trudge downstairs still in their dressing gowns, the house was sombre, no one spoke, Mary was dressed," I'll go and get a paper" Mary said, and off, soon she was back with The Argus, it was full of news, how England had run out of patience with Germany, and that a state off war had been declared on Germany at 11.00am September 3rd 1939, again everyone was silent. Some time passed, then Mary jumped up and said, "Well that's it, after Christmas I am leaving the Mill, I want to do something else, I didn't come all this way, to be a mill worker all my life", "Well said", Cynthia cried, "What would you like to do", Maggie asked, "Work in a high class store like George's" Mary replied, Cynthia was excited for Mary," I'll work on those hands of yours starting tomorrow" said Maggie, Cynthia and Maggie were now planning how to help Mary, they both could help her in different ways, as, Mary had no idea about gracious skills whatsoever, she had never really been taught.

Time was moving on and nearing Christmas again, the girls had other things to contend with, life would never be quite the same now that England was at war, each had their own different points of view and outlook, Maggie was now head over heels in love with Joe, she was fully enthralled with him, couldn't stop talking about him, "'Oh' for heaven's sake Maggie give it a rest", said Cynthia, Maggie was very upset at her remarks, Mary could see this, "That's a bit harsh Cynthia", said Mary, "Sorry", Maggie, I have things on my mind," said Cynthia. Maggie left the room, when she had gone, Mary asked Cynthia what was wrong, "Nothing's wrong, I'm just fed up, with my job, I need a change, I'm like you, I want to do something different with my life, I want excitement, I'm over qualified for the job I am doing, it irritates me no end, I'm going to give my notice in, but it will a months' notice for me", "Flipping heck" said Mary that's a long time. I'm thinking of going into the Civil Service, it pays well and gives you security, especially now, did you know I can speak German and French fluently, well I could, if I don't do something about it, I will lose it", said Cynthia, Mary knew she was clever, but didn't know just how cleaver she was, "Good for you, perhaps 1940 will be a good year for us all," said Mary

Even though Europe was at war, nothing seemed to change much in Australia, except large numbers of men had decided to go and fight in Europe, to help England's cause, some of men from the Mill returned to England to help with the war effort. Mary and the others were just going about their business waiting for the New Year to arrive, all of them where at crossroads now, and nothing would ever be quite the same again. Christmas arrived once again, everyone made the most of it, despite the horrible events in Europe, the girls had their own agendas to fulfil, Maggie inevitable marriage to Joe, who was now back in Perth and corresponding with her on a regular basis, and vice versa, Cynthia was revising her linguistics prowess and Mary was just looking forward to leaving the mill.

A week later it was New Year's Eve the girls had been invited to a party in Carlton, which they eagerly accepted, they all knew that perhaps this might be the last time that they would share a New Year's Eve party together, I hope it turns out better than last year, thought Mary.

No one mentioned anything about last Year's Party they seemed oblivious to what had gone on, then Cynthia said "I do hope it's turns out better than last New Year's Eve", Mary smiled to herself, no they hadn't forgotten. When they arrived at the House Party, everyone was laughing and smiling, and having a jolly good time, it was as though everyone just wanted to forget about the war in Europe, and just enjoy themselves for one night at least. It was now 1940 Europe was now well into the war with Germany, many Australian's enlisted to go and fight in Europe, Robert Menzies didn't stop anyone, who wanted to help the England's cause, there was a very strong bond with England, some say, that Australia is still attached to the umbilical cord and it always will be.

As promised Cynthia took charge of Mary, groomed her as much as she could, Maggie worked on her hands, to Mary it was lovely being pampered like this, the girls were becoming more like sisters to her, and she was fiercely protected about them. "Can I have a chat Cynthia" said Mary, "Of course" Cynthia replied, "Do you think I am ready to apply now for George's, "Mary asked, "I should think so Mary, you have done well, I am sure you will end up working at George's," "That's very kind of you Cynthia" said Mary and pecked on her cheek, Cynthia blushed slightly. In a way life just went on, the war in Europe didn't seem to affect them that much, except for the Poms's who had family in England, and of course Maggie and Cynthia, but they had their own dreams and aspirations to follow, Cynthia had now handed her notice in, and was looking daily for a high profile job, she had signed up with an employment agency, Mary was still waiting on news from George's Store about her application and was getting deeply anxious about it all, "Don't fret" said Cynthia "it will come".

Maggie was still writing as much as she could to Joe, but Joe's letters were becoming less frequent, so she was panicking, Cynthia noticed that the two of them were down in the dumps, "Come-on girls let's start dinner, with a lovely bottle of wine, and we can talk", said Cynthia, "Don't talk about wine to me" Maggie shouted out, my she really has it bad thought Mary, the bottle was popped opened, they just sat around still in their own thoughts. Then Cynthia said, "It's like a bloody morgue in here, put the radio on", they sat and chatted, with the radio on," then Cynthia said at, we have come a long way together since we arrived here we've been through some tough times, and also had some jolly good times. You start first Maggie said the girls, "How did you meet Joe", Maggie started to tell them the tale, I was in Collins Street, I was window shopping as usual, looking for presents for Christmas, when I heard this voice," Hello beautiful can I buy you a coffee," I turned around, you mean me" "I do" said the stranger, "I'm new in town, all I want is coffee with you", Maggie jumped at the offer and said she had no thoughts about any consequences that might happen.

He was the most charming and extremely handsome bloke I had ever met, a rugged face, very well built, I fell in love with him at once, he also had lovely blue eyes, it was love at first sight, "I knew I would marry this one" said Maggie, Cynthia said, "Well aren't you the quite one, how could you just go off for a coffee, with a complete stranger", Maggie chirped," I don't know it just seemed the right thing to do". That next week Mary's application finally arrived, and Maggie received a letter from Joe, he would be in Melbourne on Saturday and couldn't wait to see her, we will meet up at Flinders Street, you know where, and I promise you I will not be late, Maggie read the letter over and over again," it's a wonder there's any writing left, "Cynthia said in her usual sarcastic way.

After that the girls hardly ever saw Maggie, Joe was in Melbourne on business for his father, they owned a vineyard in an area called Margret's River, south west of Perth City, according to Maggie his family all lived together on the estate, he has two brothers and one sister, his two brothers were married already, his sister who is the youngest is off to agricultural college, the estate has been in the family for many years, they also breed cattle.

I've always' dreamed of belonging to a big family and quite honestly girls, if he asked to marry him tomorrow I would, I just know he is Mr right for me". Mary jumped up "Good for you" Maggie" "I'm so happy for you", "So I'm I" said Cynthia." time was moving on they decided to call it a night and retired for the night we all have a story to tell thought Mary, I wonder what will be mine. The next day being a Saturday, Cynthia asked if Mary would go to St Kilda's with her, she was in a pensive mood, Mary thought, Cynthia was indeed in a thoughtful mood, she said, have put the house up for rental and bought an apartment in St Kilda's, it doesn't need much work on it, just sprucing up really. Mary agreed to go, (Mary realised from an early start that Cynthia came from a wealthy family,) and that in fact Cynthia owned the house in Albert Street, Mary's thoughts turned to Maggie, and said," What about Maggie"," Oh' there's room for Maggie too, not that she will be needing it" they both giggled.

After lunch they set off to look at the apartment, Mary fell in love with it, it was much larger than Albert Street, it was also facing the sea with a lovely scenic views and also close to the promenade, "Do you think it will be noisy at week-ends Cynthia", asked Mary, "We can always close the windows if needed and besides there are fans in every room which will be very handy in the summer", Cynthia replied," Mary said, It's lovely, what about rent", Cynthia was very cross with her," I've told you not worry about the rent, we will work something out, I don't like repeating myself Mary" "Steady on Cynthia, I just needed to be quite sure about the arrangements for myself" said Mary they made their way back to the house in silence, it was now tea-time, I'll start dinner", Mary said and the ice was broken, Cynthia just smiled, and went upstairs.

They enjoyed their meal, and sat with a couple of beers and talked things over about the apartment, "You can do me a favour Mary would see to things for me, be my dogsbody so to speak, while I finish my notice" "Anything Cynthia just ask", Mary's replied, then they both relaxed, until a whirlwind hit them, it was Maggie out of breath, "Whatever is the matter Maggie" said Mary. "Nothing! I'm getting married, Joe popped the question, and I said" Yes", so soon the girls said, "Yes", I'm going back with him too Perth next week to meet his parents and family, isn't exciting" what the girls failed to understand was that Maggie was an only child, and she'd always yearned for brothers and sisters, she just knew she would be happy with Joe. Well we are overjoyed for you Maggie" said Mary, "Here's a beer Maggie good luck", they sat there for hours just talking, Mary then said "What about your job" I'll just take two weeks off, stuff them!" Cynthia was taken aback," Good for you Maggie that's fighting talk" they just burst out laughing.

On Sunday morning Mary asked Maggie if Joe would like to come to the house, "What a lovely idea, I've talked so much about you both", said Maggie, "Well that's settled, about 2.00pm Maggie, if that's ok and we can have afternoon tea the English way", Maggie flung her arms around Mary, "I'm sure going to miss you, you're the only one with any common sense, Mary was surprised by this remark. "What's this about common sense Cynthia said, as she walked into the lounge," Oh' nothing, I have just asked Maggie to bring Joe for afternoon tea that's all," said Mary, Cynthia just nodded too them and went back upstairs.

They had a smashing time reminiscing about the old days, what they used to get up too, going out to the dance halls in Rochdale and Oldham, looking for someone to dance with and more importantly buy them a drink, of course Cynthia didn't include herself in this conversation, she was well above all that, "I'd better watch my step" said Joe, and they all fell about laughing. "Gosh it's getting late, I got lots to do tomorrow, thanks for a lovely time, it was nice to be able to put names to faces" said Joe, "You can kip on the couch here Joe" said Cynthia, "No thanks I've a room at Hotham's," I'll walk a little way with you" said Maggie.

Well that's it, no need to mention the apartment" Cynthia said, Mary just nodded, they waited for Maggie to return then they all went upstairs together, "We've got a lot to do tomorrow girls" said Cynthia, knowing that this chapter was about to end, and another one about to begin. "The next day Mary didn't wake up till past 9.00am crumbs she thought, I must have been tired out, she raced downstairs only to find a list if thing to do, from Cynthia Mary got herself organised and set about doing the various tasks in the house, after lunch she was about to leave the house when a knock came to the door, who could this be, she asked herself, she opened the door, it was the postman, "Sign here my lovely", he said,

Mary blushed, she duly signed the slip of paper and off he went, the big brown envelope was addressed to her, it was from George's, she just stared at it, oh' bother, I'll wait till Cynthia gets home, and set off to go into town, finally the list was finished, phew this is harder than working, I hope there are no more lists tomorrow, with that thought she set off home, by this time it was 4.00pm. "Hi I'm home Mary", Cynthia said, then opened her mail, and asked about the list, Mary replied she had managed to get everything done, "Good girl, that's saves me a lot of time", Cynthia then, noticed the brown envelope, "What's this" "It's from George's" Mary replied," Will you open it Cynthia, I'm too scared" "Don't be silly Mary," It will be to say you have got an interview". Cynthia opened it for her and screamed, "You've got it you've got it", "Got what" asked Mary, "The bloody interview of course", was Cynthia's reply, and they just jumped up and down with excitement." Oh' I'm so pleased for you Mary you have worked so hard with your speech, and deportment," "Don't forget the nails," Mary said, and they both laughed out loud.

It was all go for Cynthia, she had now finished work at the Mill and was able to concentrate on the move and finding suitable employment for herself. Cynthia drilled Mary on certain questions that she may be asked at her interview, what Mary lacked in social graces, was matched by her stunning beauty, thought Cynthia, she had no doubts at all about Mary getting the job she longed for. The day came for Mary's interview, she was so nervous, "Knock them out kid" said Cynthia, good luck will meet up at 1.00pm," and went their different ways, Cynthia first call was to another employment agency to sign on, she was given an application form and other necessary documents, it took Cynthia about one half hours to fill the form in and to have an informal interview. "We will let Cynthia then went off to meet up with Mary,

"Gosh you seem to have been ages" Mary said,"

Cynthia, asked Mary how did interview went?

"I think it went alright, I was glad you prepared me on the question's, you weren't that far off, how did you know?" Cynthia just smiled.

"Come-on lets have some lunch my treat this time Mary said in an emphatic way".

Cynthia just smiled and nodded at her, they had a quite lunch by the Yarra River, just watching the world go by, "What are you thinking about Cynthia? "Asked Mary, "Oh' all sorts of things", she replied, Maggie was one of them, and other was her job prospects. A week had gone by, nothing was happening then a letter came to say Mary had been accepted on a temporary basis, with a view to full time if found suitable, Mary was cock- a- hoop," I can't believe it Cynthia". What with you working at George's, and for me, not exactly what I had hoped, but my dream job will come", "I do hope so" said Mary.

CHAPTER FOUR

Cynthia had landed a job at a solicitor's office and land agents, her boss gave her the creeps, but it was work for the time being and it paid well, she really hated the work but stuck at it. "I will be working late from December till after the New Year," Mary said, "That's ok, I can entertain myself you will have Christmas Day and New Year off won't you?" Oh' yes, that's one good thing about the job, replied Mary. The next few days were quite busy for them both, Cynthia received a letter from Maggie, it was pages long, good gracious she thought, I'll have to read it later, Mary had already left for work, and Cynthia was about to leave when the telephone went, who the hell could this be, she answered, "Is that Miss Cynthia Boardman, "It is" replied Cynthia.

My name is Charles Collins, I'm at the home Office here in Melbourne, I have been looking at your resume', and you seem to be just what we are looking for, is it possible to meet sometime today, sorry for the short notice",

Cynthia's heart was pounding," What time where you thinking of",

"Now if possible,"

"Yes" replied Cynthia, this is it she thought, he gave her details of where to meet, and outlined what the position entailed.

"See you here at eleven then" said Charles Collins.

Cynthia could hardly believe it, she was walking on air, by this time it was 9.30am the phone rang again, yes,

"Where the bloody hell are you" a voice yelled, I've got people waiting here to view properties".

Cynthia replied, "Go to hell you are a horrible little man, I won't be coming in at all, I'll just to pick up my personal things" and slammed the phone down, that outburst had given her great deal of satisfaction, he was a creepy touchy man, that breathed heavily when he was near her, he gave her the jitters.

Cynthia set off to meet up with Charles Collins, at an office block, close to Flinders Street station, wait till Mary hears this. The meeting went well, just informal chit chat really nothing concrete, but Cynthia was pleased with what she had heard and thought she was quite capable of doing the job, of course it was all hush-hush, so she couldn't really tell Mary anything, "That's a shame" Cynthia thought herself. Mary arrived home about 7.00pm," How's your day gone" asked Cynthia, Mary replied, "I am so tired I could sleep for a week, my head is spinning, and their lot's to remember, it's harder than working in the Mill, "Surely not" Cynthia said, it was two weeks off December the two girls had a lot on their minds, Mary with her new job, and Cynthia about to enter into unknown territory altogether, oh' crickey" yelled Cynthia, "Maggie's letter" she jumped up and picked up the letter. Mary went upstairs I'll just wash and change she noticed Cynthia was totally absorbed in the letter, a knock came on the door, "Are you decent Mary," "Come in," replied Mary, "Listen to this" Cynthia started to read the letter.

Hi Cynthia, Mary,

Hope everything is ok with you both, well I've done it, I have married Joe, last week, the family are delighted, I feel quite at home, everyone has been so kind. The farm is huge the family work day and night, sometimes Joe's so exhausted to do anything, Sunday is the only day we can spend time together, then there are certain jobs that he still has to do, I never ever saw dawn before, but I do now. His sister is arriving for Christmas, so everyone's looking forward to that, she has one more year to do, at agricultural college. We all have to muck in, I help his dad with the paperwork etc. His dad is hard work to talk too, he doesn't have much to say, his mum is lovely and bubbler, Joe says his dad has a lot on his mind. That's it for now, have a lovely Christmas and New Year."

Love Maggie

Well I never fancy that said Mary, "I do hope she'll be alright in the back and beyond, as far as I know it is a hell of a long way from here" Cynthia said, they thought for a while about the letter then Mary said, "I'm bushed, and trotted upstairs," I won't be too long myself" said Cynthia. The next day Mary had already left for work, Cynthia had breakfast and read Maggie's letter again, she detected that Maggie might be missing Melbourne and also Mary and herself, she was about to go upstairs and have a nice relaxing bath, when the phone rang, "Oh' bother" Cynthia was quite irritated. "Yes! who is it", said Cynthia," Glad I caught you, Charles Collins look here are you free this afternoon, I would like you meet some colleagues of mine, let's say 3.00pm same place" Cynthia was taken aback, gosh he's sure of himself, "Yes I can make that" "Jolly Good, will see you then" the phone slammed down.

Might as well tidy up and have my bath later, I'll look over my notes again and get my head together for this afternoon, for the first time Cynthia had a little apprehension about it all, it soon became to 2.00pm, Cynthia left a note saying that dinner was in the cooler, then got herself ready, gave herself the once over not bad girl, you scrub up well. Cynthia soon reached Flinders Street, she entered the block of flats, room 30 as she recalled and proceeded to walk up the stairwell as she did one of the clocks started to chime, she knocked on the door, "Come in" a voice said, she entered, a woman said, "Can I take your coat" "Sure" replied Cynthia her brain now working overtime, "This way" the women knocked on another door "Enter" Cynthia recognised the voice, "Hello Cynthia, glad you could make it" Collins said in a mellow voice, "I would like you to meet my colleagues who you will be working with, Cynthia replied, "Working with, "See I told you she was quick on the uptake" said Collins, they all sniggered, except Cynthia.

Let me put you in the picture" said Charles Collins, my colleagues and I work for HMS secret service, "Your spies!" Cynthia blurted out, "Not quite" please let me carry on"" Sorry" said Cynthia, we gather intelligence and if we find something interesting, we pass it onto the relevant departments, we also liaise with the Australian and American intelligence agencies, "I see" said Cynthia. Your job would be to scrutinise information gathered, dissect it, and if necessary bring it to our attention that is all I can say at the moment are you interested in being part of our team Collins asked" Cynthia thought long and hard, "Yes I am interested," was Cynthia's reply," Good glad we've got that out of the way". Collins then went on to tell her more, about irregular hours, pay, benefit's expenses, and so on, they shook hands, and as Cynthia approached the door "Nine o'clock sharp Monday morning, here at this office Collins said, and by the way you are governed by the Official Secrets Act", Cynthia just nodded and went out the door.

Blimey, what a lot to digest, wait while Mary gets home, then she remembered, oh' crumbs she thought, better be careful what I say, it was 4.30pmthe Store, it was very busy with Christmas shoppers and made her way up to the second floor, scouring for Mary, ah! There she is, poor thing, she looks run off her feet. Mary noticed her, "Excuse me", Mary said to a customer, and came over to Cynthia," Whatever is the matter" "Nothing said Cynthia", then told Mary of the job interview, and how she had been accepted and that from time to time, she may have to work late, "You and me both" chirped Mary, "Well I thought we could celebrate, what time do you finished? "In an hour" replied Mary, I'll get dinner sorted", said Cynthia, "Excuse me, are you serving, I would like this", "certainly Madam," Mary replied.

Cynthia, skipped through her shopping list no expense was spared she was on a high, that's it, I have everything, she looked at the time, blimey 5.00pm, how time flies, she got a taxi back to the apartment, flew in to start the dinner, she ignored what she had prepared earlier, and set about cooking something else.

They had a lovely meal, Cynthia told Mary as much as she could, avoiding the actual work involved, "I start on Monday 9.00am", replied Cynthia, it was now moving towards week-end, Mary was still very busy at the Store, and was looking forward to having time off. Mary only had to work Saturday morning, then the week-end was hers, Cynthia could hardly wait for Monday to arrive. and Mary couldn't wait for Saturday lunch to arrive and said. fancy meeting up with me Cynthia at George's

After lunch they just whiled the afternoon away, watching the world go by on the veranda, Beer! Cynthia asked, "Don't mind if I do", replied Mary, St Kilda was a very popular place at weekends, it was usually packed with sightseers and locals. Lunar Park was a great attraction for visitors, people would often come to relax on the beach or sunbathe or even take a swim, at night you could hear laughter and shouting from the amusement park, at times it could get very rowdy, then they would close the windows and veranda doors if it got too noisy, this time however the noise didn't seem to bother them at all one beer led to another. Mary didn't even remember going to bed, she was woken by the telephone, who could this be, she asked herself, she opened her bedroom door to go downstairs, when she heard Cynthia say "My God", I'll come straight away", Cynthia put the phone down, "Whatever is the matter", cried Mary. Cynthia replied, "The Japs have only bloody well bombed Pearl Harbour half the American Fleet has been destroyed with the loss of many lives,"

"I've got to get ready, someone is picking me up"

"What for" shouted Mary,

"Can't talk now will catch you later".

Cynthia flew up the stairs to get organized, Mary was bewildered, but knowing Cynthia as she did, thought it best not to press her any further. Mary just sat there in total disarray in her hearts to hearts she knew this was indeed bad news, she sensed that things would never be quite the same again, and felt very unsettled for the first time, apprehension took over, "Bye", Mary, don't wait up for me, I might be late", then Cynthia was off out the door, Mary, went upstairs to have a leisurely bath and to gather her thoughts, eventually she came downstairs, made breakfast for herself, then turned on the radio, it was all about Pearl Harbour, and Franklin Roosevelt having declared war on Japan.

Mary was getting quite depressed about the bombing sand decided to go out and take her mind off things, she caught the tram into the city, from there she went to go to Albert Street, to reminisce about happy times they had living there, she spent some time in Fitzroy Gardens it was so peaceful. Suddenly the Cathedral bells began ringing, it had been years since Mary had gone to Mass, but something told her to go, she wasn't really that religious, but being from Irish stock, was catholic and so s made her way to St. Patricks cathedral to contemplate. After the service, Mary had a thought, she went to the Roxy to see what film was showing, it was only 1.30pm, when she arrived the only film showing was Gone with The Wind, which she had already seen, but decided to watch it anyway, to take my mind off things and settled down to watch the film, thank goodness I've missed the Pathe News the film started, Mary was now fully engrossed, in the film Gone with the Wind.

By the time the film was over it was getting near teatime Mary reached home about 5.30pm no sign of Cynthia, then decided to make tea for herself, one thing was for certain Mary wasn't too happy being on her own she had got used to having Cynthia around after she had eaten Mary turned on the radio, got her book out and started to read for an hour or so, still no sign of Cynthia, so she decided to retire to bed. Cynthia arrived, at the Office, it was 10.30am, "This way Miss" the officer said, she followed him into another Office, this isn't the same place she said to herself, a lady was waiting," Hello, I'm Miss Scully pleased to meet you Cynthia, follow me" they proceeded to the end of a long corridor, and knocked on a door, "Come in" I recognise that voice, thought Cynthia. Ah! there you are, sorry to drag you out like this, but it's all hands on deck I'm afraid, but I'm sure you'll cope, have a seat Miss Boardman" Blimey, that's formal" thought Cynthia, he reiterates what the job entailed "You will be working with other colleagues dissecting snippets of information, and putting it in some resemblance of order, if you find anything of interest or a pattern emerging, then you let your supervisor know immediately, "Clear" said Mr Collins, Cynthia nodded.

"Good girl you'll fit in very well here, I just need you to sign the official secrets act, for me." Collins said, he gave her the pen, she hesitated, then thought what the hell, Mr Collins like the fact she had hesitated, he knew that she would go far, his intuition had never failed him yet, "Welcome aboard" he said and with that, pressed a button, a young man appeared, "Yes Sir" "Take Miss Boardman to room 33 will you" Collins said, Cynthia turned around to thank him but he was pre-occupied with other matters. When they arrived at room 33 they entered, a very smart lady came up to her, I'm Penny, your supervisor, follow me", Cynthia was led to a large desk were three large trays were one was for shredding, one for possible leads, the other was for definite leads, "You'll soon get the hang of it" Penny said, "You'll be working with Jo for the next week or so".

Cynthia sat down, there was a pile of telex messages, she just starred at them, her thoughts were interrupted, "Hi I'm Jo", Cynthia isn't it", "Yes "replied Cynthia, "Let's get started then we've got a mountain of work here", Jo explained the job to Cynthia, then explained that normally it was a nine to five job, but because of Pearl Harbour, information was coming thick and fast and needed to be dissected, Cynthia just nodded by this time it was 12.30 lunchtime," Jo then said, "Let's have some lunch, we can start in earnest after we've eaten."

After lunch they set about reading all the text messages, Cynthia loved it, it was like piecing a jig-saw together snippets of information gathered from different sources, eventually making a picture or pattern of events, obviously what she was reading was classified information, no wonder I had to sign the secrets act, she thought to herself, after a few hours a pattern was beginning to emerge, enough to warrant further investigation, Jo put her hand up the supervisor came over, "Found something interesting Jo.

CHAPTER FIVE

The pile of paperwork and telexes was never ending, What I usually do", is put all the telexes in date order, that way you can see what you are just dealing with, if you don't it ends up a complete mess like this",

"How did it get like this" asked Cynthia,

"Afraid I can't tell you" replied Jo.

Jo took Cynthia and showed her the common room inside was easy chairs, tables and chairs, a radio, and an area to make tea or coffee, some girls were already using the room, some just chatting others reading. Hi girls", I like you to meet Cynthia, she "has joined our little group" everyone shouted Hi Cynthia, "You'll get to know them all in good time" said Jo.

Let's get back, and start another batch", Cynthia just nodded she was trying to take it all in, suddenly Jo looked at the time come-on she said, so they toddled off to the rest room for half an hour or so, by this time Cynthia was getting a little worried about Mary,

"What time do we actually finish, my friend will be getting anxious,

"In about an hour I should think", replied Jo.

They returned to their desk only to find, Mr Collins there with the supervisor he spoke to them, "Well done girls, that information you gleaned has proved very useful to us",

He went away with the supervisor, deep down Cynthia was chuffed, the supervisor came over, "It's getting late girls, you can go now, see you at 9.00 am sharp, she said to them".

"Come on Cynthia, let's get out of here fancy a drink" Cynthia was torn, she was thinking of Mary, but then again didn't want to appear standoffish.

Ok but just a couple, my flatmate will be anxious, I just went out this morning with no explanation at all".

Jo took Cynthia to another building, they entered it was full of personnel from navy to army and men in pinned stripped suits

"This is a private club" Jo said.

Cynthia said to herself, gosh I thought she meant coffee. By the time Cynthia reached home it was late, she entered the flat there was no sign of Mary made herself a coffee, then retired upstairs, her head was in a whirl, what a day, I'm jiggered she opened Mary's bedroom door, she was fast asleep, and went to her own room.

Boy, "I'm just glad to see you, I was worried" said Mary,

"Hopefully I'll be home at reasonable hour tonight, then we can have dinner together, if something crops up, I'll ring you." "Fine" said Mary.

Mary went down to make some toast and put the radio on, suddenly, Mary screamed Cynthia, Cynthia," What is it now!" Cynthia she was quite irritated, Singapore has been bombed, cried Mary. Cynthia went numb,

"Are you listening" Mary repeated herself,

"Yes" relied Cynthia,"

Oh' Cynthia, what does, it all mean, Pearl Harbour, now this", said Mary was very perturbed, it was the 8th December 1941. Cynthia got herself organised, and went downstairs, "Coffee's ready and some toast", I'm off see you tonight, said Mary,

"Don't forget Cynthia to ring me if you are going to be late", Mary left for work.

Cynthia listened to the radio in disbelieve, so now I know what the job entails, she thought to herself the phone rang,

"I presume you have heard",

"Yes" replied Cynthia,

"Can you get here right away", it was Penny her supervisor,

"Yes certainly",

Cynthia then phoned for a taxi, and left a note for Mary,

The taxi arrived, and off she went Finders Street please," Sure",
all the driver talked about was Singapore, and how beautiful it was,
and how lovely the people were,

"Bloody nips, shower of bastards, that's all I have to say,"

Cynthia just nodded at him, there you are Miss, Cynthia gave
him a ten bob note," Keep the change" "Thank you Miss" then drove
away.

Cynthia remembered which building she went into the day before
and proceeded to enter, she was confronted by an officer, "Pass Miss"
Cynthia blushed," I don't have one" she said,

"Who do you want to see? Cynthia thought, "Miss Scully",

"You're in the wrong building for her" he took her outside,

"It's the third door down" the doorman said,

"Thanks" said and hurried to the right door she entered, Miss
Scully, was there,

"Cynthia Mr Collins wants a word with you", crumbs, Cynthia
thought, and was shown to Mr Collins office again, and entered the
room.

Sit down Cynthia" he didn't even look at her,

"I guess you have heard the news", Cynthia nodded,"

I wanted to tell you that the work you did yesterday was invaluable
to us, it will be just as hectic today I'm afraid, but things should settle
down, we are getting more recruits from other departments, which
should help us, "Anything you wish to say," Collins said.

"Yes Sir, do I need a pass,"

"Indeed you do", I'll see to it immediately that's all Miss
Boardman"

He then pressed a bell for Miss Scully, she entered, Cynthia
followed her, taking in the directions as she went along, "Here you
are Cynthia" and gave her smile

Penny the supervisor came up to her,

"Well done for yesterday, good work" and with that went away,

Jo was already at her desk, "Morning Jo" Cynthia said,

"Morning, we got heaps to do today" Jo said, they settled down to the task in hand Jo suddenly said "Crickey, time for lunch already come on" and they went off for lunch. Cynthia chatted with the other girls they were a friendly bunch and great to get on with, some were Aussies some Americans, but mostly British, all had a sense of humour and occasionally pulled tricks on each other, the office itself was quite large what struck Cynthia was it was decorated for Christmas, which to be honest was the furthest thing on their minds. The day passed very quickly, they had managed to catch up with most of the paperwork and were only a day behind,

"Are you able to work till seven girls" asked Penny, most of girls said yes they could, one or two said they couldn't they had other commitments, and left. Cynthia then asked Jo,

"Is it not compulsory to work late", Jo answered," Not at moment, but if the situation gets any worse, then everyone will have to stay, then we have a shift work system, but for now, we are still 9 till 5 girls".

It soon reached 7.00pm and Jo said "That's it till tomorrow" let's get out of here, coming for a drink" asked Jo, "Why not" replied Cynthia, and off they went to the Officers Club again when they entered Cynthia noticed most of the girls were already there, they waved to them, "Over here Jo" someone shouted, they went over,

"What you're having" "Mine's a gin and tonic,

"Cynthia" whiskey and dry ginger, coming up a voice said back,

"Who's he" asked Cynthia,

"He's in another department, quite hush hush, that's all we know, he always buys us a drink, when he's in town," What's he called asked Cynthia? "Jeff I think, not too sure" said Jo. Time was getting on it was 9.00 o'clock by now.

I'll have to go Jo, things to do, see you tomorrow" and Cynthia went outside, and hailed a taxi, "Where to Miss" the taxi driver asked, "Acland Street, St Kilda" all he could talk about was Singapore, Cynthia hadn't realised the significance of Singapore to the Australian's, they were feeling very venerable indeed.

Cynthia soon arrived home, "Hi I'm home" cried Cynthia,

Mary came to her, "I'm I glad to see you, it's been like a morgue here", Cynthia laughed, "You're so melodramatic at times Mary" Cynthia said, cuppa Mary asked her,

"Yes please Mary" replied Cynthia,

"And then you can tell me all about your new job" said Mary.

To be honest Cynthia wasn't really in the mood to talk, she just wanted to relax, have a leisurely bath and retire, but Mary kept pressing her, Cynthia started by asking how Mary's job was going, "It's hectic and hard work" but I am really enjoying it, the store was buzzing with excitement about Christmas, but today everyone that came in was very perturbed and sombre, about Singapore, which put a damper on Christmas, said Mary. Now please tell me about your job, Cynthia set about by outlining her hours, and how the hours could be changed at the last minute, when things get hectic, "But your job what is it that you actually do"? Asked Mary.

Cynthia was struggling then she said, "I am an interpreter for an Export Company that deals with clients from all over the world and in many cases needs someone who can speak French to them over the telephone, it can be hectic too Mary, because, sometimes the merchant ships get bombed, or even sunk, that's when all hell breaks loose, said Cynthia, "What sort of things do you import," asked Mary," God will this is becoming quite irritating, said Cynthia to herself, the usual stuff high end products, such as perfume, luxury items, that's all I know to be honest Mary", Cynthia said hoping this would satisfy her. "How great, any free samples of perfume would gladly be appreciated" Mary said, Cynthia then said," I'll see what I can do, I'm exhausted Mary, I'm going up, see you in the morning", "Goodnight Cynthia" said Mary, Cynthia reached her bedroom, and flung herself on the bed, her head was spinning, it wasn't long before she was fast asleep.

When Cynthia woke up she was still fully clothed, gosh I must have been tired, she looked at the time it was 7.00am, she went to the bathroom and knocked on the door no answer, Cynthia entered and had a shower. When she eventually arrived downstairs Mary was in the kitchen, the smell of toast filling the room with an inviting come and eat me, "Morning Mary" "Morning" Cynthia breakfast is ready" Mary replied," You're an angel" said Cynthia, they sat and ate breakfast together, "Will you be home late tonight "asked Mary, "Not sure yet, will ring if I have to work late" "Well I'm off see you tonight" said Mary.

The next couple of days brought further shockwaves to the Australian's the Japs had sunk the flag ships HMS Prince of Wales and HMS Repulse a battlecruiser off the coast of Malaya with the loss of many lives, the survivors were being brought to the Australian mainland to be identified and debriefed, many of the sailors had been shot whilst in the water by Japanese soldiers. Once again the Aussies were shell- shocked, it was one thing after another, the news meant that Cynthia had to work late again with her colleagues, sifting through the information that came into them from Singapore, some of the survivors where picked up by HMS Electra. As everyone knows life goes on the days were going very quickly for Mary and Cynthia, Christmas was now approaching fast, the hectic and panic buying was in full swing, Mary found it exhausting but invigorating at the same time her sales were up, the bosses were beginning to take notice of her, they could see her potential, the customers liked her for her honesty when trying on the clothes etc., soon people were asking for her, Mary had always been interested in fashion, and had always noticed what the film stars were wearing or high society, this stood her in great stead.

CHAPTER SIX

Cynthia too was beginning to make a mark for herself but she was driven by ambition and self believe, one section in particular was extremely interested in her, unknown to her, the powers that be, had other plans for her. It was a week off Christmas and Cynthia was invited to the Companies Christmas Party at the Officer's Club, bring a friend if you wish, but we will have to vet them, Cynthia declined, she thought it would be safer for Mary's sake. Mary too was invited to the Stores Christmas Party for all employee's, she was so excited and decided to splash out on one the dresses in the store, she got 10% discount but it still cost her an arm and a leg, but thought it would be worth it, when she tried it on, she looked absolutely stunning, Mary was pleased it fitted her well, she felt a million dollars, I'll show it Cynthia when she gets home.

Cynthia arrived home sooner than Mary, so she started dinner work was now at a steadier pace Cynthia was able to finish work at a reasonable time, which suited the hierarchy, they did not to draw too much attention to their department as to what they were actually doing. Suddenly the door opened,

"That you Mary, I'm in here" cried Cynthia,

"What have you got there" asked Cynthia,

"A dress" Mary replied, she showed her the dress Cynthia was most impressed this was the girl who four years ago worked in a cotton mill, she smiled to herself,

"You've come a long way Mary Conner, the dress is lovely" Cynthia commented,

"I'll try it on after dinner" said Mary.

After they had eaten Mary tried the dress on telling Cynthia about the invite to the stores Christmas Party, Cynthia was amazed at the transformation a dress could do, she looked absolutely wonderful in it,

"I've got some news too, I've been invited to a Christmas do, by my bosses, on Saturday,

"That's great news" cried Mary, we are both going to Christmas parties on Saturday",

"What are you going to wear Cynthia"

I don't know yet" answered Cynthia.

"Buy something off me" Mary said eagerly,

"I might jolly well do that", replied Cynthia, they both laughed, then settled down and listened to the music on the radio, and read for a while

It was now Christmas week, both girls were very busy, Mary was run off feet all week, but making big sales, which pleased her, the Christmas party went a treat, for the first time she felt as though she belonged in Australia, she had also made friends with some of the girls she worked with, they asked her if she would like to go out with them sometime, Mary jumped at the offer, it gave her a purpose, instead of just working and with Cynthia out most of the time with her work, it couldn't have come at a better time," I'd love to" said Mary.

Cynthia also had a great Christmas party, she got to know her superiors better, once they let their hair down, also this chap Jeff was there, this elusive man keeps popping up now and again, nobody seems to know what he does, Cynthia thought him both fascinating and intriguing at the same time, she was quite drawn to him but couldn't figure out why, he was quite tall with steely blue eyes, fair hair and he also had a lovely smile. Cynthia managed to get home she would often have piles of mail, which she would sift through, keep, bin, this amused Mary no end, as she never ever got a letter, a personal one anyway, on this occasion there was one from Maggie,

"Great we can read it after we've eaten" Cynthia said, once they had eaten Cynthia started to read the letter.

"Hi Cynthia, Mary,

Hope you are both well, and wishing you a very happy Christmas and New Year, let's hope 1942 is better than the last, with all the bombing and loss of life its awful, I have written to Mum and Dad with the news and I just wanted to give you the news too, she carried on, jeepers!" Cynthia cried," she's going to have a baby, sometime in June, "Well I never" said Mary, Cynthia carried on, Maggie goes on to say that Joe's Dad had, had stroke, so the boys have to take on extra chores around the farm, and that Joe's Dad has given his sons power of attorney "What's that?" asked Mary," they can run the farm legitimately," replied Cynthia, and carried on reading the letter, I have to do more work in the office now, so we have very little time to ourselves,(you must have had some time thought Mary).

Love Maggie.

Well that's a turn up Maggie being pregnant, she feeling low" Mary said, "Yes it's a pity she lives so far away", "Back and beyond, if ask me" chirped Mary, with and set about doing their own thing each looking forward to Christmas Day, and the New Year.

Christmas and New Year were just a memory now and once again work took over, Mary was seeing more of her work colleagues and Cynthia was also getting more involved with her work colleague's they hardly saw one another during the week, occasionally Cynthia had to go in on a Saturday and Mary always worked till lunch on Saturdays, so it was usually a Sunday when they spent time together, "It'll soon be your birthday wont it" asked Cynthia, "Early June" replied Mary, "Of course it is, silly me, I'd forgotten, it's Maggie's birthday in March isn't it", Cynthia said.

"We can do something special on my birthday when it comes" said Mary.

"That's an idea" replied Cynthia.

The war in Europe was still raging with no sign of peace, the allied forces didn't seem to be gaining any ground at all according to the news, the fight against Japanese's was deepening with terrible torture going on, reports getting back that prisoners of war were building a bridge over the river Kiwi, for tracks for a railway from all accounts it was slave labour, the Japs were a very cruel race, and anyone who tried to escape, were shot the Japanese culture was not too surrender it was cowardice in their eyes.

Soon it would be weekend, Mary was off to the Roxy with a couple of girls from work, Cynthia however had been called into work unexpectedly, "See you later Mary", Cynthia went out the door. When Cynthia arrived at work she was met by Mr Collins, "In here Cynthia" he said, she entered the room, and sat there was the man himself, "Cynthia this is Jeffrey Owen" said Collins "Pleased to meet you I'm sure" Cynthia replied," Likewise" Owen replied.

Mr Collins started we have asked you to come in to discuss a change in direction for you, here Jeff will explain it better than I, Jeff stood up, I'm looking for people with special talents such as yourself to work under cover "You mean a spy" "No not quite" let me carry on, it means you would be working with another team but at the same time working on your own, you would be expected to report back to me and only me, if anything suspicious came to your attention, you would have to evaluate the situation yourself before you sent in a report, if further investigation was warranted, then we would send in more troops so to speak.

I must warn you, it can be very dangerous, long hours, with little or no reward for the job you do, "What do you think" he said," I'll have to give it some serious thought," relied Cynthia "I'll give you a seven days" Jeff Owen said and then said goodbye to Cynthia, Collins opened the door for him "Goodbye Jeff", he turned to Cynthia, just let me know soonest Cynthia, "I will" she replied, It was 2.00pm by this time, Cynthia decided to have lunch, she went to the Bella Vista her favourite restaurant, see saw Jose',

"Ah! Miss Cynthia, nice to see you,

"Hello Jose', Cynthia ordered her meal with wine,

"How are you Jose,

Times bad Miss Cynthia, some foods are hard to get especially from Asia, he said, "I'm sorry to hear that Jose, you can still get hold of Italian can't you?"

"Oh yes, it is no problem", he said.

By now Cynthia mind was racing, she had a lots to think about it did sound like cloak and dagger stuff to her, but also exciting, when Cynthia reached the flat she decided to write to her Mum and Dad, also her Brothers, she hadn't written for ages and felt guilty and re-assured them that she was safe despite the fact that Japan had bombed Pearl Harbour and Singapore, she now had a new job in a government department and how she missed them especially at Christmas time, and also mentioned that Maggie was now married and was pregnant and that she and Mary were sharing a flat in St Kilda, you can look it up Dad, it's beautiful, the sunsets are quite spectacular. Cynthia finished her letter to her parents and set about writing to Maggie, telling her how thrilled to hear that she was pregnant, and that she was looking forward to a new job which had been offered to her and also Mary was doing well at the store, they had now move to St. Kilda in an apartment which she had bought, she wished Perth was nearer so they could visit her Cynthia carried on writing for some time then noticed the time, gosh, she decided to close the letter.

Mary's late tonight must have gone for a drink with her mates, thought Cynthia, so she sat and mulled over this morning's meeting weighing up the pro and cons, on the one hand it sounded exciting but dangerous, on the other hand she was quite happy with the job she had, she heard Mary come in, "The picture was great, I went for a drink afterwards, how's your day gone?

"You know Mary you said that in one breath sad Cynthia and laughed.

"As a matter of fact I've had another job offered me, but it may mean travelling to another states, it sounds really interesting, I have to make my mind up very quickly, Cynthia said,

"Don't worry about me Cynthia, we can sort some arrangement out about the flat, your hardly here as it is if you want to sell it" said Mary, Cynthia just smiled, "We can sort that out later Mary, I have a week to think things over."

What shall we do tomorrow, asked Cynthia wanting to take her mind off things, "I've written to Maggie, and Mum & Dad so that's out of the way, I've told her that I have had a new job offered to me and have a week to decide, she didn't want Mary worrying too much till she had made up her mind completely. Mary hadn't really thought about it much, she knew that Cynthia would do what was best for her,

"Shall we have another lazy day, then go to Lunar Park in the afternoon, it would be nice just to relax for once for both of us", said Mary,"

"How right you are, it's been one thing after another, we'll do just that "replied Cynthia.

The next day they just lazed around, Cynthia was in her room for quite some time sorting paperwork out, tidying up, getting rid of stuff she didn't want or use, and generally de- cluttering. Cynthia had written to her mum and dad as she mentioned it to Mary, there was also a letter for Mary and one for Maggie, just in case something happens to her. Cynthia left them the name of her solicitor, she would get witnesses from work for the will, well I think that's it, she said to herself, she wandered around the house and perused to see if anything else needed to go out for rubbish, after all she probably wouldn't be here all that much. They had a great afternoon and a ball at Lunar Park it was a smashing funfair it was always crowded that afternoon they seem to bump into lots of people they knew, how funny thought Cynthia, we hardly see anyone when we are out together, hope it's not an omen, she rebuked herself, don't be bloody silly Cynthia Boardman. The next day they went off to work, things would never be quite the same again for the two girls, they both had different paths to follow, as they waved goodbye to each other Mary just knew in her heart that Cynthia was going to take the new job she had been offered.

Cynthia arrived a bit earlier than usual to catch Mr Collins, she went to his office knocked on the door,

"Enter! a voice said, she opened the door

, "Ah Cynthia have you made a decision,

"Yes" she said, I've decide to take the job,

"Good girl, Jeff will be delighted,"

No need to stay here Cynthia, you may as well go home, Jeff will get in touch with you,"

"Are you sure Mr Collins"

Perfectly sure was the reply and with that Cynthia left the office to return home, well I never what a funny way to go about things, when she arrived home she made herself a coffee and relaxed, milling over things, when the phone went.

"Hello" answered Cynthia,

"Jeff Owen here, welcome aboard, you've a week to sort out your personal things, you have a passport I presume valid",

"err I think so replied Cynthia".

"If not give me a tinkle on this telephone number, if you have any problems, just ask for me",

CHAPTER SEVEN

Ok replied Cynthia, with that the phone went dead, shit where do I start, she said to herself Cynthia had collated a list of things she had to do, her passport was valid, so no worries there, the other things were, the Bank, the Solicitors and the Estate Agents to arrange for Mary to look after flat and to pay them the rent each month.

Cynthia set off for the city and went to the bank," Yes a young girl asked, "I have an appointment with the manager",

What's your name" Miss Boardman, Cynthia replied,"

Follow me" said the girl, she knocked on the manager's door," Come in,"

"Miss Boardman for you",

"Cynthia it's been a long time since I saw you" the manager said.

"Too long", Cynthia replied, without going into too much detail, she discussed her situation,

"We can sort all that out for you, when do you intend to leave",

"In the next two or three days" replied Cynthia,

"I'll get on to it right away," said the Bank Manager.

Cynthia shook hands and headed for her Solicitors,

"How nice to see you Cynthia", said her Solicitor.

"How can I help you," Cynthia again explained everything to the Solicitor and that time was of the essence,

"I'll sort that out right away for you, can you pop in tomorrow sometime after 2.00pm",

"Yes", replied Cynthia and by the way any letters for me will be at the same address" Cynthia said. she thanked him for his prompt attention then headed for the Estates Agents.

Now Barstow's, Cynthia said, to herself,

"Good afternoon, Miss Boardman, "I think I might have a property for you, there are two in fact, one on Albert Street two bedrooms near your other property, and the other one quite near the Women's Hospital in Carlton" said Barstow.

Cynthia asked", "Are the prices reasonable," They are indeed" replied Mr Barstow.

"Right I'll view them tomorrow at 10.30am", said Cynthia.

Cynthia reached George's Department Store went up the escalator to see Mary.

"Hi Cynthia what brings you in at this time of day, Cynthia said, "I need to speak to you", "You sound worried, I have a break coming up in five minutes," Can you wait," Mary said.

Cynthia nodded, this is going to be hard thought Cynthia, suddenly Mary appeared,

"What so urgent that it couldn't wait till tonight", Mary said,

Cynthia set about telling her of the phone call and how she will have to leave in the next few days and it may be for a couple of months before she would see Mary again. I know its short notice Mary, I have arranged for my mail to be sent to the same address, I will give you a telephone number just in case you need to get in touch with me urgently, but only if it is very urgent, I have arranged everything through my Solicitor also the Bank Manager and Estate Agent, I want you to stay in the apartment, as I won't be needing it just yet, if you have any worries or problems at all get in touch with my Solicitor, he is arranging for all utilities to be paid though the bank.

"I think that's covered everything Mary" said Cynthia,

"What about the rent" asked Mary,

"Oh' you will pay your rent to Barstow's Estate Agent every month it is a reasonable rent Mary so don't worry, you are doing me the favour by staying here and I know you will look after it for me", was Cynthia reply, (really Cynthia was in such a good financial position, the rent was the last thing on her mind), her thoughts were interrupted.

"When do you expect to leave" asked Mary,

"A week today" was the reply "Gosh! said Mary so soon,

Mary went over to Cynthia put her arms around her and said.

"Don't worry about me, I'll be fine I have savings so I want you to charge a fair rent and no arguing about it Cynthia" said Mary, Cynthia ignored her, "See you tonight I will have dinner ready and a nice bottle of wine", was Cynthia reply. Cynthia was so relieved, thank God that's over, she thought, but before Cynthia left she turned to Mary and said,

"There is just one more thing Mary, never ever tell anyone where I live or where I am"

Mary laughed "You're being melodramatic aren't you Cynthia" Cynthia snapped,

"I have never been more serious in my life than I am now, promise me Mary promise me"

"I promise Cynthia, replied Mary.

By the time Cynthia reached home she was exhausted, she made herself a coffee and ticked off the list that she had done, then made another list for tomorrow Solicitors first, then Estate Agent 10.30pm she wrote down, after while she got the necessary documents out for Jeff Owen and made a start on her packing.

Cynthia viewed both properties, she liked them both, she asked Mr Barstow to offer them a fair price if they accepted she wanted to rent them out and asked Mr Barstow to be the letting agent for her, he agreed, as I have mentioned I will not be around for the next couple of months, so if they agree to my price I will arrange everything with my Solicitor. I have spoken to Mary Conner, my flat mate and we have agreed a fair rent, Barstow thought the rent was too low,

"Well she is doing me the favour by staying there and looking after it for me", Cynthia said,

"I see," Barstow said," I want you to send her a monthly bill? Said Cynthia

"Yes of course, consider it done", Cynthia shook his hand.

After Barstow's, Cynthia went onto the Solicitors,

"Hi Cynthia, not quite finished",

"That's ok I have something else for you to deal with","

Wow Cynthia I don't see you for ages, then Wham, fire away" he listened intently jotting everything down, she would inform the bank, to authorise him to draw £1000.00 to cover cost for the houses plus costs for Barstow's, also any cost you might incur or any problems that Barstow's might have to deal with, I will not be available for some time.

"If I have anything serious crops up, how can I reach you",

"Just send a letter to my apartment, and address it urgent, my flat mate can then get in touch with me," said Cynthia, if that's all I must rush," Cynthia said. He shook her hand.

"Good luck Cynthia" he said, Cynthia just smiled at him and walked out, for some reason there was a great relief that=t came over her, or was it anticipation of what she was letting herself in for.

A couple of days later Cynthia received a phone call, can you be ready for Monday 10.00am someone will pick you up, make sure you have all your documents, see you then, the phone went dead, good that gives me a bit more time to sort everything out. It was now March, Cynthia had made a lovely meal for them,

"Hi I'm home" cried Mary, "Something smells good," Mary went into room, Cynthia had laid the table, thought we'd celebrate our last night together I go in the morning, it sounds like the last supper to me, said Mary, and giggled. Cynthia told Mary of all the arrangements to the last detail, "Gosh you have been busy" Mary said,

"Here is Maggie's address, keep in touch with her won't you "Cynthia said, "I will I promise" replied Mary, Cynthia had also sent Maggie a birthday card from the two of them, and arranged flowers to be sent, Mary said "You think of everything don't you Cynthia, boy I'm I going to miss you", Cynthia just smiled at her as she did, and thought to herself, and I'm going to miss you too Mary Connor.

The next day Mary said her goodbyes tears were now flowing,

"You take care of yourself and look after yourself"

"I will" Cynthia hugged Mary tightly, Mary then went out the door not daring to turn around, the emotion was just too great. Well this is a new beginning for me, Cynthia said to herself, and closed the door, it was 10.00am precisely when someone knocked on the door, she opened it to see Jeff Owen standing there, ready, "Yes" replied Cynthia, and they drove away, wonder what's in store for me now, Cynthia said to herself with a little apprehension.

There was trouble for Maggie at the farm, the two brothers were arguing for weeks, on how to expand the farm to make more profit, they had lots of acreage so there was no problem there. Jack wanted to increase the livestock, Joe and his brother Dave wanted to increase the vines which would take several years to bear fruit for picking, Jack said it would take too long, the arguments went on and on with Jack still wanting to increase the livestock, and Joe still wanting to increase the growing area for more vines to be planted, by this time, their father had, another slight stroke, which prevented him from doing any physical work around the farm, his mind had not been affected too much, except he was slow. This irritated Maggie, as she was quite capable of doing all the office work, after all with her training, it was what she did best, Maggie wanted Joe to be proud of her.

Things came to a head one day when the two brothers started to argue and a fight ensued between them, they were knocking hell out of each other, their sister Catherine threw a bucket of cold water over them to stop them fighting, she was calling them all the names under the sun. Maggie's nerves were on edge through it all, suddenly there was a commotion, Maggie went outside and asked Catherine, "What the matter was? they've only been bloody well fighting the pair of them, said Catherine, then the other brother Dave chipped in, Sis only threw a bucket of cold water over them, and he started to laugh, it's no laughing matter, said Catherine.

Maggie was upset, "Oh! Joe" why can't you sort this out, I'm getting tired of this bickering it's upsetting for me, your Mum and Dad too,

"He yelled stay out of it Maggie, this is family business",

Maggie was so upset, she didn't speak to him at all that night, instead she tried to find a solution that would suit both of them, she racked her brains out all night but eventually fell asleep. The next morning, Joe spoke to her," Sorry Maggie," I'm being a jackass, but you know how much it means to me, to get the estate in a profit making position, and wine is the up and coming market, I just want be in first, when the boom comes". Maggie just smiled at him and kissed him,

"How's my boy then", he felt her swollen tummy,

"He would be much better, if you didn't argue with your brother," I know he said it's so frustrating, he's so pig-headed", Maggie laughed, and "You're not!",

Joe smiled, and went out the door, Maggie had thought of a plan and decided to have a word with Joe's father, as soon as Joe went off to work Maggie couldn't wait and went to have a word with Joe's father, although he had, had a minor stroke, it hadn't affected his mind, just one side, his movement was impaired, it didn't restrict to doing the office work, he got on well with Maggie now he was use to her, and the family were overjoyed about the baby.

"Can I have a word" Maggie said to Joe's father,

"Sure Maggie, what is it"

Maggie outlaid the plan, she explained every detail to him,

"You know Maggie, that might just work"

Maggie felt great, to think she might have resolved the arguing between the brothers,

"Can I make a suggestion Maggie" It might sound better if it comes from me, the boys will listen to me, we can tell them later, if it comes off, Maggie was disappointed by this she wanted to show Joe, that she wasn't just a went into the office to start work.

That night the father got the boys together and discussed the plan," It might work said Joe his brothers were also in agreement, the father said to Jack the eldest, "You work on the costings of the ranch include everything mind, don't leave anything out, and Joe you work out your costings, and we'll go from there, now shake hands you silly buggers, let's have no more of it", the father said, they shook hands and embraced one another, this calls for a drink, crack a bottle open Joe.

CHAPTER EIGHT

After about a week a meeting was held in the main house all the family were present, except the kids, his father stood up, he presented the plan, which Maggie had formulated, she kept quiet, she was impressed with the father, he explained it very well, all those in favour, a show of hands went up, Maggie of course couldn't vote, it was carried unanimously, Maggie felt proud of herself. Thank goodness for that, the next few weeks she was kept busy, working out the figures for the cattle business and the wine growing business.

Maggie was now feeling really tired, the weather didn't help, it was very hot still even though they still in winter, approaching spring, she suddenly felt pain that she had never felt before, she cried for help, she couldn't move, the father came, golly, mother, mother, "Whatever is it Joe" it's Maggie I think the babies coming, "It can't be it's not due, she has a couple of months to go, quick get the doctor". It took some time for the doctor to come," I'm afraid she's miscarried," just as the doctor said that, Joe came crashing through the door, he heard what the doctor said," Maggie! Maggie! you poor thing, this is all my fault, giving you all that worry, then the extra work dividing the company into separate companies, I put too much pressure on you", the doctor said, "Plenty of rest for you Maggie", "I'll make sure she does" Mrs Yardy said." Come on my girl bed for you" Maggie was devastated so was Joe, he vowed never to talk to Maggie about work again or put any pressure on her.

It took several weeks for Maggie to get over the loss of her baby, Joe was at his wits end, he'd tried everything, no response at all from

Maggie, he went to his mother for advice," She's depressed" said Joe's mother. "I'll get doc to come over to give her a tonic", Joe seemed relieved, "Thanks Mum", now be off with you, you have work to do, Joe went out the door. As soon as Joe went, she telephoned the doctor, told him the situation, "I'll be over as soon as I can Molly" he said, then Joe's mum went into her room, sat beside Maggie," Come on girl you've got to snap out of it, you won't be first and won't be the last to lose a baby", Maggie just starred at her, and thought, but it was my baby. Then Joe's mum said," I've lost three children altogether with miscarriages over the years, you just have to work through it Maggie, I know it's hard, but you're a strong girl, and Joe loves to bits, he's so worried about you, he has also has lost a baby not just you", Maggie suddenly realised what she meant," I'll try", Maggie said,"

"Good girl, by the way the doctors coming over sometime today to see you". The next day Joe shouted, "You've got a letter from Melbourne", he was excited for her, for he knew how she looked forward to hearing from Cynthia and Mary, he knew Maggie was very close to them and missed them very much. Maggie settled down to read the letter, she read it several times over, Cynthia what have you gone and done, she said to herself, I wonder what Mary thinks about it, she couldn't wait to tell Joe. As Joe was about to leave the house, his father beckoned him to come over," Have you heard Joe? "What! The bloody Japs have only bombed Darwin, sunk most of the ships docked there, with loss of many lives mostly civilians," Bloody hell" cried Joe, that's where all the cattle go" "I know" said his dad, better let your brothers know. Joe jumped into the truck to let his brothers know, everyone on the estate was in a state of shock, to think the Japs had bombed Darwin this was bringing the war ever closer to the Australian's and they felt vulnerable.

Mary sat down she was happy, she had been in the flat for just over a week and it felt so peaceful, I wonder what Cynthia is up to, I do hope she's alright, she sat for while in her own thoughts going through her mind, what's the time better make dinner, and went into the kitchen, she turned on the wireless, not really paying any attention to it, then she suddenly heard bombing, "What's this", she turned up the sound, then she heard about Darwin being bombed, I'm fed up with this bloody war and the bloody Japs, but Mary was also frightened of the consequences of it all, for she knew that while war was still raging in Europe and the Pacific, there would be no chance she could ever return home to England, even if she wanted too.

When Mary got to work everyone was talking about Darwin, and the outcome of it all, it got Mary down, she tried to ignore it, but nearly every customer talked about it, mainly because, they were concerned about their own families, especially the ones who had sons one women, said bloody fool he's gone and enlisted to fight the Japs, Mary felt sorry for her, a new volunteer army was formed to fight the Japs. Conscription was now in force to protect the South-West Pacific area. It had been an awful week at work, nearly everyone was worried, the lads especially wondering if they might have to fight, Mary was glad it was coming to the week-end, she was going to a house party with some girls, a bunch of British sailors had arrived in Melbourne, mostly from The Repulse and the Prince of Wales which were sunk by the Japs off the coast of Malaya, she was looking forward to hearing an English accent again.

Saturday night came Mary had to look her best for tonight, she took ages to get ready trying this dress on, trying that dress on, eventually she chose a dress, this'll do she said to herself I better get a move on, she looked at herself weighing up everything, when she was sure she looked ok, Mary went downstairs. No sooner had Mary got downstairs when a knock came, "Come in Grace its open", Mary said, Grace entered wow!" What a lovely apartment Mary, and you look stunning" she said," "I'm really looking forward to this party, I've pretty down these past few weeks" said Mary, "We've noticed" said Grace, "That's why we asked you to come with us," "That's very thoughtful of you Grace," Mary said. Soon they arrived at the party when they entered, all you could see where Naval uniforms, most of the lads spoke English, a few were Aussies, golly this party is in full flow, thought Mary, "Over here Grace, Mary it was Mildred "You could hardly move for bodies, "Who's party is it anyway, asked

Mary." Not sure a girl said, someone piped up, these lads were on the Repulse and Prince of Wales, their lucky ones, said another, the Aussies that are here, are the ones who helped to rescue them, poor sods, someone else said.

Come Mary lets circulate, next thing Mary heard a voice say
"Hi what, you're having", Mary turned around,
"I'm JR"
"That's a funny name", replied Mary,
"It stands for John Robert, but most people just call me JR it's easier,"
"I'm from the South of England, my family live in Hitchin," And where's that? Asked Mary,
"It's in Hampshire" JR replied, then he said I detect a bit of a northern accent from you.
"I used to live in Oldham Lancashire", "How did you end up here" he asked, "That's long story" Mary replied, "When you two are finished how about that bloody drink" said Grace, "Make that three" said Sara, JR said "How many are there".
"Just us three, and the others, we haven't got clue", someone shouted" Gate-crashes", they all laughed, Mary quickly turned around to the others," Let's get rid of him after the beer", Ok, the girls said, and that's what they did.

The night went into morning, there were still bodies all over the place, Mary and Grace were having a great time, then JR met up with her again,
"Are you avoiding me" he said,
"Not really I just wanted to circulate, it's ages since I've been out to a party", Mary said to him,
"Me too" JR replied. Mary was beginning to like him with his English accent, and his English humour, he was very handsome, he had a look of Robert Taylor the film star, but much taller, he looked well in his uniform.
"What's them on your cuffs" Mary asked, she was beginning to sober up, JR answered her,
"I'm what you call a sub-lieutenant on a ship," Mary was no wiser,

"Now what about that breakfast, I'm starving" JR said, just a minute,

I'll get Grace" JR is coming to my place for breakfast", said Mary "Bloody hell that's quick" said Grace, "That's why I want you there with me" Mary replied.

Ok I'll come" Mary pecked on her cheek,

"Thanks" she said, they all managed to get out of the door, the sun was shining brightly, JR said

"Is it always like this, so bright and sunny" the girls said you'll get used to it, come on were nearly there, they caught the tram back to the flat and entered, JR said "Well I never, what a lovely flat" Oh' it's not mine it belongs to a friend of mine I'm flat-sitting". Time past, Grace had already left, then JR said

"Can I see you again Mary, we can go to the pictures maybe sometime next week, I have a month's leave due" (JR was unaware he was on sick leave due to the bombing of the Repulse and d that the doctors had found a small piece of shrapnel embedded in his head, the doctors thought there was no he imminent danger), Mary replied,

"I have Wednesday afternoon off this week we can meet then if you like", said Mary,

"Great, said JR, see you then", Mary watched him walk away, he waved, his face was beaming. Her heart jumped, was this the man of her dreams, like Maggie, she was elated. By now she was feeling extremely tired she decided to take things easy, as it was work the next day.

Mary saw a lot of JR over his month's leave, not every day, but most weekends, they usually went to the pictures, or for a drink, at Jackson's, Mary liked the atmosphere in Jacksons, to her it was a proper pub, and it reminded her of England, soon it was time for JR to report back, his leave was almost over, "Gosh I'm going to miss you Mary" "Me too" was Mary's reply, I'll write as often as I can" JR said, He grabbed hold of her, Mary just melted in his arms, she was in utopia, she waved him goodbye, with a tear rolling down her face, JR waved back and was soon out of sight.

CHAPTER NINE

Christmas and New Year was now a distant memory for Mary the thoughts of JR and the New Year's Eve party brought a smile, it had been a super night. Mary had received a letter saying he was stationed somewhere in Brisbane, and didn't know when he could see her again. Mary was disappointed to hear this this, she was due leave, but was reluctant to take it, so she could spend time with JR, also her birthday was coming up later on in the year, she thought it would be rather nice if JR could have his leave at the same time.

Mary's attention turned to Cynthia, she hadn't heard from her for ages, she was worried about her, in her hearts of hearts, Mary knew Cynthia had a dangerous job, involving the war, but was never able to approach her on the subject, Cynthia always brushed her off. Then her thoughts turned to Maggie, she decided to write to Maggie, and put her in the picture of what was going on in the big City, and tell her about JR, as it was sometime since she last wrote to her, she felt very guilty for not writing to sooner. Mary was now in a buoyant mood, she had received two letters one from Maggie, one from Cynthia, she sat down and read the letters, Maggie's news was upsetting hearing that she had lost her baby, the other letter was much better, Cynthia would be in Melbourne sometime in June and hoped she could make it for Mary's birthday, Mary was overjoyed to read this. Good old Cynthia, she never lets me down, but there was no letter from JR, to say when he would come.

However, a couple of months had now passed Mary carried on working, she put JR on hold as much as she could, and immersed herself in her work, then one day whilst at work, she was serving a customer, when she heard a voice say

"Is that you Mary"

Mary quickly turned around and looked at the woman, "My God is that you Kathy" Kathy nodded

"Can we talk" asked Kathy,

"Give me a minute I'm dealing with a customer", when Mary was free she went over to Kathy Pretend you are a customer buying something off me Mary said. Kathy started to tell Mary about her time with Edwina, and that Edwina wasn't too well and had decided to come back to Melbourne, mainly to see a specialist, she sure didn't know what wrong with her, all she knew that she was unwell.

"Look can we meet somewhere this weekend" asked Mary

"That'll be great" replied Kathy

"How's Cynthia what she up too" Kathy asked,

"I don't know we don't see much of one another these days" said Mary,

"Is that Edwina over there Kathy", asked Mary? Kathy looked, I can't see her you must be mistaken replied Kathy, Mary was sure it was Edwina, but didn't press the issue.

Weekend soon came Mary met up with Kathy, they had lunch at Mary's favourite place on Lyon Street, Mary asked Kathy,

"Is everything alright",

Kathy "Fine" she replied, Mary had always had great intuition something was telling her that things are not quite what they seem, and another nagging thing was. Kathy hadn't even asked about Maggie, Mary was wishing Cynthia was there, she would know what to do, then she remembered that under no circumstances had she to tell anyone where she was, Mary did have a special telephone number to ring, if anyone was asking for her or thought it was necessary to ring her, I'll ring her later Mary said to herself. Mary saw Kathy a couple more times after that, but there was still no word from Cynthia, "How is Edwina, any results yet" Mary asked, Kathy looked at her. Mary saw Kathy a couple more times after that, but there was still no word from Cynthia, "How is Edwina, any results yet" Mary asked, Kathy looked at her "Mary, I am so frightened, whatever for" asked Mary, "It's Edwina she's changed, I don't know her any more". Mary saw Kathy a couple more times after that, but there was still no word from Cynthia, "How is Edwina, any results yet" Mary asked, Kathy looked at her "Mary, I am so frightened, whatever for" asked Mary, "It's Edwina she's changed, I don't know her any more".

Kathy said she has all these strange people coming and going to the house, I'm not allowed to be in the same room as them, she tells me it's a cultural evening, but they all have funny accents, I suspect they are Germans, when I took in coffee and sandwiches one evening. I am almost sure I overheard them mention Cynthia Boardman, I looked up, suddenly Edwina said," Thank you Kathy that will be all", I just left the room not knowing what to do, I'm really scared, I don't think it's by accident that we are in Melbourne," Kathy said.

Mary was taken aback," What about you Kathy, can't you leave her?" asked Mary, "That's just it Mary, I love her" Kathy started to cry," Oh' Kathy please be careful" said Mary feeling sorry for her getting mixed up with Edwina, who Mary had disliked from the start. "Please don't worry about me, I should be alright", said Kathy, "I just needed to tell someone" Thank you for telling me and trusting me, if you ever want to leave her you can always come here", Mary wrote down the address for Kathy, completely forgetting about what Cynthia had told her. Kathy just hugged her and went on her way, she didn't even look at Mary, Mary shouted "Write me if you can at the address I've' given you," Kathy, was nowhere to be seen, it upset Mary for a couple of days or so, I must ring Cynthia, said Mary to herself.

Cynthia was in a meeting in Sydney the discussion was about collaborators, sympathiser's, call them what you will they are spies to us, said Jeff Owen, the information we have received has pinpointed cells working in Perth Brisbane and here in Sydney, especially the Kings Cross Area of the city, unexpectedly the door opened," Sorry to interrupt you, Cynthia you have a message on your special line it sounds urgent", "I'll be with you shortly", replied Cynthia," Can we now carry on Cynthia! Jeff said in a tetchy voice", Cynthia just nodded. Discussions went on for some length of time, a covert operation was implemented with Jeff and Cynthia heading the team. After the meeting, Cynthia went to see what the message had to say, she immediately connected the two.

"Thank you, Wallace" said Cynthia, she went straight to Jeff's office, knocked and entered, "Can I have a word", Jeff looked up, "What is it" Cynthia told him about the telephone call, and how she thought the two were connected,", so I'll go over and find out more" Jeff hesitated "But we need you here" Cynthia was shocked to hear this. "Jeff you know Mary wouldn't ring unless it was something important, I know Mary better than anyone, she must be worried about something, and if it is what I'm think it is, it will save us a lot of time and leg work", "You've lost me Cynthia, ok one week mind no longer" she flung her arms around him and kissed him gently on his cheek, Jeff blushed, he had a soft spot for Cynthia, "Get out of here before I change my mind" he looked up, Cynthia had already gone, he smiled to himself.

Cynthia arrived a couple of days later, she attended to her own personal business first, then went straight to George's to see Mary, Mary caught sight of her, "You took your bloody time" I've been so worried about you," "Well I'm here now" said Cynthia, Mary knew better, but left it at that, Mary suspicions were founded, that Cynthia was involved with the war more than she was letting on "I'll see you later then" Cynthia then went off out the store. Mary arrived home about 6.00pm Cynthia had made a dinner, Mary thought just like the old days, they chatted, Mary told her about JR, and how much she liked him, that he was up in Brisbane somewhere, that he writes as often as he can," I am hoping he can be here for my birthday and you can meet him", You'll love him Cynthia" said Mary, "I'll be the judge of that" replied Cynthia," Cynthia Boardman you're such a cynic at times" said Mary, then they laughed.

Cynthia was getting quite irritated by now, she wanted to hear what Mary had to say, "Now Mary tell me what was so important you had to leave a message for me", Mary told her everything about Kathy, Edwina being ill, the strange guests the keep popping in and out of the house, the fact that they spoke with a German accent, and how frightened Kathy was, and lastly that Kathy had heard Cynthia's name mentioned. Cynthia looked startled by this, how would they know my name, she thought to herself, Mary carried on I think Kathy is caught up in this, without even knowing anything, she just wanted you to know and if she could help in any way she would, of course Kathy didn't say she would help, but Mary wanted to defuse the situation, she had never seen Cynthia react like she did, it scared Mary.

Mary carried on I have asked her to write here, if she has anything else to tell you, I hope I did right thing, Cynthia wasn't too pleased to hear about Kathy knowing her address but passed it over for the time being, "Has she been to the apartment Mary" Good Heavens No! Cried Mary, "Good we'll keep it like that, do not bring her here Mary, it is for own safety, do you hear me! Mary nodded. Mary broke the momentary silence, where shall we go to have dinner, asked Mary, Cynthia replied to the Melbourne Hotel of course, knowing that Edwina might still be there, Mary thought, now who's playing a dangerous game, "Why there" asked Mary, Cynthia replied," Because that is where Edwina and Kathy are staying isn't it", Mary just stared at her speechless. Cynthia Jumped up "I have to go out don't wait up for me" and out the door she went, without a bye or leave, so much for being here Cynthia, thought Mary in a sarcastic way. Mary's thoughts turned to JR I do hope he can make my birthday, it's ages since I've seen him, and I'm missing him so much, she decided to make a cuppa, then started to read the Argus, it was full of gloom and Doom, she glanced at the time it 10.30pm she decided to retire to bed, and left the door un-locked just in case Cynthia came back.

Meanwhile Cynthia was at the office in Flinders Street, sending Jeff the information she had learned, and that she now knew who one of the activists might be, she gave Jeff a full description of Edwina Aston, but didn't mention Kathy, and where they might be staying at the Melbourne Hotel, "I'll get my men on it right away" Jeff said." There's just one thing Jeff, she has a travel companion who is totally innocent, her name is Kathy, so ask your men to be careful, "I'll mention it said Jeff, "But you know about collateral damage Cynthia,

"I know" said Cynthia, she returned to the apartment feeling very tired and very low, she entered the house it was in darkness, so she crept up the stairs, hoping she would be able to sleep with all that had gone on.

The next morning when Cynthia woke it was very light and bright. Golly what time is it she said, it was 10.00am blimey I'd better get a move on, she had coffee, then went straight to the office, they had checked out of the Hotel, we searched the room absolutely nothing, Cynthia was very disappointed. Cynthia, thanked the lads, and went, she gathered her thoughts, then set about booking a meal for them, at the Grand Hotel, as she was feeling rather guilty about leaving Mary high and dry, and it was her way of saying sorry. When Cynthia arrived back at the apartment she noticed a letter, must be from JR it had a Brisbane postmark. She put it on the sideboard for Mary, she was feeling very hungry by this time so she made herself something to eat. Cynthia just sat there thinking about the events in the past weeks "Where the hell can that Edwina Aston be, Cynthia snapped "From now on you're my number one target I'll get you even if it kills me".

Cynthia's thoughts then turned to Maggie, and her miscarriage, she decided to write to Maggie, telling her about Mary meeting a lad from Hitchin in England that Mary was smitten with him that his name was John Robert, but he was known to everyone as JR, I have yet to meet him so the jury is out until I do, she went on to ask how Joe and the family where feeling after their loss of their baby, and promised she would come over as soon as she could.

Cynthia's thoughts were interrupted, Mary suddenly arrived, Hi Cynthia" Glad to see you back, "Sorry about last night, I just had to go out" "It's Ok" said Mary "But I wish you would be more honest with me Cynthia" Cynthia said "I can't Mary, I only wish I could, and I don't want to put you in any danger", Cynthia, then changed the conversation, "There's a letter for you I think it is from JR"

Mary read the letter and smiled, "He thinks he can make it for my Birthday," Cynthia", That will be lovely for you Mary, said Cynthia, they had a smashing time at the Grand, Cynthia then said she didn't know when she might see Mary again, Mary 's thoughts were now of JR, but decided to put all thoughts of JR behind her, as Cynthia had gone to so much trouble for her to enjoy the meal. Soon it was time for Cynthia to leave, "Keep in touch with Maggie won't you Mary, it's important," God you sound like a mother hen, I've already written to her" said Mary "Goodbye then" see kissed Mary on her cheek, Cynthia hated goodbyes, she often wondered, if she would ever see Mary and Maggie again, she left with tears in her eyes. Mary was also sad to see Cynthia go, she was also worried about her hoping she would be safe.

Time was moving on; it was now April JR was to have some leave, he was expected back in Melbourne sometime in May June, Mary was so excited even though it was a couple of months away, it gave her a purpose, that's all she talked about at work, Mildred said, "For heaven's sake give it a rest, you won't be the first to fall in love and you won't be the last" Mary was amazed she had never seen Mildred so angry, Mary was so upset about the outburst. Mildred then left the room, Sara said, "You don't know Mary", "Know what" Mary asked, Sara said, Dave, Mildred's boyfriend had been killed over the week-end, "My God I didn't know, how did he die" Mary asked, it was a pub fight round by the docks, he had been badly beaten and robbed, they caught the guys, a couple of itinerants they said, Mary felt awful, and went over to Mildred put her arms around her, "If there's anything Mildred," "I know I'm sorry too" Mildred said.

Maggie received a letter from Cynthia, blimey one from Mary, and now this one, but she was always excited when she heard from Cynthia, she shouted Joe, "Got another letter from Melbourne", "I know, you are a very popular lady", Joe said and smiled, "When are you going to tell them the news", "Not just yet Joe, I want to be sure" Maggie replied, Joe kissed her, and went out to work, Maggie settled down to read the letter with enthusiasm sounds as though Mary has met her man, Maggie thought to herself, now what about you Cynthia Boardman, it's about time you stopped whatever you are doing and find a Mr right for you.

CHAPTER TEN

Maggie was now made to take things easy, for she was now four months' pregnant, and Dr Hargreaves didn't want to take any chances with her pregnancy, he wanted her to go to Royal Perth Hospital to see a specialist, this upset Maggie, the doctor assured her that everything was alright, and it was precautionary, in view of her previous miscarriage. "It's for your own good Maggie" and you'll be able to rest properly, what about the office work, we'll manage" said Joe," And we don't want you to lose this baby Maggie, chirped Dr Hargreaves", reluctantly Maggie agreed."

"When doctor" asked Joe, "The sooner the better, I'll write a letter, and arrange the Flying Doctor, to take you and Maggie up to Perth" Dr Hargreaves then said, Right I'll be off, "Can I have a quick word Joe" sure replied Joe, they walked out together, the doctor turned to Joe," I think there is more than one baby", and if's that's the case, Maggie will need all the professional help available, Royal Perth can give her," Jeepers "cried Joe, "Not a word to Maggie Joe, promise, "I promise" Joe replied.   Deep down Joe was cock-a-hoop, he felt like telling the whole world, "What did the doctor want" asked Maggie, "He just wanted to tell me the arrangements that's all" "Joe Yardy you're a terrible lair", "Strewth! Maggie, cross my heart" Joe retorted, I'd better get back to work, see you later.

A week later Maggie was in Royal Perth, she and Joe had been given the news, they were shell-shocked, the pair of them just stared at each other. "This is all your fault Joe Yardy" Maggie said, pointing at him, "Hey it takes two" said Joe, and they burst out laughing and giggling, no wonder Doc Hargreaves was concerned, said Maggie, "I still can't believe it Joe, Triplets" "That's what they said three at once making up for lost time Maggie," said Joe. Just then the door opened it was the consultant, "I just want to talk you through a few things" he said, "Sure, fine, fire away Doc" Joe replied. He went through the various procedures, the fact that Maggie was now approximately five months pregnant, he thought it best for her to stay in hospital for the full term, he explained, in many instances multiple births tend to be premature, he asked Joe to sign the necessary paperwork, which Joe did.

Don't worry Hun, I'll come up every weekend I promise" said Joe, Maggie was now crying, Joe tenderly put his arm around her, "Come on it'll be worth it in the end, "I know sobbed "Maggie. It was an exhausting labour, for Maggie, but she suddenly heard the cries, there's one coming, thank God for that she thought, as each baby was born, a slap and a cry, it's a boy, next it's a girl, and the next, Maggie waited eagerly, there was silence, then the doctor said, Maggie knew instantly, "I'm afraid, this one is stillborn", tears flowed down her cheeks "Cheer up said the doctor, you still have a healthy boy and girl".

At that particular moment in time that was no consolation to Maggie, oh' how I wish Joe was here, "Can you ring Joe, and let him know" asked Maggie, we have already rung him, he is on his way, by plane I believe said the doctor, "Now I want you to rest" said the nurse. Joe arrived the next day, the doctor had a word with him, and then he went to see Maggie, he had a smile wider than Sydney harbour bridge, and the biggest bunch of flowers you have ever seen," Where's my girl," Joe said tears flowing, "We lost one" "I know baby "but the others are fine, he held her as tight as he could. Have you seen them, I sure have Maggie, there just like you, and I thought they were just like you, they hugged one another for ages. It was several weeks before Maggie would be able to go home the babies were doing well, so was Maggie, Joe spent the weekends with her as much as he could, then the doctor said" You can go home Maggie, we'll arrange the Flying Doctor for you." Maggie couldn't get out quick enough,

Joe and Maggie thanked the hospital staff, and as a thank-you Joe gave them a box of red wine and a box of white wine, the staff were delighted by his generous offer.

Soon they were flying home, wait till Mary and Cynthia know they are Aunties, Joe squeezed her hand and smiled. By the time they arrived home, Maggie, was feeling very tired, the twins believe it or not slept all the way, the plane touched down, when they arrived home all the family were there to greet them, there was a big banner saying Welcome Home Maggie, also balloon's and bunting. Joe helped Maggie down from the waggon, the twins were now awake, and started to cry, "Their hungry Joe" I'll have to give them a bottle, everyone run up to them, to see the twins, his Mum said, just like you Joe, he was proud as a peacock., Maggie took them inside to feed them. Joe said" time for a party", all the neighbours had come from, all around the Margret River area, many had brought beer and presents for the twins.

Cynthia had been back in Sydney just over a week, she was obsessed with Edwina and her collaborators, Jeff had called a meeting, he started the meeting, our intelligence reports, suggests that the cell is working here in the Sydney area, and various regions in other parts of Australia, mainly Darwin, Melbourne and Sydney docks areas. We think that there is a major operation about to take place, to try and disrupt as much as possible, and to be a nuisance, and keep us busy, "Cynthia would you like to take over". Cynthia stood up, our main priority is the cell working here in Sydney, we've lost sight of them, our main target is Edwina Aston, Cynthia pinned a photo dent picture of her on the board, this may not be of course her real name, our research shows she is from German decent, and comes from an extremely wealthy family, the family have great influence in commerce and industry, here in Australia, so her resources are limitless.

I have it on good authority, that they meet up every week on the pretext of a cultural evening, most of them speak with a German accent, or European accent, we believe that they are in the Kings Cross area of the City, perhaps in a night club, or massage parlour, or something similar, where no-one would suspect anything out of the ordinary. It is absolutely imperative that we find this cell before they do any real damage, I want 24-hour surveillance in Kings Cross, ask your informants, no matter how insignificant it maybe it could prove the missing link. "Thank you", Cynthia then sat down, Jeff nodded at her in approval. After the meeting Jeff asked Cynthia why the Kings Cross area, "It was something my source said, "What was that" she said "You won't find her, she's inconspicuous wherever she goes, but Cynthia think outside the box Cynthia, there is always somewhere in a city, or an area that attracts a seedier side of life, "I see" Jeff said, Cynthia then said "And that's my turf Jeff" "steady on Cynthia, I hope this is not going to be a vendetta" "I just want to catch them" replied Cynthia.

The next couple of months were really busy, nothing had emerged everyone was fatigued, Jeff called a meeting, "He said we have scrutinised every scrap of paper nothing, so I'm calling off the surveillance for now, I will pass all the information on, but I can't see anything at all to warrant 24hr surveillance, go home get some rest, be back in three days," then Jeff ended the meeting. Cynthia was furious when she heard this, she bounded in the door, "What the bloody hell have you done that for" she yelled at Jeff, Jeff raised his voice, "May I remind you just who is in charge of this department", Cynthia was stunned, that was the first time Jeff had ever shouted at her, he was very angry," I suggest you go through all the paperwork again, and pass it on to the relevant departments", Cynthia just nodded and went out the door.

Jeff had had some bad news from upstairs the department was to be shut down, everything was to be transferred over to Naval intelligence, Jeff decided not to tell anyone just yet, he was hoping for a miracle he wanted to be able to report that, they had indeed found the cell, and his department would get all the glory. The next few days Cynthia, couldn't relax, she was still working through the paperwork, just in case something had been missed, but in a leisurely way, it meant she could spend some time at home, which she hadn't done for ages. One morning she was on her way to work, she felt as though someone was watching her, it was an eerie feeling, Cynthia decided to move more quickly, stopping now and again to see who it was, Cynthia caught the ferry to work, but was still vigilant, there was no one suspicious as she could make out.

Cynthia eventually arrived at the office, she went straight to Jeff's office, to tell him she thought she was being followed, "And where the bloody hell have you been, all hell has broken loose here" Jeff said, Cynthia was shocked, "Why what's" up, Jeff confided in her, "Unless we can crack this case Cynthia it's curtains for us all" "What do you mean" asked Cynthia, Naval intelligence will take over the department, and we will all get new assignments" "Shit" said Cynthia. "I hope you've got something for me," Not really, I was followed this morning, that's why I'm late, I had to shake whoever it was off well that's something I suppose," said Jeff, Cynthia felt sorry for him, "If there's anything I can do Jeff" "Catch the buggers Cynthia" and he walked out of his office.

Cynthia went to her desk, she started to peruse the information again, this time Cynthia had put them in date order, to see if a pattern had emerged, it took up most of her day, and half the night, to evaluate her notes, then it dawned on her, see noticed that some of the sightings of suspects seemed to be in one particular area of Kings Cross, an old factory building, behind a strip joint called the Blue Lagoon. Jeff had already left the office, she looked at her watch it was 9.00pm time to go and have a look she said to herself, and with that she left the office and made her way to Kings Cross. Then Cynthia realised she was too well dressed, for that sort of area, and decided to go home, I'll let Jeff know in the morning, she got a taxi, Lyon's Road please, "Right you are" the taxi didn't take long, "Here we are Miss" Cynthia said thank you and alighted the taxi. She still felt uneasy about this morning, looked around, no one in sight, and then entered the house.

The next morning Cynthia decided to take a taxi to work, as to avoid any surveillance on her if any, catch me if you can, she said to herself. It didn't take long to arrive at the office, she entered the office building, there seemed to be a lot of activity going on, wonder what's up now, she said to herself. She proceeded to Jeff's office, she knocked and entered," I think I may have stumbled on something Jeff" she looked up Jeff wasn't there, Cynthia closed the door and went to her office, she entered and sat there was Jeff and another man.

"What the Hell, who is this?" Cynthia yelled", Jeff said," "This is, Richard Stevens, Under Secretary to Peter Andrews", He has orders for you to work to at Parliament Building, Melbourne," Cynthia looked across at Jeff, their eyes met, Cynthia replied, "And what if I don't want to work for your Boss" Mr Stevens, he just smiled, "You and me both" he replied "You don't have a choice I'm afraid he said, you have two weeks to sort out your personal things and tidy up things here, you are expected to be in Melbourne, on the 22nd May. Where exactly am I going to work", said Cynthia, he gave her large brown envelope, "Everything you need to know is in there, see you on the 22nd" and walked out, "Well I never, just who does he think he is" said Cynthia in an indignant way, Jeff said," He is Government, Cynthia you have been head-hunted, your reputation precedes you" said Jeff, "What about you, where are you going" asked Cynthia," I'm to stay here and carry on trying to catch Edwina & Company, at least the Navy is not taking over, that's something I suppose", was Jeff's response.

Good I've got some good news for you, I think I know were their hideaway is," said Cynthia, It's no use Cynthia you have to drop everything what you are doing" you have no authority now, you are desk tied, I have to choose a new number 2 and I've chosen Harry Barns, he's a good man" said Jeff" I'm so sorry" Cynthia tried to convince him to change his mind." Well at least let me investigate this building, I still have a couple of weeks", said Cynthia "If I do let you, you must follow orders," said Jeff "I'll tell Barns and he can go with you, no heroics Cynthia, it's my head on the block here not yours". Cynthia wasn't at all happy about the situation, she wanted her and Jeff to catch the spies, now she hated the job, and wanted to get out of it altogether, but couldn't, she had signed up for the duration. Cynthia and Harry Barns, really didn't see eye to eye, there was something about him, that made Cynthia distrust him completely, Cynthia went with Harry barns she had no choice, and told him where she thought the cohort might be working and having their meetings, they surveyed the area, nothing struck them it seemed ordinary.

Harry Barnes wasn't that impressed, he thought it was a wild goose-chase, moron thought Cynthia, as they were arguing over the matter, they noticed some activity taking place, the large doors opened, then couple of cars, came out Cynthia swiftly took the registration numbers and description of the cars. They tried to see who was inside, but the windows were blackened," Bother" said Cynthia, come-on Harry, she swiftly, went over to see what was inside before the doors closed, Harry was three paces behind her, keep up Harry Cynthia said in an irritating voice, he just murmured something under his breath, "What was that" asked Cynthia, he didn't answer her.

Cynthia went inside to clock everything, there wasn't anything suspicious at all, then she heard in a funny accent, "What the hell are you doing this is private property" Cynthia answered," I thought this property was up for sale with Henderson's, "The reply was less than polite, Harry said come-on let's get out of here, "Sorry we've obviously made, a mistake", he said to the two chaps, and dragged Cynthia with him. Cynthia was seething with him, "You could have pressed more Harry," "It's not my style Cynthia, I will do it my way, don't worry, we'll keep an eye on the place, I'll get the team on it right away, and a camera man, just in case, and see where we go from there," Cynthia wasn't happy she wanted to crack the case with Jeff, but had to admit defeat.

Soon it was time for Cynthia to leave the Sydney Office, a knock on the door, it opened, "Bye, Cynthia best of luck with your new posting," it was Harry Barns, she just smiled at him, but loathing him at the same time, she didn't want to leave Sydney or Jeff, well not till she had apprehended Edwina anyway and her cronies. It was late-afternoon," Come back for coffee my place, as this might be the last time I see you," Cynthia said to Jeff, "ok give me 10 minutes" Jeff replied, then they got a taxi to Cynthia's place, Jeff then said to her "Open your envelope let's see what your job is going to be" Cynthia opened her envelope and started to read it, "Blimey, I am to report to Parliament Building in Melbourne and ask for a Peter Andrews" Moving up in high places Cynthia, better watch out, or they'll eat you alive" Jeff said, I don't think so thought Cynthia.

After a couple of hours Jeff said, "I'm off", "How can I get in touch with you" Jeff asked, "You can write to me at my apartment or telephone me, replied Cynthia," "That a good idea, "I'll also give you the address for Maggie's, you never know you might get over to Perth one day, and we could perhaps meet up there. Jeff grabbed hold of Cynthia and kissed her with great passion, Cynthia was stunned for once she was speechless, she too responded, and kissed him, "Boy I'm going to miss you", Jeff said in gentle voice," Don't forget me Cynthia" I won't I promise", was Cynthia's reply. "Well best of luck" Cynthia, "You too Jeff" they both looked at each other, momentarily for a few seconds, then Jeff left, Cynthia was tinged with sadness, she too was now on her own, and felt uncomfortable, not knowing where the new job would take her. Then she thought, well at least I'll see Mary more, and I'll write too Maggie and let her know.

The next day she went to her office the door was locked, Harry Barnes appeared, your downstairs now Cynthia, in the deciphering department, we'll see about that she said to herself and headed straight to Jeff's room, he wasn't there," It's no use Cynthia," "If I was you, I 'd go straight home, and take advantage of the time you have left," said Harry Barns "I'll just leave Jeff a note, can you see he gets it" I will". replied Harry. Cynthia got a taxi home, made herself a coffee, sat down and read the contents of the envelope, inside was a map, and instructions upon arrival, she was to ask for Johnathan Roberts Office, who was Commander Andrews, Superior, top brass, thought Cynthia, it went on to say that she was still governed by the official secrets act and she was expected to be Peter Andrews right hand man so to speak, "Blimey" Cynthia was elated and amazed at reading the letter, all thoughts of Sydney's operation paled into insignificance.

The following day, she got all her personal things together, arrangements had already been made for belongings be taken to her apartment in Melbourne, Cynthia was to fly there, no expense spared, she thought to herself, suddenly the phone rang, it was Jeff, "Good luck, we should have dated a long time ago Cynthia, now it's too late", Cynthia replied" Well make up for lost time, after this bloody war is over Jeff. Don't forget if you get any leave, come over and stay with me", "I will", there was a silence, that said everything, well almost, Cynthia wanted him to say, that she loved him, but the phone went dead, why didn't I tell him that I've loved him from the very first moment I set eyes on him, Cynthia said in rueful way. Then her mind turned to the task in hand, I must ring Mary tonight and let her know, I'm coming back to Melbourne I can tell her the details, when I arrive.

Mary arrived home, it had been really busy at work, she kicked her shoes off and just sat there to gather her thoughts, she too had, had some good news, the powers that be were very pleased with her sales once more, and she had been offered a raise and promotion, Mary couldn't believe it, she was delighted, it meant of course more responsibility, but they were sure she could handle it. They hadn't given her much time to consider the proposition, they wanted to know as soon as possible.

The phone went, I bet this is Maggie, Mary said to herself, "Hi Maggie" "It's not Maggie" Cynthia said to Mary," What! Cynthia is everything alright" "Everything fine Mary" Just to let you know I am coming back to Melbourne, I have been offered another position, can't go into much detail. "That's great cried Mary" "When do you expect to arrive, in the next couple of days or so, "Cynthia replied. "I too have some good news to tell you too Cynthia, but it can wait till I see you" said Mary, Well I never it's funny how things turn out, can't wait till Cynthia gets back, it'll be just like old times, Mary said to herself.

It was now middle of May, the weather was turning a bit cooler, with plenty of rain, Mary had finally heard from JR, he was due to arrive about the June 3rd approximately, and said that he has two weeks leave to come, also that he was being transferred to another ship called Kuttabul, based in Sydney, and that he had been promoted to Lieutenant. JR said, couldn't wait to see her, and all he could think about was her, and seeing her again, it kept him sane in this crazy war, Mary was walking on air, then he said the days couldn't come fast enough, the next day Mary wasted no time when she arrived at work, she asked for two weeks leave," Mary you know that June is our busiest time with stocktaking and ordering for the next six months" the supervisor said, "I know" said Mary. JR is coming over he has two weeks leave," I see" said the supervisor, "I'll have a word upstairs" the supervisor said, Mary said herself, I'll go anyway. It wasn't long before the supervisor came back to her, Mary.

The Management has reluctantly agreed for you to have your two weeks leave, with the fact that your boyfriend is coming over from Sydney to see you, they also want an answer from you regarding the meeting with them yesterday, "What am I tell them" asked the supervisor, Mary replied "Yes". They will be pleased, well done Mary, you've worked so hard for it" Mary said "Thank you", the supervisor went on her way, Mary new somehow the supervisor had put in a good word. That night when Mary arrived home, Cynthia had arrived already, "Hi Mary it's great to see you, you look great"," "You look tired Cynthia", Mary said, "I am Cynthia carried on it's all the travelling that tires you out", Mary said "I have heaps to tell you," "I haven't got any dinner ready Mary I've just actually arrived" said Cynthia, "That's ok we can eat something later", replied Mary.

Mary began by telling her about Maggie and the quins, the fact that one had died, two had survived a boy and a girl, they were born on the 19th September," Gosh!" Cynthia said, she was saddened that she didn't know, Mary carried on Maggie and Joe are delighted and the babies are thriving, we talk on the phone now, Maggie has a party line, she rings me on Saturday or Sunday it is mainly on a Sunday though, we try to keep in touch as much as possible.

"What about you and JR" Cynthia asked," He's coming over beginning of June for two weeks, I've just arranged to take the two weeks off when he arrives", said Mary, "I see "Cynthia said, we talked about going over to see Maggie by train, "That's a long way" Cynthia chirped in, it takes 2 or 3 days by train" Blimey so long, I'll have to have a re-think", Mary said. "I also have some good news to tell you Cynthia" said Mary, "What's that" asked Cynthia," I have been promoted to supervisor, it may mean working on a different floor, which I'm not happy about, I have to have some training, but it means a pay raise for me", "Well done! Mary, you've earned it, you've come a long way to get where you are", said Cynthia.

"Now what brings you back here? asked Mary, "Well, I've have been head hunted, obviously I can't go into too much detail, the work means I will be working here in Melbourne, I may have to be away from time to time, but I will definitely be based in Melbourne more often than not, I am to start work next week, so that gives us plenty of time to catch up, Mary pipped in," And you can tell me if you have anyone special in your life Cynthia". Cynthia just smiled and didn't answer, "I'll go up and have a bath now, "Your bed needs making up, and needs airing, I'll see to it for you", Mary went upstairs to make the bed up, she filled a couple of hot water bottles to warm the bed, then proceeded to go downstairs to make something to eat for them both, It's nice to have Cynthia back. Thought Mary. Cynthia came down after her bath, "That's better, it was nice just to soak, and not worry about time, It's been so hectic these past few months," Have you seen anything of Kathy since we last spoke, asked Cynthia," No replied Mary I haven't"," they ate supper, and just chatted all night, catching up on gossip and Maggie, it was also nice for Mary, to have someone to talk too.

Time past by very quickly, Cynthia was getting so excited about her new job, Mary was also getting excited, about her new role as a supervisor, after her holidays, to help her to settle into management she would have to attend courses in-house, it would entail every aspect of her new role as a supervisor, she was also, eagerly awaiting news from JR to confirm the correct a date when he would arrive.

Cynthia made the most of her time off, she went to the Bank, Solicitors, and then onto the Estate Agents, to see if everything was in order, she had purchased another couple of houses in the Carlton area which were going cheap, that Barstow had informed Cynthia of, she was now building a very nice Business for herself for the future. Cynthia also needed to know if there were any documents that had to be signed, or any outstanding bills to be paid. Later on she decided to go shopping, for new clothes, of course she went to George's and saw Mary, Mary was delighted, Cynthia wanted to completely change her wardrobe, which she did, it meant, Mary would have a big bonus at the end of the month, just in time for her holidays with JR.

CHAPTER ELEVEN

Cynthia asked, "Fancy dinner out tonight Mary, "We'll probably be ships passing in the night, once I start work, well at least, till I get organised, said Cynthia "Sounds great" let's go to the Bella Vista, we always enjoy it there, book for 7.30pm, it'll give me time to change." said Mary. "And it is my turn to pay for the dinner, as you haven't charged me the full rent, no arguing Cynthia I mean it. Cynthia just looked at Mary and smiled.

They talked all night reminiscing about how far they had come, Maggie and her twins, Kathy the enigma, also wondering how the folks back home were coping with the war, "I've written to Mum and Dad, to reassure them I'm fine" Cynthia said, "You'd better let Maggie know your back in Melbourne too" Mary said, I'll ring her in the morning" replied Cynthia. I was thinking where I could take JR, it would do us both good, to get away from everything, and just rest and be waited on, "Can you think of anywhere Cynthia" asked Mary," I suppose you could book a tour, there are lots of places you could go to," After all none of us have seen anything yet, it is a vast country, if you have time tomorrow, get some information from a Travel Company." Cynthia replied.

That's an idea, Mary said, "I will". They finished their meal and took a leisurely walk past Collins Street, then onto Finders Street Station, where they hailed a taxi home, by this time it was 10.00pm, blimey, Mary thought how time flies, it didn't take too long to reach home," Goodnight Cynthia thanks for a lovely evening, just like old times", said Mary, "Goodnight Mary. "Cynthia replied Cynthia went into the lounge, and sat for a while, then poured herself a glass of Sherry, she was in her own thoughts again, why did I not tell Jeff how much I loved him, why did I let him go, why didn't I run after him, Cynthia Boardman, you're a bloody fool to yourself at times, her thoughts then turned to the job, and her new boss wonder what he is like this Peter Andrews, hope I like him, and we get on. I must remember to phone Maggie tomorrow, her mind was racing, and then she poured another Sherry, and retired to bed, trying not to wake Mary. When morning came Mary was already up making tea and toast, the smell of toast wafted through the flat, Cynthia eventually came downstairs she was greeted with, "Morning Cynthia, best of luck with your new job", Thanks Mary, "Not too sure when I'll get home tonight," That's ok I'll rustle something up for dinner" replied Mary, I'll see you tonight, bye," and Mary was off.

The taxi driver for Cynthia, chatted all the way to Parliament Building, Cynthia wasn't paying too much attention to him, then he said "Here we are Miss" Cynthia paid him," Keep the change" she said, "He doffed his cap, "Thank you Miss," he then drove away. Cynthia then read the instructions as to where exactly she had to go, and which department, she entered the building it was beautiful, it had a lovely tiled floors, very high ceilings, all the woodwork was in mahogany, a lovely big open tiled stairway, Cynthia was delighted, back in Sydney it was a dingy office, in fact you wouldn't have noticed an office was even there.

"Can I help you", she looked up, it was the receptionist, "I have an appointment with a Richard Stevens" "And your name Miss" asked the receptionists, Cynthia Boardman? "One minute please".

The receptionist picked up her telephone and rang a number, she waited, a voice said yes, "A Cynthia Boardman is here" "I'll be right down" was his reply, "If you could wait over there, Mr Stevens will be down shortly. Cynthia thanked her and went to sit down, it seemed ages before Stevens arrived "Sorry to keep you waiting Cynthia," Follow me" they took the lift to the first floor, room 24, and entered, "Here she is Mr Andrews,", Thank you Richard, then Peter Andrews turned to Cynthia. We are pleased you have decided to join us here"

Cynthia said to herself, I really didn't have an option did I, she followed Mr Andrews into another room, which was very spacious," This is your Office," he said to Cynthia, she was shell-shocked, gosh, she said to herself, it was huge, "You should have everything you need here, you have your own wash-room through there, Andrews said.

What exactly will I be doing here Cynthia asked, "You'll be working with me of course, most of the work will be undercover, we will also be away days sometime weeks, if necessary, "I see" said Cynthia, "It's not as bad as it sounds, we get to move around a bit stay in decent hotels, not just in this country but abroad, mainly Singapore, and parts of Asia, it is dangerous work of course, do you have a firearm certificate" he asked, "No I don't, I have never needed one, I can shoot though if I have too" was Cynthia's reply. He looked surprised, "We'll have to get that sorted out right away, you will need to protect yourself, oh' crumbs what have I let myself in for, thought Cynthia, "I'll fill you in with more details over lunch," then he left, Cynthia just stared at the desk and sat down, well I never she said to herself, she opened the drawers of the desk, they were empty, that's a good start, do I just twiddle my thumbs now till you come back, she said in her usual sarcastic way.

The door opened, I've brought you some coffee, Stevens said, "Gee thanks" replied Cynthia, "No worries" was his, reply to her, he also gave her an exceedingly large file, all the information you require is in there, take your time, if you have any questions let me know, "I will" she replied, she was dumb-struck really, what the hell am I doing here, she poured herself a coffee. Cynthia just looked at the file then opened it, it was dossier on all the activities taking place here in Australia, and elsewhere, especially in Singapore, Malaysia, and Indonesia, this was more like it, something to get my teeth into, Cynthia sat down to take it all in. Cynthia was still engrossed in what she was reading, when suddenly Andrews came in, Cynthia it's lunchtime, "Stevens lock this away will you," he took the dossier, to give to Stevens, "What do you think so far" he asked her, "It makes very interesting reading, I have one or two ideas" he looked at her surprised, "So soon" Oh' there just observations, she said," We can talk this afternoon, come on let's have lunch, with that they went out the door.

Andrews and Cynthia, sat and talked over lunch, it was very informative, Cynthia was impressed by him, he explained to her that she would have to have some training in armed combat, that it was only a precaution, if she ever needed to protect herself, he also explained that she would be working for him and nobody else, that they would be a married couple from time to time, especially in Singapore, she would also have an Irish passport like his, when necessary. He carried on, the work is dangerous, long hours, mainly surveillance, except in Singapore, where we can rest up and pretend we are on holiday, any questions, "Yes" Cynthia said, "What happened to your last co-worker," "Nothing" he said, this is an entirely new operation, and I wanted someone with some background knowledge with undercover work experience, you came highly recommended to me, it also helps that you speak German and French". "I see" replied Cynthia.

The lunch took longer than expected, when they arrived back at the office, the receptionist said you have six messages, Mr Andrews, and she gave him slips of paper, he took them off her without a word, they proceeded to the lift to the first floor, Cynthia thought he had something more on his mind, but dismissed it as being paranoid. In the afternoon, they carried on chatting about all sorts of things, filling in each own background, after while he said, "I must attend to these messages, ask Stevens for the dossier for you to peruse over, any thoughts let me have them", then walked out of her office, this is a man who knows what he wants, Cynthia thought.

That afternoon she studded the dossier and made notes of interest to her, in particular the Sydney connection, there was no mention of Edwina whatsoever or anyone else for that matter or any activity in the Kings cross area, or anywhere else in the Sydney area, Cynthia was taken by surprise, now what is he up too, she said to herself, I'd better keep an open mind about Peter Andrews. The afternoon went very quickly, a knock on the door, it disturbed her, it was Stevens, "Sorry to bother you, but it is past 6.00pm" How long will you be" he said, Cynthia jumped up, "Give me a couple of minutes", she replied and gave him the dossier. Cynthia closed the door and walked to the lift, as she entered the lift, a voice said hold the lift, it was Peter Andrews, "How's your day gone" "Fine" Cynthia replied, "Find anything interesting", a couple of things, but nothing major" Cynthia replied, he looked surprised but didn't say anything. Finally, Cynthia arrived back at the apartment, Mary was already in the kitchen, "Dinners almost ready, smells good, thought Cynthia, then went upstairs to change, "Did you ring Maggie" asked Mary" crumbs I completely forgot said Cynthia, "I ring when I've eaten", "It'll be too late now Cynthia, your best bet is to ring Saturday or Sunday morning about 12.00 noon" Mary replied.

The next day Cynthia arrived at work, there seemed to be more activity than yesterday, "What's going on" to the receptionist, "There's a big pow wow today in the boardroom, you have to go to the room on your right, when you get out of the lift Cynthia" she said, "Thanks" said Cynthia. On reaching the first floor, she looked for the boardroom, and saw Stevens waiting for her, he gave her an agenda and minuets, also motions to be carried, crickey this is more like a Company, than a government office, she said to herself, then entered, Andrews beckoned her to join him, "Morning" she said, he didn't answer, He stood up are we all here, everyone nodded, "Then we will begin the meeting went on till about 11.00am then broke for coffee.

Andrew's said "Follow me I'll introduce you to a few people of interest", he introduced Cynthia, to nearly everyone, most of them high ranking officials, there was one chap who was very interested in meeting Cynthia, he was very high up in government, his name was Johnathan Roberts, in fact (he was Peter Andrews boss), which was hush hush, Andrews introduced Cynthia to him, "Mr Roberts, this is Cynthia Boardman. "Well finally we get to meet" he said to Cynthia, he shook her hand firmly, and said "Welcome aboard", my dear, Cynthia said likewise, then Roberts walked away," Well what a to-do." said Cynthia. An extremely busy man Cynthia, I wouldn't pay any heed to it", He was very persistent that I offer you the job "Andrew's said, "I can't think why, I have no idea who he is" replied

Cynthia, she then took it as a complement, after all she was loving every minute of her new role.

After about half an hour or so, they all entered the boardroom again, some of the motions got quite heated, some just sat there, and took it all in till it came to the voting, some talked amongst themselves before they voted, Cynthia was fascinated by it all, most of the discussions were top- secret of course.

The meeting closed about 3.00pm Andrews turned to Cynthia, "Glad that's out of the way" he said to her, Cynthia just looked at him, "It can get a bloodbath sometimes", "Really!, I would never have guessed", Cynthia said in her sarcastic voice, he laughed, they each went back to their own office, about an hour had passed, a knock on the door, and Andrews walked in, "Can we go over your comments, and observations Cynthia, time is of the essence, there is quite a lot of Jap activity going on with their reconnaissance planes especially over our ports". Cynthia was in a quandary, should she tell him what she and Jeff knew, or was he just fishing, then she thought Oh' what the hell in for penny in for a pound, she said "I have read the dossier, and there are a lot of holes in the reports, she went on, it was as if someone was trying to hide the information or even give a false impression that everything was fine, she couldn't make up her mind".

Andrews was listening intently, "Carry on he said" engrossed, "There is one significant piece of information, that isn't even recorded anywhere", "What's that" he asked, Cynthia told him about the Sydney cohort that her and Jeff Owen had been working on for nearly a year, they knew the ring leader, but she was very evasive, it was as if someone was tipping her off before they got to her as far as she knew, Jeff Owen was still working on the case when she left. Andrews was very quiet, then he spoke I have suspected for some time, that we might have a mole, amongst us, I haven't a clue who it might be, I sat in that meeting today, eyeing everyone up, most of them I know very well, not a hint from anyone, Cynthia interrupted him," I have an idea, because I think Jeff and I have thought that for some time we might have a traitor, and we were quite sure something big is going down, sooner than later" "And what's your idea", asked Andrews.

Would it be possible for me to go back to Sydney, "I have an informant there so I could go back to help finish the job Jeff and I started," He just starred at her, "Say something at least" she shouted, "Sorry, I was just thinking, we could go over together and work with Jeff Owen, undercover"," Can you set the ball rolling with your informant," I'll try" replied Cynthia, "I'll arrange everything else" Andrews said. Cynthia looked at her watch it was turned six, "I'd better get going, she said to Andrews" He didn't even look at her, "Very well see you in the morning" Goodnight Sir" Cynthia said, He just nodded and stared out of the window. Cynthia thought he was strange at times, she hoped she had done the right thing telling him everything.

Cynthia, hurried on home, Mary was already there, "Sorry again for being late Mary, I'll make it up to you" "No need Cynthia you've made many a meal for me it's been difficult in getting fresh vegies lately, I don't know why" Mary said," Cynthia said I think it's because of the war, then said, "I may have to be away for the couple of weeks" said Cynthia, "The week after is when I am seeing JR I am hoping we can have a few days away" "Have you booked anything yet" asked Cynthia "No I thought I'd wait while JR gets here, then we can choose together" said Mary, "Great that will work out fine for the both of us, said Cynthia.

Cynthia then changed the subject, you haven't seen Kathy lately have you, "Why" asked Mary, "I just wanted to thank her for the information she gave me, it helped a lot, Mary looked at Cynthia, you want to get in touch with her don't you, thought Mary. So how do you talk" asked Cynthia, "I take her into the changing rooms, she tries clothes on, then buys something off me" "I see", so you can't get in touch with her if needs be, Mary was in a spin, "You do know how to get in touch with her don't you, don't you" Cynthia was pressing Mary for an answer, "Stop it Cynthia your shouting" yelled Mary, "Sorry Mary it is really important I get in touch with her, she might be in danger, I just want to warn her that's all, I'll be in heaps of trouble for telling you this, after all, I am bound by the official secrets act" Cynthia said.

Mary went upstairs and came down with an address it read 300 Lyons Road, Sydney, well I never, Cynthia said out loud, she only lives on the same road as me in Sydney, then said to Mary, thank you Mary, I really appreciate this, and don't worry I'll keep Kathy safe, "What will you do now," Cynthia asked Mary, "I can't tell you anymore Mary, but I promise you this she will be safe", was Cynthia reply. There was silence for some time, each in their own thoughts, Cynthia jumped up, fancy a drink Mary, yes was the reply, she came back in the room with a bottle of Malt Whiskey, wow! "Where did you get that Cynthia? "Don't ask" said Cynthia and smiled, she then poured the whiskey out for them both. I wonder how Maggie coping with her two little ones, they both started laughing, you can imagine her, shouting Joe every time they cry, or want their nappies changing, I wonder how the nails are coping with all that washings, what a culture shock for her, by this time they were giggling, shall I pour you another one, asked Cynthia, Mary said no I have to be up in the morning, still giggling, I'm off upstairs tripping upstairs all the way.

Cynthia felt guilty about how she had treated Mary, but it was essential to find these people, Cynthia was sure that they were planning something big, then she thought about the informant, she went through all her working colleagues back in Sydney, she had one or two ideas but nothing concrete, if I get a chance I'll have a word with Jeff.

The next day was a Wednesday, luckily for Mary she had the afternoon off, her head was spinning from the whiskey she drank the night before, I'll kill that Cynthia when I see her, she said to herself, she opened the door, the brightness was too much for her eyes, she had to put her sunglasses on, it wasn't really that sunny, but light bothered her, she walked towards the tram, then stopped. That's Kathy, she said to herself, with that Edwina, they got on a tram for Brunswick Street, Mary jumped on the same tram, it took her near to where she worked, she watched them from a distance, Edwina was bulling Kathy, she grabbed Kathy's arm, and sat down, Mary kept her head down, she didn't know what to do, whether to follow them or go to work, she decided to go to work, but made a note of the tram number.

Your late Mary, said the supervisor, I'm sorry Mary said, I was sick on the way here, I think it's something I must have eaten last night, I really don't feel at that well, I think you had better go home Mary, said the supervisor, you have never had any time off for illness all the time you have worked here, go to see the doctor Mary, you might have a stomach bug, Mary just nodded to her, and made her way out of the store. Mary couldn't get home quick enough, she hailed a taxi, bother the expense she said to herself, St Kilda's they soon reach the destination, "How much" 7/6d gosh that's a lot thought Mary, she gave him, 10 shillings keep the change, and ran into the flat, she flung opened the door, Cynthia, Cynthia are you still here, suddenly Cynthia came into sight, she looked fantastic in her navy suit, and white blouse, it suited her to a treat, Mary stopped in her tracks, Cynthia looked great, just look at her, and I look a complete wreck, Mary thought.

"Whatever's the matter", asked Cynthia, Mary blurted out I've seen her, "Who! Edwina of course getting a tram to Brunswick, I had to get off at Flinders Street for work, when I arrived at work I said I wasn't feeling too well, that I felt ill this morning, which wasn't a lie, I really don't feel that rosy, the supervisor suggested I came home, and here I am.

Cynthia immediately telephoned Andrews, she turned around to Mary, "If you wouldn't mind Mary, this is a private conversation", "I understand" Mary went into the lounge.

Cynthia entered the lounge, "Do you think you could retrace your steps Mary,

"I can" said Mary, have we any pictures of Kathy with Edwina, asked Cynthia, "I'll have a look" Mary came down with a big tin box, it was full of photos of them all, from Tilbury to Melbourne, "Gosh so many" said Cynthia, Mary handed Cynthia a fistful, they started sifting through them," Here's one of Kathy, it looks recent enough" said Cynthia, Mary said I'm sure we took one of them both when she came out of hospital", but it doesn't seem to be here," Perhaps Kathy took it with her" said Cynthia. They headed back into the city, this time taking the same tram as Kathy and Edwina, and getting off at Brunswick Street, Mary recognised the conductor, and showed him the picture, did you notice this girl this morning about 7.45am she was going to Brunswick Street, Carlton, "I sure do my lovely red hair, didn't like the woman she was with" Can you remember the stop they got off at", asked Cynthia. Brunswick Street or was it Grattan Street they wanted, I told them to get off and go down Johnson Street,", "Can you let us know which stop" Mary asked, I will, he replied, it didn't take too long before the conductor, said Johnson Street, Mary and Cynthia alighted the tram.

Where do we go from here thought Mary, "Follow me Mary" Cynthia said, Mary followed Cynthia, do you know where they are, "No I don't Mary" let's just pretend we are looking for a house to rent around here, leave the talking to me" Mary didn't answer. hey knocked on a few doors asking whoever answered if they knew of any properties up for rent around this area, no-one seem to know, "It's a lost cause Cynthia let's go home, Mary really wasn't feeling too well" "Just a few more, they went onto Elgin Street, then onto Swanson Street, by this time Mary had, had enough. I'm going home Cynthia, I'm tired of walking around", "Just another street and I promise, then we'll go back" replied Cynthia, suddenly they arrived at Grattan Street," Look Cynthia, Grattan Street," Mary said, "Leave the talking to me", they stated to knock on a few more doors again. Cynthia asked whoever answered a door, had they seen two girls who had recently moved in, they were there friends, and couldn't remember the house number, one or two didn't know, then one said I think someone has just moved into no 25 a few days ago, can't be sure it's them you're looking for. Cynthia smiled and said "Thank you ever so much" Cynthia was overjoyed, come-on Mary we'll, have a look at the house, to see what's inside, "They might be in and see us" said Mary, "That's a thought, let's go back the way we came" which is exactly what they did.

Cynthia left Mary and went onto work, it was nearly lunch by this time, it didn't take too long to reach the office, she entered and went straight into the lift to her office, Stevens was there, she asked if Andrews was in, he replied I think so, she proceeded to Andrews office, knocked on the door, a voice said come in, Cynthia entered, "Any news" Andrew's said. Cynthia replied "Yes I think so. Cynthia then began to tell Andrews, what exactly had gone on this morning, she mentions Mary her flat mate, coming home from work not feeling too well, and told Cynthia that she had seen Edwina and Kathy who are one of the gang Edwina especially, Kathy is the one who is in danger from Edwina, and has to do what she says, Edwina bullies her," I'm digressing aren't I", Andrews nodded."

"Well the long and short of it, I think I've found one of their safe houses, on Grattan Street number 25 to be exact", Andrew's jumped up "Well done girl", I'll mobilise the troops," Shall I come too" No! You stay here its best this way, said Andrews" Cynthia was very disappointed, but understood. Meanwhile, surveillance was put on the house, in teams of two, Andrews went to the rear of the house, to observe if anyone was still in, looking through windows during the day was not recommended by the department, it draws too much attention.

Andrews came back, got into his car, he said he thought the birds had flown, but it would take 24hrs before they would get permission to go in, once they had the clearance, they would enter the building by which ever means they could. When Andrews returned, he said to Cynthia "No joy I'm afraid, it looks though they have gone in hurry too, so they may have left something, who knows" I'm waiting for the right paperwork to come through, it will probably take 24 hrs. Cynthia just said" I see" "Don't worry Cynthia we'll get the bastards," he then went to his office, by this time it was 4.00pm, Cynthia decided she would leave early as Mary wasn't feeling well. It didn't take long to reach home, "Hi Mary" Cynthia said, "In here" Mary was laying down on the settee," Oh' you poor thing, are you still no better", Mary nodded, then said "No more whiskey for me especially in weekdays", I'm thinking I'll take another day off, it will do me good, JR should be here next weekend, it will give me chance to catch up on a few things".

"How's your day gone any luck, drawn a blank I'm afraid" replied Cynthia,

"I've been thinking" "Careful Mary" Cynthia replied in her usual cynical voice.

Do you think you might have a traitor here in Melbourne, or Sydney? "You've been reading too many books, or watching too many films Mary", Cynthia tried to laugh it off, but how right Mary was.

CHAPTER TWELVE

Why don't you take an leisurely bath and relax for once" said Mary, which is exactly what Cynthia did, it also gave her time to dwell on things, and try to determine just who was giving them (meaning Edwina and Co) the information, and just how much was Kathy is involved voluntary or under duress, and what about Harry Barns, she didn't take too kindly to him, he seemed evasive and unwilling to pursue any leads with her, so many unanswered questions, which sent her alarm bells ringing again, I think I will give Jeff a ring tonight, and talk things through with him, I am certain something is going to happen, but I can't think what, Cynthia came downstairs, fully refreshed, and in her loungers, Cynthia opened a bottle of wine, which was from Maggie, a case in fact, which Maggie was always sending cases of wine to them, it was good wine too, which Cynthia enjoyed with her meal.

Mary wasn't always bothered about wine, she preferred a beer," Have a glass of wine Mary, hare of the, Mary winced at the thoughts of it, "It really will do you good, just have a small glass" Cynthia insisted, Mary begrudgingly took the glass of wine off her, and took a small sip. After dinner, Mary was feeling much better, Cynthia was right, that wine did help, plus the meal of course, Mary put the radio on to listen to the music, then picked up her book and began to read, Cynthia poured herself another wine, and went into the hall to ring Jeff, what time is it 7.30pm he should be home hopefully, she said to herself, she started to dial the number, it began ringing, pick up Jeff, she waited for a while, he mustn't be in, then a voice said hello" Jeff Owen here," Hi Jeff Cynthia here". Jeff spirts were down, but hearing from Cynthia raised them again, "So how's things with you in Melbourne, "Fine, then she started to tell him the tale, about the safe house, Kathy's involvement or non-involvement, that she still thinks, something big is going down call it intuition Jeff, I just feel it makes sense, and I am definitely sure that someone is leaking information, "You and me both" said Jeff.

Cynthia also mentioned that her and Andrews were thinking of coming over to Sydney, sometime next week to go over the operation with him, "It will be lovely to see you Cynth" Jeff said, Cynthia just smiled, and said me too. Cynthia carried on, I sometimes wonder whether Edwina is just a distraction to keep us off the scent. "I see" said Jeff, "It's been pretty quiet here too, we still have people wondering around Kings Cross, nothing so far," I think it is a ruse Jeff "However I've got some information for you to follow up, it might be worth looking into, "We'll be glad of any information Cynthia", Jeff said, she carried on, try this address 300 Lyons Road Drummoyne, that's where Edwina actually lives with Kathy, and that's where all the meetings apparently take place every Friday,

"Wow!!, that's near where you used to live, cried Jeff"

"I know bloody cheek of it, that's all I have for now", said Cynthia,

Take care Jeff keep me posted, you might just get lucky for once, see you sometime in a couple of weeks hopefully. The telephone line went dead, it was nice talking to Jeff, I do miss him, Cynthia said to herself, I think I'll ring Maggie now see how she getting on with the twins, Cynthia shouted to Mary what time is it in Perth, Mary didn't answer, Cynthia entered the room, she had fallen to sleep, Oh' bother. Cynthia tided up and secured everything, left a note for Mary, then retired to her room, she enjoyed the solace it gave her time to think, she decided to write to Mum and Dad, and then to Maggie, to tell her what was happening, and when would be the best time to ring her, (she had forgotten about what Mary had told her, about ringing at weekends) she hoped the babies were doing well, also Joe and the family

It was now approaching weekend, Cynthia had not heard from Jeff, which she found frustrating, her office had reports of reconnaissance flights over Sydney harbour, which where a great concern at the office, Andrews especially was very concerned, "What are they up too Cynthia" Andrews said," I don't know, but I tell you this I would put everyone on Red Alert, cancel all leave, check what ships are docked in the harbour, and see if there is anything that the Japs would love to destroy, like they did in Darwin," said Cynthia," I can see you going far and one day replacing me" Andrews said. Cynthia just laughed it off, deep down she was chuffed. Andrews immediately put everyone on Red Alert, increased the skeleton staff over the weekend and all personnel to be extremely vigilant, get this communique off immediately Steven" Andrew's said. There was still had no word from Jeff, she was getting very agitated about it, I'll ring him when I get home the day couldn't go quick enough for her, she went to Andrew's office, "Do you mind if I leave early, I have one or two irons in the fire, that I need to check up on. "Fine" Andrews replied. She left the office, and hailed a taxi, St Kilda's please, "No problem" he said, and drove off, soon they arrived at St Kilda's, "Where about Miss" "This will do, she paid him, and walked to the apartment. Once she got home she started to get dinner ready, made a cuppa, went to wash and change, by this time it was 5.00pm, I'll give it another hour or so before I ring Jeff she said to herself, she poured herself a sherry, and poured one for Mary.

Once again Cynthia pondered over the days happening, she was racking her brains to see if a spark would trigger something off, then it came to her in a flash, I bet they are going to bomb Sydney Harbour Bridge, she jumped up, ran to the phone to ring Andrews, a voice said the office is now closed, our hours 9.00am till 6.00pm Monday to Friday. Oh' bother, shit she said to herself.

Cynthia's thoughts were interrupted by Mary coming home, "Hi Mary" Cynthia said with a smile on her face dinner is almost ready, "Great I'll nip upstairs and change," "You look in good spirts" said Cynthia, "Yes a couple of more days and JR will be here" Mary said, oh' crumbs Cynthia thought, I'd better keep strum. "What day is it exactly is he due to arrive" asked Cynthia "I'm almost sure it's the 3rd or 4th, he wasn't that precise, he just said, about that date, I suppose when there is a war going on things can happen." Cynthia just nodded and said "Well let's hope he arrives on time, and then you will have the time to spend together." "Thank you Cynthia what a lovely thing to say" said Mary, and went upstairs. 'O' crumbs, Cynthia felt very guilty, knowing what she had suggested to Andrew's, but like Mary had said when you are at war, and you have different priorities. Mary came down to dinner, saw the sherry, pondered whether to drink it, then said to herself, what the heck, it tasted lovely the other night, the whiskey can stay in the bottle for me, the sherry left her with a warm glow.

I've written to Maggie and Mum and Dad, Cynthia said, "What the time difference in Perth and Melbourne" asked Cynthia, Mary replied "Three hours, that's why I said you have ring at her at 12.00 noon here so it is 3.00pm in Perth, Maggie said that's the best time, "Good" Cynthia (didn't mention that she had forgotten about the time difference), we can ring her this Sunday. They had a quiet evening as usual which both girls enjoyed, their company was enough, for them to relax, Cynthia suddenly realised, the time, "Gosh I'd better ring Jeff" as she approached the phone, it started to ring, she picked up the phone, before she could say is that you Jeff, a voice said "Andrews here" you rang the office, Cynthia hesitated, I'm at home, can I meet you somewhere, "I'm outside your apartment right now" blimey thought Cynthia, does this man never switch off or sleep", Cynthia went outside, got into to Andrew's car and said, "I think it might be Sydney harbour Bridge the Japs want to blow up, think about the morale booster it would give them, and just the opposite for the Australians, it would be mind-blowing".

Andrew's was speechless, "Say something" Cynthia said," I'll pass it on immediately" "I sincerely hope you are wrong" then he bade her goodnight and drove away, Cynthia felt sorry for him, poor sod... Suddenly Cynthia felt cold there was a nip in the air, she crept back into the house, Mary was deep into her book hadn't even noticed she wasn't there, Cynthia spoke to her, is the book interesting, "Yes" said

Mary, "I just have to ring someone Mary I won't be too long, "No worries" was Mary's reply.

Cynthia once more tried to ring Jeff, he answered, "Is that you Cynth" you could be onto something, we checked the house, it was empty, as though they had left in a hurry, we searched every nook and cranny, and lo and behold we came across a map, of Sydney Harbour, with various pin-point markings, we have passed the information onto Harbour Control. Jeff carried on I believe they have had notification from the Melbourne Office, about an imminent attack," "I don't suppose that you had anything to do with that, in a sarcastic voice", Cynthia just smiled to herself, "Please be careful Jeff, it is lovely to hear your voice, I sure do miss you" and I miss you Cynth said Jeff, "When this is all over we'll meet up and have a few beers" "You're on" Cynthia replied.

The following day being Friday, Mary was in buoyant mood, she was singing along to the music, and all was well in the world, she was hoping JR would come walking through the door, just like they do on the pictures, when suddenly she was interrupted by Cynthia, "What the hell or you doing Mary" she said in a sarcastic way, which used to irritate Mary enormously, "Nothing", replied Mary, and got on with her breakfast, there was the usual two or three minutes silence, then Cynthia said "Sorry Mary, I've a lot on my mind at the moment, I'm really happy for you and JR". Mary was magnanimous as ever, "See you tonight Cynthia, I'm going to do some shopping, and get my hair done," "Steady on girl splashing out" Mary just giggled, and went out the door.

The day was going very slowly for Mary, even though they were busy, the supervisor came to her, your last day Mary, do you have any plans or anything with JR? "Yes" said Mary, we are going on a tour, up by the Dandenongs," I haven't booked anything yet, I'm waiting to book it with JR" I've never seen anything of Australia all the time I've lived here, I believe the scenery is fantastic," "Yes" the supervisor said, "Australia is a beautiful Country, and so vast Mary, it would take a lifetime to see it all", then the supervisor gave Mary her salary for the month. Mary opened the pay packet, she had good sales this month and was hoping for a bumper bonus, to her surprise, she had more than she thought, great she said to herself that should help us enjoy our time together.

Her thoughts were once again interrupted, "Excuse me" Mary, she knew that voice, Kathy she said to herself, and swung around, Kathy, looked dreadful, she took her into the changing room,

"I really do need to speak to Cynthia, it is very urgent", Kathy was in a right old state,

"You look awful Kathy

"I'm alright really haven't been too well lately that's all" was Kathy's answer. she started to tell Mary,

I have left Edwina and her pals they are dangerous people Mary, and I have some papers that I've taken from Edwina's safe, which I think Cynthia needs to see, it is all in German, I remembered that Cynthia once said she could speak German. Edwina or somebody will be after me, I'm sure, they will try to kill me, I'm scared Mary", Mary said," Do they know you are here in Melbourne". "No" I've tried to leave a trail with a suggestion that I have gone up to Brisbane, I know they go up there a lot, somewhere near Townsville I think" Mary pondered on what to do, "I can't see Cynthia wanting her at the flat, how do I get in touch with her? "Look Kathy my lunch is 1.00 – 2.00pm, stay here in this changing room, I'll look for some clothes for you".

Mary went off to look for clothes for her to try on, she looked on the bargain rail, to see if she could get anything cheap, but it was not a cheap shop, oh' bother Mary said to herself, I'll get the clothes on my tag, and that is what she did, with a handful of clothes and undies she went back to the changing room, "Here you are Kathy, but Kathy had gone, Mary was mortified, she had left everything there, with a note don't look for me Mary, I'll find you. Mary was upset, the day went downhill from then on, all she could think about was Kathy and what danger she might be in, Mary was beginning to hate Edwina Aston for what she had done to Kathy.

It was nearly time to close the store, Mary in her hearts of hearts was hoping Kathy would be somewhere outside the store, she had bought some clothes for herself, so she put all the papers Kathy had left and concealed them in her new clothes, as not to draw too much attention when she left everyone wished her a happy holiday and good luck with JR, Mary just nodded, her mind was on other things, now I know how Cynthia feels at times.

Mary said to herself. Mary didn't even think about having her hair washed, she went straight to Parliament buildings to see if she could speak to Cynthia, she entered through the main doors, she was amazed how big it was and busy, she went to the receptionists, "I'm sorry we are closed for the day" she said to Mary, "I must speak to Cynthia Boardman if she is here it is very important I must see her, it is very urgent."

Mary was very persistent, "Just a minuet I'll see what I can do" the receptionist went across the hall, and into the lift. Upon arriving on the first floor, Millie made her way to Cynthia's office, she knocked on her door, "Come in" Cynthia said, she was taken aback when she saw Millie, "What is it Millie you looked flustered", I have a very irritated women downstairs she is insisting she speaks to you immediately, something about a Kathy, Cynthia jumped up, "Show her up here please Millie" said Cynthia, Millie nodded and went out the door, upon her return to the reception area she beckoned Mary to come over to the lift, "Miss Boardman will see you, I'll take you up. Follow me, by this time Mary had managed to calm herself down.

When they arrived at the first floor, Cynthia was waiting for them, "Thank you Millie" Millie said goodnight and went back down in the lift. Cynthia took Mary into her office, Cynthia had thought it might be Kathy herself, but how would she know where Cynthia worked, suspicion was awe with Cynthia, could she really trust Kathy, and now she's put Mary in danger as well, all this was going on in Cynthia mind, when suddenly, "Say something Cynthia, I'm at my wits end here" said Mary. "Tell me what's brought you here, I'm just surprised to see you, at my place of work, it was a shock Mary", "I knew you worked here, I've seen you quite often go in and out of the building, sometimes with a rather distinguished gentleman" again Cynthia was flabbergasted with Mary. "Kathy came to the store again", Mary told Cynthia that Kathy is very frightened that they might try to kill her.

Cynthia immediately got up "Just a minuet Mary" she shouted Stevens, "Can you make us coffee and is Andrews still in"? "Yes he is" Stevens replied, with that Cynthia went out the door, whilst Cynthia was away, Mary took out the papers that Kathy had left, and put them on Cynthia's desk, Stevens came in with the coffee, and sat with Mary for a while, "White or Black" he said to her, "White please" Mary replied.

CHAPTER THIRTEEN

Cynthia knocked on Andrews door, it took some time for him to answer, she knocked again, and opened the door, he was on the telephone, he looked grim, he pointed to a chair and indicated to Cynthia to sit, he finished his conversation, then turned to Cynthia, and in a stern voice said. You were right about Sydney harbour Cynthia, but wrong on the target, Japanese mini subs have bombed the Kuttabul a converted ferry boat as well as Allied ships, with the loss of nineteen lives and several casualties, Cynthia was shocked, she just stared at him, they both looked at each other not speaking.

Andrews broke the silence, "What was it you wanted" he asked Cynthia, she began to tell him about Kathy, and Mary, and the various papers that was left by Kathy, for Mary to give to her, that Mary was in her Office, with the documents and they are in German, He immediately rose from his chair, Cynthia caught hold of his arm, "Before you go in, Mary's fellas is a lieutenant on the Kuttabul that has been sunk, they are due to meet up this weekend for a fortnights holiday they haven't seen one another since the beginning of this year," So please no mention of the bombing".

"He was angry, bloody hell Cynthia what do you take me for" and he headed straight for the door, Cynthia trotted behind him like a scolded little schoolgirl, she was seething inside idiot she said to herself.

They reached the room, and entered, then Andrews said, "Hi now what can we do for you Mary isn't it", in a warm and friendly way, this guy never ceases to surprise me, thought Cynthia, Stevens left the room, Andrews shouted, "Make some more coffee will you Richard, it's going to be a long night" "Right you are Sir" was Stevens reply. "Now young lady I'm afraid we have lots to get through here I'm sure you will understand, we are very grateful for your help, Cynthia see that this young lady gets home safely, I will expect you back here by 9.00pm" Cynthia just nodded, the worst had to come for Mary, and how could she tell her, that it was she that had ordered more personnel on watch at Sydney harbour over the weekend, she couldn't bear the consequences if Mary ever found out especially if JR is one on the causalities or even worst has been killed.

Mary gave Cynthia the note it read," Please do not try to find me I'll find you. Mary said, I'm more upset because I won't' be at the store for the next couple of weeks," Cynthia faced grimaced, if only she knew what was in store for her. Then Cynthia said, "Mary why don't you go upstairs put your clothes away, I'll make something to eat and hopefully we can try to relax, at least you have something to look forward to seeing JR after all this time, "I have to go back to work", Mary reluctantly went upstairs, and got herself organised, when she came down, the meal was nearly ready, "Smells good" Cynthia, I am really starving I missed lunch through Kathy." "Cynthia poured Mary a large wine, blimey Cynthia are you trying to get me drunk, Cynthia just smiled at her, "Who me" and they laughed, Cynthia wasn't at all hungry, and couldn't eat a thing, "What's wrong Cynthia, you normally have a good appetite, you're just playing with the food". "I know "Cynthia said, I'm worried about Kathy, she has put her life at risk, to give me these papers, I do hope she will be ok". Mary said, "Look Cynthia Kathy's a fighter, she has had to be all her life, she's a survivor", "I do hope you are right Mary" Cynthia said in a wistful tone, Mary wasn't used to seeing Cynthia like this, she wondered if there was something else Cynthia wasn't telling her.

Mary went to put the radio on, but unknowing to her, Cynthia had taken the fuse out so it wouldn't work, I don't understand this, Mary said," it was fine this morning," Cynthia pretended to have a look, well we have had it a long time, said Cynthia, "I suppose so, it's just like the music, and the noise of it, that's all, somehow you just don't feel alone, especially when you're not here." Mary replied. Gosh Mary I really do have to go, she telephoned for a taxi, and hurriedly ran out the door when it arrived, she yelled "Don't wait up for me, not sure how long I will be" then the door slammed, Mary just stared at the glowing fire, it was winter now, the nights could get very cold, she washed the dishes and cleared the table, decided to put her loungers on, came back down, poured herself another drink, then settled down to read her book. Mary tried to read, but her mind was working overtime, she couldn't think of anything only Kathy and the state she was in, she felt an affinity towards Kathy it was as though they were soul mates, which is something Cynthia would fail to understand whether it was their backgrounds she wasn't sure, then she decided to retire.

The taxi arrived at the office, Cynthia went to open the door it was locked, she rang the bell several times, after some considerable time someone opened it, Cynthia yelled "About bloody time it's freezing out here" the security man replied" You should have a key" Cynthia replied "Well I bloody well haven't" charming, I must say thought the man, a bit of a bitch if ever I saw one.

Cynthia arrived upstairs, went straight to Andrew's office," Ah! There you are just the girl, there lots to get through here, we have tried to put in some resemblance of order, by dates, that as far as we've got, as most of us have very limited knowledge of the German language" Andrews said. "My German is a bit rusty too" replied Cynthia, "But here goes let's see what we come up with," Cynthia then began to peruse the letters notes and maps, it took most of the night and early morning, to make any sense of what they had. It was about 7.30am by this time, Stevens knocked on her door. "Coffee and Toast Cynthia" "You are a darling Stevens" she said, he just smiled and left the room, after half an hour or so, Cynthia went to the wash room, too tidy herself up, luckily she always had a change of clothes, just in case she couldn't get home, her office was very accommodating with all the necessary amenities, chance any of the staff had to stay overnight.

It wasn't too long before Andrews came to her office," Any luck Cynthia" he asked, "There is plenty of information, nothing specific as yet, lots of addresses of safe houses across all the states, mainly near industry or the docks, also dates, some I have managed to tie up with events that have already happed, there is no doubt in my mind that we have enough information here to smash the cohort once and for all". Cynthia gave him the information, it was all written down in an articulate way for everyone to understand, Andrews was most impressed, he looked at her, she's been up most of the night, and yet she looks stunning, he said to himself. "You get home now Cynthia we'll take it from here" "There is just one thing, could you find out, if Lieutenant John Robert Harding is safe, it's Mary's boyfriend, they are planning getting married sometime this year, or early next year", he looked at her, "I'll see what I can do no promises mind" Cynthia smiled at him, "Thanks." and Cynthia he said, "You owe me one", she looked at him, now what does he mean by that I wonder?

When Cynthia arrived home, Mary was still in bed, so she crept upstairs to have a nice soak in the bath, and clear her head, she knew at some stage, Mary would find out about the bombing at the Harbour, she decided to take her out to lunch and do some window shopping liked they use too, it would be nice for them to unwind. A knock came to the door "Is that you Cynthia" asked Mary, "Well who the bloody hell would it be she yelled" Mary didn't even answer her, she went back to her room, Cynthia chastised herself, at being so thoughtless, at times Cynthia Boardman you are an arsehole, she finished dressing and went downstairs, Mary was still in her bedroom, sulking.

Cynthia said to herself, I must ring the office, suddenly the phone began to ring, Cynthia ran to pick it up, "Is that for me Cynthia" asked Mary, Cynthia just waved her arm at her, as if to say shut up, it was Andrews, "Cynthia that chap JR, he is safe, we tracked him down, we have arranged to fly him over here, he will be in Melbourne sometime tomorrow lunch time" "Thank God for that, thought Cynthia. It was a heavy load off Cynthia's mind, "Thanks a lot", "No worries remember you owe me big time Cynthia, "Again alarm bells started to ring, I don't like the sound of that, she said to herself, then put the phone down. Mary had gone back into her room, she was very upset with Cynthia, and she couldn't understand why, then there was a knock on Mary's door, "Can I come in" asked Cynthia, Mary replied" If you must" in a tone Cynthia hadn't heard before, "Gosh I must have really upset her, "This will cheer her up, I need to speak with you Mary it is important".

When Mary opened the door, she looked at Cynthia, "What is it" Cynthia entered the room, I have some news to tell you, "You sound serious Cynthia" said Mary, "Look sorry about this morning, I had something on my mind concerning you and JR", Mary was taken aback, "What do you mean", We learnt last night that Sydney Harbour had been bombed, well the ships that where docked there, and one of the boats was the Kuttabul that JR is serving on, there were fatalities, and casualties, I asked my boss if he could find anything about JR whether he was safe or not. Mary went numb, Cynthia could see she was in shock, Mary blurted out "He's dead isn't he" and started sobbing uncontrollably, Cynthia got hold of her, Mary was screaming and crying at the same time, Cynthia slapped her face hard," Calm down Mary he's alive! Mary just looked at her and didn't move, "What did you say" Cynthia repeated herself, "He's alive! And the best news is, he's being flown over to Melbourne, he should arrive sometime tomorrow lunch time, my boss fixed it for you. "As a thank you for yesterday, bringing the documents to his attention, they helped us a lot, we shall be forever in Kathy's debt too.

Oh' Cynthia, I'm fed up with this bloody war, it has ruined everything, I hate it when I hear of people we know who came with us being killed, or taken prisoners by the Japs, the tears where flowing down her cheeks, Cynthia grabbed hold of her," Mary, JR is safe! and that's all you should be worrying about, come on pull yourself together, get organised for tomorrow sort yourself out, then later on this afternoon we will have a slap up meal at our favourite restaurant on Lygon Street" my treat. It soon got to 3.00pm Cynthia had gone back to bed to sleep for an hour or so, she felt so tired, the emotion was just too much for her, Mary did get herself together, and washed her hair, and tried on clothes, deciding what she should take or not, they were touring after all, so she needed good shoes, but also dress shoes, as well as causal clothes and evening clothes, it was a 10 day tour so it was important to get it right, also she wasn't sure about the weather, but she knew one thing she had to look her best for JR.

Mary looked at her watch, crickey, its 6.00pm, I'd better give Cynthia a shout, Mary was already dressed for the evening, she knocked on Cynthia door, "Its six o'clock Cynthia" Mary said, "I'm getting ready Mary won't be too long", "Did you manage to sleep" asked Mary, "like a baby" was Cynthia's reply. Soon Cynthia arrived downstairs she looked radiant, she was tall, slender and had an air about her, she also had lovely blond hair, which sometimes she wore up, her eyes sparkled like diamonds, Mary often wondered why she had no man in her life, or perhaps she had a reason not to mention anyone, with the kind of work she did, she had heard her mention Jeff once or twice, but that was all. The night went pretty well, every man and his dog seemed to be out, nearly everyone was talking about Sydney Harbour incident, and what was the government was doing, there was plenty of advice being offered as to what should be done.

CHAPTER FOURTEEN

Cynthia found it intriguing, and she was quite bemused by it all, Mary did wonder if it was spoiling her night," Is it upsetting you Cynthia hearing all this criticism" asked Mary, "Not in the least, everyone is entitled to have their say, that's what a free society is all about", was Cynthia's reply. Mary thought flipping heck, that's a bit heavy for a Saturday night.

It was now about eleven," Shall make our way back Mary asked Cynthia, I've quite a lot on tomorrow" Cynthia just nodded, they asked for the bill, "My call Mary I told you my treat" Cynthia said emphatically, Mary said ok, they made their way home, when they reached Flinders Street, they hailed a taxi, back to St Kilda's, soon they arrived home. Mary went straight upstairs, "Thanks for a lovely evening Cynthia" she replied "Your welcome", "I'll be up shortly" Mary I just have something to do first, she went to telephone Jeff, I hope he is in, but the phone just kept ringing, bother, she herself decided to go upstairs and retire for the night.

Sunday morning was soon came around, Mary was up with the larks, her spirits were high once more, she tried to be quite so not to wake Cynthia, Mary made herself breakfast, sat down with a cuppa, it was strange not hear the radio on Mary wasn't used to it, but it gave her time to think about where she was going, and what might be in front of her, she had every intention of marrying JR if he proposed to her like he said he would, then it would mean moving out of the apartment, and getting a rental property somewhere else. It could even mean going to live in Sydney, who knows, thought Mary, her thoughts were broken by the telephone, she went to pick it up, her heart was thumping, "Yes" is Cynthia there, a voice said, "Just a minuet" Mary turned to go upstairs, Cynthia was half way down, "It's for you" Cynthia took the phone off her and didn't say a word.

"Hello" "Jeff here Cynthia", Just thought I'd let you know, what's happening here, we received quite a lot of info from your end, I have been up most of the night following the tip offs, we have captured a lot of dissidents around Parramatta and the Drummoyne area, about thirty in all, So many thought Cynthia, but no sign of the elusive Edwina, but it won't be too long before we catch up with her, there is just one thing Cynthia, and that is why I am ringing, we found your informant, Kathy she is in a terrible state, drugged to the high heavens, well out of it, she's lucky to be alive, I think they tried to kill her off with a massive drug overdose., she's lucky we found her when we did. Cynthia went cold, "You will look after her Jeff" she has helped me so much over these past twelve months or so, in fact she has been invaluable" We'll take good care of her Cynth, we'll put her in a safe house, when and if she recovers, from the overdose.

When Cynthia entered the lounge Mary was sat there, reading her book, she noticed that she had already had breakfast, "Some bad news and some good news Mary" Cynthia said, I know you won't say anything to anyone, "They have found the people responsible for the bombings, but no Edwina as yet, the good news is that Kathy is safe, they found her in a terrible sate, they had given her a drug overdose, enough to kill her, she is in hospital now, and if she recovers they will put her into a safe house. "The bastards Mary said, "I know what I would do with that Edwina if I had my way", "Steady on Mary you're talking murder here" "I don't care" people like that deserve everything they get, and quite often they get away with it" Cynthia got hold of Mary "I promise you now, Mary! Edwina will never ever get away with what she has done to Kathy we just have to hope Kathy pulls through.

Suddenly the doorbell rang, Mary jumped up and ran to the door, standing there was JR, she flung her arms around him, and kissed him, "Thank God you are safe" she said to him, He just stared at her, he didn't say too much, Mary could see that the bombing had affected him, he looked so tired, she took him in.

This is Cynthia my flat mate, Cynthia JR" Cynthia went to shake his hand, "It's nice to meet you, I heard so much about you" "All good I hope" he replied, Cynthia then said," Well I have to be off now Mary, have a good day and enjoy your holiday". JR sked to her "What holiday" I thought we could go on a tour in the Dandenong region here in Melbourne, it would only be Bed and Breakfast and evening dinner, we don't have to go on any tours if we don't want too, I just thought it would be nice for us just to be together, and do just what we wanted to do. "You look tired my darling, have you eaten? "No" bacon and egg, he looked at her and smiled, ""That'll be lovely" her heart was saddened at the state of him, she wondered whether it was a good thing to go away, or just to rest up at the apartment, or perhaps book into an hotel in Melbourne for a few days, after all she hadn't booked anything. It was now 4.00pm Mary said," Do you fancy going out for a meal, or I could cook a meal here, if you like", JR looked at her "I'm not hungry, I'm just tired," "Ok you rest JR and I'll put your things away for you", Mary picked up his suitcase and took it upstairs into the spare room, and started to unpack his clothes, she noticed, medicines and a letter, she began to read the letter, oh' my word Mary was shocked.

Mary sat and ponded what to do, her heart was heavy, with what she had read, all she could say was Shell-shock to herself, she knew only too well what it meant, a lot of service men from the first world war suffered with it. There was a chap that lived near her family in England, he suffered for years with terrible nightmares, you could hear him screaming especially at night, it had a psychological and a physical impact on the man, everyone thought it was funny and made fun of him, of course these people had never been to war, Mary felt sorry for him, she used to take him meals on the quiet, her dad was one of the many who said he was a nutter.

Mary went back downstairs, went into the lounge JR was still fast asleep, he looked dreadful, she tip-toed around the house as to not awaken him, he needs some peace, she said to herself, a couple of hours went very slowly for Mary, she was in tis-was, as to what to do, then she suddenly made her mind up, she went over to JR, he started stirring, he opened his eyes, he smiled, is that you Mary? She answered, "It is JR"." He closed his eyes and said "My Guardian Angel" and smiled at her again, "Now what about food, shall I make something" said Mary, He got up, "Where is the bathroom Mary, she told him where to go, he then went upstairs, "Your bedroom is on the right" Mary yelled "Thanks" JR answered.

After about half an hour, JR entered the lounge, he looked absolutely wonderful, he had changed in to shirt and slacks and casual shoes, he had a lovely tan, his blue eyes sparkled, was this the same man who arrived this morning, she said to herself, He looked himself now, "My that smells good Mary" they sat down to dine, Mary poured out a beer for him, she had a glass of wine, JR said "Wine, I didn't know you were so rich Mary" Mary explained that Maggie was always sending cases of wine over to them." JR said "Who is Maggie", Mary replied I'll tell you after we have eaten, it's a long story", they settled down to finish dinner, "Another beer JR," JR nodded, then he said "No more for me Mary I'm on medication", Mary pretended to be surprised, "What for" JR explained, that after the bombing of the Kuttabul, the explosions had triggered something off, it brought back the memory of the Repulse and The prince of Wales, being sunk by the Japs. It was terrible Mary, The Japs were firing at us while we were in the water, I saw many a man hit, and drown, the Doctor said, I had put it in by sub-conscious box, but when Sydney Harbour was bombed it brought it all back to me the horror of the sinking's, the tablets are supposed to help me keep calm and to prevent any anxiety I may have. You poor thing my sweet, well you will be safe now, I been thinking, we won't go on a tour, I am going to book us into the Menzies Hotel for two or three days, it is very posh, and expensive, but I have been saving up for this moment with you, and it will do us both good, to pamper ourselves", said Mary.

JR looked at her, "I too have savings" Mary, it sounds good to me, let's do it" Mary jumped up, I'm going to book now, for Wednesday

Thursday and Friday, JR chipped in, "And Saturday," Mary said, the money won't go that far JR, I have done my homework, JR just smiled at her. Soon Mary was back, well that's done, we have a whole day together here and tomorrow, so we can just relax, and perhaps have a slap up meal at our favourite restaurant, it would be nice if Cynthia could join us, I'll, ask her". "You seem to be close to Cynthia" JR said, "As a matter of fact I'm close to them all" JR looked at her, "I'll explain", so they sat down and Mary explained everything to him, about the four of them, travelling over to Australia together and staying friends, but leaving relevant things out, which were privy only to them. "I'm tired now Mary, my head is spinning, I can't take it all in, you'll have to be patient with me, till I know who's who", Mary replied "No worries JR, take as long as you want", Mary looked at her watch, golly it is late, "I'll just tidy up here JR, I won't be too long "Goodnight" JR turned around and went to her, he grabbed her, "Thank-you for being so understanding my lovely, I love you so much", then he kissed in the most tenderly way, Mary just succumbed and responded to him.

The next day there was a glow in Mary's face, she knocked of JR's bedroom door, no response, she knocked on the bathroom door, no response from the either, He must be downstairs, she said to herself, she went into the lounge, there he was, he looked much fresher, and calmer, "Good morning Mary, did you sleep well? "I slept very well thanks JR" was Mary's reply. They made the usual tea and toast, JR preferred coffee, they just whiled away the morning, it was nice not to have to rush out to work, thought Mary, I could live this life, soon it was 12.00 noon, Mary jumped up, "I'm going to ring Maggie up" "What now" said JR, "Yes, it is the only time we can talk to each other". The phone started to ring a voice said, "Hello" "Is Maggie there", "Just a minuet" a few minutes passed, "Maggie here" "It's Mary" Maggie screamed, and yelled "It's Mary Joe, It's Mary Joe", "I heard you Maggie" Joe said with a smile he knew deep down that she missed her friends, and sometimes felt guilty whisking her off to Perth at the other side of Australia

Mary set about telling Maggie everything that had gone on since they last spoke to each other, Sydney Harbour, Cynthia, finding Kathy, then she said JR is here we have about 10 days together, we have booked ourselves into the Menzies Hotel, for three nights at least, JR says four nights, but we will have to see how far the money goes, "Gosh Mary you are splashing out, you'll have Cynthia jealous if you are not careful" and they both laughed. "I have to go now Maggie, keep in touch," said Mary, "I'll ring you next time" Maggie said, then the phone went dead, Mary replaced the receiver, and went back to JR. The telephone began to ring again, Mary picked it up, "Hello" "It's Maggie", Mary, I've just had a thought, tell Cynthia, if she sees Kathy again, tell her that I am looking for someone to help me with the twins, and if she is interested, she can come and live here with us in Perth, Mary was overjoyed, oh' Maggie you are the most wonderful person. It was Joe's suggestion, Maggie said, "Tell him I'll give a big kiss when I see him, said Mary, "No you won't "cried Maggie "I hope JR is not listening to this conversation, then both started to laugh again.

JR asked, now what, Mary said, Let's go into town, and have peak inside the Menzies Hotel, have a drink or two in a pub nearby if you want, I'll show you where we all used to live in Albert Street, then we'll have dinner at Lygon Street, "It's a good job I have my walking shoes" said JR in that wry humour he had, Mary just laughed, "I'll leave a note for Cynthia chance she comes home, tell her about what Maggie has suggested about Kathy living in Perth with them, and that we are dinning at our favourite restaurant, if she wants to join us. They caught the tram into the city, Mary took him into the George's first, where she worked, he was most impressed with the store, the girls thought he was wonderful, JR said it wasn't quite like Harrods's but close enough for the Aussies, Mary said, "They'll skin you alive if they hear you JR", he was most impressed with, Finders Street Station, Melbourne's Town Hall, Parliament House, and the Shell Building, there are so many beautiful building to see, but they were running out of time, and JR was getting tired. "Where to next asked JR"? The Menzies Hotel, it was the Grandest Hotel in Melbourne, it wasn't too far from where Mary worked, and she wanted to have a look inside the Hotel, before they, they were due to arrive the next day.

They entered the building it looked really grand on the outside, but when they actually went into the foyer, it was magnificent very plush, JR whistled, Mary nudge him with her elbow, he just grinned at her, she gave him a dirty look, "Sorry Mary" he said still grinning, "Are we going in or what, "asked JR, Mary replied," I don't think we could afford a drink in here, let's wait till tomorrow, we still haven't seen everything, come-on", so they set off once again. Mary just looked at him, and thought, what the hell Mary, that's enough for him today, don't push it girl, let him get his breath, "I know let's just go and have a couple of beers, and watch the world go by" Mary said, "Sounds good to me", replied JR, and that's what they did, Mary took him to Young & Jackson's, they ordered a couple of beers, Mary always enjoyed a pub more, the atmosphere was better she thought, than a cocktail bar, which Cynthia always preferred.

It was getting close to 5.00pm they decided to get a taxi back to St Kilda's, so JR could rest up for a couple of hours, it didn't take too long to reach home, they entered the apartment, Cynthia had been home, she had read the note, was delighted with Maggie's suggestion, was sorry but she couldn't join them at the Bella Vista, maybe another time. That's a shame thought Mary. JR did if fact go upstairs to lie down, which gave Mary time to sort everything out for the next day, she put one or two things aside for packing, then gathered her thoughts, she was of course very upset about JR, and wondered if it was the right thing to do, to marry him, after all, she knew in her heart that she was totally besotted with him, and she also knew what shell-shock was and the effects it had on the people closest to them. Violent outbursts were quite common, with sufferers, who usually took it out on their nearest and dearest.

Mary wasn't sure if she could cope with that, also she had a good job, that she had worked so hard for. Her thoughts were interrupted by JR entering the room, Mary just melted when she saw him, he was such a handsome guy, she dismissed all negative thoughts, went over to him, and kissed him, he responded, and held her so tight, that she could hardly breath, "God I love you so much Mary "I don't know what I would do without you" Mary never answered him. They enjoyed the night out in little Italy as the locals called it, it was always busy, with its bars, cafés and restaurants, Mary took it for granted, but JR was fascinated by it all, although it was winter, and a chill in the air, it didn't seem to bother, Mary or JR, they just kept smiling at one another, it was strange, they knew people where all around them, but to them they were in the distance somehow.

When they arrived back at the apartment, JR grabbed hold of Mary again, he was more passionate than ever, Mary just succumbed to his charms, and one thing led to another. The next morning, Mary was walking on air, her negative thoughts, well and truly behind her, she was looking forward now, to having a few more days with JR, eventually JR came downstairs, he went straight to Mary, and said in a gentle voice, thank you for last night Mary, and I still want to marry you! Mary just lashed out at him, you oaf, she said, he was grinning, like a Cheshire cat, suddenly Mary saw the funny side, "You do have a wrapped sense of humour JR"

They had breakfast, then headed for Menzies Hotel, an air of excitement, and expectation, filled Mary's mind, as they linked one another, Mary felt so safe and secure, "Here we are" said JR, they entered, a porter came up to them," Carry your cases Sir, the boy said, JR just nodded at him, JR and Mary went to the reception desk," We have a booking" "What name is it" as the receptionist, Mary said, "Harding, JR Harding", JR just looked at her, Mary blushed slightly. The receptionist, beckoned a porter, "Room 202" she said, "This way Sir" so they followed the porter to their bedroom, Mary whispered to JR, "Have you any change for tip" JR just nodded, after all he had stayed in four and five star Hotels back in England with his Mum and Dad, so this experience was not new to him, he realised, that it might be something Mary hadn't done before, in his mind he wanted to help Mary ease her way into the plush surroundings.

The room was spacious, not much of a view, but plenty to watch, as people went along doing whatever they had to do, it was quite fascinating really, for Mary at least, JR wasn't too bothered, he just rang reception for coffee, not before too long a knock on the door, JR said, "Come in" a maid came with coffee, "Thank-you Miss" JR gave her a tip, she nodded and went out again, Do you fancy a walk now we can go to Albert Street, it's not that far away the walk will do us good", JR just nodded in approval, they set off, a few it didn't take long too Albert Street it looked spectacular, with Fitzroy Gardens, just across the street, she stopped at house number 332. "This is it JR, I just love this house, it felt really homely here, oh' don't get me wrong the apartment is sumptuous, but to me it is not as homely like this one was, I can't stay forever with Cynthia's, sooner or later I will have to move out.

"Cynthia has her life and I have mine, so I am thinking of trying to rent it, if I can afford it, all good things do have to come to an end", Mary said, come on JR let's have a beer somewhere. They headed back towards the Hotel, went pass a few independent shops, along the way, browsing, as one does, JR noticed a jeweller's shop, couple of doors away," Won't be a minuet Mary". Mary was too busy looking at a fashion shop, it was full of individual designs, and whoever did the window dressing, was very clever, Mary was taking it all in, one day I'll own a shop like this, but it won't be in Australia, she said to herself, then looked to see where he was, where the hell is he, then she noticed him, he was waving to her, and gesturing for her to come.

He grabbed hold of her and pushed her inside, what the hell Mary thought, and then she realised it was a jeweller's shop, "Try this one Miss if you please", Mary looked at JR, He just winked, she smiled, she eventually chose a ring, it was a beautiful single stone diamond engagement ring, then JR said in the shop," Marry me Mary", without hesitation she said yes," He picked her up, "You have made me the happiest man on this earth", then he kissed her, but Mary's thoughts were, Oh' My God, what have you gone and done!. Mary and JR, had the most wonderful four days anyone could wish for, JR had swept her off her feet, she was dancing on air, they shared lots of interests, going to the pictures was one of them, walking along the beach at St Kilda's, watching the sunset, even on a chilly evening, having a few beers, although, JR was careful about drinking, but most of all they loved dancing. All too soon the holiday was over, JR had to be back at base on the 14th and work for Mary, on Monday morning, so it was goodbyes, with tears and kisses, not wanting to let go of each other, the train arrived for Sydney, JR just looked at her, and slowly drew his arm away.

Mary wanted him to stay a while longer, with a huge sigh, he pulled himself away and entered the train, he looked at her through the train window, blowing her kisses, as the train edged out of the Station, Mary was heartbroken, sobbing uncontrollably, as she watched he train disappear.

CHAPTER FIFTEEN

Mary arrived back at the apartment, no JR, no Cynthia, she was now completely on her own once more, Cynthia had left a note, saying see would be away for approximately six weeks, on a course, Mary decided to take a bath and soak, it helped her to think about her future, and what might be in store for her, she still had the weekend to come, so she made arrangements to meet up with Grace, and the girls over the weekend. To Mary it was strange having all this time on her hands, it would have been better if Cynthia had been around, and Mary could have chatted about JR, on what to do, she was in a tis- was, about JR, her heart told to marry him, her head was telling her to think about it very deeply, she kept the engagement to JR to herself for the time being. The telephone began to ring, it was Cynthia, glad I've caught you in Mary, "I got your note" said Mary, "Good sorry its such short notice, I dearly wanted to meet JR another time perhaps", Mary told her that he had go back to base, and that she was seeing the girls over the weekend. On Monday she would be starting her new role as supervisor, "That's right, I'd forgotten, well that'll keep you out of mischief Mary", they both laughed, "Have to go now, will try and ring again, best of luck" the phone went dead, keep safe Cynthia, Mary said to herself.

Meanwhile back in Sydney, Kathy was responding to treatment and feeling more herself, apparently, unknown to her, Edwina had been systematically giving her drugs over a period of time, the doctor's explained to Kathy, that the drug dose they gave her was lethal, and that she was very lucky to be alive, the doctor also told her, that as far as they could tell no permanent damage had taken place but obviously couldn't be sure at this stage, Kathy didn't feel lucky, in fact she was depressed and upset that Edwina could do such a thing, and now she was on her own, her thoughts were interrupted by a nurse, someone to see you Kathy. Kathy's heart jumped, could it be Mary or Cynthia, "Hi my name is Jeff Owen", Kathy was deflated, "I need to ask you some question's if you're up for it", Kathy just nodded, Jeff could see she was down, the doctor had warned him, about her being depressed and the side effects from the drugs, "I believe you know Cynthia", Kathy's eyes had a tiny gleam in them, Jeff noticed the response.

Kathy gave him as much information as she could remember, giving him various addresses, that they visited in Brisbane, Broome, and Freemantle, and that they frequented a place in Kings Cross called the blue Lagoon, Cynthia was right all along, I wish she was here, said Jeff to himself, Kathy then said she was feeling tired and needed to rest. Jeff said he would come again and thanked her for her help, but just before he went, he thought she needs something to cheer her up, by the way, your friends, Kathy stared at him, "What about them" she said in an aggressive tone, Jeff looked at her," Oh not them, the three musketeers" was his reply, they all send their love, Kathy gave him a lovely smile, so they know I'm here, she said to herself.

A couple of weeks later Jeff returned, by this time Kathy was getting stronger, and was more herself, the doctor said she was well enough to leave, if she had somewhere to stay, Jeff knocked on her door, and opened it, "Can I come in" "Sure" Kathy replied, "Well you look great" Jeff said, "I believe you can leave now" "Yes" Kathy said in a hesitant voice, "Where will I go? I don't know anyone in Sydney. Jeff then said "No worries Kathy" you are to stay with Maggie and Joe in Perth, the girls have arranged it for you," Her face lit up, she had a beautiful smile, her deep auburn hair catching the sunrays, Jeff thought, what a looker she is. Now I thought I would just let you know, the information you gave us enabled us to catch more dissents, and we have gleaned valuable information from them, so we would like to thank you, "And what about Edwina, "No joy as yet I'm afraid, but we will find her, have no fear on that score" Jeff assured her. After a further week Kathy was discharged from hospital Jeff had arranged for Kathy to travel over to Perth on a bi- plane, where Maggie and Joe, would meet up with her in Augusta, there was a makeshift runway there, Jeff wished her well," Give my love to Cynthia, when you see her" Kathy looked at him and smiled," Thanks' for everything and I will".

Jeff then said, "You have been extremely brave, and thank you for helping us, we are very grateful to you". The plane took off, Jeff stayed till it, went out of sight, his thoughts turned to Cynthia once more, God I miss that women.

Maggie and Joe were waiting patiently, for her to arrive, Maggie was so excited, Joe was bemused, all he heard from her was we must look after Kathy Joe, she's been through a lot, Joe was only too pleased to help, he knew what it meant for Maggie, the plane landed as softly as it could. Maggie was straining to see Kathy, "There she is Joe" Maggie cried, "Over here Kathy" she shouted, Kathy saw her, and waved, Maggie took one look at her, My God she looks dreadful, she needs a few good dinners down her, Maggie didn't realise, the extent of Kathy's illness, or what had brought it on. Joe and Maggie ran up to Kathy," You look tired", "I am, it's a long journey," Kathy replied, come on let's get you home, "This is Joe my husband", "Pleased to meet you Joe", "likewise" answered Joe, it took a good hour to arrive at the estate, Kathy didn't say much, Maggie was waffling on, "You'll love it here" I'll show you your room" Maggie took her to the bedroom, it was quite spacious, the bathroom is over here, We'll let you rest up now.

It was evening now, and no sign of Kathy, Maggie went to the bedroom, knocked on the door, it's me Kathy, dinners ready, Kathy came to the door, do you mind Maggie, if I just stay in my room, I'm not hungry, "But you must eat something Kathy," replied Maggie, "I'll bring a tray" "Please Maggie I don't want to be a nuisance" Maggie could be very persistent when she wanted to be, and insisted that she must eat something, Kathy finally gave in. Kathy stayed in her room, Maggie was upset, she wanted to introduce her to the family, Joe said, leave her be Maggie, give her time, from what Jeff said, she's been to hell and back, Maggie nodded, "I suppose your right, I'll ring Mary at weekend to let her know Kathy's safe. The next morning, Kathy was still in her room, Maggie, went to see if she was alright, and knocked on the door, "It's Maggie Kathy, can I come in, no reply, Maggie knocked harder, Kathy, then opened the door, Kathy still looked distant, breakfast Kathy, asked Maggie, I'll rustle up tea and toast, I know you and Mary always had tea and toast, at weekends, Kathy nodded, I'll bring it to you, Kathy smiled and said thank you, Maggie got hold of her, your safe here, no- one knows you are here, except, Cynthia, Mary and Jeff.

Mary was enjoying her new role as supervisor it was challenging, she didn't realise all the work that was involved, complaints, exchanging clothes, making sure stock was correct, and checking tills, if they didn't tally to the cash total, the only advantage Mary could see, that it paid more, and you could walk around your department and meet the customer, she was into her second week, no letter from JR as yet, and nothing from Cynthia, no letter, or telephone call. In a way Mary was glad of the respite, she was feeling very tired, and wondered if she was getting a cold, she was hoping to rest up at weekend, which was only a couple of days away.

Meantime Cynthia, was having to train in combat fighting, which she absolutely loathed, firearm practice, which she didn't mind, the bulls-eye was Edwina, hence the fact that she got full marks for her shooting ability, her keep fit regime wasn't going down too well either, the sooner all this crap is sorted the better, I could be doing something more worthwhile than this, it was her fourth week, at the special unit of armed combat, she still had two more weeks to go. Andrews was kept informed of Cynthia progress, and had a wry smile when he learned she was kicking at the traces, he was impressed with her shooting ability, he wasn't at all surprised, at the lack of enthusiasm for the combat and keep fit programme, but it had to be done, she would then be a special undercover agent, part of an elite force, working abroad, and home.

Peter Andrews, was also busy, trying to sus out the informant, it had to be someone privy to top top-secret information, there were only a handful of personnel who had this access, to his mind, he had to devise a plan, to draw him or she out of there comfort zone, and he needed Cynthia for this job. That was the favour, Andrew's had for Cynthia when returned, he had someone in mind, but he would have to tread carefully, as this person was very high in the hierarchy, and extremely ruthless, as Andrews knew only too well from personal experience, he needed Cynthia back in situ as soon as possible. A knock on his door, interrupted his thoughts, it was Stevens, "Yes Richard", Johnathan Roberts, he is insisting on speaking to you," Here Stevens, take these out" he handed Stevens, his papers, use the other door, put them in the safe, for your eyes only Stevens, Andrews said, suddenly the door burst open.

'Hi', Andrews, was in the neighbourhood thought I'd pop in see how you are getting along, any news on the recent bombings, I'm afraid not was Andrews reply, then Andrews said, I think we might have an informant, "What" replied Roberts, "How do you know this" Roberts asked, "I don't, call it intuition, but they seem to be one jump ahead of us all the time, while we are chasing out tails" Andrews said, "Nonsense" Peter, you'll get the bastards," Do you need any more men, I can arrange it for you", "No thank you, we have adequate ground troops" it's probably me just being paranoid, was Andrews reply. A knock on the door, it was Stevens again, with coffee, which he left on the desk, "Thank you Richard," You're on first name terms Peter that can be dangerous, people might talk" said Roberts, Andrews ignored his remark, coffee, Roberts nodded, they chatted for about half an hour or so, then Roberts, said keep me posted and went out the door, Andrews rang for Stevens, "Were his henchmen with him" Stevens nodded, "Did they see anything" "No, I locked it in the safe" "Good lad", I have some phone calls to make now, "Yes Sir," Stevens said and went out the door.

Andrews looked at his watch, they might be in, he started to dial a number, it rang for a couple of minutes, a voice said, "Can I help you," Andrews here Melbourne", Can I speak to Commander

Simon Atkinson please" "Just one moment" "Atkinson here what can I do for you Peter" "You have one of my senior operatives with you, I was wondering if she is ready to leave, I need her in the field immediately if possible, would you have a problem in releasing her," "Can I get back to you Peter, I'll see what I can do" "That'll be great", was Andrews reply. It was a couple of days, Atkinson rung Andrews up, Hi Peter, about Boardman, she has passed shooting with flying colours, not so hot on the keep fit side of things, her marks were very low, as for the combat, just passable, which you knew, "Have you passed her that's what I want to know", "Well yes as a favour to you" was Atkinson's reply, "Many thanks Simon, a nice bottle of red on its way to you, Andrews put down the phone.

"Will you send for Miss Boardman," asked Atkinson, Cynthia arrived at Atkinson office, a sergeant said "You can go in now Miss", "Ah there you are, you're a lucky lady if ever I saw one", "You can leave as soon as possible, and report back to Peter Andrews immediately, here is your firearm certificate, and one for the course," Cynthia was most surprised, "Do you mean I can leave now!!" asked Cynthia, "Of course I mean now" Atkinson retorted, and led her to the door, no goodbye, or well done, or any comment whatsoever, "Well I'm damned", Cynthia said to herself. It didn't take Cynthia too long to arrive back in Melbourne, but instead of going straight to the office, she went to see Mary, at first Cynthia couldn't see her, then she noticed her with a customer, Mary could see Cynthia out of the corner of her eye, when she had finished, Mary went over to her. "My Mary you look great, said Cynthia "I don't feel great, I think I am pregnant", said Mary, "Good God women how old are you!"," Don't chastise me Cynthia, I'm at my wits end here as to what do."

"We'll talk tonight, I have to go into the office from here, if it's any different, I'll ring you", said Cynthia, Mary felt much better for telling someone, it was a relief. Later on Cynthia arrived at the office, "Good afternoon Cynthia, nice to see you back, he is expecting you" "Thanks Millie" Cynthia replied, and she headed for the lift, upon arriving, she made her way to Andrews office, and knocked "Come in Cynthia" said Andrews, "Boy I'm I glad to see you, I hear you just

119

managed to pass, Cynthia said "Don't ever send me again on any course, I'll resign first", Andrews just laughed at her, Stevens came in with coffee, "Nice to see you back, you have been missed". "Well that's something I suppose, was her reply.

Cynthia was never any good at doing physical work, she couldn't see the point of it, however now she was now to embark on a more intriguing assignment, Mr Johnathan Roberts, and what about you Mr Peter Andrews, what skeleton have you got hidden in your cupboard? She said to herself.

Cynthia, I had a long chat with Jeff Owen, we have agreed to join forces at last, but we will be strictly undercover, and we will only liaise with Jeff, our main task to eke out this Edwina Ashton, if that's her real name, which I doubt, "So do I" chipped Cynthia, we also are aware of a traitor or traitors in our midst.

I have a very strong feeling, as to who I think it is, this is where you come into it Cynthia, this is the favour I need you to do for me, I want you to get to know Johnathan Roberts, "Your Boss", let me finish Cynthia, I have to tell you, he is a very dangerous man if you cross him, which I learnt, at a very high cost to me personally!, so do not take him lightly, he also has a couple of heavies, that go everywhere with him, "I see, do you suspect him," said Cynthia, "And others who are in the process of elimination", replied Andrews. Here is a dossier on him, where he goes, what he gets up, clandestine meetings, etc., for your eyes only Cynthia, study it well." When do you want me to start on this? Enquired Cynthia, "As soon as possible" was Andrews answer, "I'm I allowed home for at least for two or three days, I'm exhausted", Andrews looked at her, you look in good nick to me, he thought to himself. "First thing then Monday morning, have your passport, suitcase ready, we could be away days or weeks, was Andrews reply.

When Cynthia finally reached home, she slumped in the chair, mulling over what had been said, she was glad they were still on the case, of course she couldn't wait to see Jeff again, the door went and it interrupted her thoughts, it was Mary, "I've only just arrived Mary, I have three days, then I will be away again for a couple of months", So about your situation, I do happen know someone who can help you, but you will have to make up your mind very quickly" "You mean abortion" said Mary, "Don't sound so horrified, do you want my help or not" again Cynthia got very irritated with Mary. Mary pondered, and then said "Yes" I have money saved, the sooner the better, with that Cynthia went to the phone, Mary could hear her talking to someone, is next Saturday afternoon Ok, Mary just nodded, "How much" £50 was Cynthia's reply. "Bloody hell" Mary said to herself. Cynthia gave Mary all the details. "Don't go soft on me Mary, see it through, or you will regret it for the rest of your life, remember Mary, under no circumstances must you ever tell JR, promise me" Mary could see Cynthia was adamant, "I promise" was Mary's reply, "There are lot of catching up to do", said Cynthia, "It is my half day tomorrow, so perhaps we catch up then", said Mary, Cynthia nodded, "Do you mind Mary I'm exhausted, I need a long soak and an early night, "I'll start dinner" said Mary, "I only want a snack Mary.

Cynthia went upstairs, she unpacked, and went into the bathroom, after about an hour, Cynthia came downstairs, Mary had made her, sandwiches with a side salad, it looked very inviting, "You shouldn't have gone to all that trouble Mary, I could have made something, there was even a glass of wine", Cynthia smiled.

CHAPTER SIXTEEN

Have you heard from JR" asked Cynthia," not a sausage", then Mary said "I have heaps to tell you, but it can wait till tomorrow, perhaps we can meet for lunch somewhere by the Yarra", Cynthia nodded. Mary put the radio on," Oh' I see you had the radio fixed, Mary answered "Yes Cynthia you took out the fuse, that's why it didn't work, JR fixed it for me". Cynthia just smiled at her, Mary knew why she had done it, so she wouldn't hear about the bombing in Sydney, by now it was 9.00pm Cynthia said" I'm off Mary see you tomorrow", she made her way upstairs with the glass of wine, "Goodnight Cynthia" shouted Mary the next day when they met for lunch, Mary told her all about JR.

The news came as shock to Cynthia, Mary mentioned about getting engaged, but was now having second thoughts about it, she mentioned that he is suffering from shell-shock and has shrapnel in his head which could move at any time, which the doctors only found out after the raid on the harbour, that he is on medication, which the doctors have said that he might get completely better. But there was always the chance something might just trigger everything off again "I'm in a quandary Cynthia, my heart tells me to marry him, and my mind tells me to dump him." Cynthia pondered for a while.

Mary, why don't you see how it goes, get all the facts from the doctors, and make your mind up then, and make sure he keeps his trousers up" "Don't be crude Cynthia it doesn't suit you", Mary was very indignant Cynthia just laughed, Mary didn't think it was funny. Mary was getting quite nervous about having the abortion, she knew of course it was the right thing to do, but her conscientious was telling otherwise, "It's your catholic upbringing that makes you feel guilty," said Cynthia, Mary didn't answer her.

Maggie was still mothering Kathy, still trying to fatten her up, Kathy was beginning to like the attention, she was more relaxed now, and loved the farm, and the children, it would soon be their birthdays, Maggie had learnt to drive, so Kathy and her would take the odd afternoon shopping or meeting up with Maggie's many friends, this time it was special, Maggie went to see the doctor, and Kathy, went looking for birthday presents for the twins, Maggie had arranged to meet with up with Kathy and the girls later at the tea rooms. Dr Hargreaves greeted Maggie," Nice to see you, how are the twins, and the family" he asked, "Fine" replied Maggie, "Now what can I do for you"," I think I'm pregnant again" said Maggie, Dr Hargreaves, eyes lit up, "Well let's see shall we", the Doctor examined Maggie, "I would think you are about three to four month" the doctor said, Maggie nodded, "I thought perhaps three months, do you think I will have any complications this time asked Maggie, "I don't really know Maggie, we'll have to see how it goes, but I know one thing, you will have to rest, and I mean rest" replied the doctor.

"We have a young woman who helps with the twins, she is very good, also Mrs O'Day our daily comes in, so I should be ok, Joe has someone in the office to help him, since his father had another stroke, and Molly helps when she can, so we should be alright", "Tell me Maggie, does Joe know" her reply, was "Not just yet", and you Maggie, "Oh I'm delighted, and I'm sure Joe will be". Joe was never quite the same or the family since the terrible accident at the farm which involved his older brother Jack, he was driving a load of cattle bound for the train depot to go up too Darwin, when the herd he was carrying, stated to get spooked, and were actually rocking the waggon, Jack went to investigate, he opened the back of the waggon, the barriers had not been secured properly, the herd headed straight for Jack, there was nothing anyone could do.

The police arrived, and the doctor pronounced Jack dead, the cattle hands managed to capture the cattle, and placed them back onto the other waggon's to take them to the train depot, Joe's brother Dave was traumatised, the doctor gave him medication as he was in shock, he was taken to the nearest hospital, which was several miles away, the police said they would ring the Police at Augusta to let the family know. The rest of the cattlemen, carried on taking the cattle to the depot, they too were deeply upset, at what had happened, some of them gave statements to the police, the ones who saw the accident, the rest were allowed to carry on their journey, the police checked the other waggons, just to be sure everything was secure, Joe had noticed that time was moving on, and wondered why Jack hadn't rung, he usually rings before now, I hope everything is alright, he said to himself, he went to the farmhouse, and asked his father, had Jack rung up, his dad was about to answer, when a knock came to the door.

Joe went to open the door, he just stared at the police officers, then Joe said quietly "It's Jack isn't it", the police officers, just nodded, they told him what had happened, "From all accounts Joe it was quick" by this time there were tears trickling down his face, he thanked them the best way he could, then thought about Dave, "What about Dave" the officer replied, "He's ok the doc gave him a sedative for shock, he is in York, at the local hospital there". Joe couldn't face the family, he left the farmhouse, went straight to Maggie, he entered the house, "That you Joe, your home early" Maggie came from the kitchen, she took one look at Joe, "What is it Joe, your dad? "No it's Jack, he's been killed" by this time the tears were really flowing, "I can't face them Maggie" Joe blurted out," Sit their Joe, you need a cup of tea for shock" Maggie shouted Kathy, "Make us a cup of tea will you Kathy, there's a love" "Sure Kathy replied".

After a while, Maggie said "You stay here Joe, while I go over and let your Mum and Dad know what's happened" "Go easy Maggie," it could kill Mum and Dad," Joe said, "Don't worry I will be sensitive, but we have to let Catherine, Elizabeth Dave's wife and Jack's wife Josie know" said Maggie, Joe looked up at her" I'd forgotten about, Elizabeth, Josie and the kids" Joe then said. "You go and tell Josie and

Elizabeth and I'll tell Mum Dad and Catherine", Maggie nodded, so they both set off together, holding each other for a while, then each going their separate ways, it was terrible when Maggie told Josie, she was hysterical, Maggie couldn't calm her at all, she ran back to the house, and shouted for Kathy, Maggie explained what had gone on, and could she help Josie, as she needed to be with Joe, Kathy went over to Jose's house, with no hesitation, to sit with Josie and the kids while Maggie came back.

For the next couple of weeks, it was unbearable, the funeral had been held, Catherine and Dave, plus Joe, were in sombre mood, their father had had another stroke, more severe than the last, and Maggie had yet to tell Joe, about her expecting another baby, she wanted to tell him, but it was one thing after another, Joe was worried about the harvest, if the bad weather persisted, it was bad news all round as everything depended on a good harvest. Kathy had noticed that Maggie was pregnant, "When is the baby due Maggie", Maggie just looked at her, and burst into tears, "Kathy it's awful, I can't find the words to tell Joe and the family, they are grieving so much", Kathy then said, "Do you not think that it might be just what the family need, it will give them hope, no matter what, it gives them something to look forward too, after all they do live on a farm, they must realise that life goes on". Maggie jumped up and kissed Kathy on the cheek, "Oh I'm so glad you are here Kathy, I'll tell him tonight".

Maggie was playing with the twins, by this time they were about nineteen months old, they looked just like Joe, Maggie was thinking, when Joe came in, Joe pecked on her cheek, and then said "How's my little angels, and picked them up, Maggie chirped in" There handful Joe Yardy, never mind angels".

Joe seemed in a better frame of mind, she was about to tell him, when the door was thrown open, "Quick Joe it's dad" said Dave, Joe rushed out to the house, Maggie shouted Kathy, "Will you see to the kids for me, something happened to Joe's dad", Maggie then rushed across, when she entered, she could see all was not well, Joe looked at her tears again flowing from down his face, he couldn't speak, Maggie went over and just held his hand, he responded by squeezing her hand. The funeral was held at the farmhouse, everyone from all around came to pay their respects to Jack Yardy, Joe and the family were deeply moved by the comments and kindness shown to them, Joe's mum in particular was proud to hear all the nice things said about Jack Snr. Kathy came up to Maggie, "Now's the perfect time to tell Joe and the family, about your news", Maggie nodded, she asked the family to join her in the lounge.

What's up sis you being mysterious" said Dave, Joe just looked at her, "Well we are all here" Joe said, Maggie hesitated, then said, "I'm pregnant, I'm four months I think", been to see Doc Hargreaves, everything seems fine", they all looked at her in amazement, the first to congratulate was Joe's mother. Mollie then said to Maggie, "This calls for a celebration, I am overjoyed for you both" then all the family joined in, Joe in particular went to her and said," How are you feeling I had no idea," I wanted to tell you Joe, but so much has been going on, there was never a right time" was Maggie's reply.

A month had passed, and Mary was feeling down in the dumps, she wasn't proud of what she had done Cynthia had now left, so she had time to think more clearly, but the guilt was always there, it would take time, she said to herself, Cynthia was right it is my Catholic upbringing. Mary and Mildred (Mary's old supervisor) had been invited to Sara's wedding, Grace was her lady in waiting, and a few more girls from work were also invited to the night do, Mary was pleased to get out of the flat, and meet up with her friends, she really enjoyed herself, and all thoughts of self-doubt disappeared for a while at least. the next day being a Sunday, Mary decided to ring Maggie at the time arranged, she had a leisurely bath, read the Argus, the war in Europe seemed to be edging a bit closer to ending, the war in the Pacific was still raging, causalities are inevitable in war, Mary just wanted everything to return too normal, so she could get back to her beloved England.

Then the phone started to ring. Gosh is that the time, Mary said to herself, she picked the phone up, "Is that you Mary, its JR" Mary went numb, she couldn't speak, she wanted to say it was Cynthia, speak to me Mary for God's sake, Mary then said," Well you've took your bloody time, no letters no nothing did you get my letters" she retorted, "Yes I did, I know I'm sorry I have been in hospital all this time they give me tablets which make me sleepy, I am really not that well at the moment, I don't know when I will be able to see you again", said JR. "Well this is a fine kettle of fish JR Harding, and what am I supposed to do wait?, it's months since I last heard from you and you expect me to wait till you get better has it not occurred to you, that you may never get better I am 29yrs of age, I can't wait forever, I've made my mind up, the engagement is off, I'll send your ring back, It's no use you phoning me again she yelled", down the phone, the phone just went dead, Mary was in tears she was distraught, but she knew it was the best thing for both of them.

Mary sat for while wondering what to do, she rang the clinic up and asked for a Doctor Jenkins, he was one of the psychiatrist dealing with JR case, Dr Jenkins here. Mary explained what she had done and broken off her engagement to JR, she was to return the ring to him, "I see" replied the doctor "It probably is the best thing Mary in the long run, he may never be fully fit, you have to do what you think is right for you", "Thank you Doctor Jenkins" and put the receiver down.

The phone started to ring again, Mary hesitated, she let it ring, eventually it stopped ringing, she then picked up the phone, and dialled Maggie's number, it didn't take long for Maggie to say, "Hello" "It's Mary" Maggie said "I've just rung you, I got someone here that wants to say something" "HI, Mary it's Kathy". Mary was overjoyed to hear her voice," Oh' Kathy we have been so worried about you, Cynthia will be pleased when I tell her, is Maggie treating you well? "Yes very well" I can't thank her enough Mary, she's been wonderful", Maggie grabbed the phone off Kathy," that's enough I've loads to tell Mary", Maggie then starts to tell her everything that has gone on at the farm, and finally says, "And I'm pregnant again Mary" "Good for you, is Joe thrilled", "All the family are overjoyed Mary" Maggie then said" I'll have to go now, keep safe, God Bless", then the phone went dead.

By this time it was mid-afternoon, Mary got herself ready, and went into the city, she decided to window shop, and went to the arcade, where there was a variety of shops, to look at, in particular the fashion shops, with their unusual window dressings, for greater impact, I'd love to be able to do that sort of thing, Mary said to herself, she wondered around a while longer, then went to Flinders Street Station for a coffee, she sat there just watching the world go by, trying to forget what had gone on with JR and breaking up with him, deep down she knew it was the right thing to do. Then a voice said," And what are you doing on a nice Sunday afternoon", she looked up, it was Mr Charles from George's," I'm just having a coffee, and watching the world go by" Mary said, "Can I join you" Charles asked ""If you wish" she replied

Mary couldn't explain it, but suddenly she burst into tears," Oh' I'm sorry Mr Charles don't mind me", "Whatever is the matter he said, surely it can't be as bad as that? Charles was quite concerned, He liked Mary, and he had always thought, if he were the marrying kind, she would be the one, but he knew she was engaged. I've just broken my engagement to JR", Mary started to tell him all about it, how wonderful he was at first, and how deeply in love she was with him, that they had a great four days together, staying at Menzies, Charles eyebrows raised, "Really" he said, Mary nodded and carried on, it was then I found out that he was suffering from shell-shock and other things, this upset me very much, I thought he might get better with the medication, but there seems no end to it at all. Mary carried on telling him every tiny detail. Charles was so sympatric, and understood, how she felt, "I don't know why I'm telling you all this Mr Charles, it's not your problem" Mary said, "Can we have two more coffees over here please" Charles said in a commanding voice, he smiled at Mary, "Look Mary, from what I can see, you are just chastising yourself, and feeling guilty", Mary looked up at him, "You are right I do feel guilty and frightened, I don't want to spend the rest of my life alone", Charles laughed, "What a lovely looking woman like you ending up being a wall flower, I think not", Mary then also started to laugh, "That's much better, now drink your coffee, before it gets cold" said Charles.

After about half an hour, "Well I must dash Mary, see you tomorrow" Mary looked at him and said "Thank you for being a good listener", and she pecked him on his cheek, he blushed, and then he whispered goodbye. Mary was feeling relieved that she was able to talk to someone, and was surprised that she could tell Mr Charles everything that had gone on, and how he had listened so intently, and that she wasn't at all embarrassed. The next day Mary was going about her business at the store, when a voice said, "How are you feeling today" Mary looked around it was Mr Charles, "I'm much better and thank you for being so kind yesterday, I don't know whatever got into me, telling you all my troubles", "No worries Mary, I was only glad I could help.

I was wondering if I could take you out for a drink sometime" Charles said, Mary blushed, "Are you sure Mr Charles", "Yes, I'm sure and please just call me Charles, Mr Charles is so irritating", Mary looked at him," it's awkward for me, just to call you Charles, especially here, all the girls are looking at us now and giggling", "Let them giggle I don't care, nor should you" said Charles, with that Mary agreed to meet up with him on Sunday at Finders Street Station, at the same café 7.30pm.

CHAPTER SEVENTEEN

Mary was quite bemused by it all, as she had heard rumours like everyone else about his liking for the men, rather than the women, "What's going on with you Mary and Mr Charles, you've no chance there from what I've heard, said Jenny, Mary turned to her, Jenny Rhodes theirs a customer waiting see to it!! In a most indignant manner, which even surprised Mary, gosh I'm sounding like Cynthia, she said to herself. The week was going pretty slowly for Mary, but at least she had the weekend to look forward too, still no phone call or letter from Cynthia, she had so much to tell her, I wonder what she is up to, no doubt ruling the roost, Mary smiled to herself.

Her thoughts then turned to Maggie poor Maggie, all that trouble she's had, and how well she has coped Cynthia would be of proud of her, and helping Kathy it is really kind of her and Joe, it couldn't have been easy for them, Kathy sounded great, I sometimes wish I could be there with them in Perth, but it's ever such a long away. It was nearly time to closing, Charles came up to her, "Can you make it tonight Mary, I have a proposition to put to you, which could suit both parties", Mary looked at him, What the hell is he blabbering on about, she said to herself, "Same place 7.30pm" he said to her, for some reason unknown to herself, she just said "Yes", "Fine I'll see you then" Charles walked away. When Mary reached home she wondered why did you say yes for, sometimes girl you are so bloody stupid, what have you let yourself in for now.

Unexpectedly the phone went, oh' God please not JR again, once more she hesitated, "Well you took your time, "Cynthia I am so glad to hear from you, when you are coming home? "Not just yet Mary is everything alright? "I have so much to tell you, do you have the time", "Don't pussy foot about Mary", Just tell me," Mary smiled, she back to her old self again, Mary began by telling her about JR and calling off her engagement, she then mentioned, Mr Charles at George's store asking her out tonight, that he wanted to talk to her about something, "Is this the owner's son Mary?" "Yes", relied Mary, "I'm just wondering whether to go or not". "At times Mary I do wonder about you, of course you should go and find out what he wants, he might want to marry you for God's sake" I have to go now Mary, write to me let me know how you get on, at the old address in Sydney" "But Cynthia I have still lots to tell you" "Write to me Mary I must go", the phone went dead.

Mary felt much better telling Cynthia, she always recognised that Cynthia was worldlier than she was and was always grateful when she gave her advice, even though she had a nasty habit of getting very agitated, when Mary didn't cotton on right away what, Cynthia was saying to her sometimes. Mary looked at the time, gosh I'd better get ready, after about an hour, she was ready and made herself a bite to eat, a knock on the door, she wondered who it could be a sudden panic engulfed her, she just stood there motionless, another knock on the door, eventually she slowly opened the door, it was Mr Charles, Mary was shocked he noticed her face.

I'm sorry for intruding on you like this, but I really must speak to you" he said, Mary gathered herself together, "I thought it might be JR, she said, come in, "Have you eaten" Mary asked, "Not yet was his reply", Mary made another batch of sandwiches and gave him a glass of wine, "Now what is so important that it couldn't wait till later" Mary asked, He took a deep breath, "First of all will you let me finish what I have to say before you say anything" Charles insisted, Mary agreed to listen to what he had to say. After Charles had spoken, Mary was absolutely dumb- struck, she just stared at him, "Say something Mary" Charles said" I'm thinking", then she remembered what Cynthia had said, "Before I give you my answer, I can't give you a definite answer because yes I am attracted to men, but also very attracted to women, that doesn't mean I won't have another affair with a man I just don't know and that's my problem, But I promise you this, if you marry me, you will be well cared for and we will definitely try for children, I know it will be a marriage of convenience for us both, but it gets you out of a sticky situation with JR, and me with my Mum and Dad" was Charles reply, well at least he is honest, Mary said to herself.

Mary poured herself a glass of wine, "Fill up Charles" he nodded, "Well just so we know where we stand, I too have a skeleton in my cupboard also a few months ago I had an abortion I am ashamed to say and I am not proud of what I did in fact it still haunts me, I'm not too sure if I can have any children, I liked to think so", say something Mary said to Charles, "Is that a yes then?" Charles said, Mary nodded, "Well if you're sure Charles" said Mary, Charles was absolutely ecstatic," Thank you Mary, you will never regret it.

Mary then said," We must come to some understanding, about the marriage, what if I can't have any children, do we get divorced?, "I think we will have to cross that bridge if it comes to that" was Charles reply, "There is just one more thing, what if you are caught up in a scandal regarding your taste in men, I do not want the humiliation of the gutter press Charles, I just couldn't handle it, I need some sort of reassurance off you, that I can just walk away, with or without children." Charles looked at her in amazement," You really have given this some thought haven't you" Mary nodded, "I will get papers drawn up with my solicitor detailing what you have just said, we will both sign it, a sort of pre-nuptial" was Charles reply. Mary hadn't a clue what a pre-nuptial was, I'll have to ask Cynthia, she said to herself, "Mary then said. "Ok I'll Marry you, but please don't let me down like JR did", Charles got hold of her and just held her briefly, "Thank you Mary" and kissed her tenderly on her cheek.

Charles then said," You know Mary I have always admired you from a distance you always look so radiant and your lovely with the customers", Mary interrupted him," Charles what about my job? "Well I don't think you need to worry about work anymore do you" was Charles reply. Mary was disappointed about what he had said, after all, she had worked so hard to become a supervisor, but realised it would be impossible to carry on working." Mary then said, there is one thing I would dearly love to do Charles, I would just love to go out and look at fashion and look for one off designs, we could set a trend in designer only clothes, I'm sure it would bring more customers in, high end of course", Charles just looked at her, this woman is quite incredible, Mum is really going to like her, they have so much in common.

Charles looked at her," If that's what you want to do then it's ok by me, but my old man he's a different kettle of fish", Mary then asked, "What about your mother, how is she going to react to her son marring a shop girl marrying her only son", Charles replied, "I don't think for one minute she'll react, because she was a shop girl when she married my father, he then said and I must tell you, that they want me to marry so they can have grandchildren, they know about my indiscretions' shall we say and they are not too pleased about them, so I have been given an ultimatum get married or leave the family business said.

Charles had really thought things out, "I think we should marry later in the year give it six months or so, let people get to know us as a courting couple, around Eastertime I should think, then we perhaps could go away for two to three weeks", "That would be wonderful, replied Mary. They then went out to celebrate, Mary was overjoyed it didn't matter to her, about it not being romantic, she'd had all that and look where it got her, he was kind she could see that, he was also very gracious, they had a few drinks at a private club which Mary didn't know existed. Now what can I get you," asked Charles, "A small sherry please" Mary replied, he waved his finger a waiter came over, he told him the order and off he went, Mary was fascinated by it all, wait while Cynthia finds out about this she thought.

By the way, that wine you gave me, where did you get it from, it was really a very good red?", asked Charles, Mary smiled at him, "It comes from one of our friends in Perth who's married to a wine grower, they own a vineyard, she is always sending us boxes of the stuff", "I gather you know absolutely nothing about wine, well to be honest I prefer a beer any day, Charles laughed out loud, everyone stared at him, but Charles was oblivious to it.

Mary thought, he knows how to treat a lady, even if doesn't mean too, his mother has taught him well, It's getting late Mary he called the waiter over order a taxi for me would you, the waiter nodded, a few minutes later the waiter nodded, "Taxi 's here Mary" "Where too Sir" St Kilda's please, Mary was panicking a bit I hope he doesn't want to stay soon they reached the apartment, Charles got out first, then helped Mary out, then said, "Stay here driver I won't be a minuet" "Right you are Sir". Charles took Mary up to the door, "Thank you for a lovely evening" I won't see you tomorrow, I have to tell Mum and Dad, see you Monday morning at the store, he then gently kissed her on the forehead.

Meanwhile, Cynthia and Andrews also Jeff were busy, trying to work out how to lay a trap for the suspected traitors, Andrews said, "Cynthia I want you to concentrate on Johnathan Roberts, and remember what I said about him being dangerous be very watchful of him, he is a sticky character, not to mention his sidekicks", Cynthia nodded in agreement," Jeff you and I will liaise with Cynthia daily, and keep tabs on her at all times", Jeff also nodded in agreement. Andrews carried on, "Jeff I want you watch Harry Barns, he's another slippery customer, Andrews said, that he had, had no reports whatsoever about your surveillance on Edwina Aston and her cohorts, so there is something fishy going on there in Sydney" Jeff agreed," I have some devices here that are in experimental stage, but I am assured they work very well, he showed them, walkie – talkies the range I'm told is adequate for close proximity, there was also camera's again to use close by but with no flash, infra-red I believe, the image comes out later, let's hope they work".

It was agreed to set up shop at Cynthia's place as it was closer to the city and transport was easier, Cynthia agreed to this she also said," She would get provisions", and made a list of what they needed. Andrews then said," Well I think that's it, here are your passport just in case we have to travel overseas, Cynthia you're with me, Jeff you will be in the background watching and taking notes, meet tomorrow 10.00am Cynthia place, enjoy the rest of the day, make the most of it", Andrews then walked out the door. Jeff turned around to Cynthia," You and me again Cynth, just like old times", he caught hold of and kissed her, "I have missed you more than you will ever know" he said to her, "I've missed you too" Cynthia replied, "Now let's paint the town I'm hungry and you promised me a few beers" said Jeff so they set off into the city centre, caught the ferry over to the rocks, it was full of tourists, even though there was a war on, there were lots of service men with girl friends or just girls for the day who knows, Jeff and Cynthia just walked arm in arm till they reached a pub, they entered, it was packed with sailors, some yanks, some brits, but mostly Aussies, Jeff said "let's get out of here" so they moved on.

They decided to go to an Italian restaurant, that Cynthia frequented a lot when she was in Sydney, "It reminds me of Melbourne" she said to Jeff, "You miss the girls don't you, I do especially Mary", "Why Mary", asked Jeff. Cynthia carried on, "When Mary came over to Australia with us she was the proverbial rough diamond thought she knew everything, but didn't, oh' nice to get along with, but no social graces whatsoever, but thought she had, "Kathy" she was totally different, had a hard upbringing from what Maggie told me, but a different nature than Mary, more loving more caring, would make a good wife for someone one day.

What about Maggie, Jeff asked, he was fascinated by it all, it was the first time that Cynthia had let him into her private life, "Well, Maggie's Maggie always chirpy, very well laid back, takes everything in her stride, spoilt rotten by her mother, we were brought up together, went to the same school together, had different friends of course as I was a year older than she was. Our fathers both have business, where we used to live, we ended up doing secretarial work for our respective fathers, I graduated for university but never went instead, I studied languages in Manchester instead. Our fathers bless them still send us money each month, I keep telling my father, that I am ok, but he is most persistent, Jeff chirps in, "A chip off the old block then" and laughed Cynthia just looked at him.

135

The day became night they did some shopping from a local store nearby where the house was, eventually arriving home, "I'm having a bath now Jeff", keep yourself occupied after about an hour, she arrived downstairs, Jeff was fallen to sleep, Cynthia draped a blanket over him, and retired to bed. Cynthia was up bright and early, Jeff was up and about getting organised, he'd had a good sleep, Cynthia said, "Have you got everything", Jeff said, they waited for Andrews to arrive, "It's not like him to be late" Cynthia said, then the bell went. Jeff went to open the door, Andrews fell in, "Cynthia quick get an ambulance, he's been stabbed", "Oh my God" said Cynthia, they had a special number if they needed medical attention, it wasn't' long before a black ambulance arrived, Jeff was quite perturbed about what had happened, "Stay away from the windows Cynthia, we might be being watched", "How the hell do they know where I here" Cynthia yelled.

The next two or three days everything was in turmoil, Jeff manged to leave the house via other people's back yards he was very good at disguise, so if someone saw him he would not be recognised, Cynthia stayed in the house it was the first time she had really been frightened and wondered, if they would ever discover who the traitors were, she sat and pondered over things as she always did to try and find a solution. The phone disturbed her, she let it ring, it went dead, it rang again, it went dead, then it rang a third time, Cynthia picked it up, "Good you remembered" Jeff said, "Well I'm afraid he died Cynth", Cynthia nearly fell over, with the news's, you still there asked Jeff, "Yes" replied Cynthia, "Get everything together, we have to get out, make sure you have everything Cynth, leave no stone unturned, I believe we will be the next" "Stop it Jeff you're putting the fear of God in me"," I sorry Cynth, will be back as soon as I can". Said Jeff.

Cynthia set about gathering all the information they had, luckily they had packed anyway, she then set about cleaning the house of all fingerprints as much as she could, she disconnected the phone, closed all the curtains, it was high summer so no one would notice, she packed all her belonging, and finally burnt all the unwanted notes and paperwork that wasn't relevant to the case, by this time she was exhausted, she sat and made herself a coffee. It got mid-afternoon,

Cynthia must have dosed off when she heard a noise it alarmed her then a tap on the kitchen window," It's me" Jeff said in a quiet voice, she gingerly opened the shutter slightly she sighed," Its' Jeff thank God for that".

Jeff looked around the house, good girl, he said to himself, then went back down to see Cynthia, "I've cleaned as much as I could", in fact she was still wearing her gloves, I packed up best way I could, burnt all the bumf we had, disconnected the phone, I can't think of anything else, just double check for me Jeff" she asked, "I will" was his reply.

CHAPTER EIGHTEEN

Now can you think of any place we can go, that no one knows where we are" asked Jeff," I can Jeff" Cynthia said, "And where's that? asked Jeff, "Perth with Maggie", was Cynthia's reply, Jeff nodded, "But first Jeff we need to go to Melbourne, my place, I need to get a dossier on Johnathan Roberts, so we can bring the bastard down once and for all" Jeff agreed, then he said, "We leave tonight, I have a van parked at the back, as soon as it is dark, we'll pack everything, now what food I'm starving?", I'll make up some sandwiches and flasks, "Bring the whiskey, Jeff said, Cynthia laughed, she set about making as many sandwiches as she could and put everything in a cardboard box, water, booze, food, flasks, medical box, personal belongings, handbag, the list was endless, Jeff came to her "What the hell Cynth, we can't take all that with us", "We might have to drive to Melbourne, they may be watching the train stations, and airports", was Cynthia's reply.

By the time they had checked and double checked everything, they finally set off for Melbourne by road, it would probably take them a good couple of days or so, one thing was for sure, they would sure be glad to see the back of Sydney, one thing was puzzling Jeff, "You look worried Jeff" Cynthia said, "I am, how can we go to your apartment, they could be watching it" Cynthia said "No need to worry, I have a safe house in the Carlton area, no one knows about it, that's where the info is, we can rest up there, we should be safe", Jeff breathed a sigh of relief. They had been travelling for about 8 hours, Jeff pulled over, "I just need to check the water and petrol,

138

we can rest up here", Cynthia started to take out the flasks and sandwiches, she handed Jeff the food and drink, Cynthia had made salmon sandwiches, my this is tasty said Jeff, he devoured the lot in less than five minutes, "Steady on Jeff we have a long way to go" said Cynthia.

He just smiled at her, Jeff then said, "We shall have to get petrol when we can", then he settled down to have a nap, Cynthia couldn't sleep a wink, and cat napped through the rest of the night, she watched dawn rise, and thought how beautiful it was, the scenery was just breath taking, this really is a beautiful country she thought to herself. Cynthia got out of the van to stretch her legs, where the hell are we, she wondered, she looked at the map, all she could see where winding roads, no sign posts at all, in fact it was very quiet they seemed to be in the middle of nowhere, Jeff appeared, "Did you manage to sleep" he asked "Not a wink" replied Cynthia, Jeff laughed, "Not use to roughing it are you Cynth", she threw the road map at him, "Temper, Temper" Jeff said still laughing, just then they heard a waggon, Jeff waved him down, "Can you tell me nearest gas station", "about two hours mate further down," the driver answered, "Is this the Princess Highway" the scenic route" "Sure is mate just keep driving, be seeing yah," the driver rode off.

Jeff looked at his watch, "I reckon we have about another 8 hours' drive if we are lucky, before we reach Melbourne, let's have coffee and eat something" Jeff said, "Is that all you can think about food" Jeff said, look you have to eat it's a very long drive, it can be hazardous so you need our wits about us and besides at some point when we get near the main Highway.

Cynthia never said another word, she could see he was cross with her, eventually Jeff pulled over, you take over from here stay on this road, do not whatsoever deviate follow highway 53, I'm bushed", he crawled into the back of the van, and laid down, Cynthia was furious with him, not a word had been spoken since they stopped for a bite to eat, she just stared at him, he was unaware of this of course, as he said he was absolutely exhausted.

Reluctantly Cynthia got into the driving seat then started to drive off following his instructions, it took Cynthia four hours' to reach the outskirts of Melbourne, then another two hours for her to reach the safe house, it was now 7.30pm in the evening, luckily she had a lock up with the house, she drove the van into the lock up, as she opened the doors, Jeff began to stir, he opened his eyes. "Where are we" his eyes hadn't focused just yet, "Where the bloody hell do you think we are! Cynthia retorted, "Strewth girl, I only asked a simple question" Jeff yelled, they were both extremely tired, and tempers were frayed. Cynthia opened the door to the house, it felt stuffy and stifling, she opened a few windows to let whatever air there was, she left everything in the van till morning, got out a couple of sleeping bags, threw one to Jeff, who was still half asleep, secured the house and then she just flopped. By the time she woke up, it was well past lunch, Cynthia looked at her watch, good grief is it that the time, she opened the blinds, it was a beautiful summers day, the sun caught her eyes, I need my Sunnis, which she took from her handbag. Jeff was nowhere to be seen," Now where the hell is he" she said to herself, I need a shower, Cynthia went upstairs to freshen up, she was in no mood for Jeff or anyone, it had been a nightmare for her, if this undercover work they can stick it, she said to herself

After about an hour Cynthia emerged, fully refreshed, and looking more herself, she made coffee, sat pondering what to do, still no sign of Jeff, what is he up to now, she asked herself, it was now 2.00pm Cynthia decided to empty the van, and went to the lock up, it wasn't there, all the baggage was there, but no van, "Now where has he gone", at times Jeff Owen, you're an idiot" she was again furious with him, she took all the baggage into the house went upstairs, and put everything in order, Jeff in one room, her in the other.

Eventually Jeff returned he called her name, she didn't respond at first let him think I'm not here, "I hope you are not playing mind games with me Cynthia, this is deadly serious, unless we pull together, we are dead" he was raging with her, Cynthia cracked on she hadn't heard him." "What did you say Jeff and where have you been, I've been worried, I thought you might have been caught", Jeff mellowed on hearing this, but Cynthia had just made it up to appease him. Jeff said, "I've been watching Robert's office most of the time, I hope these camera's work, we need someone we can trust to have them developed, do you know anyone? "asked Jeff, "I'll have to think about it, my brain is frazzled at the moment I need a good night sleep, replied Cynthia, but I do need to go out and get some personal things for myself, "Be careful out there, just do what you have to do, and get back here, as quickly as you can" Jeff said, it irritated Cynthia no end, that Jeff was calling the shots, she wasn't used to it now and didn't like it at all.

After about an hour and half Cynthia arrived fully laden with stuff," What have you got there" Cynthia said, "I may need to change my appearance", so she took out dye to colour her hair also a wig, and different clothes to what she is used to wearing, and finally she had brought some food, and a bottle of wine, "That's more like", said Jeff and he smiled, Cynthia gave him a wry smile, she still wasn't too happy with him, "What have you got there" asked Cynthia, "Some notes I took this morning, while watching Roberts office, there is a lot of activity going on there, can you not think of anyone who can help us with these pictures?, asked Jeff. Cynthia sat and thought for quite some time, "The only one that may be able to help, is Richard Stevens, he was or Peter Andrews right hand man, said Cynthia, in more ways than one would think, Cynthia said, Jeff just looked at her puzzlingly, "What do you mean?", asked Jeff.

You know what I mean" retorted Cynthia, "No I don't "replied Jeff and they both started laughing. Jeff looked at Cynthia seriously and asked, "How do we get in touch with Stevens, we can't very well go to the office, "Do you think you could go out and get today's paper or papers, there just might be something reported in them or information regarding Andrews death", asked Cynthia, Jeff replied, "Good idea, but I'll eat first, I'm starving, "What again, have you got worms or something", Cynthia said in her sarcastic manner, He just laughed again, "No when I get stressed, I have to eat for some reason", replied Jeff.

Jeff wasn't too long before he returned, "There wasn't much choice at this time of day" he said, Cynthia poured them both a wine, each reading a newspaper, "Well nothing in here", "Or in this one" Jeff said, "I wonder if they know at work, after all he was undercover", asked Cynthia," I'm sure they will know, Roberts, would make certain of that, perhaps your right", replied Jeff "What shall we do next" asked Cynthia was most eager to get on with things, and she needed to get to her "I think we should rest up here for a couple of days, whoever is after us, may just give up then report back to Roberts" said Jeff, "I need to get to my apartment, I have private papers there that I need to get hold of," What sort of papers? asked Jeff, Cynthia answered, "All sorts with address of people I know, also personal letters, the usual stuff", "I'll go now", "What at this time!!, I'll come with you to the apartment", Jeff said. Cynthia said, emphatically "No! "You stay here, I'll be quicker on my own," she went upstairs, and shortly came down, she shouted Jeff, he looked, "Good heaven's what you done, I didn't recognise you", "It's a wig" said Cynthia, "Well be careful out there, I'll study these papers again, we might have missed something" Cynthia had already left.

Cynthia knew her way around Melbourne now with buying properties she had rough idea of the area, she caught a bus, got off as near as she could to St Kilda's, and walked the rest of the way, stopping every now and again, to make sure she wasn't being followed, eventually she reached home, she entered the back way into the apartment her heart was pounding, her adrenalin was sky high. She knew Charles and Mary were co-habiting and knew only the cleaner would go in, which is what her and Mary had arranged. Still she was very hesitant approaching the apartment, Calm down Cynthia, keep your head, she said to herself, she let herself in gingerly, taking out her pistol, she started to perspire, she pulled out a torch, and surveyed the dining area, everything seemed ok, she entered the lounge, no sign of any intrusion, same in the bedrooms, and bathroom, to Cynthia's great relief, her first job was to pick up all her post, there was one from England, Maggie and Mary, it was the girls she was most concerned about, she wanted to keep them safe if she could.

Cynthia, systematically went through every drawer in the house, perused every scrap of paper, put everything that was relevant into a night case, suddenly the phone rang, it startled her, she waited, till the third ring, then picked it up, Where the hell are you,", asked Jeff," I'm still in the apartment" replied Cynthia, "Why what time is it" Jeff said it's 2.00am, "Gosh I'm sorry Jeff", I'll come immediately. Better to come tomorrow and buy some morning papers, we need milk and bread also, "What did your last servant die of", "Don't be flippant Cynth, it doesn't' suit you" in that tone which says it all, then the phone went dead, in a way Cynthia was glad, it meant she could read her mail, and her other correspondence in peace. Her first letter was from home, she started to read it, oh 'My God she said to herself, it was from her eldest brother, telling her that their father had had a massive heart attack, and died, her mother had passed away a couple of years earlier, the tears just flowed like a tap, "It's just one thing after another, I'm fed up with this war.

Mary was right, it ruins people's lives, but not the bloody Politian's. Cynthia, carried on reading the letter, the burial had already taken place and could she ring as soon as possible as formalities had to be resolved, regarding the will, her brother gave the name and address of the solicitor in charge, he carried on saying how much they missed her, and wished she could be back home with them and signed off.

The next letter was from Maggie, this will cheer me up, Cynthia said to herself,

Hi Cynthia,

Hope you're keeping well and safe, it's been ages since you last wrote, I know Mary has been in touch with you, but even she hasn't heard from you. Joe and I have some good news, I am pregnant again, everything is fine, I am now 7 months, Kathy has been wonderful, she is very good with the twins, and I now have a daily Mrs O'Day, I expect Mary's told you all the news, so I'll close now, write when you can, or ring.

Lots of Love Joe Maggie& Kathy,

The next letter was from Mary,

Well you're like the Scarlet Pimpernel, "They seek her here, they her there, where the hell are you, I need your help and advice, as always". Mary then filled her in on what had been going on with her and Charles, that she had left the store, that they were now living together, in an apartment near Cynthia's in St Kilda, she mentioned the pre-nuptial whatever that is, Cynthia did her usual wry smile, that also she and Charles had arranged to go over to Perth to see Maggie in Charles's Father's private plane. Alarm bells started to ring, that's it we can go over to Perth with them, Cynthia said to herself, she carried on reading the letter to spend Christmas and New Year with Maggie, Joe and family, it would be absolutely wonderful if you could come too, and lastly I want you to be my maid of honour when I get married, Maggie and Kathy have agreed to be ladies in waiting, don't get any idea's Cynthia, it is going to be a very low key wedding.

I have to close now. Love Mary & Charles

Ps Look after yourself, and bring that Jeff along, it's about time we met him.

The next letter she opened was more disturbing it was in fact from Peter Andrews, telling Cynthia of his involvement, in an undercover operation that went badly wrong, and a number of innocent people got killed, he was in charge of the operation at that time, and felt responsible for the disaster, unknown to me at the time, I had been seriously misinformed and set up, by Johnathan Roberts, my number two, at the time.

Andrews went on to say, that he was up for the top job at the time, which he never got due to Roberts, later Roberts was promoted to the job meant for him it was years later, that I learned of Roberts treachery, Roberts had deliberately given me the wrong impression that everything was ok and that everything was in order to go ahead with our raid, which I acted on. That led me to my downfall. If anything happens to me, Cynthia, I want you and Jeff to expose this man for what he is, I know he has a safe in his office and that he keeps files on people, for his blackmailing business, hence the heavies he has with him all the time for protection, can I remind you once again how dangerous he is and ruthless, this is the favour you owe me Cynthia, I hope you can finish him for good.

Peter Andrews.

Well I never, Cynthia was reeling from what she had read, she looked at her watch by now it was 6.30am, she decided to have a bath, she could think more clearly when she was relaxed, she started to tick of boxes in her head, that's what we'll do she said to herself. Eventually she came downstairs, it was too early to ring anyone, except Jeff, which she did, told him about Andrews's letter, and said she had formulated a plan that she would see him later. Soon it was 7.30pm "I'll try the office, ask for Stevens, if he's in, said Cynthia, the phone rang, "Hello" a voice said, "Is Richard Stevens in the office yet?" asked Cynthia, "He's just arrived", It's for you" "Who is it?" asked Stevens, "I don't know some women" the man said. "Hello" Stevens here, "Hi Richard, it's me, don't say my name, we need your help", Cynthia told him where to meet her at about 4.00pm, and was he able to get away, without any one knowing, Cynthia, "I can manage that, I wish you could tell me what's going on, all this cloak and dagger stuff isn't really my style", Stevens said, to Cynthia, she put the phone down.

She looked at her list, I'll try Maggie, hope the timing right, the phone started to ring, someone picked up the phone, hello, "Is Maggie there", "Just a minute, Maggie phone" someone said, "Hello said Maggie, "It's me, don't say my name, just listen to me, Maggie listened while Cynthia told her as much as she could, and would it be alright if her and Jeff came over for Christmas with Mary and Charles, "You don't need to ask, you will always welcome here" Cynthia interrupted her before she could mention her name. Maggie it is very important that you get in touch with Mary, I need you to give her this address in Carlton, ask her to meet me there at 1.00pm today, Eastern time, it is very important that you get this message through to her Maggie, I'm depending on you, "You can count on me" said Maggie, then the phone went dead. Maggie went to the office, there was no one in, she picked up the phone to let Mary know what was going on and to give her the address, she needs you to meet her at this address for 1.00pm your time, "Sounds melodramatic that's Cynthia all over, Mary said." Mary she is in trouble, I could sense it in her voice, you must go" Maggie was cross with Mary, "I didn't say I wouldn't go Maggie, did I" Mary retorted", "Let me know what's happening" was Maggie's reply. "I will" said Mary.

Cynthia disconnected the phone, switched off the utilities at the apartment, carried her suitcases downstairs to the door, and waited for the taxi to arrive, "Where too?" "Flinders Street Station" Cynthia replied, as he drove off she checked her list, just a couple of more things, then I'm done. "Here we are Miss" the driver said, she gave him the fare keep the change, he helped her with the cases," Blimey going to Tim- Buk -Tu with this lot are we?" Cynthia didn't answer him, she just walked away and hailed a porter to help her to put the two larger cases in a locker at the station.

Cynthia just had two more things to do before she could make her way back to Carlton, by the time she arrived back it was 12.30, she entered, "Boy am I glad your safe, I tried ringing you", said Jeff, Cynthia told him everything that she had done and what she had in mind, also that Mary was coming over for 1.00pm today to meet up with them also Stevens at four.

Cynthia then showed Jeff the letter from Andrews, he just whistled, "We'll get him Cynth the bastard", just then a knock on the door, Cynthia opened it, she put her finger to her lips, for Mary not to speak, Mary just looked at her, she entered, "I Mary I'm Jeff", "Well about bloody time we met you, we all thought it was a phantom romance", Jeff then burst out laughing, "No wonder you and Cynth get on", "What's with the Cynth" Oh' it's just my way of winding her up" Jeff said, "I can see you and I are going to get on.", "What are you two talking about?" asked Cynthia, "Nothing" they said together, and they looked at one another and smiled.

CHAPTER NINETEEN

Drink Mary" asked Cynthia. "Don't mind if I do" was her reply, Cynthia then said, "I believe you are travelling over to Perth in a plane, to see Maggie," "That's our intention, "What's all this cloak and dagger stuff" Mary said "Cynthia was not amused at being interrupted, Jeff had a smirk on his face, she withered him, "Get on with it Cynthia, I haven't got all day" Mary said, "Can you take me and Jeff with you?", Mary looked at her, "I don't know I will have to ask Charles", was Mary's answer, "Can you let us know soon as possible, time is of the essence" said Cynthia, Mary nodded.

Jeff butted in," Mary, we are in a tight spot here and we would be really grateful if you could take us, do you think we could meet up with Charles, then I can explain the situation to him", Mary replied, "Why not come over tomorrow for dinner say 7.30pm and discuss it then", Jeff said "Great we'll do that, can we park our van somewhere as not to be seen", "I think so I'm not sure" said Mary. They sat and chatted for about an hour, "I have to go now, see you tomorrow, I will ring you" Cynthia then cut in "You can't ring us here the phone is dead, any chance you could pop over in the morning, we might be able to fill you in with more information", Mary said she would and went on her way, Cynthia saw her to the door, "Thanks a lot Mary it is really appreciated, it will get us out of a real jam here", Mary gave her a peck, "See you tomorrow about eleven".

When Cynthia came back, she poured them both wine, and told Jeff all about what she had done that day, that all the planning was still in her head, but they could work on the plans together, when

Steven's arrives. Cynthia also mentioned that her father had died, that the funeral had taken place already, that she had to get in touch with the family Solicitor in England, which she had taken care of with her own Solicitor here in Melbourne, to liaise with her brothers, she also mentioned to Jeff, that she had put the apartment up for sale, and if anyone asks she had moved to Singapore for the foreseeable future, "My you have been busy" Jeff was amazed, how she could turn a situation into something that suited her, she was always one step ahead of anyone else.

There was a knock on the door, Cynthia opened it," Come in Richard, would you like a drink, "Yes please" he replied, he looked nervous, "This is Jeff Owen, Sydney Office" Oh' Hi Jeff I do remember you" Andrews always spoke highly of you, said you were one of the good guys. Jeff interrupted, "You told him Cynthia", "It was the right thing to do Jeff", "May I speak" Stevens said to Jeff. "I'm glad Cynthia has told me, we were more than work colleagues, we were involved, I would have been so upset at Cynthia had she not told me, no one knows at the office, Roberts keeps coming as though he owns the place, when we ask where Andrews is, he says he's working in Singapore, that's all we know".

Richard said, I can call you Richard" he nodded, Jeff carried on, here's the thing we have two cameras that are infra-red, don't ask, they take pictures at night apparently, we need to get them developed, as soon as possible, can you help us in that quarter, we also need your help in gathering all the information you might have regarding the undercover work we were working on with Andrews. Richard' reply was, "I can help you with both requests", "Good" said Jeff, "I must warn you this could be dangerous, it may not be safe for you to stay here in Melbourne, are you due any leave asked Jeff. Again Richard replied, "I am due leave, a month to be exact".

Great, that will fit in nicely with our plans" Jeff said, Cynthia then told Richard of their proposed plans, and that Richard would be really valuable to them if he could help in surveillance, at the property in Little Burke Street, watching who comes and goes", "I suppose I could, but it is not my forte'," said Richard, Jeff asked,

What is your forte' "Planning, articulate planning, that's what I do best", was Richard's reply, Cynthia piped in "That could be very useful to us Jeff".

"We can do the surveillance in shifts, let Richard do the planning, I do have a plan formulated in my head Richard, Jeff and I were going to work on it tonight, so if you could meet up with us here, tomorrow afternoon about 4.00pm, would that be ok with you" Richard nodded too Cynthia. That's settled then and you can let us know how you get on with cameras" Richard said goodnight to them both, "Be careful Richard, Roberts is no fool", said Cynthia, "I will" he then went on this way.

"Did you buy any food? I'm starving", asked Jeff, "Oh' bother I forgot", Cynthia replied, "I'll go and get a Chinese shall from the local shop?", Jeff said he would go, as he needed to stretch his legs, Cynthia set about setting the table, it wasn't long before Jeff was back, "That smells good," Cynthia was now feeling quite hungry. They dined and talked about what to do next it was all about prioritising. Cynthia told Jeff about her proposed plan," It might just work, we have three weeks before Christmas, so hopefully we will have everything in place by then," said Jeff, after about an hour, Jeff said, "I'm bushed I'm off for a kip," he kissed Cynthia gently on her cheek, then said "Sleep well, if you can." Cynthia just nodded, she too was she feeling extremely tired by now, so it wasn't long before she too retired upstairs. By the time Jeff appeared the next morning, Cynthia was already busy, papers all over the place, papers, ripped in shreds "Who's been busy then" said Jeff, in a jocular manner, Cynthia didn't even look up at him, she ignored him, which used to infuriate him, "Are you going to tell me what's going on or not?".

Jeff by this time was really cross, she looked up," Cynthia and said to Jeff, "I'm deep in thought here, make us some breakfast", Jeff shovelled to the kitchen like a naughty schoolboy being told off by the head, murmuring, "What's that your saying now" asked Cynthia, now it was Jeff's turn to ignore her. An hour later, Cynthia looked at him, "Well I think we covered everything and every eventuality, Jeff just looked at her and waited for her to speak, by this time he was in no mood to be dictated to by Cynthia, Jeff stormed out of the house in a temper, Cynthia just carried on with her planning and all the preparation that needed to be in place, as if nothing had happened when she had finally finished it was nearing 10.30am, "Gosh Mary will be here soon, Cynthia thought, I hope he comes back before Mary arrives."

The door opened it was Jeff, "Look what I found wandering around" Cynthia looked up, it was Mary, Cynthia was so pleased to see her, she greeted Mary warmly, put the kettle on Jeff, he trudged to the kitchen again muttering, "What's wrong with him" asked Mary, "Nothing he's just playing silly buggers that's all" they both laughed. Cynthia waited for Jeff to return, then meticulously went through every detail with them both, Mary jotting down her and Charles role, then took down instructions for Maggie and Joe, they also had a part to play, Jeff and Mary just stared at her in amazement, "Well say something why don't you" Cynthia yelled, "There's nothing to say Cynth, it's bloody marvellous I don't know how you do it" was Jeff's reply. Jeff gave Mary the Instructions for Charles, "Well I'm off see you both tonight pick you up about seven, I'll show Charles these then Jeff can answer any questions that Charles might have", Cynthia said "Hang on here" Mary butted in, "You and I Cynthia Boardman are having a girlie night, no talk of war spies, undercover agents or whatever you call it, do you hear me!"

Cynthia just nodded sheepishly, wow that's put Cynth in her place, thought Jeff, "See you tonight" then Mary left. Look Cynth, why don't you go and relax now, I'll see to the van and tidy up here, get rid of what we don't need, take your usual leisurely soak you have to look your best tonight for Charles," "What do you mean?" asked Cynthia, "You need to win him over to our way of thinking" was Jeff reply. The dinner went well at Charles and Mary's, it was small talk and congenial over the dinner table, later would be the time to be serious, it was lovely for Jeff and Charles to see Mary and Cynthia in a different light, both happy and completely relaxed, their eyes dancing as they spoke about the old days.

Soon it was time for the hard talk, Charles and Jeff went into the games room, while Cynthia and Mary talked about Mary's forthcoming wedding, Mary had left Maggie to make all the necessary arrangements, which Maggie insisted on doing, Maggie and Joe wanted Mary and Charles to marry on the estate, Mary was overjoyed that Cynthia had agreed to be her maid in honour, Cynthia said, she didn't have any honour, Mary replied Nor' do I, and they both laughed out loud, suddenly the boys came in, "We'd better get going Cynth" said Jeff, Mary and Cynthia embraced one another, while Jeff and Charles shook hands, "See you soon thanks for a lovely evening" said Jeff. The next day the reality of everything that taken place over the last ten days or so, was beginning to slowing sink in, about the massive undertaking they had taken on, Cynthia was in no doubt that everything would work out, Jeff was concerned that they didn't have enough troops, for full surveillance on Roberts Office, "We'll manage don't worry, let's do a rota and start in earnest over the weekend, said Cynthia, which is what they did.

Unknown to Cynthia and Jeff, Richard Stevens was also plotting and planning the downfall of Johnathan Roberts, he had arranged to see his Uncle Matthew, who is very high up in the Melbourne circles and not without influence, Richard had decided to tell Uncle Matt everything he knows about the stabbing of Peter Andrews, the saboteurs and the possible connection with Johnathan Roberts in the conspiracy. He needs his Uncle Matts help in uncovering Johnathan Roberts blackmailing business, and hopefully get proof to expose him for what he really is, however this needs the resources that Stevens doesn't have, and which his Uncle Matt can provide.

Stevens arrived at the Carlton house exactly 4.00pm, knocked on the door, "Come in Richard" said Jeff and shook his hand, Stevens told Jeff about his uncle Matt, Jeff whistled, "Wow you kept that quite" said Jeff, I am meeting up with Uncle Matt over the week-end, I briefly explained the situation, he said he probably can help with the cameras, He wondered if you and Cynthia would also come to dinner he would like to meet you both. Jeff pondered, I'm not sure what Cynthia has in mind, Stevens than said," Jeff, I really don' t think you, me and Cynthia, can do this surveillance on our own, Stevens then asked, "Where is Cynthia" Jeff replied," She's already watching Roberts office, "I see" said Richard. Richard carried on "It's a mammoth task which requires a great deal of manpower, this is where my Uncle might be able to help". Jeff looked shocked, "For God's sake keep this thought to yourself", Cynthia will go ballistic if she hears this, listen to what she has planned, before you voice an opinion," Richard Stevens agreed.

By this time, it was 5.00pm Cynthia arrived, "Hello Richard, has Jeff filled you in" "Not just yet Cynth, I was about too, I'll leave it to you now, I'll put the kettle on", Cynthia got herself organised, then went through every single detail with Stevens, outlining every role that each had to play, but mentioned no names. "What do you think?" Cynthia asked Stevens, "It could work I suppose" was his reply, "What do you mean it could work!" yelled Cynthia, Steven's caught Jeff's eye, Jeff just shook his head, for Stevens not to pursue it any further.

Jeff jumped in," Richard wants us to meet his Uncle Matt for Sunday dinner, which I have accepted on our behalf," Cynthia just withered Jeff, and said nothing, "Well if that's it I'm off Stevens, a car will pick you up say 2.00pm" Jeff said "Fine" and bid him good day. Cynthia was absolutely seething, she was spitting feathers, little upstart, she said to herself, Jeff kept quiet, let her stew for a bit, was his reaction. The planning had gone to plan, Jeff and Cynthia were convinced there was a mole in Parliament Building, but finding proof was difficult, there plan for Roberts Office, had already been successful unknown to Richard Steven's, the documents and files account books, etc., where already on their way to Perth thanks to Joe Yardy, the suitcases full of paperwork from Andrew's office where dumped at Jonathan Robert's office, to confuse the issue. Sunday arrived, at precisely 2.00pm a car drew up to house to take them to Box Hill, a salubrious part of the town, "Wow Cynth, look at these houses, they've cost a few shilling", Cynthia didn't answer him, the car turned up a drive, the house sat on a hill overlooking the city below, the views were fantastic, you could see for miles.

Cynthia was impressed, but showed no emotion whatsoever, they entered, a maid took Cynthia's coat, then they were shown to drawing room, "Ah, there you are", said Stevens, after formal introductions, they all went into another room much cooler than the drawing room, Cynthia was still on her guard. "Now tell me my dear, how do you know Richard" said Aunt Becky, Cynthia answered" We are just work colleagues, "Oh' I'm sure your more than that, Richard speaks very highly of you both" said Aunt Becky, Cynthia just smiled, and glanced across to Jeff, their eyes meeting momentarily, "And you Jeff work for the Allies I believe" Matt Hunter said, "Steady on, I'm only a general dogsbody for my gaffer" Jeff said, "Surely not! From what Richard has told us", Jeff looked across at Stevens, Richard blushed, "That's enough Uncle your embarrassing me", "Nonsense my boy" then his Uncle laughed out with a raucous sound.

After dinner the boys went into the den, "Come along my dear" Aunt Becky said to Cynthia, Jeff looked at Cynth and shrugged his shoulders, she just acknowledged him for she knew Jeff would take it all in, to tell her later, Cynthia and Aunt Becky went back into the drawing room, it was too hot to sit outside, Cynthia began small talk, trying to glean as much information as she could, "What about Richard's parent's ask Cynthia, "Oh' very tragic my dear, killed in a motor accident, about five years ago," "I'm sorry to hear that", said Cynthia. Then Cynthia said to herself, here goes, "Where do you or your family come from originally, I detect a slight accent," "How observant you are" said Aunt Becky, "My parents were originally from Austria, my great grandfather, emigrated over here after the Prussian war, we are third generation".

Aunt Becky then got out a family photo album. Cynthia wasn't in the least interested, she was preoccupied with what was going on in the den, she tried to look interested of course, and this is my brother's daughter Gertrude, like all families my dear we all have skeletons in the cupboard my mine is my own brother, we had a great fall out when war broke out in Europe, let's say we didn't see eye to eye, alarm bells should have started to ring with Cynthia, but she was too distant with what was going on in the den. Eventually, Cynthia started to pay attention, but the moment had passed to what Aunt Becky had said, "What's your brother called? asked Cynthia, Aunt Becky, didn't answer her, Cynthia then noticed family photograph's on the top of the piano, Cynthia not to miss a trick, "Do you play Aunt Becky", she asked, "Not anymore, I used to, it's my hands you see", Richard usually plays for me when he visits., said Aunt Becky, "I see" Cynthia was straining at the neck to look at the photos.

CHAPTER TWENTY

Then the men came in, "Night cap Jeff, Cynthia", asked Uncle Matt, "Don't mind if we do" was Jeff's reply, Cynthia just nodded, Richard helped himself, and poured Aunt Becky a sherry, they chatted a while longer. Jeff said, "Thank for a lovely dinner, we really must get going, he shook hands with Uncle Matt, and acknowledged Aunt Becky Cynthia never followed up on her conversation about Aunt Becky's niece to Jeff, if only Cynthia had mentioned it, things may have turned out so differently. When they got in the car, Jeff squeezed Cynthia hand, as if to say everything was fine, it wasn't too long before they arrived home, they bid the driver goodnight then entered the house, as soon as the car disappeared Cynthia and Jeff got the van out of the lock up, secured the house, and went to alternative bolthole.

How did it go" asked Cynthia, Jeff told her everything, from start to finish, the American's and Australians or now taking over, "What!" cried Cynthia, let me finish, it takes us out of the equation now Cynth, we can go over to Perth knowing we have done all we can, "And what about bloody Edwina Aston, cried Cynthia, oh' Cynthia, forget her she's just not worth it, she'll get her comeuppance at some stage," Jeff said. They soon reached their destination, it was in a quiet suburb of Melbourne, not too far from the airport, near the Universities, Jeff dropped Cynthia off, "I'll go and dump this van somewhere Cynth, don't wait up for me, we have a busy day tomorrow", Cynthia pecked him on his cheek, "Be careful out there" she said softly to him, "I will", Jeff replied, Cynthia retired upstairs, most of the things they needed were already packed for the trip over to Perth, she waited a while for Jeff to return, but fell asleep.

Jeff woke first and knocked on Cynthia's door, "Wake up Cynthia", Cynthia muttered something, and it was the first time in weeks that she actually had a goodnights sleep, eventually Cynthia came downstairs, we have about 3 hours, Jeff said to her, "Let's go over everything make sure we have not missed anything", so they set about checking everything, "Well I think that's it Cynth, Perth here we come", said Jeff, he was like a schoolboy on his first trip to the seaside, Cynthia just smiled, he was so relaxed, it suited him, she thought, "Time to go Cynth" said Jeff. When they reached the airport hangar 34, Charles and Mary where already waiting. Mary greeted them both warmly, Cynthia looked at Mary, radiant, confident, bubbling with excitement, I just can't wait for us all to be together again, after all this time Cynthia", said Mary. "How long will it take for us to arrive? asked Jeff, "About 6 hours approximately, depends on headwinds etc." replied Charles, Jeff whistled so long, "You will see some fantastic views as we fly over Jeff", Charles said.

The girls were already comfy and chatting, about the wedding, both looking forward to seeing Maggie and the kids and Kathy, none of them had any idea what to expect, Perth was the back and beyond to them, except Charles, who had been a couple of times with his father on business. The journey was uneventful, it seemed endless to Mary and Cynthia, Jeff was very interested in what was going on, the vastness of it all nothing but desert, but with the occasional farm dwelling, stuck in the middle of nowhere, it fascinated him, Charles said, "Not long now Jeff if you look down there you will see Esperance, a beautiful beach and resort".

Soon they landed on the make-shift runway, it was a bumpy landing, Charles said, "Steady on James", the pilot replied, "I did my best Mr Charles", Charles ignored him, they alighted the plane, there was Maggie, Joe, and Kath waiting for them, Maggie was jumping with excitement, Cynthia had to smile, she said to Mary, "I see Maggie hasn't changed, still excitable as ever, they both laughed. After about an hour's drive or so they reached the Yardy Estate, it looked huge to the four visitor's, lines and lines of grape vines, as far as the eye could see, Mary looked at Cynthia, they smiled, Maggie was still chattering, no one taking any notice of her. Charles was really impressed with what he had seen so far, Jeff just wanted to get there, he was feeling jaded, then the waggon stopped," Here we are, come on everybody, follow me!" Maggie run up the steps to the farmhouse, they entered, Mummy, Mummy, the twins came running up to her, Maggie put her arms around them, come on I want you to meet my best friends in the whole wide world, Aunt Kathy too, said the little girl Maggie laughed of course your Aunt Kathy too.

After being introduced to the children, someone brought iced lemonade, which everyone was grateful for, it was stifling and extremely hot, "Is it always like this Maggie so hot" asked Mary, Maggie said, "Only in the summer months, but it cools down in the afternoon with the Freemantle doctor", Mary just stared at her, "You'll see what I mean, a little later" they all went into the large lounge, which was so much cooler, and met the rest of Joe's family, then Maggie said, "Here she is our latest edition, Catherine, meet your Aunts", Mary jumped up, "I'm so sorry Maggie, would you believe it, I forgot to tell Cynthia that Catherine had been born early". Christmas and New Year went swimmingly, Mary and Cynthia hadn't had such a good time in years, it was as though the separation over the past years had never happened, the four girls just joked and giggled all the time, the boys were quite bemused, Joe was proud of Maggie and what she had achieved in hosting the get together, even though she had just given birth to young Christine who was just a couple of months old, he just marvelled at her and her enthusiasm for life.

Jeff, Cynthia, Charles, Mary, had the most wonderful time with Maggie Joe and the rest of the family, they had been everywhere the sightseeing took them to Perth City, Fremantle, Guildford, York, in the north and also the Margret River area there was so much to see, they visited so many places like, Mandurah, Dunsborough, Busstleton, and many more places, Perth indeed was vast, with many diverse qualities. Jeff and Cynthia loved Cape Leeuwin also Cape

Naturaliste, each place being of interest in a different way, most where only a few miles from Maggie and Joe's Estate, Cape Naturaliste, and Cape Leeuwin reminded Cynthia of Cornwall for some reason, Jeff liked it for the fishing, each had their own preference, Charles and Mary loved Perth city, Mary also fell in love with Fremantle with its carefree spirit.

It was getting ever so nearer to saying goodbye, Kathy had indeed come out of her shell, and told Mary and Cynthia about Mrs O'Brien who came from Connemara, same place as her mother, she ran the tea rooms in Dwellingup and that Mrs O'Brien read tea leaves, everyone came from miles around just have their tea leaves read, it was a thriving business, she mentioned that on her days off she would go to Yellingup and help Mrs O'Brien out. Cynthia said "I'm so pleased Kathy that you have found peace at last, Mary and I have been so worried about you over these past few years", "I know" Kathy said, "I just want you to know that I am very happy here and I can't thank Maggie and Joe enough" in fact, for what you have all done for me, I will be forever grateful, Cynthia just hugged Kathy. It was now a couple of days away from leaving, so they took themselves off for one final outing, Joe arranged a flight to Perth, Maggie and Kathy stayed at the estate, the events had caught up with Maggie she was feeling really tired, she was happy for them to go up to Perth for one final look.

Charles had a business proposition to put to Joe, Jeff was just happy to watch the cricket have a few beers and watch the world go by, he could live this life, he said to himself. Joe had booked an apartment for them all at the Holiday Inn near the WACA, he and Charles carried on with the cordial business chat and proposal for Joe to extend his wine growing business, Charles could see great potential for both of them.

Mary and Cynthia shopped till they dropped, they caught a taxi back to the Holiday Inn, after a brief respite, they sat on the veranda Mary showed Cynthia the pre-nuptial agreement that her and Charles had agreed on, Cynthia read it, "My Mary this will make you an extremely wealthy woman", "I know" said Mary, "But remember I have to conceive first, or it's null and void". "So what's stopping you" asked Cynthia "Charles" Mary said, "I don't quite follow you Mary" Cynthia said, "You know Cynthia you talk about me, but I wonder about you at times, a woman with your intelligence and knowhow, and yet you can be so naive it's beyond belief", Mary was so exasperated that Cynthia hadn't grasped the situation." Do I really need to spell it out for you?" Mary cried, after all it is a marriage of convenience for us both.

Cynthia sat and pondered, then the penny dropped, "Oh 'you mean because he is that way inclined", Mary nodded, thinking to herself, "Thank God for that, "I shouldn't worry about that, just buy a drug that relaxes him, "was Cynthia's reply, "And where do I get this drug for him? Asked Mary, "You can buy it in China town, just tell them what it is for and bobs your uncle" replied Cynthia. Mary then changed the subject, "What about you and Jeff are you going to marry him, he besotted with you" said Mary, Cynthia looked at Mary, "We have unfinished business to carry out first, we have been assigned to Singapore, so we have to report back to Sydney on the 12th January, then we'll see "was Cynthia reply. Soon they heard a rumpus, what the hell, it was Jeff he fell in, he looked up Hi Cynthia in a slushing voice, Cynthia was not amused, Mary said," Come on Jeff bed for you", her and Cynthia managed to get him on the bed, and left him, Mary then left to go to her apartment, "See you later". she said.

An hour later Charles arrived with Joe, "Nightcap Joe", asked Charles "Don't mind if I do" was Joe's reply, Mary asked if they had enjoyed the cricket, Joe replied" We would have done if we hadn't lost", Mary didn't reply she knew absolute nothing about cricket, "Did Jeff get home alright Mary" Charles asked, Mary said, "Yes drunk as a skunk" Charles and Joe laughed out loud, a knock came to the door it was Cynthia, when she saw the boys there she said, "What the hell has he been drinking, I have never ever seen him in this state before", Charles and Joe just laughed out loud. The next morning after breakfast, it was time to make tracks back to Margret river, Jeff had yet to emerge, Cynthia left the three of them to see to Jeff, the other three just grinned at one another, bet he has a sore head this morning" He doesn't drink much" Mary said, Joe said "You could have fooled me, he knocked the wine back like someone who drowns pints", Anyhow, let's get a move on and hit the road, an hour later they were on their way back to the estate. Upon arrival, Maggie came to meet them with Kath, took them back to the farmhouse. After a long chat over lunch, everyone said their goodbyes, then Charles, Mary, Cynthia and Jeff set off to return to Melbourne, Mary shouted, "See in May Maggie thanks for everything" they all waved slowly as the plane took off.

Cynthia and Mary just watched as the plane soared into the sky, they could no longer see any land only sky and clouds, "It was great to see everyone Mary, said Cynthia, Mary "Yes it was, I can't wait till May, when we will back together again" was Mary's reply, "Just remind me of the date again", asked Cynthia, Mary replied, 20th May and" Don't you let me down Cynthia Boardman", "Would I do that to you" replied Cynthia. The journey didn't seem quite as long going back home as it was going, they soon arrived in Melbourne, Mary asked Cynthia and Jeff who was about just coming too from his binge, if they would like to stopover with them for a couple of days, which Cynthia accepted, she still hadn't forgiven Jeff just yet.

It was now the 10th January, farewells were in order, Cynthia embraced Charles, "Thank you for a wonderful time, you look after Mary you have got a good one there", Charles nodded "I know I have", Jeff shook hands firmly with Charles, "Thanks for your company really enjoyed it" Mary came over to Cynthia, they embraced, Cynthia whispered in her ear, China town don't forget, Mary acknowledged her. When Cynthia and Jeff arrived back in Melbourne, they immediately booked into a hotel not too far away from the airport, they had decided to rest up and catch the next flight out to Sydney the following day, as far as they knew they had left no stone unturned and felt safe.

They had a quiet night together remembering about their travels over the past month, and how much they had enjoyed the company over in Perth, Jeff in particular got on very well with Mary, he sensed a kindred spirit with her, he also liked Maggie, and how she was mother hen in more ways than one, Cynthia laughed, then Jeff said "You know Cynth, I have never heard you laugh as much as you did in Perth, you looked so relaxed and enjoyed every minute, it did you good" Cynthia agreed with him, "You too looked relaxed Jeff I think it did us both good, I do feel so refreshed."

Soon they were on their journey back to Sydney which only took a couple of hours at the most, by this time each were in their own thoughts, wondering what might lie ahead, Cynthia was looking forward to Singapore, she had heard so much about the place, and a wave of excitement crept over her. Jeff on the other hand was more apprehensive about the move over to the Orient, after all the Japs occupied Singapore along with Indonesia, Burma, Vietnam, Cambodia, and many more countries, in the South China Seas, although part of the 7th Fleet of America had been destroyed by the Japs, America was still a force to be reckoned with. Upon arriving at Sydney, they booked into a hotel near the Darling River and just relaxed the day away, each preparing mentally for their next assignment.

Meanwhile in Perth, Joe told Maggie about the proposal Charles had put to him, on the one hand he would be grateful for any financial support, on the other he doesn't want to lose control of the family business, he also has to put the proposal to his brother and sister, who have an equal share in the business, Maggie usually does not get involved with the running of Joe's business, so she was surprised that he had mentioned it to her. Maggie pondered for a while then said, "What's troubling you Joe, you usually know just what to do", "Well it's a lot of money Maggie, and it is tempting to say yes", "Why don't you ask Dave and Catherine what they think, then make up your mind, I'm sure Charles would answer any questions that you might have if you ask him" Joe just looked at her, "That's why I love you so much you are so simplistic" and he kissed her. Back in Melbourne Mary just knew she had to get pregnant, for her own wellbeing and security for the future, she took Cynthia's advice and went to China town, and explained the best way she could what she needed, the penny finally dropped, she was given a prepared portion. The aged

Chinese lady said, "For you" and "For him" in pigeon English, Mary pushed her potion away, and shook her head, and pointed to the one for Charles, the old lady persisted that she takes both. In the end Mary ended up with one for Charles and one for her, the instructions were written in English, then the Chinese woman said, you keep in touch yes! Mary said she would.

Back at the house Charles was out when Mary returned, which deflated her, she was hoping they could have spent a quiet night in together, but no joy, he had gone out and left no message, which meant he would not be home till the early hours, Mary was so disappointed, after a great holiday together, Mary actually thought she might be winning him over. The next day Mary decided she needed to tackle Charles on his commitment to children, she was determined to get the matter resolved one way or another, she entered his bedroom door, no sign of him, that's it she said to herself, I'll sever all ties with him sod the wedding, just as she was about to leave, Charles appeared, "What is it Mary" Charles asked, she entered the bedroom, and sat down, "I think we need to think long and hard about this marriage Charles and your commitment to this forthcoming marriage," Mary replied, "Why do you say that" asked Charles.

CHAPTER TWENTY-ONE

Well since you came back you have been out every night, not even asked me if I would like to with you, we used to go to the picture at least twice a week, I want to know what you are doing" was Mary's reply, Charles came over to her, "I haven't been doing anything that would hurt you Mary, in fact just the opposite. I have been looking at houses for us, if we have children I want them to have a back yard" was Charles answer, Mary kissed him, "I'm lonely when you are not in" Mary said, "I promise you when we are married you will not be lonely", with that Charles went over and embraced her tightly. A week went by for Charles and Mary, it was very amicable for them both, Charles was trying his best to please her, for he knew that so much depended on him being a good husband and hopefully a good Father, his whole future with his family was at stake.

Mary kept going to China town for the potions, from the old Chinese woman, who spoke pigeon English to her, this particular day the old woman, grabbed Mary's hand, "You pregnant yes", Mary replied "No", the old woman repeated herself, "You pregnant yes" again Mary said no, the old woman then went towards her put her hand on Mary's tummy and rubbed it, she smiled at Mary, then she took her hand to read her palm, she kept smiling, you have a good life. Then she frowned, and stopped reading her hand, Mary was perturbed by this, and kept asking her what was wrong the old lady went away, Mary was bewildered, then a younger Chinese girl came out, "My grandma says, you are pregnant, and that you are having twins, but there is danger lurking around you, not you in danger but someone you know". Mary rushed back home, she was so upset at what had gone on, made herself a cuppa, then sat down to take it all in, she suddenly screamed, "Oh my God! Cynthia is going to be killed.

I had better warn her, I must write to her tonight, her thoughts then turned to the old woman telling her she was pregnant with twins, how odd she thought, she could be wrong on both accounts, she was probably after more money, so Mary dismissed the episode and decided to stay away for a while, after all it was only four weeks off her wedding. Charles and Mary were kept very busy with all the arrangements, even though Maggie was seeing to everything, Mary and Charles wanted updates every day just to make sure, the invitations had gone out to Cynthia and Jeff, with a note from Mary, threatening Cynthia not to let her down, and to let her know soonest, so they could travel over to Perth together.

Charles had chosen a beautiful house, he asked Mary if she would like to look at it before his final decision, by this time he was fed up with looking for the right property, but he thought this one was the best he had seen, he wanted everything in place before the wedding. It was now a week before the wedding no word from Cynthia as yet, Charles was getting agitated about it, he knew how much it meant to Mary," I assure you Charles, Cynthia will just show up no announcement whatsoever, then suddenly she is there", "I wish I had your faith Mary, I have to get these documents sorted in the next couple of days" said Charles. Sure enough Cynthia cut it fine she arrived at Mary's and rang the bell a maid answered, "Who is it Sara" Mary asked, Cynthia brushed passed the maid nearly knocking her over, "It's me" yelled Cynthia, "Boy I'm I glad to see you, I'll let Charles know right away he needs you to fill in some documents, "Where is Jeff? Asked Mary, "I'm afraid Jeff can't make it Mary, the company would only allow me to come over" "That's a pity, Charles will be disappointed," said Mary.

When they all arrived at the Yardy's Estate, everything was in full flow, "It's funny Mary it's as if the war isn't happening over here, no one seems to talk about it" Cynthia said, Mary agreed with her,

"Perhaps they don't get the news over here as often as we do" was Mary's reply, "Anyway no talk of war, Cynthia, it's my wedding" they both grinned at one another, "On a serious note Mary, how is it going for you? Asked Cynthia, "Fine, I just want to get this marriage out of the way, then I can set my stall out", said Mary, there was no mention of the old Chinese woman. Mary kept that to herself, they were interrupted by Maggie smile beaming, with excitement, she greeted them with open arms, and embraced them with loving affection, which took Cynthia by surprise, Mary just gave Cynthia a look and shrugged her shoulders, Kathy wasn't too far behind, hers was a more genteel greeting, which Cynthia was grateful for, Maggie showed them the barn, Oh it's lovely Maggie then, Mary embraced her, said thank you ever so much I will always appreciate this, Maggie blushed.

Charles was in a buoyant mood let's all go to Dunsborough I liked it there, so the four of them, Charles, Mary, Cynthia and Kathy piled into a lorry which Joe had lent them, "How's things with you Kathy" asked Cynthia, Kathy replied, "Do you remember Mrs O'Brien, I told you about having tea rooms in Yellingup," Cynthia and Mary both nodded. Well her family want her to go and live with them up country somewhere, Baldivis near Rockingham, I think. Joe said he knew where it was, her family said they would give me first choice to rent it off them, their Mother was insistent upon it," Kathy went on "I can't live with Maggie and Joe forever, the tea rooms are only open nine months of the year depending on the weather, so I'm thinking of combining the two jobs, I just need to sort out the finances, to see if I can afford to do it.

After they had spent a couple of hours at Dunsborough, Cynthia said, "How far is this Yellingup"," "Oh' not too far about half an hour's drive" Kathy replied, Charles interrupted them, "Can you direct me Kathy," Kathy nodded, so they set off to look at the tea rooms, when they arrived everything was locked up for the winter. Mary, and Cynthia peered through the windows, Cynthia wasn't that impressed with what she saw, but didn't say anything to the others, Mary was more gracious, "I can see you can do a lot with this Kathy",

"Yes" Kathy replied with excitement," I do have plans to improve it" Charles looked at his watch, "I think we had better make tracks, we have got a big day tomorrow", Cynthia chirped up, "Want to save your energy Charles with a wistful smile", Mary was not amused and withered Cynthia.

The next day Maggie was running around like a scolded cock, Cynthia cried, "For heaven's sake Maggie calm down, you've done everything you can," Maggie stared at her" Cynthia realised she had upset her and went over to her, "Sorry Maggie, but there is really no need to rush around, go and get ready, the preacher will be here in an hour" with that Maggie went to sort herself out.

Cynthia went to Mary's room and knocked, "Can I come in", "Of course you can" said Mary, when Cynthia entered the room, she was in awe with Mary, she looked absolutely stunning, "You look beautiful Mary, if Charles heart doesn't melt when he sees you, all I can say, take him for every penny he's got", Mary just smiled, "You're are definitely a cynic Cynthia Boardman", another knock what are you two talking about, it was Kathy, she too looked lovely too, her golden red hair catching what bit of sunlight there was, "Are we ready girls" asked Maggie, and they all nodded, Mary took a deep sigh, then they made their way to the barn.

It was a beautiful service, the preacher had done them proud, Joe gave Mary away, Andrew Charles best man and Cynthia being her maid of honour, the two others being her bridesmaids, the rest of the folk were made up of Joe's and Maggie's family, and a few neighbours from around the area. It was all too much for Charles, tears were falling from his face, Mary took out her hankie and wiped them away, Charles said "I have never been as happy as I am now Mary" "Why the tears then", asked Mary, "Tears of Joy Mary" Charles replied, and he embraced her, Mary was also ecstatic with joy and hoped in her hearts to heart that things would work out for them both.

The partying went on till the early hours of the morning, everyone was drunk, Joe and Charles in particular, Maggie and Kathy had both left the shindig and retired for the night, Cynthia and Mary just watched as everyone made a fool of themselves, that is not to say that they were sober, "Are you happy Mary" asked Cynthia, "As happy as I will ever be" Mary answered. "Well I'm off myself Mary, you go and drag Charles away from Joe" said Cynthia, Mary did just that, "Come on Charles I've waited long enough", all the lads started giving Charles advice, Mary just said "I'm sure he can manage quite well thank you" all the lads started sniggering, Mary took no notice of them and dragged Charles with her, once she was in their room, she could see what state he was in and left him on the floor, while she went to bed.

By the time Mary woke up, it was well into the morning, she had a slight headache but nothing she couldn't handle, but Charles was a different story, he was very fragile indeed, and for Joe, he was definitely in Maggie's bad books for not looking after Charles, Cynthia found this very amusing. Mary entered the farmhouse, Maggie started to apologise to Mary, Mary interrupted her, "No need to apologise Maggie, did everyone have a good time? Maggie said "I think so" "Well then that's all what matters, it will be the talk of the Margaret river, on what a good spread you put on" Maggie beamed, "I will won't I", Cynthia asked where Charles was, "Still sleeping it off, I don't know what they were drinking, I've never seen him in that state before" Mary said.

A couple of days later it was time for them to return to Melbourne, Mary and Cynthia, were always sorry to leave Maggie and Kathy, "Keep in touch both of you" said Maggie, they said their goodbyes and off they went. Charles was himself now and was very upset at what had happened, Mary wasn't all that bothered, and she didn't feel all that well and just wanted to get back home, Cynthia too was itching to get back to Singapore to see Jeff, Cynthia stayed the night with Mary, that is when Cynthia broached Mary, on the idea of buying the tea rooms for Kathy, Mary was in full agreement, Cynthia asked Mary to fix it with Maggie, and find out how much the property was worth and to get back to them, hoping they could sort it out before the summer season started, Cynthia left the next day, first to Sydney then onto Singapore.

The next couple of days Mary was still feeling off colour, she was thinking it was something she had eaten, Charles insisted the Doctor came to see her, which he duly did, he examined Mary, and said "Congratulations you are pregnant" Mary couldn't believe it knowing what the Chinese woman had said, "Did you hear me Mary" asked the doctor, Mary just smiled, "I'll let myself out".

Mary quickly got herself organised and went to the store, she went straight upstairs to see Charles in his office. Guess what darling I'm pregnant" to her surprise, not only was Charles there, but his father also, they both jumped up, Charles was fussing around her, his father said, Charles she won't melt you know, Mary chuckled, then they all started to laugh, his father said, "Wait while Eleanor hears of this, she will be overjoyed, well done son", Mary thought hang on, it takes two.

That week brought better news, the war in Europe was virtually over, which brought even more joy to Mary it meant that going back to England was still an option for her, let's see how we go, she said to herself, Mary couldn't wait to tell Maggie and Kathy, Maggie was so pleased for her, "Hang on you have only just got married" Maggie! Exclaimed. Mary laughed I know, "Oh 'well we'll skip that" said Maggie, Mary had a chat with Maggie about what Cynthia had suggested about buying the tea rooms for Kathy to run in the summer months, would she look into the possibility of buying the property without Kathy knowing, Maggie said she and Joe would find out all they could, "I have to go now Maggie, need to write to Cynthia now and tell her the news.

Mary felt the need to let the old woman know in China Town, she took herself off to see her, deep inside she was really happy, the prospect of having a child, filled her with pride, at last I will have someone who will really, really love me, I will be a great Mum she said to herself, soon she arrived in China Town and saw the old woman there, she smiled, Mary went over and greeted her warmly, she asked her, "How did you know" the old woman shrugged her shoulders, and went into the back. The old Chinses woman came back with her granddaughter, "What is it" asked the girl, "I just wanted to know how she knew I was pregnant" Mary said, the girl said, "She couldn't tell you if she wanted too, she has a gift, that's all she knows".

Mary then asked if she would be offended if she could visit her grandma on a regular basis, and that Mary would pay her for her time, the young girl went into the back to tell her grandmother, they were quite some time before they returned, the old woman was smiling and went to Mary, she put her hand on her tummy, then put two fingers up, "I'm having twins" Mary said, the girl asked her grandmother in Chinese, then the girl said "Yes twins", with that Mary warmly shook hands with her and said thank you". By the time she arrived home she was feeling quite jaded and decided to lie down her mind was spinning with all that had gone on, she felt drowsy and fell into a deep sleep, she was wakened suddenly by the telephone, it took her a while to come around, she picked up the phone "Hello, my dear Eleanor Winfield here, I am overjoyed for you both congratulations", Have you got a date" Mary replied "No I have only just found out today.

It will take some time for me and Charles to get used to the idea" then his mother asked if they are going to announce it, Mary thought she's fishing here Charles hasn't told her anything, "I will leave that to Charles, now if you don't mind Eleanor, I am rather tired", "Keep in touch Mary let me know how you are getting on, said Eleanor then she put the phone down. Mary couldn't wait for Charles to arrive home, he was later than usual, "Shall I put dinner out for you Mrs Charles?", asked the maid, Mary said she would wait for Mr Charles to arrive, after about ten minutes Charles arrived with the biggest bunch of flowers you have ever seen. "Where's my lovely wife he went over to her and kissed her, thank you for making me a very happy man". After dinner Mary told him about his mother ringing and fishing, asking her all sorts of questions, do they know that we are married," Not just yet" replied Charles, "Why not? Asked Mary,

Charles said he was planning on asking them to dinner on Sunday to give them the news.

Well I suppose we can still ask them if you still want too." The news that the Pacific war was edging closer to ending, was music to the ears of the Aussies, everybody, had, had enough of war, with so many soldiers maimed and so many deaths, the cost of human lives was something governments seem to overlook, people trying to pick themselves up, and try to forget about the monasteries of war. Mary was in a thoughtful mood and wondered about JR, she was hoping he was getting better with his treatment, she didn't know why she had thought of him, she just did, Mary was resting, Charles went to her room, "Mary the Doctor has rung me, and made arrangements for you to see a Paediatrician next Thursday", Mary was most indignant, and why did he not ring me"! "Mary that's not the way it is done". Said Charles.

CHAPTER TWENTY-TWO

Meanwhile in Singapore, Cynthia and Jeff, were still undercover, trying to eke out defectors, they were based in China Town, Pagoda Street to be precise, a flat in one of the apartments, it was an area where everyone kept to themselves, their contact was a Mae Ling who liaised with them, with snippets of information, half the time Cynthia thought she was making things up for the money, they were to meet her at 12.00 noon at the boat Quay. "This is going to be a wild goose chase again, she's using us" said Cynthia, Jeff answered, "Let's just wait and see", it was approaching 12.00 noon when they arrived at the Quay. Jeff ordered two beers, there were many bars and restaurants, each with their own particular cuisine, from western too eastern, Jeff and Cynthia loved this part of Singapore, Mae Ling soon showed up, she was very nervous, she quickly handed Jeff a piece of paper, then rushed off, Cynthia was put on her guard by this Jeff also, "Let's get out of here" said Jeff, their drinks still on the table. They split up, "Meet at the usual place at 4.30pm", Jeff said, Cynthia nodded, each looking over their shoulder as they went their separate ways, Cynthia made her way to Stamford Road, and went into the Oriental Hotel, and ordered coffee, sitting at an advantage point.

After about an hour, Cynthia was about to make her way out, when she spotted, Johnathan Roberts, she quickly sat in the background, watched as he asked for his key to his room, now this is interesting, thought Cynthia, she decided to have lunch, made her way to the restaurant, were again sat in a discreet area of the dining room, a waiter came up to her, give her a menu, then she ordered something, in a broad Irish accent, the waiter nodded, Cynthia then used the menu to observe as much as she could.

By the time Cynthia returned to China Town Jeff was already there, she told him everything that had gone on and how she manged to get Johnathan Robert's room number, "Good girl" said Jeff, I'll go to the Embassy and pass this onto the powers that be". Just a minuet Jeff, don't be too hasty, we can break into Roberts room and see if there are any documents or any information, if so, we can scrutinise it for ourselves", Jeff was adamant, No! We will pass it on now" Cynthia wasn't at all happy about this, she made her mind up there and then to go back to Sydney, after all she wasn't supposed to just watch and pass on any information she found out, she had a Senior role in Sydney. Jeff was gone for ages, Cynthia was getting restless, she went outside the apartment, there seemed to be quite a lot of activity going on, she decided to get everything together just in case, they had a planned escape route if needed, Cynthia peered gingerly out of the window she could see Japanese soldiers stopping people and asking for their papers, "God dam it" said Cynthia.

Suddenly the door burst open, it was Jeff breathless, quick Cynthia, "There onto to us", Jeff grabbed the two rucksacks, Cynthia grabbed the cases while surveying the room to see if she had overlooked anything, "Come on Cynthia! Cried Jeff.

They managed to get out of the building without being seen, Jeff said, "We've been set up" "I just knew it" yelled Cynthia, I'm going back to Sydney" "You can do what you like, I've had it here", Jeff was taken by surprise, "You can't just leave like that, what will the Embassy say" Jeff said, "I don't give a shit! What they say, I'm wasted here" was Cynthia's reply.

Let's get to the Embassy then we can talk things over with the powers that be", Cynthia agreed, they set off to the Embassy in Tanglin Road. When they arrived at the Embassy, it took some time for them to enter, the longer they waited the more vulnerable they became, Jeff and Cynthia trusted no one now, and felt betrayed by Mae Ling, Jeff was kinder about Mae Ling, but Cynthia was furious with her. "By the way what did the message say?" asked Cynthia, Jeff replied "I don't know I just handed it over to Mackintosh, who said he would pass it on". "At times I wonder which planet you're on Jeff Owen, your problem is you're too trusting," Jeff retorted, "Well I'm not a cynic like you!" He yelled at her, there was now uneasy silence.

Finally, they were allowed in, Cynthia said, "About bloody time it's our lives on the block here not yours", the attaché said "Calm down", "Calm down", Cynthia was about to say something when Jeff interrupted her, he then said, "Do you go out and gather information on what the Japs are up too, or do you just sit in your cosy little office all day, and at night sip Singapore slings in Raffles and just talk about the war? "Good buddy, I've got news for you, we are the ones who put our lives in danger, so don't you ever patronise people like us or criticise, you have no idea what you're talking about," Cynthia was proud of him, the phone rang, he picked it up sheepish, "Yes Sir", the attaché said "You can go up now, Jeff and Cynthia didn't even look at him, Cynthia thought that's put you in your place you little shit! They entered the Ambassador's office, "Jeff it seems we have been betrayed, we have a mole, we must have", he said, Cynthia chirped in, "It's that bloody Mae Ling" I knew we couldn't trust her, the Ambassador replied, "I'm afraid not, she has been found murdered", Cynthia blushed.

Jeff then said "Look Sir, we are no use to you here now, we might as well go back to Sydney" the Ambassador looked surprised, "I don't think there is any need for that Jeff, Cynthia jumped up, "Well I'm not staying here, I'm used to working on my own with Jeff, and I must say we have been very successful over the past few years, we work better when we don't have to keep passing on our information onto someone else, that's when the information can get distorted, I don't trust anyone, not even you" Cynthia was seething, "Steady on girl" Jeff said. The Ambassador, looked at Cynthia, "I've had good reports on you and indeed Jeff your reputations precedes you, but I didn't know you were so outspoken, you take no prisoners do you? Cynthia didn't even look at him, "Just what do you want? The Ambassador asked, Jeff looked at Cynthia, he waited for her to speak, "Are you going to say something" Jeff said in a sarcastic note, reluctantly Cynthia got up then said, "Unless we can do the job in our way, and report to no one except you, I'm not interested in staying in Singapore, in fact we haven't had a day off since we came here, we have been in dingy smelly apartments. I have been trained as an elite and specialist undercover agent.

Jeff said, "Cynthia does have some very good information on a certain Johnathan Roberts, if you would allow us to follow this up, hush- hush, and report only to you, perhaps a rendezvous of your choice daily, we can then pursue Roberts, who we suspected when we were in Sydney, you can confirm this with Allies Headquarters in Sydney if you wish".

The Ambassador pondered for a while," Ok we'll do it your way, you set everything up, book yourselves into a decent Hotel, not the Oriental, it's too expensive," "Get some extra funding from the accountant?" The Ambassador then said, "Jeff shall we say the Recreation Club Connaught Drive every other day at 8.30pm. "Sounds good to me" was Jeff's reply, The Ambassador bid them both goodnight and wished them luck. When they reached the reception area, they went to see the accountant for more funding, the attaché was still on duty, Cynthia just walked right passed him, Jeff acknowledged him, then they went on their way, Jeff then said, Blimey Cynthia you went a bit over the top, Cynthia replied, "I hate people who sit in Ivory Castles, and haven't a clue what they're talking about.

Well at least we can now get on with it ourselves now, I'll book into the Oriental, said Jeff, you book into the Peninsular it will be safer for you there, The Oriental was close to the Marina, with its restaurants and bars, Cynthia was not too pleased about being in a three star Hotel while Jeff was in a five star Hotel, you would Jeff Owen, Why can't I stay at the Oriental?, she said to herself, Jeff was much happier about everything now, he felt better that they were to split up, it was safer for them both. News was filtering through that the Allies had the upper hand in Europe, it was hoped that a major operation being planned would once and for all put an end to the war. Singapore knew only too well what it was like to be invaded, the japs were everywhere, Cynthia and Jeff had to be very careful when they went out, pretending to go sightseeing, they were getting very good with their Irish accents.

When they could they would survey the Oriental Hotel with a view to breaking into Jonathan Robert's bedroom, every last detail had to be made, it was while since they were on such reconnaissance, that they suddenly saw Edwina Aston, Jeff had to put his hand over Cynthia mouth shush' he said, Jeff waited while she went out of sight, Cynthia wanted to trail her, but Jeff said "No, one job at a time, Cynthia, that's when mistakes are made, Cynthia loathed her for what she did to Kathy, Jeff interrupted her thoughts by Jeff. "Tonight we'll do it tonight" Cynthia just nodded, Jeff insisted that they go back to the Hotel, Cynthia wanted to do some shopping, to replenish her wardrobe, "Are you sure it's clothes shopping, or Edwina Aston shopping" said Jeff," It is definitely clothes shopping, come with me if you don't believe me" replied Cynthia. Jeff went back to the hotel to go over everything, Jeff was very meticulous in his planning, Cynthia went on a shopping spree, it was her way of relaxing, after all she never had time to spend her own money, she bought Jeff a couple of shirts, aftershave, and perfume for herself Chanel was her favourite and the most expensive of course, then she saw Edwina again this time she hid out of sight, she watched as Edwina meet up with Johnathan Roberts. Cynthia was gobbed smacked, Jeff will never believe this, she said to herself, she watched them for some time, then went their separate ways.

Cynthia wanted to follow Edwina, but didn't want to jeopardise the plans for that night, she couldn't wait to get back to tell Jeff. Unknowingly to Cynthia, she had been spotted by Edwina, Cynthia was so caught up with seeing her and Roberts together, for once Cynthia had let her guard down, it was only by chance, that Cynthia stopped at a shop to look in the window and noticed Edwina in the background, Oh' crumbs she said to herself, she went into the shop made her way near the back hoping she could get out, as luck had it she was able to slip out the back door of the shop, she slowly and gingerly made her way back to the hotel, not daring to tell Jeff what had happened, but Cynthia was unnerved by it all. That night they set out to break into Johnathan Roberts bedroom, they entered the Oriental separately, Cynthia first, and went into the lift, she looked like a guest, she had evening wear on befitting for a five-star hotel, Jeff went to the receptionist and asked if Johnathan Roberts was in his room, "Let me check Sir" she came back, "I'm afraid Mr Roberts is out, who shall I say called"., "Oh' that's Ok I'll probably meet up with him at Raffles."

It was a very busy hotel despite the prices, the receptionist went over to another customer, Jeff hurriedly ran up the stairs, Cynthia was waiting patiently, Jeff took out his tools to pick the lock, after a couple of minutes the door opened, they entered, he looked for the safe while Cynthia searched his clothes, draws and wardrobe, even the bathroom, Jeff was still working on the safe it suddenly opened, he took all the contents out and put them into Cynthia's handbag. Cynthia then left for Raffles, Jeff closed the safe, and locked the door, he went down the back stairs, which brought him to the kitchens, he slipped by a couple of chief's the doors were already open. Half an hour had passed, Cynthia was getting nervous, what's taking him so long, she thought to herself, then she saw him on the balcony, she went up to meet him, "Ok" Jeff asked Cynthia nodded, they then slipped into the background, surveying everyone in the bar below.

Jeff nudged Cynthia, Johnathan Roberts had just entered the room, "There he is" Cynthia looked over, a little later on Edwina Aston came into view, "And there she is" said Cynthia, they both looked at each other, Jeff said "Let's get out of here", which they did and headed to their hotel, Jeff had decided to stay at the Peninsular that night instead of the Oriental with Cynthia, for safety.

When they reached the hotel they went straight to the room, Cynthia took out all the documents out of her bag, and gave them to Jeff, Cynthia ordered drinks, soon the waiter arrived, Cynthia went to the door, "Just a minuet Cynth" Jeff whispered, he went behind the door, with his pistol ready, Cynthia opened the door slowly, the waiter came in with the drinks, Cynthia signed the receipt and gave him a tip, he nodded and left. Jeff was very jittery he decided that they should move out first thing in the morning he wasn't taking any chances, "The trouble with this place, you don't know who you can trust, I'm not too happy at seeing Edwina Aston here, if she spots us were dead meat", Cynthia kept quiet and agreed with him, in hearts to heart she knew she should tell him about Edwina but he was so uptight it wouldn't help the situation.

Jeff had decided to stay somewhere nearer to the airport, they hailed a taxi taking everything with them, once they had found something suitable two stay, Jeff went back to the Oriental to settle his bill, as he arrived the police were there, he went straight to the reception desk, "Can I settle my bill", Jeff asked "Certainly Sir" a young man replied, "What room is it", Jeff said "Just a minuet I think I've forgotten something be back in a jiffy", with that Jeff rushed up the stairs, he just had this feeling things were not quite right he made his way to his room, then moved onto Johnathan Robert's room, the police were all over the place, he walked passed the room and glanced inside, he noticed the safe door was opened but nothing else, "Keep moving Sir" Jeff just carried on walking, he went back down to the reception desk, settled his bill, "By the way what's all the commotion? "I'm not sure Sir, someone said a body had been found in one of the guest's room, that's all I know" Jeff gave him a tip, "Thank you Sir", Jeff just got out of the Hotel as quickly as he could.

Jeff told Cynthia about a body being found in one of the guest rooms, he wasn't sure which one it was, thought it might be Roberts's room but when he passed the room which was open, all he could see was the safe door was opened, he was told to move on by the police, "You know Cynthia I think we should leave today separately back to Sydney, let the powers that be sort things out from now on, it's getting too dangerous for us here". They booked a room a motel for two nights, after a bite to eat they left for the airport, they decided to leave keys in the room, it didn't take too long to reach the airport, security was tight, they got their papers out, Cynthia had the documents hidden upon her person, she was going back to Ireland via Australia to see relatives, when asked by the Japanese soldiers, he stamped her papers she was now safely in the airport lounge waiting to board.

Jeff papers were to say that he was an attaché,' at the Irish Embassy he had been ordered back by his Government to Sydney and showed them the relevant paperwork, he too had his papers stamped. Jeff arrived in the airport lounge and slowly looked for Cynthia, she was already chatting to an elderly couple, who were returning to Sydney to stay with their daughter, Jeff smiled to himself, it was Cynthia heavy Irish accent that made him smile, an hour passed, then the announcement for all passengers to go to gate 17 for the flights to Sydney, first class passengers first, slowly the remaining passengers made their way, with documents and passports ready before they boarded. Cynthia of course was in first class, Jeff was in economy, it was an eight-hour flight to Sydney. Cynthia removed the papers and place them back into her hand luggage and was able to settle down and relax.

CHAPTER TWENTY-THREE

By the time they reached Sydney it was 8.30pm they both managed to get out of the airport by 9.30pm, hailed a taxi to Jeff's place, Cynthia was relieved to be back in Sydney, she couldn't wait to get Jeff's place, Jeff also was in this own thoughts he too was glad to be back he was now looking forward to a good night's sleep.

The next day it took Cynthia some time to realise she was back home, she went downstairs, Jeff had already left, he had left her a note back in a couple of hours, he had taken all the documents with him, Cynthia was furious she wanted to look at them before he handed them over, so she decided to have a nice leisurely bath, made herself a coffee, took all her mail up with her, and went into the bathroom. After an hour Cynthia was dressed and was reading her post, she heard a noise, she shouted, "Is that you Jeff," no answer, she shouted again, still no answer, a sixth sense came over her she gingerly went to her room, took her pistol out of her bag, and waited, she knew if someone came upstairs, she would hear them, as one of the steps creaks quite loudly, sure enough she heard the creak, by this time she was definitely on her guard,

Cynthia hid behind the door, it opened slowly, she was about to pull the trigger, she closed the door slowly her heart pounding so hard she could hear it, then she heard "Don't shoot! Please don't shoot" Cynthia took one look, it was the cleaner, "For heaven's sake Lizzie, didn't you hear me shout twice! Cynthia yelled, the cleaner said "I'm deaf in one ear", and started to cry, Cynthia just looked at her then put her arm around her, and said "Carry on Lizzie, I'm so sorry I startled you, it's been a hell of a week". Cynthia, then went into the lounge to read her mail, she noticed a letter from Mary and one from Maggie, she opened Mary's letter first, it read

Dear Cynthia,

Well it has happened Cynthia, I am pregnant, due sometime beginning of December, I must tell you the old Chinese woman is adamant that I am having twins, but the paediatrician hasn't mention twins to me, he just says the baby is healthy, Charles is a different person towards me, (I bet he is he's got what he wants) thought Cynthia, his parents are also different towards me now especially Eleanor, I know it's just for show. I hope his parents don't get their hands on the baby with their fancy lawyers, Charles say he has made sure that it won't happen in his will, and that no way his parents will have anything to do with the upbringing of their children if something happens to him or me, I just have to trust him I suppose.

Now on a lighter note, I have managed to buy the tea rooms for Kathy. Joe said it was a fair price, so being as you were not around, I've bought the tea rooms in Kathy's name, at the moment she is paying rent to Maggie and Joe, we are waiting for you, so we can give her the deeds. I don't know where the hell you are, Maggie and I are both worried sick about you get in touch as soon as you can.

Lots of Love
Mary and Charles

Cynthia opened Maggie's letter it was similar to Mary's except she too was pregnant again due sometime in late March early April, (God! Maggie when are you going to stop having babies), Cynthia thought to herself, then carried on reading the letter, her and Joe are extremely happy about it, Maggie carried on about tittle-tattle which was Maggie all over, Cynthia wasn't remotely interested in tittle-tattle she just closed the letter.

There was still no sign of Jeff, Cynthia rang Mary first, a maid answered, "Is Mary there" the maid asked "Who shall I say is calling, "Cynthia was the reply, blimey this is very formal", thought Cynthia, "Charles here Cynthia, Mary can't come to the phone we are about to take her to the clinic, she is in labour, and not handling at all well", Oh' my word, "I was planning on coming over, to see you both". By all means please do, Mary will be delighted, she has been worried about you", "Will Jeff be coming over? "I'm not too sure" was Cynthia's reply, Charles then said, "We have to go now Cynthia".

Jeff still hadn't arrived all at once the phone went, it was Jeff, he told her what had gone on that he had met with the Top Brass, mentioned to them Edwina and Co., in Singapore and so on, "You'll never guess," "What! Cynthia was agitated Jeff had this nasty habit of dramatizing everything, Jeff went on to say that Johnathan Roberts had been found murdered in his room at the hotel, stabbed, they have one suspect a woman, Cynthia interrupted him, "Bloody Edwina I bet!!", Jeff replied "Yes". I have to go now Cynth, see you later. Eventually Jeff went to Allied Headquarters, he slipped through the official entry, and proceeded up the back stairway to General Howard's office, he picked the lock and entered, he expected to see General Howard sat at his desk but no sign of him, it was an hour later that he heard Howard's voice say, "Coffee Miss Chadwick", Andrews entered his room, "What the hell", Jeff put his fingers to his mouth.

Howard moved towards his desk, that when he noticed the documents, passports, time tables and so on the list was endless, General Howard noticed two black notebooks and more passports which were from Robert's safe in Singapore, then a knock on the door, Jeff hid behind the door, Howard went over to take the tray off Miss Chadwick, then he said," I do not want to be disturbed at all Miss Chadwick, no phone calls, say I am out", she replied "Yes Sir", Howard closed the door.

Jeff briefed, General Howard on his and Cynthia, safe breaking activities and surveillances on Jonathan Roberts in Singapore he was certain that top secret information had been leaked from Allied Headquarters, and now he had the proof. The rest was from Roberts's safe in Melbourne, which was ordered by Peter Andrews, this information and all the paperwork and documents were passed over to Matt Hunter in Melbourne to deal with, a warrant was issued for Jonathan Roberts arrest, but he managed to evade them. He showed Howard one of the notebooks, it had a list of names, of collaborator's whose allegiance was to Hitler or Japan, the other notebook was a list of assignations some of which had been carried out, with further names written down to be dealt with, quite a few were in senior posts in Government, and a few like Cynthia and Jeff who were undercover agents, General Howard was speechless, he knew most of the names in both books.

Jeff asked Howard, if he could set up a task force, "I intend to hand pick my fellow agents who I believe are loyal to the Crown, said Jeff. General Howard contemplated a while then said, "Keep me informed" Jeff replied, "With all due respect Sir, it is better if you don't know anything", Howard deliberated again, "Look I may know someone who can help you put this task force together, he is one of my most trusted friends, and he's not on any of the lists", Jeff agreed. Jeff rang Cynthia, "The department have assigned me to set up a task force to eke out and destroy these collaborators once and for all, no holds barred, "I am to be in charge of the task force said Jeff, Cynthia asked, "Am I in this task force of yours", Jeff replied, "That's why I am ringing, you are not included".

Jeff waited for a tirade of abuse from her but no such thing, Cynthia had a different agenda now, "So when will I see you" asked Cynthia, "Not sure when it's over I suppose", replied Jeff, "I can't really say any more Cynth, you know how it works", Cynthia was tinged with sadness, "You come back save Jeff Owen, I love you", "Jeff was taken aback he knew she was fond of him, this put a different prospectus on his dangerous mission now, "I will Cynth and when I get back we'll get married and make everything legal," they both laughed.

A week later the task force was up and running, Howard was true to his word, his chap was invaluable to Jeff, he cherry-picked people with different skills, he had obviously done this sort of thing before, names were never mentioned, only numbers, Jeff was number one, Pete if that was his real name was number two and so on, there were ten in all. Jeff had no time to think of Cynthia, he was too caught up with the assignment, at last it was something he could do which was constructive.

Cynthia on the other hand missed Jeff, and was wishing he was with her safe at Mary's and Charles in Melbourne, Mary had indeed given birth to twins, apparently one baby was behind the other, that's why the doctors thought she having just one baby, when the first baby came which was a boy he had an imprint of a foot on his face, which was the other baby pushing him out, of course the second baby was a girl. The babies were now in incubators, as they only weighed a couple of pounds each, Mary herself was still at the clinic, it had taken its toll on her, Cynthia visited her every day for an hour in the mornings so Charles could visit in the afternoon or late evening.

Christmas and New Year went, as quick as it came both Charles and Cynthia never really noticed it pass by, after a further week Mary was allowed home, the twins still had to stay at the clinic as their birth was premature, which Mary and Charles were upset about, Cynthia helped them get through it with her tales of travels. One night at dinner Mary told Cynthia they had decided to have the twins baptised at St Patrick's Cathedral, Cynthia was shocked, "Can you do that? Are you not excommunicated or something? "asked Cynthia, Mary blushed, "I don't think so", Charles butted in, "My best friend Andrew is Catholic, we both went to a Private Catholic School and that is what I want for my children" Cynthia didn't pursue the conversation any further, she changed the subject very quickly.

I wonder how Maggie's getting on with this pregnancy it will be her fourth won't it." Mary chipped "It is her fifth if you count the miscarriage, "Of course I had forgotten about that" Cynthia replied.

After six weeks the twins were allowed home, Mary and Charles were absolutely delighted, so was Cynthia, it was now nearing the end of February, Cynthia decided It was time for her to leave Mary and Charles, and go over to Perth, to see Maggie, Mary was disappointed, "I was hoping you could stay a while longer, we have so much catching up to do, we were also hoping that you could come to the Christening, we have already asked if Joe, Maggie and Kathy if they can make it," said Mary. "When do you expect this Christening to happen" asked Cynthia

"Where're not sure yet", a couple of months or so, we have to wait while the twins are that much stronger" said Charles. Well obviously I can't promise, but if I can, I will come, and you have two beautiful children Charles, (the footprint was no longer there on the boy's face) Charles embraced Cynthia, "We think so too".

A couple of days later Cynthia was ready to travel over to Perth, Mary had instructed her to give a letter to each of them, outlining the proposed Christening, Mary also gave Cynthia the deeds for Kathy, "I want you to give her the deeds with our love" said Mary, "I can't do that, you should be there! Cynthia said, in a commanding tone, I need to talk finances with you about the purchase of the tea rooms", "We'll discuss it later when I'm fitter", (Mary had no intention of taking any money off Cynthia, it was now her turn to do Cynthia the favour). Charles came in.

Will you give Joe this for me Cynthia" Charles asked, "God I feel like the "Pony" Cynthia yelled, Charles and May just smiled. With goodbyes out of the way, Cynthia left for the airport, travel was much easier now, she recalled how her and Jeff had driven from Sydney to Melbourne, and a wry smile came over her face, she was missing Jeff more that she thought, she crossed her fingers, and looked up at the sky, keep him safe, she said to herself, soon she was up in the clouds on her way to Augusta, it was closer than Perth City, and more convenient for Joe to pick her up. Cynthia opened her book and started to read, a stewardess interrupted her, "Drink Madame", "Whiskey and Dry" Cynthia replied.

Cynthia looked out of the window, she could see the Nulabor Plain and later the Kalgoolie desert which many have tried to cross with dire consequences, it so remote thought Cynthia there's nothing for miles and miles, it took ages to travel over it, another glance out of the window she saw Esperance, it was a beautiful place it was just the opposite to the Kalgoolie, the sea was a turquoise colour, the beaches were white, she knew it wouldn't be long now before she arrived, as they flew further in, greenery was everywhere, in a way it reminded her of England, I wonder if that is why Maggie and Kathy like it here so much, she said to herself. The plane touched down it was a bumpy landing, after formalities, Cynthia emerged sure enough Joe was there as well as Maggie, You-ho! Maggie waving in excitement, Cynthia thought this woman never changes, Cynthia went over to them, Maggie made a dart towards her, Cynthia was having none of it, she turned her back towards the plane, then turned back again, Maggie was in her face, 'Oh' Lord! Cynthia said to herself.

Joe said, "Come on let's get out of the heat," they made their way to the make shift car park, Cynthia looked for the lorry, this time it was a Land Rover, Cynthia said, "My we have come up in the world", Maggie said, "Wait till you see mine", "What another Land Rover" asked Cynthia, "No silly" said Maggie, "A car! Maggie said jumping up and down, "You drive now Maggie?", "I've been driving for ages, but this is my first brand new car" Maggie was so indignant with Cynthia. It was a good hour's drive before they arrived at the farm, everyone came out to greet Cynthia, they were so pleased to see her, Cynthia was taken aback she wasn't used to so much fuss, then Kathy appeared," Cynthia it's so lovely to see you", and kissed her gently on the cheek, that's more like it, thought Cynthia, they all entered the house by this time it was late evening. Maggie had put on buffet for everyone, that's very thoughtful of you Maggie, said Cynthia, of course the wine was flowing, it was as though Cynthia had never been away, after an hour or so Cynthia was feeling jaded, Maggie took her to her room, "See you in the morning Maggie, thank Joe for me" I'm jiggered", said Cynthia. Maggie left her to return to the lounge.

The next morning Cynthia was woken by noise she looked her watch it was 6.00am, Cynthia groaned, gosh so early with all the activity going on she couldn't get back to sleep, she put her dressing gown on, and ventured into the lounge, she was greeted with "Hello Cynthia did you sleep well," Cynthia just nodded, Kathy came to her, "Coffee Cynthia," in a much calmer voice, Cynthia smiled, after while Cynthia began to focus it was a hive of activity, the twins were running around for dear life, and the little one was walking and shouting, Cynthia just wasn't used to this, especially in the mornings. "Where's Joe? asked Cynthia, "He's in the vineyard, this is a crucial time for us Cynthia, It's harvest time all hands on deck I'm afraid", said Maggie "I see", Cynthia said, and Kathy? 'Oh' she will be going to the tea rooms in another hour", replied Maggie, "Is she happy Maggie?" Cynthia asked, Maggie replied, "What you and Mary have done for her is absolutely wonderful, I'm sure she is happy," was Maggie reply.

CHAPTER TWENTY-FOUR

Cynthia then said "When will Kathy be free I have to speak to her at some point today"? Maggie answered, "Well I'm not sure Kathy took time out yesterday to meet up with you," "Is it possible for me to go with her Kathy too the tea rooms Asked Cynthia, Maggie was quiet," Then said, "Kathy will soon be leaving for the tea rooms, if you would like you can take her there instead of me, it will be of great help to me". Cynthia then said, "You know Maggie Mary and I really do appreciate what you and Joe and your family have done for Kathy, we can never thank you enough, at times it must have been difficult. Maggie went over and pecked her on her cheek, "You know Cynthia we made a pact that we would look after one another, don't you remember the Four Musketeers, (Cynthia had forgotten about the pact), "Yes I do remember Maggie," replied Cynthia, "I'll go and get myself organised and take Kathy to Yellingup isn't?", "That's right Cynthia how did you remember that?" Asked Maggie, Cynthia replied "I don't know", by the time Cynthia returned, Kathy was waiting for her, "I hope you know the way Kathy" Kathy said she did and they set off to Yellingup.

After half an hour they arrive at the tea rooms, Cynthia wasn't all that impressed it needed a good lick of paint they entered it smelled musky, the layout looked fine, the tables were set out in checked gingham, some blue some red, a bit provincial for Cynthia's liking. However, Cynthia decided to be gracious and not criticise, as she could see Kathy was overjoyed about the place, "Oh' Cynthia I have so many plans for this place, I am thinking of getting a loan from the bank and completely modernising it into the Twentieth century, the kitchen definitely needs attention, I'll put up with it for this summer, but next year I'm hoping to have it completely revamped," Kathy said. Cynthia said, "I hope I'm not delaying you this morning", "Of course not I'm so pleased you have come to see it, "Tell Mary all about it won't you and Mary's twins are they beautiful? Cynthia just gestured to Kathy, (Cynthia didn't want to make too much of a fuss about it knowing Kathy can't have children). It took some time for Cynthia to get Kathy's attention, the tea rooms were now open for business and Cynthia could see the potential it was very busy with customers, Kathy had arranged for a local bakery to provide the scones, the local farmer provided her with the milk and butter, and Kathy had a lady who made homemade strawberry and raspberry jam, another farmer provided her with homemade honey.

When the tea rooms had quietened down Cynthia said, "Can we talk now Kathy", "Sure", Kathy tossed her a tea towel, Cynthia just looked at it, Kathy said, "You wipe the tea the dishes with it", Cynthia, (her thoughts weren't worth repeating). "What do you want to discuss" asked Kathy, 'Oh' it can wait till tonight I suppose, I presume we are going back to Maggie's and Joe's tonight".

Kathy said "Yes of course", Kathy was a person with very few words that's why Cynthia liked Kathy, so much. By the time Kathy and Cynthia arrived back at the farm it was 8.30pm Cynthia was exhausted, Kathy was just the opposite, they entered the farmhouse, Maggie greeted them, "Well!" asked Maggie, "I never got the chance I ended up working on the tables," Maggie laughed at the thought, "And if you tell Mary I'll kill you Maggie Hughes", Maggie then said "Cross my heart", with a smirk on her face, Cynthia just withered her, "Well there are some eats for you and Kathy in the lounge" Cynthia kissed her, and said, "You're an Angel".

A while later Cynthia arrived changed and refreshed, Kathy was already there, "Kathy was telling me and Joe what a great help you were today, being as her young helper couldn't be there", Cynthia was not amused, Joe poured her a glass of wine "Try this Cynthia, this is our new wine, we have called it' Maggie Mae', Cynthia took a sip,

"Wow this is wonderful so smooth, I must take some back with me," after Kathy and Cynthia had eaten, Cynthia said, "On a more serious note, I do have couple of things for Kathy", Kathy looked bewildered, "No need to look worried Kathy" said Maggie, "I also have a letter for you Joe from Charles. Joe opened his letter he read it looked at Maggie, he was shock, "What is it Joe" asked Maggie, "It's funding for the marketing of the new wine, Charles wants me to send him some boxes for the store for when they have fashion shows, Charles and Mary have also sent the company a significant cheque which should cover any expenditure", Maggie went over to Joe and kissed him, "I told you Mary and Charles would come through".

Cynthia stood up" Mary and I have something for Kathy", "For me" Kathy said, "Yes" said Cynthia, she gave Kathy a brown envelope Kathy opened it, she looked at it, she just stared at it, then said "I don't understand", Maggie chirped in, "Cynthia and Mary have bought you the tea rooms for you Kathy, you now own the tea rooms, no more rent to pay, except expenses which Joe and I will help you with," Kathy eyes filled up tears began to fall, she ran over to Cynthia. "Thank you", "thank you," that's all Kathy could say, Cynthia was quite embarrassed she then changed the subject, "When is the baby due Maggie? March 6th, "I must say you do look well, it suits you being pregnant", Maggie said "Now tell me how Mary is after her birth of her twins," "It has taken it out of her Maggie, she looks frail, but I am sure Charles will look after her, Cynthia then handed Maggie and Kathy another letter from Mary.

They both opened up their envelopes, it was an invitation to the Christening with a covering letter, Mary and Charles wanted Kathy and Maggie to be Godmothers, and Joe to be a Godfather along with Andrew, Charles best friend, they were so pleased, Joe said "I'll have a word with Charles, it is better in the winter time for us". Cynthia was happy for them, she was also pleased that Mary had included Maggie, Joe, and Kathy, after all she knew deep down that Mary couldn't really rely on her or Jeff to be available. When Cynthia eventually arrived at her bedroom she opened her letter from Mary and Charles, it was a notelet, telling Cynthia, that her and Charles had decided call their son Charles Andrew, and their daughter would be called Grace Cynthia, Cynthia was chuffed to bits.

Two weeks had gone by, it was now time for Cynthia to leave the vineyard, and to return to Melbourne, then onto Sydney, everyone was lifted with Cynthia's visit, Kathy was a different person, and had finally come out of her shell. Maggie and Joe had noticed a big difference in her, Maggie said to Cynthia, "She has big plans for the tea rooms "Can you cope without her" asked Cynthia, "Well I can manage, and she will be around when the baby is born in March, the children are getting older now young Mollie and Jack, will be able to help with Catherine, then I have Mrs O'Day my daily", Maggie replied. Cynthia had just one day before her farewells, she had enjoyed her stay with Joe and Maggie, even though she really wasn't used to domesticity, she often thought she wasn't the marrying type, Mary has it right marry someone super rich, and just look glam. That night every man and his dog came over to wish Cynthia farewell Cynthia found it daunting, she just wanted to get away, one glimmer of hope came to her rescue, Kathy, she took Cynthia by the arm and led her away from it all, she handed Cynthia an envelope, Cynthia looked inside, it was full of notes.

"What's this" asked Cynthia, "It is the rent I have been paying to Maggie and Joe, "Well we don't want it Kathy, Mary would be mortified if I took this money off you, use it for the alterations on the tea rooms", Kathy glowed, "Are you sure", Cynthia said "Definitely, Mary and I both want you to be happy". Kathy gently kissed Cynthia on the cheeks, "Don't leave it too long to see us again" "I hope I will see you at the Christening with Maggie and Joe" Cynthia said, "Of course I will be there I hadn't forgotten about it," Kathy said, they both returned to the house were the party was in full swing, Cynthia decided to retire early for her journey the next day. Cynthia arrived back in Sydney her first thoughts were of Jeff she finally reached home, no sign of Jeff, no note no nothing, she noticed her mail glanced through it this looks interesting, it had a government postmark, Cynthia read the letter, "Wow" it was to tell her she had been promoted and would be head of the linguistic department, she was to report to a Captain James Leigh 10th June she was to ring Captain James Leigh as soon as possible. For once Cynthia was happy no more running around no dingy rooms, she would actually be based at home which suited her, the prospect of being the head of the department enthralled her.

Mary and Charles were well into parenthood, Charles's mother and father came weekly to see how the twins were getting along, they were getting stronger and stronger, Mary was glad of the nanny, the twins were very demanding, she asked Maggie if this was normal, Maggie laughed, you'll get used to it, listen Mary you make the most of it they soon grow up," "Well you're no help" said Mary, Maggie just laughed," Mary Kathy wants a word with you", "Hi Mary just wanted to say thank you for what you have done I really appreciate it, I have big plans to make it the best tea rooms for miles around", Mary replied "No worries Kathy I'm just happy for you are happy, I have to go now Kathy the twins are crying, take care of yourself, see at the Christening".

Jeff was now up and running with his task force, the plans were made for each of the named collaborator's, each undercover agent having their own orders unknown to each other, with a time and date to liaise only with Jeff upon completion, so he could give them a solid alibi if needed. Jeff was feeling much happier now, and thought of Cynthia, he knew she was safe and would enjoy her new job, for unknown to her Jeff had fixed it up for her, he so much wanted to see her, but needed to see the task in hand come to fruition, then he could concentrate on the other notebook which had their names in it as well as others.

Cynthia met up with Captain Leigh it was a cordial meeting she liked him he was quite handsome definitely had an Aussie accent, he outlined the procedures of the work involved, then took her to her department, there was about a dozen people there, two at a desk, some with headphones on listening to conversations, they didn't disturb anyone as they were all very busy, Captain Leigh explained that quite a lot was going on with the Allies, in England, France, and of course the Americans, General MacArthur's office in particular, every so often she would be expected to report on any activity going on and if needed it bring it to the attention of the Big Wigs. Cynthia left the department, she was in a buoyant mood, and never really noticed anyone observing her, her mind was on the job and how she would handle it, she was being stalked her guard was down, she caught a taxi back to the house, it was only then that she was made aware of anything, it was the taxi driver, "Have you upset your boyfriend or something" he asked, Cynthia looked at him puzzled.

There's a black saloon following us I'm sure of it" he said, "Then lose him" was Cynthia reply, "Yes Mam, where too", Anywhere" was Cynthia's answer, the driver took her out of the city, Cynthia pretended she was sightseeing, "Are you able to see the number plate"," I might be able to", he got out of the taxi lit a cigarette, and leaning on his taxi, trying to catch the number plate. They drove around for some time, "Take me back to the city now please" said Cynthia, the driver nodded and made their way back, "I Manged to get the number" the driver said, "Good man" Cynthia said, he gave her the registration number.

As time went on Cynthia was completely absorbed with her work she liked being in charge, it turned out the car that was following her for a couple of month's was, Jeff's idea he just wanted to make sure she was safe and up to now she was, Cynthia called them her bodyguards they are always in the background, but their assignment was about to too end, they had to report back to headquarters for another surveillance. Time was going quickly, Christmas, Cynthia thought, I must give Mary and Maggie a ring, tell them I can't make it this year due to work commitments, this was Cynthia's only drawback about the job, she had to be available at all the times, she thought of Jeff, he popped home now and then and left her notes, no indication what he was up to, at times she was lonely.

Kathy had been working on the tea rooms over the winter month's weather permitting, she had befriended, a group of ladies from Pinjarra, a church group in fact that visit each year, on a day out, sometimes they visit with their husbands, some of the ladies came from the Mandurah area, so her clientele was beginning to increase, a sheep farmer who lives in Yellingup, helped Kathy with the alterations, Joe recommended him, he was well known for his handiwork. Kathy was pleased the way the tea rooms were looking, she wanted to open in November which wasn't that far off, Maggie popped down now and again with Mrs O'Day to give her a lift with the painting, Maggie loved it, she was so proud of Kathy, she took photographs of the place and sent them onto Mary, with up to date photos of the family, especially the children. Maggie also mentioned to Mary that Kathy had found someone called Pete, that he was a carpenter by trade, but helped out on a sheep farm for some reason, Maggie didn't know why.

The Christening had been and gone, Cynthia and Jeff couldn't make it, Mary was so disappointed, but realised they were caught up with important work, everyone else came, the motley crew from Perth came over, Charles Mum & Dad, Andrew, the Best man, the celebrations went on all night, Charles had booked rooms at the Menzies Hotel for everyone, Mary wasn't too pleased, why had he not consulted her, if Mary had any gripes at all, it was that, Charles would just do things without asking her, it was a family trait. The Menzies's Hotel, brought back memories of JR, she still had trepidations about him, however, everything did go well for them and their guest, except for one thing having to have their picture taken for the social pages, Charles was furious with his mother, his mother retorted, "You seem to forget Son that we have a social standing here.

Mary had every right to be apprehensive about the photographs of the Winfield family, along with her and Charles and the twins, there was also a picture of their wedding photo too, not only did his mother send them to the Melbourne Herald but also the Sydney Morning Herald as the family had many ties in Sydney, "That bloody woman why does she have to meddle in things", Mary couldn't wait for Charles to arrive home.

Mary's misgivings proved to be right, for JR had indeed seen the photos, an inmate had cuttings from the Sydney newspaper, he recognised Mary from the picture JR carried around with him, JR went absolutely ballistic, "No! No! She's mine. She's mine! She can't be married, she's mine", He just kept repeating it over and over again, eventually the medics had to give him a sedative to calm him down, from then on it preyed on his mind, he just kept holding the picture and saying she's mine Melbourne he kept saying to himself.

Meanwhile Jeff's task force had eliminated two or three of the suspected spies, either by early retirement or an unfortunate accident one offered to be a double agent, Jeff asked every one of them did they recognise this woman, it was a picture of Edwina Aston they all said no, which was not surprising. The next three were to be imprisoned for the duration of the war and then tried for treason, he was waiting for the necessary paperwork to arrive, with no appeal whatsoever, which left just three more, then that assignment would be complete, there was still no sign of Edwina, Jeff assumed she was lying low, every man and his dog had a picture of Edwina, it would only be a matter of time before they would catch her.

When Cynthia arrived home, there was a note from Jeff, meet me in the Officers Club tonight 8.30pm Cynthia was overjoyed, she quickly organised herself, got a taxi to the Club, in Kings Cross, when she arrived she was early, she decided to go in, an attendant at the door asked, "Do you have your pass Miss," Cynthia looked up, she rummaged in her wallet, "Will this do", "That's fine, then he said Major Owen has arrived second door on the right" Cynthia just smiled, it's all very formal Cynthia said to herself. Cynthia opened the door sure enough there he was at the bar, his face beaming when he saw her, "Gosh have I missed you" then kissed her, Cynthia responded, "So have I it's very lonely in that house, they sat and chatted the night away. Cynthia's phone rang, it was Captain Leigh, "Can you come to my office Cynthia please" he was always polite, which was unusual for an Aussie, "Yes Sir" was her reply, she trotted off to his Office, Jane was there, she said, "Go right in he's expecting you" "Ah there you are" he gave Cynthia a couple of bulky files "Can you translate this lot for me Cynthia, it is very urgent get one of the other girls to help if necessary", Cynthia looked at the file, crickey, she thought, "Yes Sir right away". It was a couple of weeks off Christmas Cynthia was hoping for some time off and spend time with Charles and twins.

Cynthia arrived home earlier than usual she had ordered her meal from her favourite Italian, they were happy to deliver it for her, she picked up her mail, Good one from Maggie one from Mary, the rest she put on the dresser she quickly changed put the radio on, and waited for her order to arrive, then a knock on the door. Cynthia went to open the door suddenly there was a loud noise, Cynthia slumped to the floor, her head was in a whirl, her senses were going dimmer, she felt something wet, she lifted her hand up, it was blood, slowly she realised she had been shot, she tried to get up she couldn't, luckily for her the delivery boy had just arrived from the restaurant, he was shocked to see her lying there blood oozing out of her, he didn't know what to do, fortunately a couple were passing by he shouted them to get some help. The ambulance arrived, by this time Cynthia was unconscious, they gave her oxygen, still no response, they wasted no time in getting her to the hospital, she was rushed into theatre, X rays were taken, the surgeon operated on her.

Time was of the essence, the police were waiting to question her, the doctor immerged, "You'll have to leave it a few days' lads", she is in a critical condition, the police bade the doctor farewell, then one of the policemen said, "Did you manage to retrieve any bullets? the doctor replied, "Yes two in fact", The doctor asked a nurse, to give the bullets to the policeman. The police made their way back to the house, to investigate further, "Poor bugger, she didn't have a chance", they examined everything, as you would expect, a Detective arrived, but not from their division, he was Special Branch, he had a long chat with them, they showed him the bullets. Jenkins took the bullets off the policemen so they went on their way, it suited the policemen, as they thought they might have to be there all night guarding the place, the special branch detective took over, he perused everything they knew Cynthia's identity from her personal papers, he then made a call, "Jenkins here Sir, it's one of ours I'm afraid" shot at point blank range, she had no chance, better inform Major Owen".

Jeff was on reconnaissance that night with a fellow agent, their target was a retired Bank Manager, he had strong ties with Germany and held very strong views about the Americans in particular, no one knew where Jeff was the General had been informed of what had happened by Jenkins, "You had better let Captain Leigh know" Jenkins nodded and bid the General goodnight. The following day Jenkins went back to Jeff's house, the carpenter was already there fixing the door to make it secure, Jenkins entered the house, "Anything he asked his colleagues," "We have found another bullet lodged in the stairway," one of the men answered, Jenkins proceeded to the stairway, took out his penknife, and gently prised the bullet out, he then said to his colleagues, "I think this came from a Smith and Wesson revolver no doubt it was a hit man who carried this out, I think I know just the man who can help, see you later", "Yes Sir they both replied.

General Howard still couldn't get in touch with Major Owen, he rang Captain Leigh, and asked him a question, "What work was Cynthia Boardman working on", Captain Leigh replied," Nothing as yet, she was about to start on two hefty files, first thing Monday morning", "Pertaining to what?" asked General Howard, Leigh replied, "Transcripts, telex messages, recorded conversations, all in German" Howard asked, "Does she ever take work home", "Never" replied Leigh", "Good" said General Howard, "Excuse me Sir do we know how Cynthia is doing", Howard replied, "She is holding her own at the moment I believe" then the phone went dead.

Mary was getting very anxious not hearing from Cynthia, Maggie too, Cynthia had not replied to any of their letters, and this bothered both of them, Mary felt like asking Charles if she could travel over to Sydney to see if everything was alright, but didn't like leaving the twins, Maggie too was tied up with her brood, then Mary decided to look up the old Chinese woman to see if she could help her again, heaven only knows why Mary thought she would be able to help.

Mary came back from China town very disappointed, the old Chinese women still said danger was lurking around her, but no mention of Cynthia, the twins interrupted her, Mummy, mummy they said together, Sara arrived, "There's a man waiting to see you in the study", "Thank you Sara", Mary went to the study and said, "Yes can I help you" I'm Inspector Jenkins Special Branch". Mary froze "Its Cynthia isn't", "I'm afraid so, she is in Royal North Shore Hospital in Sydney, she has been shot and is in a critical condition", "Oh' my God," Mary yelled she was beside herself, "Why are you telling me this, where is Jeff Owen? Jenkins replied "We can't locate Major Owen at the moment, he went on to say he had been through her private papers and found, two envelopes one addressed to her and one for a Maggie Yardy". Jenkins then handed her the envelope, Mary looked at him, "Does this mean she is going to die" tears streaming from her face, he answered it looks that way, "Would I be able to go and see her" Mary asked, "I don't see why not,

"I could make arrangements for you and Maggie Yardy if you would like me too" Mary just nodded. Can I leave this envelope with you then, I can't seem to find Maggie Yardy in the Sydney or Melbourne directory", said Jenkins, Mary then said, "But how did you find my address? "That's easy I saw your picture in the Sydney Herald" Jenkins replied, Mary went cold two shocks in one day was just too much to take in. "You will have to excuse me now, I have things to do, I'll see Mrs Yardy gets this," said Mary, with that Jenkins bade her good day.

Mary went to the children's bedroom to see if they were alright, Sara was reading to them, when they saw Mary, they jumped up and put their arms out to Mary, "Are you alright now" they both nodded, Mary decided to take them with her to the Store, "I'm going out Sara, I'll take the twins with me, tell cook to make a cold buffet for tonight", "What time will you get back? It's my half day", "Of course it is, sorry Sara you can go, see you Thursday", Mary said.

Finally, Mary got the car out, "Jump in you two", there were fighting to be the first in, "Hurry up Mummy has things to do", Grace started to cry, "What's the matter now? "He hit me", "No I didn't" said Charles's Jr, "Oh' for heaven's sake be quiet you two, Mummy has things on her mind, they both went quiet, soon they arrived at the store, Mary parked the car up, and entered the store, everyone was pleased to see Mary and the twins, Mildred came over to her, nice to see you again Mary, it was Mary's old supervisor, Mary greet her warmly.

CHAPTER TWENTY-FIVE

Mary was dying to go up to Charles office, but she didn't want to appear rude, suddenly Charles's came into view, "Well this is an honour, how's my little ones, do you want to go to the children's department, "Yes please Daddy they both said", Charles looked at Mary he could see she was upset, "What's the matter", "Not here Charles in your office" "Mrs Taylor would you take the twins to the toy department, till we get back", Mrs Taylor nodded, come on you two the twins skipped away. Mary burst into tears, Charles was shocked, "What's happened surely it can't be that bad," said Charles, "But it is", Mary then told him what had gone on with Inspector Jenkins of the Special Branch in Sydney, that Cynthia had been shot and was in a critical condition, he gave her two envelopes one for her and one for Maggie, "I think she is going to die" she blurted out.

Charles went to his Secretary, "Can you make us tea Jenny, Mrs Winfield is not feeling too well", then Charles asked "Were does Jeff fit into all this," Mary answered he doesn't know yet, they can't get hold of him, Jenny the secretary came in with the tea, "Thank you" said Mr Charles, he poured Mary and himself a cup of tea, "Here drink this" Mary took hold of the cup, "Now where's this envelope have you opened it" "No" said Mary, "Why not" asked Charles, "It says the last will and testament of Cynthia Boardman, Charles took it off her. "Cynthia is not dead yet Mary, I'll put this in the safe until she is", you may never have to open it", "I hope you're right Charles, I will have to let Maggie know," said Mary, "I'll do that for you, I'll give Joe a ring, Maggie will think it's about the wine, no need to upset Maggie if we don't need too is there, said Charles," Mary just nodded, Mary didn't mention Jenkins seeing their picture in the Sydney Herald, they both had a lot to deal with for the time being.

Charles then said "Feeling better now, we'll go and pick the twins up, when they arrived at the toy department, it suddenly struck Mary that Christmas was only a week away, it had gone completely out of her mind, the twins ran up to Charles, "Can I have this Daddy, can I have this Daddy" they said at the same time, Charles turned to Mary, "I'll be glad when they start talking separately and not together, Mary smiled, apparently that's what twins do she replied. As soon as Mary left, Charles rang Joe, to tell him of the situation, and to break the news too Maggie best way he could, that also there was a copy of Cynthia will which was addressed to Maggie as well one for Mary, no mention of Kathy I'm afraid, perhaps Maggie might fill you in on that.

"Mary 's too upset at the moment, I think she may be planning on going over to Sydney, it would be nice if Maggie could go and see Cynthia also, let me know what you decide,", Joe then said "It's a difficult time for us with Christmas, everyman and his dog wants orders for Christmas and especially the New Year, but I'll see what I can do", "I'll fly over if that makes it easier for you Joe" said Charles, Joe went quiet, "I'll let you know as soon as possible". When Charles arrived home, Mary was in the kitchen, "Where's cook", Mary then said "I forgot all about Christmas Charles, I let them go early cook left us a nice buffet, and it Sara's half day, my mind was completely in a spin, the twins are still up, there're in the lounge.

Charles went to see the children, Mary got out two glasses of wine, and set the table, Mary actually enjoyed doing things around the house, but Charles was adamant about Sara doing the cleaning and cook doing the cooking, unknown to Charles, Mary did do some cleaning, especially if they had entertained the night before. The phone went, Charles answered, Jeff here Charles, "Is Mary there", Charles passed the phone over to Mary, Charles indicated to Mary that it was Jeff, "Hi Jeff", it took a while for Jeff to speak, "You know about Cynth, I'm told, "Yes" Mary replied, an Inspector Jenkins came to the house, and told me, it was a terrible shock Jeff", "A shock for me too" Jeff replied. I feel responsible for the whole bloody mess" he blurted out, Mary tried to pacify him it was no use, he needed someone to talk too, Mary then said, "Look Jeff as soon as Christmas and New Year are over, I'll come over to Sydney and stay for a couple of weeks, I need to clear it with Charles and make arrangements for the twins, it's the best I can do right now", Jeff said "That'll be great she might have regained consciousness by that time, Mary was shocked to hear this, "Why is she in a coma", Yes I'm afraid she is" replied Jeff.

Mary felt great relief on hearing this, "Cynthia's a fighter Jeff, she stronger than you think", "I hope you're right, I have to go now, things to do, said Jeff then the phone went dead, Mary thought it was funny how people never said goodbye to anyone after they had phoned them. Jeff indeed had plenty of thinking to do, he did blame himself, for had he not gone after the spies and dealt with them the way he did, perhaps Cynthia would not never have been shot, he had procured the files that Cynthia was about to investigate. Captain Leigh had graciously seconded an interpreter for him to work with, to see if they could obtain any useful information, Cynthia had already made some notes she had entered in her journal, but it was spasmodic so Jeff had somehow to put it in some resemblance of order, this is going to take some time, he said to himself, he had been given compassionate leave so time wasn't an issue.

Cynthia was still holding her own, no significant improvement as yet, but she was still breathing albeit by a machine, Jeff spent as much time with her as he could, the doctors asked him to talk to her, as a familiar voice can jog the memory, Jeff talked about the sticky situations they would get themselves into, the odd holiday they spent together, especially Bali, Cynthia just loved Bali, "When you are better, we will go to Bali for as long as you want, and forget about this bloody war" Jeff was both upset and angry, he looked at her lovingly, but it was time to leave.

Jeff didn't even notice Christmas approaching, he was too focused on the files, Julie the girl who was working with Jeff, said "Excuse me Sir it is Christmas eve, everyone left except us" Jeff looked at his watch, it was 6.30pm," Oh I'm so sorry Julie, yes you must go" he said, Julie than said, I'm off now for a week, but there will be someone here after Boxing Day, I'm sure they will help if you need it" Jeff just nodded at her he was too absorbed in what he was doing, "Merry Christmas then" then Julie left. Christmas and New Year as usual came and went with a blink of an eye, it was now 1945, and the Pacific war had been raging for four years, with no sign of abating, Cynthia was still in the coma, the doctors were pleased, because there was some sign of her eyelids flickering, which meant to them, her brain box was working, they wouldn't know the full extent till she regained consciousness.

This was great news to Jeff, the doctors asked Jeff to keep talking to her, Jeff told them that her two best friends were arriving in a couple of days, and boy can they talk when they all get together, he explained that he worked for Ministry of Defence and had to report back as soon as possible, the doctors understood perfectly, shook hands with him and wished him the best of luck., Jeff was so relieved that there was a sign of improvement small as it was. It took several months for Cynthia to slowly recover from her traumatic experience, it was a great relief to everyone that Cynthia had managed to somehow pull through, Jeff of course was delighted, so to were Maggie, Joe, Kathy, not and forgetting what Charles and Mary had done for Cynthia, Jeff would be forever grateful to them all.

Jeff was now able to concentrate on the task in hand, his assistant Julie had done a wonderful job in piecing together all the telex messages sent to the cohort, Julie had put everything into priority first, Jeff was amazed, "You've done well Julie" she answered, "Well I have had over six months to wade through it", then laughed, Jeff looked at her, and had a thought, "Look what are you doing tonight, you deserve a night out, fancy a meal and drinks" he asked her. Julie didn't hesitate for one moment, "Don't mind if I do, what about your girlfriend Cynthia" she asked Jeff, "Oh she's not my girlfriend, we are just great mates that's all", As soon as Jeff had said the word's come out of his mouth he was mortified and wished he could take them back, the truth is he just wanted company, a lady's company just for one night, he missed Cynthia tremendously.

The night out went well enough, Jeff really did like Julie, and vice-versa, he decided to forget about Cynthia for a while, and concentrate on his needs and wellbeing, after all Cynthia was improving day by day. So Jeff and Julie became an item, to Jeff it was just a fling nothing more nothing less, to Julie it meant so much more, she was infatuated by him, Jeff still looked in on Cynthia when he had time, they would chat, trivial talk really.

Cynthia still looked drawn and it took her some time to respond to him, to Jeff she had definitely slowed down, the doctors assured him that her medical condition would improve and saw no reason why she should not have a normal life, with specialist medical help and staff, this was great news to Jeff. He explained to the doctors, that he had to return to work, after all there was still a war on, he mentioned Mary and Maggie, would try to get over whenever they could, and gave the doctor details of how to reach them if necessary. Jeff seemed relieved somehow, Julie was waiting for him, "How did it go" she asked him, oh' you know ok I guess, Jeff didn't know if she understood what he was saying", Julie of course misinterpreted what Jeff was saying and assumed he meant that he had dumped Cynthia, Julie desired Jeff all to herself, she didn't want to share him with another woman, not even Cynthia, and she had plans for Major Jeff Owen.

As all things do after a crisis, live goes on Jeff and Julie settled down to the task in hand perusing the messages, it was much easier now, with the hard work Julie had put into it Jeff was impressed with her work ethic, it took another two weeks for a picture to emerge, Jeff and Julie were absolutely delighted, all that hard slog had paid off, they now knew all the names of the agents, but more importantly knew their true identities. Jeff was on high, "Come on he said this calls for a celebration" so off they went, first to Allied Headquarters to see General Howard with the information, Howard was most impressed especially in the circumstances, "You've done well Jeff", Jeff replied, "It wasn't me really Sir, Julie has done all the hard graft, as you know I have been at the hospital for the past few months, so I could do little to help Julie.

General Howard then asked, "How is Cynthia now", Jeff replied she is improving every day, that's why I've come back to work, "I'll see this information gets to the right people Jeff" Howard said, Jeff then left to meet up with Julie. They had a great night, the meal was great so was the company, Jeff was walking on air, it had been months of worry, he could now finally relax and start to enjoy life again, it was getting late by this time, Julie then asked Jeff, "Why don't you come back to my place tonight" without hesitation Jeff accepted. Little did Jeff know that his decision to go back to Julie's house, would have an impact on his life?

Over in Perth, Maggie had given birth to their fourth child, she named him, Joseph Albert, after their fathers, she missed her mother and father from time to time, but wrote when she could, Maggie could see the frailness in her parents writing, and worried about them, Joe on the other hand was pleased as punch it was a boy, his thoughts were on preserving the family estate for future generations to come, Maggie said, "No more Joe I'm jiggered" Joe got hold of her and kissed her gently, "I mean it Joe no more!" Joe looked at her, "Bloody hell she means it" he thought to himself, the next day a letter came from Mary.

Hi Maggie,

Just to let you know Cynthia is doing well, the doctors are very pleased with her progress, Charles and I are hoping to get over sometime next week to see her, congratulations on your new edition. Trying for a cricket team are we! Haven't seen or heard from Jeff lately must be on his travels again, great news is coming from England it looks like the war is nearly over according to the Pathe News.

Of course Charles who keeps a watchful eye on world events, he says it can have a damaging effect on the store if it is bad news, never told me how it might affect the store when it was good news, it never seemed any different to me when I worked there good or bad, that's men for you.

Hope Kathy is still enjoying her tea rooms, it would be nice to think if she could meet a nice bloke, it seems that she may just have met one, I do hope so she deserves happiness, I wouldn't like to think of her being a spinster all her life. The terrible twins are still terrible still bickering between themselves, I just shut off and read my book, hope yours are different than these two.

Love
Mary and Charles.

Ps. write soon

As soon as Joseph Albert was fast asleep,

Maggie put pen to paper Mary Charles,

The new edition has truly jiggered me, I've told Joe no more and I mean it, glad to hear Cynthia is doing fine.

Kathy is also ok she has indeed got a new friend called Pete Wilson, he is a carpenter but works as a sheep farmer as I have already mention to you, here in Yellingup, quite near where the tea rooms are, do you not remember he was the handyman Joe found for her when she completely changed everything around at the tea rooms to make it larger, well they have been seen a lot together lately, so I guess she is happy, you know Kathy, never tells you anything, keeps everything close to her chest. Glad to hear the war is nearly over, wish it would end here, you hear so many tales of people you know who's fathers have been killed, maimed, or are a prisoner of war, it's terrible, I don't like talking or thinking about it, The twins are just the same as yours, fighting all the time, one trying to boss the other, and the other having none of it, Give Cynthia our deepest love, and hopefully I will be able to come over in the winter time.

Love Maggie and Joe

When Charles arrived home in was in buoyant mood, looks like the Jerry's are getting fried he said, "What do you mean" asked Mary, he answered, the German army are on the verge of collapse, the men are leaving their posts and going home to their families according to Reuters, "Do you fancy the pictures tonight Mary, let's go out and celebrate" Charles said, Mary replied, "I'll see what's on". Charles came down from upstairs, "What's on" he asked, Mary replied, "This film looks good", 'Mildred Pierce' with Joan Crawford, "Well get ready then" said Charles, Mary took no notice of him she knew the picture didn't start till 8.00pm, instead she went to settle the twins down for the night, and then let her nanny know that they were going out, "Probably be back about eleven Nanny Williams", Mary said.

CHAPTER TWENTY-SIX

Finally, Charles got the news he wanted to hear, the film was interrupted by an announcement that Germany had indeed surrendered to Allied forces, it was the 7th May 1945, which would forever be indelible in everyone's mind. Everyone clapped, whistled, cheered, then the picture restarted, Mary really enjoyed the film, she couldn't stop talking about it, as they arrived at their favourite restaurant. People kept coming up to them, in a joyous mood, one said, "That'll show them not to trifle with the English", Charles was bemused by his remark, for he knew that England would have had no chance had it not been for the Americans and Roosevelt, another chap came up to Charles, "Now let's sort these bloody nips out once and for all", everyone said, We'll drink to that!

When Charles and Mary returned home, they were exhausted, Charles went straight upstairs, Mary went to the children's room, both fast asleep, just look at them both they look like little angels, she thought to herself, then she went to see Nanny Williams. "Everything alright, have you heard the news?" asked Mary, Nanny Williams nodded at her, "This calls for a celebration Nanny", and Mary produced a bottle of sherry, she offered Nanny William's a glass and sat with her for a while, but her thoughts were now on returning to England at the soonest opportunity, she wished Nany Williams goodnight, and retired to bed. The next morning Mary had a terrible headache, she wasn't used to drinking, or eating late at night, Charles had already left for work, she crept downstairs, the twins saw her, Mummy, mummy they yelled, Mary's head was splitting, she shouted

Sara, "Where's Nanny Williams" she asked her, "In the Nursey I think", replied Sara, "Can you take the twins in, I've got a spitting headache, I don't want to be disturbed just yet" Mary said to Sara.

It was lunchtime before Mary emerged, she went to the nursey, the twins were reading for Nanny, Mary entered, Nanny Williams asked if she was feeling better, "Much better now Nanny, I'm just going ask, cook to fix me up with a light lunch, would you like to join me" Nanny Williams was shocked, she had never ever been asked to join her employee for lunch, she just nodded at Mary nanny was speechless. Nanny Williams entered the drawing room, Mary was sat there feeling much better and looking much better, "Ah there you are sit here Mrs Williams", Mary started her lunch, "Dig in Mrs Williams" and try to relax, I'm not going to sack you or anything.

I just wanted to thank you for all your effort with the children, and the enormous pressure I have put you under with the twins, when I have gone over to Sydney, my friend is improving all the time, and of course I will still have to go from time to time, so here's a little something that Mr Charles and I want to give you as a big thank-you, Mary then gave her an envelope.

Mary did the same with Cook and Sara, they were overjoyed, "It's just a big thank-you for steadying the ship while I have been away, in particular this year, Cynthia is improving, but I will still need to go over from time to time, Sara kissed Mary," Thank you very much Mrs Winfield I really appreciate it, Cook did the same, after all they had been with Mary from the beginning and liked working for her, in many ways she wasn't like the other wealthy women they had worked for in the past. The phone went, Sara quickly went to pick it up as not to disturb the twins, it was the hospital in Sydney, Sara handed the phone to Mary, and they both left the room, Mrs Winfield, "Yes" Mary answered, I have someone who wishes to speak to you, Mary feared the worst, a voice said, "Is that you Mary" Cynthia said, in a laboured voice, Mary shrieked, "Is it really you? Cynthia replied, "Yes", "I just wanted to hear your voice again. The doctor carried on saying, that there was absolutely nothing more the hospital could do for her, and that he didn't want her get into a comfort zone with the hospital, she was now ready in his opinion to start doing things for herself and become independent once more the clinic would probably vet your house to see if it was suitable.

Cynthia talked very slowly, then doctor spoke to Mary, he thought it might be a good idea to move her to a private clinic in Melbourne to recuperate, he explained to her, that she would need help in speech therapy, and in building her muscles up again, also physiotherapy, and to start mixing with people she knows to help her, Mary interrupted the doctor, "If she goes anywhere it will be here with me, Mary was most indignant to think the doctors could whisk her off to some clinic Mary did not hesitate for one second, "Will you make the necessary arrangements then over at your end, and liaise with the clinic over here, ask them to get in touch with me, so I know what exactly is involved if Cynthia comes to our house, and not the clinic". The doctor agreed to Mary's request, she then spoke to Cynthia again, but spoke slowly to her, to let her know what was to happen. Cynthia just said thank you, then put the phone down.

When Charles arrived home Mary mentioned what had gone on, "Are you sure you know what you are taking on Mary, it is a huge responsibility, and what about the children, I don't want them to suffer", Charles said, Mary answered, "I won't neglect the children I promise, if it doesn't work out with Cynthia, we can still see to it that she gets the right treatment over here can't we instead of her being in Sydney on her own", by this time Mary was in tears. Charles looked at her and capitulated, "Ok but if the children or the house suffers in any way she goes to the clinic agreed," Mary went over and kissed him, "Thank you Charles I love you so much" Charles grabbed her, "Show me then it's been a while" Mary just said, "Follow me". It wasn't often that Charles showed her affection.

Jeff Owen was beginning to tire of Julie Harris, he was fed up with all the bitching and bickering between them, whenever he mentioned Cynthia, he wanted out, he thought she was vindictive and a very possessive woman, she was stifling him, he just knew he had to get away from her, for his own sanity. Julie sensed that things weren't quite the same as they had been, she was not about to lose him now after all the hard work she had put into their relationship, in her way she did love him, too much really, too much in fact for Jeff's liking, if only Julie could have taken a step back and given Jeff breathing space that he needed, their relationship might have just worked out. To Jeff's delight he received a phone call it was from General Howard, "Jeff I want you to come back to Allied Headquarters tomorrow 8.00am sharp, Jeff replied "Yes Sir", he was delighted Jeff made up his mind there and then he would finish with Julie. The next morning, he arrived at work as the clock struck 8.00am as he proceeded to General Howards office, he knocked on the door, "Come in" said General Howard in a strong Aussie accent. Jeff entered, "Good news Jeff, Cynthia Boardman is to be transferred to a private clinic in Melbourne I'm told for rehabilitation", Jeff was so relieved, he was now feeling guiltier about his affair with Julie Harris.

I won't beat about the bush Jeff, I need you here now, things are about to change in the next few weeks, and it's all hands on deck I'm afraid, I want you back in Singapore immediately be at the docks usual time tonight no later than 11.30pm. Jeff could have kissed him, but of course didn't, "You can manage on your own over there can't you? We have a good team there waiting for you to work with, here are your papers and orders," Howard then shook Jeff hands and said good luck. He ran out of the office he so glad he was back doing the job he loved, also it would get Julie Harris off his back, Jeff however, did ask General Howard about Julie Harris, Howard answered, "No need to worry about Julie Harris, she has been reassigned and is well out of the way", Jeff was puzzled by his remark, but decided to leave it at that, he was just pleased he had a chance to redeem himself.

Jeff's thoughts now turned to Cynthia, he got in touch with Mary, he had a long chat with her, for some reason, he told Mary everything, about Julie Harris, that he had done unmentionable things in time of war, he also thought the bullets were really meant for him and not Cynthia, that he was so guilty about everything, he just couldn't stand to see Cynthia fighting for her life. He felt so guilty he poured his heart and soul out to Mary, eventually he managed to say, he had been re- assigned abroad again for the duration of the war, he sends his love to Cynthia and wishes her a speedy recovery.

Mary sympathised with Jeff, then said she would pass on the message, "Do you think Cynthia will forgive me?" Jeff asked, Mary thought for a moment, then said "What good would it do now Jeff, the damage is done, best leave it at that, if you ask me there is no need to mention anything at all, I'm sure if the boot was on the other foot Cynthia wouldn't blink an eye, take it from me! With that Jeff said goodbye to Mary.

Charles came into the drawing room, that was Jeff on the phone, remarked Mary, "At last" Charles replied, Mary carried on, "He was sorry that he couldn't get over to see Cynthia as much has he would have liked, now it seems he has been reassigned to go abroad and doesn't think he will be back for some time. That he is thinking of Cynthia and sends his love and best wishes for a speedy recovery" Charles made some remark under his breath, "What was that Charles" Mary asked "Oh' nothing in particular", was Charles reply. (Charles didn't realise the importance of Jeff's involvement in the Pacific War). Cynthia was responding to the treatment quicker than the doctors had hoped, the doctors were astounded that she had pulled through one doctor thought it was a miracle, Mary had, had a great influence on Cynthia, in a way the whole family helped.

Charles would give Cynthia daily reports from Reuters News Agency, the twins popped in now and again, Grace in particular loved her Aunt Cynthia, it warmed Cynthia's heart, quite often Grace would creep in and sit on the sofa with her, and tell her all sorts of things, till Mary came into the room, "Come on Grace, your Auntie needs her rest now", Mary would just smile at Cynthia, and take Grace with her.

One night Charles came rushing in, he put the radio on, he insisted everyone went into the drawing room, including the children, everybody was just looking at one another bewildered, "What is it Charles", asked Mary Charles replied "You'll see", he turned the radio up. It was a message from President Harry Truman he had announced the dropping of an Atomic Bomb on Hiroshima and Nagasaki, the world gasped at hearing this news, and that immediately the Japanese Imperial Army have surrendered and all hostilities between the two countries have ceased. So on the 6th of August 1945 war with Japan was over, Charles then said, "What a way to end a war", Mary went to him, "But at least the war is over Charles, and that is all that matters? Charles just looked at her, she is so naive at times, he thought to himself.

Like anything else in life the war soon becomes a memory, unless you have lost someone, by now Cynthia was well on her feet, her speech was more or less back too normal, her wit had returned somewhat, her movement was much better, it had taken its toll on her she looked older, Cynthia and Charles had become great chums, they were both extremely intelligent, and their conversations stimulated both of them. It was September by now, Cynthia shouted for Mary, "In here Mary "shouted back, Cynthia entered the dining room, Mary looked at Cynthia, "What is it" asked Mary, Cynthia hesitated, "I think it is time for me to stand on my own two feet, will you help me to find a suitable house or apartment for me, somewhere with a sea view, Mary answered of course I'll help you", Cynthia replied, "I will always be indebted to you and Charles, you are truly wonderful friends to have.

Both Charles and Mary were glad Cynthia had decided to move out, they had done all they could, and were only too pleased to help her to become independent again. It also meant that Charles and Mary could take a holiday that they so badly needed, Charles had always liked Bali, and with the war over it meant they could travel anywhere they wanted too.

Cynthia soon found a place overlooking a sandy beach, she eventually settled for a lovely cottage at Warrnambool, about a two hours' drive from Geelong, it was in a lovely setting and so peaceful, she turned to Mary, "I like this Mary, I could start painting again", Cynthia said, "I didn't know you could paint", said Mary, "I'm a woman of many talents", replied Cynthia," Mary just smiled at her, then said to herself, yes she's back to own self again and ready to do her own thing. It took another month to make the necessary arrangements, Cynthia still had to have medical check-ups, and stayed with Charles and Mary overnight when she needed too, Mary and the twins would drive down to see her sometimes on a Sunday, or when the twins had school holidays, the twins loved it there, they were getting on much better now, school helped of course, Charles Jr went to a boy's prep school, and Grace to a girl's prep school, which had done wonders for them both.

One Sunday whilst visiting Cynthia, Mary noticed she was in a pensive mood, "What's the matter now", asked Mary, Cynthia looked at Mary her eyes welling up as if to start crying, "I can't stop thinking about Jeff, and the thoughts of him getting killed, I miss him so much Mary it hurts, "Next time you are over at our place we can go to the Library and look for a list of survivor's, at least you would know one way or the other Mary said, Cynthia smiled, I'll do that", then pecked Mary on the cheek, "Now let's have lunch" Cynthia said. With the war ending expectations were now high, girlfriends waiting for boyfriends, wives waiting for husbands, each ship that arrived in Melbourne brought some grief to someone, Mary felt so sorry for the women, she wanted to do more she approached the Royal Voluntary Service to see if she could help.

Mary got a group of her pals to help in any way they could, either by fund raising or voluntary work, to help the more unfortunate people whose lives had been affected through the war years, the work the Royal Voluntary Service they did was incredible to say the least. Charles was so proud of Mary and her little band of women, who went out daily to see if they could help people in need, the Service gave every member a list of people for them to visit, some came to the centre, for lunch, there was always clothes that had been donated as well as other household items, which again had been donated by the public's generosity. Mary hadn't seen much of Charles as of late, she decided to ask cook make a special meal for them both, and spend a quiet night in, with the children being at boarding school, both of them had more time to spend together.

When Charles did arrive home he was in a good mood, sales were up significantly on last year's figures, "See I told you Mary, it matters a lot when it's good or bad news", Mary just shrugged her shoulders, she completely ignored what Charles had said, cook then said, "Dinners ready", they both went into the dining room. Charles had a serious discussion with Mary about, if anything happened to him, he wanted to let her know that her and the children were well taken care of, this upset Mary, she could never face reality in the face, she was a romantic and often dreamed of being swept off her feet, it could never happen of course, but she could have her dreams at least, especially with Charles taking about wills and dying, she was very superstitious and thought it might put the mockers on things.

Charles could see that this was upsetting her, so he changed the subject, "I have a surprise for you and Cynthia and me of course, I have booked a box for next year's 1947 Melbourne Cup, I have invited Joe, Maggie and Kathy if they can get away, and The Winfield Group are one of the main sponsors for next year."

CHAPTER TWENTY-SEVEN

Mary was thrilled to bits she was like a little schoolgirl, with a new toy, she absolutely loved going to the races, and it was one of her favourite pastimes. Summer was just around the corner, people began thinking of holidays, also Christmas would not be that far off either, Charles wanted to go to Bali and take the children, Mary wanted to go to Perth to see Joe and Maggie, "Can't we do both Mary" Charles said, Mary looked at him, "I suppose we could after all the children are getting older now and behaving better", I'll book us an apartment for us at my favourite place in Bali, you'll love it I promise", said Charles.

A week went by when Joe rang Charles, Sara answered, "Is Charles there", Joe asked, and "Who shall I say is speaking? Asked Sara, "Its Joe from Perth tell him", Sara went to Mr Charles, "It's for you a Joe from Perth" she said to him, Charles snatched the phone from her. "Hi Joe, how you're doing hope you can make it, I intend to publicise the wine at the Melbourne Cup, it is a golden opportunity for us there to push the brand," Joe was about to refuse, but how could he now, Charles had mentioned the publicity for the wine, "We'd love to come there will be four of us is that ok", Fine replied Charles. Charles went into his study, and pondered who the fourth would be, but then started to plan his campaign for launching of Yardy's Wines.

With the war in the pacific ending the British Government and Allies started contingency plans to bring all the troops back home, there were also a lot of expatriates that had been held prisoners of war by the Japanese Army in Singapore, Malaysia, Burma as well as British American and Aussie soldiers. There were women and children who were held in terrible conditions in camps, and the inevitable casualties of war, who were receiving medical attention in Australia the Allied Forces were determined to get everyone back to their own Country as quickly as possible, it was a huge undertaking, and it would take many months for everyone to return home, as passports documents etc., couldn't be checked. Jeff meanwhile, was still in Singapore, he was part of an elite team making sure law and order was enforced, he worked alongside the Singapore police, as insurgents were beginning to cause mayhem for independence from the British, He loved Singapore but longed to get back to Australia, and especially Cynthia, he was biding his time for his papers to arrive then he would be able to return to Sydney, then onto Melbourne.

When news reached Joe and Maggie about the war ending, there was huge celebration on the estate all the neighbours came from miles around, it seemed to last for days, Maggie just wanted peace and quiet, just look at the big oaf she said to herself meaning Joe, she hadn't realised that most of them were growers or farmers who would have loved to go and fight if they could have, but the nation needed to be fed and so did the soldiers. A week later things began to get back to normality, the twins by this time were helping out, and doing little chores for Joe also Maggie was waiting anxiously from news from Mary.

Kathy, however, had been dating Pete Wilson for quite some time now, he was much older than her, Kathy liked him, he was kind and considerate, he helped Kathy as much as he could in the tea rooms, their friendship blossomed from then on, they were able to see more of each other in the wintertime, that's when Pete asked Kathy to go to Perth with him, to meet his family they lived in place called Toodyay a farming community, the journey was long and arduous too Kathy she was wishing she hadn't agreed to go with him. Kathy was warmly greeted by Pete's family everyone was there Aunts, Uncles, and cousins and so on, the family were hoping that this time it would work out for Pete, their farm was small in comparison with the Yardy Estate, it meant nothing to Kathy, she felt so at home with them all, and just knew that this was what they call a family, with love and affection and laughter all round,

After a day's rest Pete took her to the main Street, with its quaint post office, a Hotel come pub, where farmers probably did their business, a store that seemed to stock everything, to Kathy it was so quaint, people would ride into town as they would call in or drive a tractor, or if lucky even a car it fascinated Kathy. Everyone knew Pete and shook hands with him, "Glad to see you back Pete, hope you're staying this time, your Pa and Ma aren't getting any younger you know" said one farmer, come and have a drink, Pete hesitated, then said "I would like you to meet Kathy", by this time there were a group of men, some whistled, Kathy blushed, Pete said, "Another time perhaps we must be getting back", Pete bid them farewell.

Ignore them Kathy, they mean no harm, I grew up with most of them," said Pete, Kathy said, "Is it true your Dad wants you back at the farm? Pete answered, "I guess so, I suppose I haven't thought about it, I was hoping my two brothers would take over the farm eventually, I like living in Augusta, do you think that is selfish of me Kathy? Kathy thought about it, "If it was me I would want to be with the people that love me, and boy do they love you". Pete just looked at her, he gave her a kiss that seem to last for ages, so long in fact Kathy was fighting for her breath, she broke away. Pete looked shocked "What's the matter he asked? Kathy replied, "Nothing I just couldn't get my breath", "Oh is that all" said Pete laughing.

When they reached the farm, dinner was ready, "Kathy you sit next to Pete" his Mother said, his two brother arrived, ribbing him, his Mother got angry with them both, then Dad said, "That'll do now boys" and no more was said, after that polite conversation took place by his Mother with Kathy, it was a sort of interrogation, but in a nice way which Kathy was totally unaware of, Pete then jumped up, "That's enough Ma" Kathy didn't know what to do she was embarrassed, the room went quiet, Kathy then broke the silence, asking all sorts of questions herself, for Pete's Mum to answer.

It was mid-afternoon Pete and Kathy said their goodbyes, Pete's Mum was crying, "Don't leave it so long next time, and bring Kathy back with you" Pete just nodded, he hated leaving them, but needs must, the farm wasn't that financially secure to support the whole family, that's why Pete left in the first place, so he could send them money every month, His Dad just said, "Keep safe Son" and hugged him, Kathy could see he was upset, she waved goodbye to everyone, Pete then drove away. For the next hour Pete was in his own thoughts, Kathy just kept quiet, she was also reflecting on whether she should be honest with him, it was the same niggling question that kept popping up, the guilt was still there, and it haunted her whether to tell him or not about her darkest moments, she was in a dilemma.

It was a while before Pete finally spoke, "You know Kathy it breaks my heart every time I leave, I look at them struggling, and somehow wish I could do more for them, Pete then started to explain the situation to Kathy, about the farm not being viable any more, it barely feeds the family as it is, if he went back it would be another mouth to fed, he thought he was doing the right thing sending them money every month to help with the bills. Kathy said, "Why don't they just sell up and move out", Pete looked at her, because it has been in the family for three generations, but for the past two years the harvest has been poor, and the larger farms are swallowing up smaller farms for more land, but they don't want to give a fair price, so they try to squeeze the smaller farms out, by getting Banks to refuse long term loans, credit becomes tight, "I see" said Kathy, but really hadn't got a clue what he was talking about.

By the time Pete dropped Kathy off it was well past 10.00pm, Pete drove off, no mention of I'll see you in a couple of days, he just drove off, Kathy entered the house, everyone had retired for the night, so she tip-toed into her room. Kathy was now feeling very sleepy; it wasn't too long before she fell asleep. The next morning Kathy went into the kitchen, "Well how did you get on" Maggie asked, Kathy replied, "You know ok I guess", Maggie was so exasperated, "Kathy O'Brien, I want to know every single detail from you, do you hear me, Kathy just looked at Maggie and nodded. Kathy then began to tell Maggie everything, about his family, the problems they were having with the farm, she did like Pete, even though he was much older than her, suddenly it all came flooding out, I don't know what to do Maggie, should I tell him of my past, or keep strum about it, what if he wants children, Maggie could see she was upset, she took Kathy into the lounge.

"Look Kathy I can't tell you what you should do, I'm the last person you should ask, what does your heart say," Kathy answered "To say nothing, "Then leave it at that tell him nothing that's my advice for what it's worth". A week went by with no news from Pete, Kathy was so upset about this, so much in fact that Maggie asked Joe to go and see Pete on the pretext that he needed some work doing on the estate, he found Pete tending the sheep, "Hi Pete" Joe said, Pete looked up, "Hi Mr Yardy", Pete replied back", "Been some time since we saw you everything ok? Joe asked, "Pa's had a heart attack, he's in Royal Perth, "Sorry to hear that Pete, I have a couple of jobs for you, but it can wait", Joe could see something was on Pete's mind, but didn't broach him about him about it, Joe was about to leave, when Pete said.

Can I have a word with you Mr Yardy? "Sure" replied Joe, Pete then started to tell him about how the farm was in financial difficulties, about the loan on the farm, which never seemed to reduce, the fact that the Wiggins family had offered him a way out, by paying off the loan and if there was any more debts the farm had, plus solicitor fees. Joe listened intently to him, then asked "So what's the problem," Pete answered the Farm has been in the family for three generations, it would kill my Pa and Ma, but the bottom line is, if they sold the offer they made is well below market price.

Joe entered the house, he didn't speak to either Maggie or Kathy, he went into the workplace to ring Charles, Maggie followed him, "Maggie do you mind this is private business, Joe said, Maggie was shocked and closed the door. Charles was unavailable, Joe emphasised the need to speak to him urgently, "I'll pass the message on Mr Yardy" said Charles secretary, "Please tell him no matter what time it is" the secretary said she would, when Joe came out he went to Kathy," It's nothing to do with you Kathy, Pete is having family problems. Kathy said I know", Joe looked at her, "How long have you known" Oh 'a couple of months, Kathy replied, and you never thought to tell me, Kathy blushed, "Pete told me in confidence Joe" I'm sorry Kathy but he is in danger of losing the family home, his father is in Royal Perth he has had a heart attack, "God please no" Kathy cried, I must go to him, he's not there Kathy he has gone up to Perth. Joe eventually told Maggie all about Pete's family problems, "So we need to tread carefully. Kathy's, been through a lot", Maggie just looked at Joe, "Don't you think I don't know that!!! Joe Yardy, Maggie was furious with him.

Charles didn't get back to Joe till the following day, Joe filled him in with the details, and asked Charles if he could do some digging on the bank in Toodyay and also a family called Wiggins, who seem to be buying farmland from farmers who are in financial difficulties, Charles was very keen to help Joe, especially as it involved Kathy, "Not a word to Mary Charles, I don't want the girls to get involved with this, or it will be all over Perth and Melbourne", "Mum's the word" Charles said. When Joe had finished his conversation, he said, "See you Maggie, then went out to the vineyards, "Well I never" Maggie was furious that he hadn't mentioned what Charles had said, she looked at Kathy, has Joe said anything to you, "No not a thing" was Kathy's reply, he's up to something, thought Maggie.

It took a week for Charles to get back to Joe," According to my sources, there is a blue print for major road to be built skirting Toodyay, to link up with the main highway too Albany, nothing concrete as yet, it needs State funding, a feasibility study has been carried out, the findings have not yet been released to the general public, I suspect that the Wiggins family have somehow got hold of this information", Joe said "I see". Charles carried on. "Can I make a suggestion Joe, if this is the case, it could suit our needs to be first in, as regards to your friend's farm, we could buy the farm from them at a fair price and allow them to stay on the farm till such time they wished to leave, we could give them a ten year lease on the property, if the plans are approved for the link up road to the main highway, it could very well take ten years or more to get the full plans off the ground, you know how fast Governments work".

Joe listened attentively, he was all for Charles proposal, "Look Mary itching to come over, why don't we go up to Toodyay, and have a word with the family see what they think, let the girls do what girls do," Joe agreed, Joe then said, "I really appreciate this, it's a matter of pride with farmers, growers, and sheep farmers, especially if the land has been passed down from one generation to another. "Think nothing of it, see you next week" said Charles. It took several months to finalise the sale of the Wilson farm, Pete's father heart attack proved fatal, the deeds of the property were now safely in the hands of Joe and Charles solicitors, Charles could now set the wheels in motion to stop the Wiggins brothers and their bullying tactics once and for all.

The next time all the gang would meet up was for the Melbourne Cup, of course Mary kept in touch with Maggie and Kathy, however being that much closer to Cynthia meant Mary kept in touch on a more regular basis when Cynthia was available, they often met for coffee or lunch depending on their calendars. Mary hadn't seen much of Charles lately with work commitments, she was bored and feeling very neglected, so much, she was down in the dumps, she longed so much for England that it hurt, had it not been for Cynthia she would have gone mad, she kept herself busy with social engagements, but it really wasn't her scene, in Mary's heart she knew it was a marriage of convenience for both of them, deep down she yearned for just a glimmer of hope to ignite something between them, she so disillusioned.

Charles arrived home early, he was in good mood, "Not long now Mary, I can't wait", Mary looked at him puzzled, "The Melbourne Cup! He retorted," Oh' I'm sorry Charles I had something on my mind yes I'm really looking forward to the races, I might even pick a new outfit for the occasion", Charles laughed, "You don't need an excuse to buy clothes", Mary smiled at him, it was the first time for ages since they have had a proper conversation. All at once Charles became serious, I'm sorry I haven't been attentive as I should have been I'll make it up to you I promise, Mary went over and kissed him gently, he grabbed hold of her, kissed her with intent, Mary was flabbergasted at this, but responded as if her life depended on it.

Meanwhile, the ocean liners were arriving from England approximately every six to seven weeks or so that the British Government had charted, to pick up army personnel and evacuees returning home, most of the walking wounded soldiers had already left to return home, it only left the very seriously injured, nursing staff, wives of service men, plus officer's wives, the ship was almost full by the time it reached Sydney, after calling in at Darwin, Freemantle before moving onto Brisbane.

CHAPTER TWENTY-EIGHT

Among the seriously injured according to the doctor's records was JR, but his records just said, brain- damage due to bombing, no mention of shell-shock, or violent behaviour, and so along with other injured service men, he was deemed fit to travel, he along with others were being transported to the docks, when a lorry collided with the ambulance, the impact was felt immediately by those inside the ambulance. JR suddenly began to scream and shout, the nurses tried to calm him down to no avail, his arms were flailing all around, he went towards the back of the ambulance to open the door, it was locked, he ran towards the door, he kicked at the door, all the time, the nurses and doctor tried to calm him down, he was like a madman, the doctor tried to tranquilise him, then suddenly the doors flung open, and he was off like a rocket. Everyone was in shock by this time, eventually the police arrived, the doctor explained the situation to them, the nurses themselves needed medical treatment, also the other patients. After the police questioned everyone, the patients were transferred to another ambulance, to carry on with their journey.

The police Sergeant who was investigating the accident with his police constables, thought there was something fishy about the crash, he arrested the driver of the lorry and his mate, and took them to the police station for further questing, after four hours of questioning, one of the men said, I want my brief, the Sergeant said, "You've got form then" the chap answered, "Yes, then tell us what happened, "Not till my brief gets here" he replied. An hour later his brief appeared he was taken to a small room, where he could chat to his client, the brief came out and said, "We are ready to talk a deal", the Sergeant replied in a stern voice, "No deal, till I hear what he has to say, then we'll talk deals", the brief went back inside the room, a couple of minutes later he came out his client had agreed.

It transpired that an orderly at the medical unit where JR was hospitalised had arranged everything for JR, the driver carried on, the orderly told him that this chap had a wad of notes and saw a way to making easy money, "Do we have a name for this orderly" asked the policeman, the brief turned to his client, then said, "When we have a deal", the Sergeant was furious, there used to be a time when we could lock up bastards up like you and throw away the key, he said to himself. The driver went on to say, that the orderly had arranged everything for JR to travel to Melbourne, he had a girlfriend there, the Sergeant interrupted him again, "Do you have a name? he asked, the driver said, "I think it's Mary can't be sure", the driver carried on, the orderly has arranged for someone to meet this JR at the Sydney station to put him on the right train. "That's all I know honest", the driver said, with that the sergeant went out of the room a constable remained, after about twenty minutes the Sergeant came back, "Write it down just what you have told me, then we can talk about a deal" said the Sergeant. Meanwhile, JR was still trying to find his way to the station, he was getting very agitated by this time, he kept bumping into people, the noise of the traffic, people talking was doing his head in, he went into a pub, and sat down, he sat for ten minutes or so, a waiter came across, "What're having? JR just looked at him in a vacant expression, the waiter repeated the question, again JR didn't respond, the waiter went away to speak to the boss, JR could see they were looking respond, the waiter went away to speak to the boss, JR could see they were looking at him, he made his way to the gents and scarpered out the back, picking up a jacket that was hung up.

Somehow he managed to find the main Station, he opened the envelope, and showed it to a porter, he stated to tell JR what platform, when JR put his hand to his ears, of course it was the noise he couldn't bear, the porter thought he was deaf and took him to the platform he wanted, JR showed him the ticket in the envelope, the porter nodded, and made a thumbs up sign, the train was already in, he gestured for him to get on, which JR did hesitantly, the porter then left him, but went to find the ticket collector on the train, he asked him to keep an eye on the deaf chap seat no 24 going all the way to Melbourne. The train arrived mid-afternoon, sure enough there was someone to meet JR, he took him to a flat in the Geelong area of Melbourne, provision had been made for JR to stay there for a while till the heat died down, just in case he was followed, which agitated JR no end, before the guy left he gave JR a couple of pills then locked JR in the flat, until he returned the next day, the guy returned the same day gave Jr a couple more tablets, as prescribed by James O'Connell, these where to keep JR peaceful and reduce any anxiety.

The following day at the police station the lorry driver was able to leave after he had signed his statement, and given the police the name of the orderly and other relevant information, he was due to attend court with reckless driving resulting in an accident, which would mean a fine. Upon further investigation by the police, they realised that the hospital was for mentally ill patients or for people with mental problems, the Sergeant was keen to arrest the orderly, as he now has his name, how many poor blighters has he duped for money, he said to himself. It was too late for anything more to be done that day, for the hospital was well out of the city a couple of hours drive at least, so the Sergeant arranged a couple of his constables to travel up and arrest James O'Connell.

O'Connell was indeed arrested and charged with obtaining money with menaces, for not only was there JR, there were at least three more who had been giving him money for certain privileges, the Sergeant wanted his guts, for what he had done, he wanted to make sure he had an airtight case before it went to court. O'Connell's brief went to Sergeant Ashworth," My client wants to make a deal," the Sergeant said, "Definitely no deal, he's a scumbag," the brief looked shocked, he went back to client, "No deal" O'Connell said, "On his head be it then.

"Hurry up Mary" Charles was pacing the floor, Cynthia was just bemused by it all, he didn't want to be late for his big day Mary came downstairs, "Wow Mary! You look stunning" Charles said, the taxi was already ready waiting for them. The atmosphere was fantastic it reminded Cynthia of Royal Ascot, but with no Royalty they arrived at the racetrack and were shown to their box, they were the first to arrive, that's Charles for you, thought Mary always the first. Joe and the rest of the gang arrived shortly after, then Charles's Mother and Father, also Charles's cousins, Amanda and Philip, as well as business associates, Charles his Father, Joe and Philip made their way to the enclosure, to view the horses, Charles Snr had a horse in the first race, called Bluebell, Mary turned to Charles Mother, "I didn't know, Charles Snr, owned a horse", Eleanor replied that it was a syndicate of about ten people who own the horse", "I see" Mary didn't see at all, but left it at that.

Mary circulated, she eventually made her way over to Cynthia, Maggie, Cynthia said," Kathy has something to show you Mary", Kathy suddenly thrust her hand in front of Mary, it took a second for Mary to realise that Kathy was showing her an engagement ring, Mary wanted to shout for joy but couldn't, she just hugged Kathy as much as she could, "So where's the lucky man" Mary asked, "He couldn't make it Mary but when you come over you will see him, "I want you to be my maid of honour", Mary was chuffed, "Of course I will", Kathy kissed Mary on her cheek. Like everything else at these functions, it is always business as well as pleasure, the men were grouped together, while Mary, Eleanor and her friends along with other women chatted amongst themselves, Cynthia loved it, Maggie and Kathy were awed by it, Maggie was wishing Joe would come over, Mary noticed Maggie and Kathy sat on their own and went over to them "Come on you two join us over here".

The big race was about to start, the build up to main race of the day was tremendous excitement filtered all around the racetrack, the expectation was unbearable then a deathly silence, suddenly, "Their Off!! the noise was like thunder with hoofs clattering on the ground the crowd was ecstatic, as they passed the grandstand the noise was deafening the race continued around they came again, this time to the line everybody shouting for their horse to win first, the noise grew even louder the, then it was over, the winner was Rain Maker the euphoria subsiding as quickly as it came, then Charles said "You had a bet on that? Didn't you Cynthia", Cynthia nodded, Cynthia Boardman your dark horse, said Maggie, everyone fell about laughing. The men joined the ladies for the buffet, business now concluded, it was just informal chatter, Cynthia found it easy to talk to people no matter what their standing was in society, Maggie and Kathy both wishing they could go back to the Hotel they were out of there comfort zone, Mary just circulated being the hostess, Charles Mother had grown fond of Mary, "How are the twins, you don't bring them enough to see us," said Eleanor Winfield, Mary replied, "Blame your son not me, I'm forever chastising him about not visiting you enough".

The day came to an end, each guest thanking Charles and Mary for inviting them promising to keep in touch, "We will" said Mary, knowing full well she may never see them again, "Well done Charles, I'll let you and Joe know as soon as I have details", "Thank you Henry", said Charles, by this time nearly everyone had left, Joe came over, "See you tomorrow Charles," Charles shook hands with him, Joe gave Mary a peck, "You look great Mary", Mary blushed.

Traffic was heavy it was a barmy night people were still lingering around the racetrack wanting to soak in the atmosphere and take in the moment again, perhaps never to return there ever again. Cynthia was staying with Charles and Mary, while Joe, Maggie and Kathy had booked rooms at the Menzies, they all left together each going their separate ways

At last they reached home, Charles went straight to his study, Mary and Cynthia went upstairs to change into something more suitable, Sara knocked the study door, "Come in" he turned round, "What is it Sara?", asked Charles, "A message Sir" replied Sara, she gave Charles the message, it was from Jeff Owen, asking Charles if he knew where Cynthia was, that his was back in Sydney, and planned to come over to Melbourne, there was also a telephone number,

"Thank you Sara that will be all" said Charles. He looked at the time thought it might be a touch too late to ring him, however, he changed his mind and decided to ring Jeff, the phone rang for ages, Charles put the phone down, I'll try again tomorrow, he said to himself.

The girls came down, Charles poured Mary a sherry, Cynthia a whiskey and dry, Mary asked Charles how did things go, "Very good Mary, some positive leads," I'm so pleased Charles you and Joe have worked so hard lately".

Enough about work Mary, we have a guest" Charles was about to say something, when the phone rang," Hello Charles Winfield", he listened, "As a matter of fact Cynthia is here" Charles turned to Cynthia, "It's for you" Cynthia gave Charles an inquisitive look and took the phone off him, "Hello! Cynthia", It's Jeff", "My God what part of the woodwork did you crawl from!" she exclaimed, "Still the same old Cynth I see", Cynthia just smiled to herself, "Come on Mary let's leave them to it", said Charles Jeff was full of apology, and remorse for not being around, Cynthia said, "Jeff no need to explain, I'm just glad that you are safe" they seemed to talk for hours, eventually the phone cut out, oh' bother said Cynthia, but she knew he would get in touch with her again.

Cynthia joined Charles and Mary in the drawing room Mary was expecting Cynthia to tell all, but she didn't, Charles said he was bushed, he retired upstairs, Mary and Cynthia chatted about the day, both Kathy and Maggie were in their conversations, they knew very little about this Pete Wilson, but they were determined to find out more. The next day Charles had already left for work, Mary and Cynthia went to meet up with Maggie and Kathy at the Menzies, while Mary chatted to Kathy, Cynthia was giving Maggie the third degree, Maggie got all tongue- tied, "Stop it Cynthia you're giving me a headache". "Sorry Maggie, we are just surprised you never let us know that's all we only want what is best for Kathy after all she been through" said Cynthia, Maggie replied, "I did mention him to Mary briefly", Cynthia ignored her.

Mary asked Kathy about Pete Wilson, when did they meet where did he come from and so on, Kathy told Mary everything, how Joe and Charles had helped Pete's family keep the family farm, Mary was surprised to hear this, Kathy carried on, he was the handyman that helped me with the tea rooms, the friendship started from there, I so much wanted to tell you about the engagement, it happened so fast, Mary vaguely remembered Maggie telling her something on those lines. "Then Kathy said can I have a word Mary about Pete, I had a chat with Maggie asking her advice, on you know what, "What did Maggie say?" asked Mary, Kathy said, she offered me some advice, mainly to keep quiet. Mary then said, "So you want to know if you should tell him about what has happened to you" "That's it Mary", "Kathy only you can do that", "My advice to you, is to really think about it, you don't have to tell him every single detail, but my advice for what it is worth, 'Let sleeping dogs lie', Have you thought of asking him why he is not married after all he is a lot older than you", Kathy replied, "No I haven't", "Nearly everyone has skeletons in the cupboard Kathy just remember that", that was the final word on the subject from Mary.

Joe arrived back at the hotel about 4.00pm the girls were still out, mainly shopping, after all it was near to Christmas, Mary had taken them to the Department Store, Maggie and Kathy had a ball, Cynthia and Mary just watched, Maggie just wanted the children's department, Kathy on the other hand wanted Mary and Cynthia to reinvent her, Cynthia thought, this is going to be a challenge as Kathy had no idea of colour co-ordination, or style.

They waited an hour, Cynthia was getting bored by this time, "Gee them along Mary or we will be here another hour" just as she said it, Charles appeared," Mary Joe is getting worried, he wants to fly out before it gets dark," Mary replied nothing to do with me Charles, we can't drag them away" said Mary, Charles went over to Maggie, and whispered something into Maggie ear, suddenly she said," Come on Kathy Joe waiting for us", Charles said, "I'll see you get these Maggie". Goodbyes were said all around, Kathy whispered, I'll keep you posted Mary," Mary just nodded, Cynthia said her goodbyes, with warmth, Maggie and Kathy were saddened at having to leave, but Maggie knew Joe had a lot on his plate.

When Mary and Cynthia arrived back at Mary's they were both exhausted, "Thank God that doesn't happen every week, Cynthia said, Mary just smiled at her, Mary then asked her about Jeff, "He's coming over as soon as he can", was Cynthia reply, "I'm so pleased that you and Jeff are finally going to settle down together," Mary said in wistful way, Cynthia noticed, "What is really the matter Mary, there is something I can sense it", Mary looked at Cynthia, tears were now flowing, I don't know whether I can take it any more Cynthia, I know we both married for convenience, but there isn't t any love there really, not from Charles anyway we just seem to go through the motions. Cynthia said, but what about the twins, that's just it Mary, he waltzed them off to boarding school, which I never wanted, I miss then so much, even though they are little devils in disguise.

CHAPTER TWENTY-NINE

Cynthia laughed surely not, "Oh' there all sugar and spice when they see Auntie Cynthia", Mary said. I am so lonely here in this big house, when I go out, I am Mr Charles Winfield's wife, not Mary Winfield, in my own right," "Have you told Charles" asked Cynthia, "No, but after the Christmas holiday, I am going to have it out with him once and for all". Replied Mary, do you fancy Christmas with us Cynthia? asked Mary.

Cynthia replied," No I don't think so, Jeff and I have a lot of catching up to do, maybe after the New Year, perhaps you and the twins can come over to me and Charles could come down at a weekend, it is a lovely place Mary as you know." Charles suddenly entered the room, "What are you two talking about, Cynthia instantly replied," We were saying what a great day we had yesterday all of us being together", Mary just agreed. Cynthia then excused herself, I'm off see you in the morning, which left Charles and Mary alone, it's been quite hectic for both of us Mary, Charles said, "When the twins are home, I suggest we have two or three days away, for a break, this was Mary's great opportunity. "I suppose we could go down to Warnambool, the kids love it there, it so relaxing Charles you would really 1 like it, and I think Jeff will be there, Charles agreed, he realised he had been neglecting Mary, he just wanted her to be happy.

Despite Mary being unhappy about the marriage situation, her and Charles had a wonderful time at Christmas spending it with the family his Mother and Father were overjoyed at them staying over, his cousins where still down from Brisbane, so it was a real get together, Mary did in fact enjoy every minute of it. New Year's Eve arrived, Mary had let the staff off for Christmas and New Year, to spend with their families much to Charles annoyance, Mary took no notice, she thought it was only right for them to have the time off, after all they were very good and very loyal to her. They had a quiet night just the two of them, the twins were asleep, they drank the New Year in, Mary whished Charles a prosperous 1948, and vice-versa, then they both retired to bed.

The next day the twins woke Mary up, she looked at the clock, it was 7.30am, she wondered were Sara was and cook, she put her robe on then looked into Charles bedroom he was already up Mary proceeded downstairs, there was no sign of cook or Sara, "What the hell is going on" the twins said to her, Mummy, Mummy, there is a strange man in there pointing to the drawing room. Mary immediately sensed something was wrong, she put her fingers to her mouth and took the twins into the study locked the door, then immediately rung Cynthia, it was Jeff who answered, Mary started to whisper, Jeff said "I can't hear you," Cynthia snatched the phone from Jeff, "Thank God it's you, he's here, "Who's here", asked Cynthia" Mary said still in a whisper, "JR!!, get help I'm locked in the study with the twins, suddenly the line went dead.

Mary froze she whispered to the twins, "Let's pretend we are dead when Daddy comes to find us", the twins thought it was great fun, she heard the door handle, she again put her fingers to her mouth, to the twins, they were very still, Mary laid there it seemed a lifetime, suddenly she heard a shot, "Oh' my God she said to herself, please God No, I know I haven't been good, I know I took a life, but please, please, spare Charles, if anyone deserves to die let it be me, but keep my babies safe. The door handle went again, it was JR, "I know you are in there Mary, why didn't you visit me, I missed you," Mary didn't say a word, by this time the twins were whimpering, she got hold of them held them closer to her she moved nearer to Charles desk went behind it, just in case, he started shooting again, he was still ranting and raging banging at the door with his body, suddenly there was a lot of gunfire, Mary was petrified she couldn't move, she was numb with fear, the twins were now crying, "Please God keep us safe", that's all Mary kept saying. Then banging on the door," It's me Jeff, your safe now open the door," Mary are you alright? open the door the police are here" said Cynthia, Mary went to open the door, she didn't open it right away, "Is it really you Cynthia," she asked, "Yes Mary, please open the door, Mary gingerly opened the door.

There was mayhem and police everywhere, an ambulance had arrived, the twins were crying and clinging to Mary, Cynthia took Grace and Charles away to their playroom, Nanny Williams followed them, Jeff took Mary's arm, there was blood everywhere, Mary looked for Charles, "Where's Charles", a policeman came up to her, "He's gone to hospital, as the policeman was talking to her, a stretcher was being wheeled out with a white sheet draped over it. Mary went to lifted the sheet, she was stopped by Jeff, "You don't need to look Mary", said Jeff," Charles is alive, injured but alive", Mary crumpled to the floor the medics helped her to a chair, they examined her, the medic told Jeff she was in shock.

The police wanted a statement off Mary, Jeff was emphatic that they left her alone, as she was in shock, hesitantly they went into the drawing room, then started asking the staff, what had happened, cook went to make Mary a cup of tea the police waiting for cook patiently, cook was in no hurry, she took the tray into the lounge, where Jeff had taken Mary. Here you are Mrs Charles, a nice cuppa for you, Jeff could see Mary was in no fit state to be left, Jeff turned to the cook, "Can you ask Cynthia to come into the lounge please", a couple of minutes and Cynthia arrived, the children were with Nanny Williams, who had told Cynthia exactly what had happened. The family doctor arrived and insisted that Mary should rest, he gave her a couple of pills, and instructed Cynthia, to give her two more, before she retired for the night, now where are the children, Jeff took him to the playroom, he examined them both, he could see they were still upset, he asked Nanny Williams to keep a close eye on them, any change let me know immediately no matter what time, Nanny Williams.

It took the police about two hours before they were satisfied, statements had been taken, except for Mary Winfield, "We'll come back tomorrow" said the Sergeant, Jeff asked if they could clean up, "I don't see why not we have everything we need," was the Sergeant's reply, "Will be back about eleven." Jeff showed him to the door. Jeff went back into the lounge, Mary was now fast asleep, and Cynthia decided to ring Charles's parents to take the children for a couple of days.

Mr Charles Senior wanted answers, he couldn't understand how a mentally ill patient managed to get from Sydney to Melbourne, and so he hired a private detective, as far as the police were concerned, it was an open and shut case. Mary by now was feeling much better, and was able to visit Charles at the clinic, he was so glad to see Mary, he started to cry, Mary, just held him, all the emotion was flowing from Charles, "I've never been as freighted in my life Mary, Charles said. "All I could think about was you and the children, I just knew I had to do something," "I know Charles Cynthia told me what had happened, it was self-defence," said Mary, Charles looked at her tears still trickling down his face, "I didn't mean to kill him Mary", Mary replied, "I'm glad you killed him Charles, he would never have left us alone", Mary then hugged Charles the best way she could.

Mary began to tell Charles's about his father wanting answers, which he already knew about, "How is mother coping with the twins? asked Charles, "She's loving every minute of it, they are of course giving her the run around" said Mary, Charles managed to laugh, Mary stayed for an hour or so, she could see he was tiring, "See you tomorrow, I'll see if I can bring the twins in to see you", Charles smiled, "That'll be good" he replied. It took another month before Charles could return home, he was frail, the doctors assured the family that he would get stronger, and provided he took things easy for the next month or so, they saw no reason why he couldn't a lead a normal life.

The twins were so pleased to see their Daddy, they were both fighting for his attention, Eleanor their Grandma, said in a stern voice, "Now what did I say to you two", they looked at her, and sheepishly stopped squabbling, Charles look at his Mother, "Do you want a full time job Mother" his mother glared at Charles, "Indeed I do not! She said emphatically, Charles just laughed.

Mary came in, "Hello Eleanor, we can't thank you enough for taking the twins, it was a big help, Eleanor smiled, then said "You can have them back now, I'm exhausted, I don't know how you do it, they never stop." Eventually there was a big enquiry into the shootings, and questions to be answered by the Police who handled the case in Sydney, Charles senior wanted heads to roll, Mary and Charles junior just wanted to forget about the whole episode, and get on with their lives with the children. Mary especially had come to crossroads in her life, her thoughts of seeing England again was ever diminishing, she made her mind up that she would pursue her dream of revamping the department store she also wanted her children to come home daily from school and spend more time with her and Charles. It was always her ambition to completely change the fashion department to be the place were designer clothes would be available, as well as off the peg clothes, she knew it would be hard work but it would be worth it in the end, Grace's then would have a reputation for service, quality, and also uniqueness.

Charles wanted to expand Yardy wines into distribution and marketing with their own transport, he asked his most trusted colleague to look at failing business's at auction's for this purpose. He told Mary about his vision for the vineyard, Mary was a little wary, "Have you mentioned this to Joe", asked Mary, "Not yet" said Charles, he looked at Mary, "Why", "Well it is after all, it is his business Charles, I would hate you to take over completely, you are better letting Joe do all the legwork and you take a back seat, we have enough to do with the refurbishment of the store", Charles thought about it, "You're absolutely right Mary, I think I will ask Joe to buy me out of Yardy's Wine,

"That's the wisest thing you've said all year", Mary said, Charles just laughed out loud. Do you miss going over to see Maggie and Kathy, "I do and I don't, besides we keep in touch by phone, I was disappointed that I missed Kathy's wedding, Cynthia said she looked lovely". Pete has gone to town on the farm from what Cynthia told me, his mother now lives in one part, while Kathy and Pete live in the larger part of the house, apparently he has set up his carpentry and handyman business at the farm, from all accounts he is doing very well, from what I can gather off Maggie, they are all hoping to fly over to see you when you are up to it". Another year went by, Cynthia and Jeff were taking things easy, Cynthia with her painting, Jeff with his fishing and sailing, it was an idyllic world for them both, they too had different agenda's now, like Mary and Charles, the friends were quietly drifting apart, unknown to any them at that moment in time. It was now the grand opening of the store after a full refurbishment, invites had been sent out, Charles was running around like a scolded cock, "For heaven's sake Charles calm down you'll have a heart attack if you are not careful, the doctors have warned you not to do too much," Mary yelled at Charles, he just laughed and ignored her, they had invited a few guests to the boardroom, for cocktails etc., Charles's Mother and father were so proud of their son.

Mary took their guests on a tour of the Store, the reaction was very positive indeed, everyone remarked on the contemporary style, Mary showed the ladies the fashion department, her own domain. The ladies were amazed at the transformation, the Designer department was completely on its own, with separate changing rooms, and the main floor space was for off the cuff clothes, by this time the place was buzzing. Charles and one or two of the most senior assistants helped to show prospective customers around, Mary noticed her old supervisor, she went over to her, to greet her warmly, Mildred it's lovely to see you, Mildred introduced Mary to her niece, "This is Rebecca, and would it be alright if I pop in tomorrow to see Mr Charles?" she asked. Mary smiled to herself, you can tell me Mildred if you like, Mildred hesitated, she was old school, "I'll tell you what you pop in tomorrow about 2.00pm we can take it from there, I have to go now" said Mary.

The evening was a resounding success, Mary, Charles and Cynthia were exhausted by the time everyone had left, Charles poured them a glass of Champagne, and made a toast, to a new era and decade,

"To the 1950s" said Cynthia, they all raised their glasses, it was well past midnight by the time they reached the house, they all just retired upstairs. The next day Mary didn't wake up till after 9.00 o'clock, she strolled downstairs, Cynthia was eating breakfast, Charles had already left for the office, "Morning sleepy head", Mary muttered something under her breath, "What was that Cynthia in a sarcastic way", and smiled, for she knew Mary was not really a morning person.

Morning Mrs Charles, Sara said, "Morning Sara, tell cook just toast for me", Cynthia looked at Mary, this Mrs Charles, a bit archaic isn't", "I know it drives me potty, I've asked them to call me Mary or, Madam, but they don't, Sara not quite as bad, she will call Madam, when she thinks about it", the toast arrived, "Tell cook I won't be in for lunch", Sara nodded and returned to the kitchen. "I had a chat with Charles about the twins, he was reluctant, but finally agreed for them not to board at school, I will pick them up each day to bring them home, said Mary, "Well that's a start Mary, just keep chipping away gently", said Cynthia. Cynthia then told her that Jeff would be coming over to Melbourne from next month, he has to report to the Australian Embassy to discuss his new position, Cynthia then asked Mary if she was free in the afternoon, so they could have a look for an apartment near St Kilda for them both, Mary immediately said yes, then, Mary remembered Mildred, "It will have to be about 3.00pm I have an appointment at 2.00pm, Cynthia smiled then left.

Mary sat for a while thinking of last night's event, and how well everything had gone, she was so proud of Charles for all the hard work he had done, it was no easy task, he was looking tired he was never really the same man after the shooting, and she did worry about him. The phone interrupted her thoughts, a voice yelled," It's Maggie just looking at the papers, you and Charles are all over the place", Mary was stunned, "I haven't seen the papers yet Maggie", "Well you should", Mary couldn't get a word in edge ways, Maggie went on and on about what the kids, what they had been up too, how Joe was working far too hard he was looking tired she carried on she hadn't seen Kathy since the wedding, and was furious about that finally she stopped. "Look can I give you a ring tomorrow Maggie I was just about to go out I have an appointment", just to say Charles is doing well and also the twins, speak to you tomorrow", Mary just put the phone down." Well I never.

Maggie was very annoyed with Mary just who does she think she is, the fact was Maggie was missing the girls and yearned for some excitement in her life, she loved Joe dearly, but they never went anywhere not even on holidays, there was a tinge of jealousy, she thought Mary and Cynthia were having a ball going out to lunch every day, off shopping doing what rich people do afternoon teas, Maggie was reading too many social magazines, she was totally wrong of course.

When Mary arrived at the Store she went straight to the office and headed for Charles's office, as she entered Sophie was there, "Mr Charles is not here, he is with his father in the boardroom", Thank you Sophie, said Mary, she proceeded along to the boardroom, she knocked on the door, Mr Charles's Senior assistant opened the door, he turned round to Mr Charles Jr, and said, "It's Mary Winfield", Charles immediately went over to see her, he was embarrassed, then said, "Mary I'm sorry this is something that doesn't concern you, see you later", he blushed, then closed the door.

CHAPTER THIRTY

Mary just stood there not believing what she had just heard, she was flabbergasted to say the least, nevertheless, she looked at her watch and went onto her office, Sophie was there, Mary asked Sophie if she knew what the meeting was about, "Haven't a clue" Sophie replied, Mary left it at that.

Mildred arrived with her niece Rebecca, and was shown to Mary's office, "Come in", Mary greeted her warmly after all Mary had a lot to thank Mildred for, she knew it was her who pushed Mary for the supervisor's job. "This is my niece Rebecca, she has just finished college, I was wondering if you could find her a job in your Fashion Department", Mildred asked. Mary shook hands with Rebecca, Mary noticed an extremely large folder, "What have you got there, Rebecca replied, "I've brought some of my sketches to show you," Mary was intrigued, "What college did you go too? Mary asked her," Royal College of Art", was Rebecca's reply. Mary was really impressed with her fashion designs and drawings, she was a very creative, young woman, and Mary could see her potential they chatted for a while, then Mary said she would let her know as soon as possible, and could Rebecca drop in sometime next week, to see Mr Charles, Mildred was so pleased, Mary showed them the door, "Till next week then" and closed the door.

The phone went," Where the hell are you" Cynthia yelled, Mary looked at her watch, oh' crumbs she said to herself, "On my way", Mary arrived breathless, Cynthia withered her, Mary just ignored her, she was used to Cynthia idiocrasies.' Time was going so quickly for Mary, she had very little time for herself and saw less and less of Cynthia, Mary had decided to return to work part time, in a less demanding role till she was satisfied that everything was running smoothly. Cynthia and Jeff were inseparable, Mary was on the school run picking up the children, which she really enjoyed, she spent less time at the store, but would pop in just to make sure that the fashion department, was maintaining its high standards set by Mary herself, Rebecca proved a great success with her own individual style, she was in great demand for her designs.

Maggie had not rung Mary since their spat a few months earlier, Joe was frustrated with Maggie for leaving it so long, but Maggie had dug her heels in, and refused to ring first, Joe had business in Melbourne with Charles, and begged Maggie to go with him, but she still refused. Joe crashed out of the house and never even said goodbye when he left, it made no difference to Maggie, although it hurt her that Joe had left without saying goodbye, the fact was Maggie wasn't feeling that great, she seemed to be tired all the time, the prospect of traveling over to see Mary and Charles daunted her also Maggie wasn't needed as much now the children were getting older especially, Mollie, Catherine and Jack, they were getting very independent, the youngest one Joseph still needed her attention, and boy did she spoil him.

Kathy too had not got in touch with Maggie for ages, then Kathy rang Maggie up to see why she had had a fall out with Mary, Maggie said to Kathy, "Mary should ring first she is the one who put down the phone on me," so for the first time in Maggie's life she was feeling very lonely, neglected and unwanted all because of her silly pride and jealousy. When Joe arrived at Charles's house, he was greeted warmly by Mary, and how's Maggie still sulking, she asked Joe, Joe was about to tell Mary something, when Charles arrive, they went into the study, Mary asked cook to make coffee and toast, which cook promptly did, the post arrived, Mary perused through it, there was one from Sydney, it looked official, but it was addressed to Charles, just then the study door opened. Mary, "Have you got a minuet I need you to sign something for me," said Charles, "Sure",

Mary entered the room, Joe looked dumb founded, Mary looked at him he didn't respond, Charles handed Mary a pen, she looked at the document then realised why Joe was in shock. Charles had given Joe his shares in the Company they set up together along with paperwork detailing what plans Charles had in mind to expand the business further. He explained to Joe, that after the shooting he had, had a lot of time to reflect, and realised, that after all it was Joe's family business and not his, he went on to say that he and Mary had a long chat and decided to give Joe the shares, and they were both happy to do so.

Joe spluttered, to find the words, he eventually said, "I can't afford to buy you out Charles, It's a lot of money," Charles replied, "We don't want any money, it's our gift to you, for being there when needed, if you feel you need to contribute, you can pay the solicitor's and any costs that are incurred", Charles shook Joe's hand, "There is only one clause Joe, keep sending the wine". Joe was ecstatic, he was also embarrassed, Mary came over and kissed him on the cheek, "Now tell me about Maggie", Charles asked to be excused, "I hope you'll dine with us tonight Joe then we can celebrate". Joe told Mary about Maggie, "I have never seen her like this before, she is so pig headed about not ringing first", Mary wasn't surprised, she explained how it had happened, that she had to cut her short on the phone because she had an important meeting to go to. I don't think she realises just how busy we are here, even Cynthia and Jeff are now back working, we don't have the same time as we used too, I haven't even been in touch with Kathy for some time either, I did have it in mind to come over when the children are on their summer holiday for a couple of weeks but now I might leave it for now". Mary said.

Joe said "You will do no such thing, you and Charles must come over, and hopefully Cynthia and Jeff, I'll also invite Kathy and Pete," Mary said, "She won't like it", Joe retorted, "She won't know", Mary then said to Joe". We must try to do something for Kathy, Joe looked at her puzzled, I'm meaning financially, is there any way we can give her the deeds to the farm, oh' I know Charles has helped, but it would be nice if you and Maggie could do something for her on that side of things, will you have a think about it Joe, "I will Mary and let you know when I do my homework" replied Joe. The evening went well, Joe couldn't get over how grown up the twins were, and polite, "You've done a good job Mary", Mary laughed, "You must be joking, school has done a good job you mean", Charles entered, "What's this", "Joe thinks I've done good job with the kids, I told him it's the school that's done a good job", Charles said, "Credit where it's due Mary, they have come on leaps and bounds since we took them out of boarding school", Mary blushed.

Mary retired from the dinner table, she could see that the men were itching to be on their own, she went into the kitchen, I think they may have finished now cook, Mary grabbed a tray," What do you think you are doing Mrs Charles," Cook! "I've told you to stop calling me Mrs Charles, just call me Mary, times are changing, and that goes for you Sara". "Now collect the dishes and I'll help you, we will say no more about it", Mary was adamant, she loved to help them in the kitchen, usually it was fair to say when Charles wasn't around, he had been brought up in the old ways.

Joe said goodnight to Mary, "See you all in the New Year at our place don't forget," "How could I, safe journey, love to the family, and Kathy", Mary and Charles watched as Joe went. Mary went into the study after Charles, "This is an interesting letter Charles from Sydney", said Mary in an inquisitive tone, Charles took the letter off Mary and said nothing, "Well aren't you going to open it", Charles looked up and then said "No", and Mary was not too pleased she hated secrets. Cynthia rung Mary up, right out of the blue, do you and Charles fancy meeting up for dinner sometime next week, she asked Mary, "I will have to let you Cynthia, somethings a foot and I can't find out what it is, when I ask Charles he is evasive". Have you got your invite from Joe? Asked Cynthia, "Yes this morning, we are planning on going over, how Maggie will react I don't know" replied Mary, Then Cynthia said, "You know Maggie she runs hot and cold all the time when she doesn't get her own way.

Mary called into the Store to see Charles, he was in a meeting with his father, so she tootled down to the fashion department it was really busy, a couple of ladies from the WVS spotted Mary, "Mary how lovely to see you, the store looks great, you must be really be proud of Charles", Mary acknowledge them both, "You'll have to excuse me, Charles is expecting me", "I Hope we see at meeting next month" one of the ladies said, Mary just nodded and proceeded to Charles Office once again, she entered his office," Charles is in a meeting with his Father, "What's going on Sophie? asked Mary, "Haven't a clue" replied Sophie.

The meeting with Charles's Father lasted well over an hour, Charles had done his homework on the Wiggins family in Toodyay, and wanted his Father's advice on how to handle it, whilst Charles was recuperating, he had, had plenty of time to set his stall out, his first priority was Joe Yardy, which had already been resolved, his second, were the Wiggins brothers which he had obtained damaging information from various sources about their financial background which was rocky to say the least, everything seemed to hinge on the new link road, the next one was the report from the Detective Agency, that his Father had hired to find out more about John Robert Harding and the orderly James O'Connell. After the meeting Charles went to see Mary, "Fancy lunch Mary" Charles asked.

Mary replied, "Fine", they set off to have a quiet lunch, Charles then told Mary everything, about the private detective agency that his Father had hired, also about the Wiggins family in Toodyay, that he was sorry he couldn't tell her anything, till things were sorted out and he had spoken with his Father before he made any decision. Mary was stunned at hearing about Pete's family farm, she did have an inkling because Maggie had mentioned something to her which she had forgotten about, till now. "What you are going to do about this orderly, James O'Connell, Mary asked, "Father's going to have a word with the Chief of Police in Sydney", "Wow" Mary exclaimed, wheels within wheels, she said to herself. It was a couple of months later that the date had finally been fixed for the trial of James O'Connell and his associates, they had been charged with aiding and abetting of the unlawful shooting of Charles Winfield, O'Connell was also charged with obtaining monies through menaces he was found guilty on both accounts and sentenced along with his accomplices.

By the time the trial was over, Charles was drained, both he and Mary missed out on the get together at Joe and Maggie's place, Charles decided to ask his mother if she would have the children for two or three weeks, so he and Mary could go over to Bali, his mother was delighted she loved having the twins now, as they were no trouble at all.

Mary was so pleased the trial was over, she thought on many occasions that he was never quite the same after the shooting, she cursed JR and hoped he was in hell "Welcome Home Mr Charles" said Sara, "Glad to be back Sara", answered Charles, as he moved towards the study with his pile of letters, he flipped through them, this looks interesting, it was from Joe, inside was a paper clipping, it read the Wiggins & Sons had filed for bankruptcy, Joe had written, nothing to do with you then! Charles gleaned a great deal of satisfaction. His next letter was more disturbing, whilst he was in Sydney he sought medical attention, as regard to his wellbeing, it read.

Dear Mr Winfield,

I write to inform you of the tests which were carried out, unfortunately our findings need you to have an urgent consultation with one of my colleagues, I have arranged an appointment for Wednesday 19th March 1956 at 2.00pm at the Royal Hospital Melbourne.

Regards,
Dr Tweeddale FRCP.

Upon reading this Charles had to sit down, I'm not going to tell Mary just yet, he said to himself, he thought better to tell her when the doctor had seen him, then take it from there, no need to worry her I can't tell her anything.

He opened another letter it was Singapore, it was from Jeff and Cynthia, to tell them, about Jeff's posting, to the Australian Embassy and already in situ there, he apologised for not getting in touch sooner, but hoped they could all meet up in Singapore when they had some time, there was also a letter for Mary, Charles presumed it was from Cynthia. "Hi where're back, the children ran up to Charles and put their hands around him, "What's this? What do I do to deserve this Charles said to them", "Grace said, "We missed you so much Daddy", a lump came to Charles throat.

Mary looked at him and smiled, totally unaware of what was to follow, he managed to compose himself, there's a letter for you Mary, I think it is from Cynthia, "About time too, she's dreadful these days returning letters, mind you she's not as bad as them in Perth, meaning Maggie and Kathy, "Oh' your speaking to Maggie now", said Charles, "No not yet, but I will, it's about time she buried the hatchet", said Mary, "How was Mother, fragile? "No just the opposite, she said Grace was very helpful, Charles on the other hand kept to himself, she said Charles Jr just reminded her of you at that age", Sara appeared, "Mr Charles a telephone call for you", Charles went back into the study, "Charles Winfield speaking," it was the doctor from Sydney, "Glad I've caught you, I been trying to get hold of you", Charles explained about being on holiday. The doctor said it was imperative that he keeps his appointment and not to cancel for work reasons, Charles said that he understood and he would attend, he then thanked the doctor, and hung up.

After dinner Charles was very quiet he was in his own thoughts really, Mary interrupted him, "Are you going to tell me what's wrong" she asked, Charles was taken by surprise, he was about to tell her, when the children came in to say goodnight, "Goodnight my little angels", Charles said, before Nanny Williams took them upstairs, Mary looked at him she just knew he was keeping something from her, "I'll be up shortly Nanny".

Charles changed the subject, "Who was the letter from Cynthia" he asked Mary, Mary set about telling Charles, that Cynthia had played holy hell with Maggie for being so pig headed, she explained to her why I had to put the phone down, Kathy was also cross with Maggie, Kathy said she blamed Joe for letting her have her own way all the time, anyhow, apparently Maggie and Joe are coming over in a couple of weeks' time to see us, did you know about Jeff and Cynthia being in Singapore, "Only today like you", Charles replied. Mary left Charles to kiss the twin's goodnight, she decided to change into something more suitable, eventually she arrived downstairs, only to find Charles in his study, she got her book out and began to read, after sometime something distracted her an anxiety crept over her she went towards the study. Charles hadn't moved, she went over to wake him, Charles, Charles, then started to prod him, no response, it was then and only then, that she realised, she let out one squeal, Sara coming running in, "Sara ring for the doctor tell him its urgent its Mr Charles".

CHAPTER THIRTY-ONE

Mary was numb by this time, Nanny took one look, she knew instantly that he was dead, she took Mary out of the room, and made her a cup of tea. It was well past midnight before everyone had left, Charles Mother and Father arrived, Mary was in tears when she saw them, they were beside themselves, the twins had woken up with all the noise and had started to go downstairs, Nanny Williams said, "Come on you two we'll have none of this bed! In a stern voice.

There was an inquest into the death of Charles, it transpired that he had a fault with his heart, which Dr Tweeddale had noticed, he explained that an appointment had been made to see a specialist, with a view to surgery, the consultant who was to perform the operation, gave his opinion, and just said, his heart just stopped beating due to a blocked aorta. The body was released, the funeral took place at St Patricks' Cathedral, it was to be a private family burial and close friends only, Mary was distraught with grief, the girls were very concerned, to help Mary, it was decided that Cynthia would stay for a couple of weeks, before returning to Singapore, most of the two weeks were taken up with solicitors, Mary couldn't take everything in, it was a good job Cynthia was with her to digest everything.

It was time for Cynthia to leave, she felt awful about leaving Mary, but knew the longer she stayed the more reliant Mary would become on her, so with tears in her eyes, Cynthia said goodbye, the twins hugged their Auntie Cynthia, they too were crying, Cynthia didn't look back at Mary, she knew she just had to leave. Six months had now passed, Mary had to steel herself for the sake of her children, by this time the twins were eleven, that is when she made the most monumental decision of her life. Mary went to see Charles Father for advice about her assets, and the decision she had made about her future and the twins, Charles senior was most upset to hear what Mary had to say, he accepted that it was her life, then said "Eleanor will be mortified when she hears what you are planning to do". Mary answered I know, but I fear they will never get over the loss of their Father living here, also don't forget the shooting, we assume it didn't affect them but who knows, they had many a sleepless night after it happened, I know you and Eleanor dream of Charles Jr taking over the Company one day, I will assure you that I will never stop Charles or Grace from returning to Australia, once their education is over, Charles Snr, got hold of Mary, we will miss you all, and gently kissed her on her cheek.

Charles Senior than said, I'll get in touch with the solicitor, with your instructions, it will probably take a few weeks, I hope you'll come to dinner, then we can discuss everything then. Mary said she would and thanked him for being so understanding, Charles Senior had always had a soft spot for Mary, and he was forever grateful to Mary for taking Charles on, with his reputation, deep down he was aware it was really a loveless marriage, but said nothing.

Mary had made a list of things to do, gosh I'm getting like Cynthia and laughed to herself, when she arrived home, Mary set pen to paper, asking Cynthia and Jeff, also the gang over in Perth to come over for Christmas, she thought it was time to circulate, as she put it, hoping that might help them to say yes, for Mary and Maggie, hadn't really spoken properly since their spat, except at the funeral, which was awkward for Maggie. The twins had a great birthday, Grandma Eleanor had been ever so gracious with Mary, but deep down she was heartbroken, Mary took her to one side and said, "Look Eleanor no matter what happens, they are your grandchildren, and they love you dearly, travel is becoming easier these days, I hear that commercial flights are being planned by Qantas, to fly from Sydney to London, they already fly to Singapore, so who knows, what the future might hold, all I know I have just got to get away from here".

Maggie and Joe received the invite, Joe said, "Good for Mary", "You're not thinking we're going are you? What about the children" said Maggie, Joe retorted, "What about the children, they are old enough and Catherine will be here while we are away", "I'm not going! Said Maggie in an emphatic tone. Oh' yes you are going and I will tell you why, Joe than started, "May I remind you Maggie Hughes about what Charles and Mary have done for us over the years, giving me the financial help we needed to expand the vineyard, you seemed to have forgotten about that Maggie, then to give us sole control of the Company that Charles and I had set up together, with Charles's money I might add, which in total at today's value is worth a lot of money, not forgetting that we were able to help Kathy and Pete out with the farm, we couldn't have done that for them had it not been for Charles and Mary!", Joe yelled, he was furious with Maggie.

"So don't you ever say to me you're not going because you are still sulking because Mary hasn't rung you, you owe Mary big time!!" said Joe, who was by this time really angry, Maggie didn't say another word she was feeling very low, and didn't have the energy to argue with Joe, "Now write to her and tell we would love to come" Joe insisted, not another word was spoken on the subject ever again.

Kathy on the other hand was delighted, Pete was pleased for her, for he knew that Kathy was very fond of Mary, Kathy hadn't really spoken to her since the death of Charles, and felt guilty, she has so much to tell Mary, but decided to wait till saw her. Pete was reluctant at first, "You don't want me there, I'll feel out of place, with all those money people", "Don't be silly Pete, Mary's not like that, you're coming with me and that's that. Pete just nodded, for he knew it was a waste of time to discuss it any further with Kathy. When Cynthia eventually received her invite, she was delighted, she couldn't wait for Jeff to arrive from work, when Jeff eventually arrived home, he seemed pre-occupied, "What's wrong" asked Cynthia, Jeff looked at her, it looks as though Communism is raising its ugly head again, we are having trouble with insurgents, Singapore is heading for Independence as well as Malaysia. You mark my words. Cynthia, changed the subject, we have had an invite from Mary, she hopes we can make it for the Christmas holiday, "I don't know Cynth, things are a bit hectic at the moment," Jeff replied, "See what you can do, pull some strings if you have to, if not for me, for Mary", pleaded Cynthia.

Mary was now in full flow with her planning, finding out about shipping her furniture and valuables working out dates, checking passports, keeping in touch with Mr Barstow to see if anything suitable had turned up, whether to use the Australian or her English passport, the twins just had Australian passports, investigating private schools in the area, only the best would do for Charles and Grace, it would have been what Charles would have done. Most of May's time was taken up looking for the most suitable place to live in England, she certainly didn't want the north of England, not for her children, she was looking for a warmer climate for them, the winters can be a killer in the north of England, her strategy was to move over sometime in May, when the clocks had been put back for the summer, she gleaned as much information from the library as she could.

Christmas was around the corner, Mary was getting apprehensive now, was she doing the right thing dragging her children half way across the world, she began to chastised herself, all she wanted for her children was to know their English heritage, after a great deal of thought Mary finally made her mind up and chose to live in the Oxfordshire Cotswold, rural England, she got in touch with Barstow, to find her a place to rent for twelve months, this would give her plenty of time to look for a place to live permanently in the Cotswolds. A couple of days before Christmas Eve, Mary invited Eleanor and Charles Winfield to dinner mainly to see the children, and to asked them if they would have them for a couple of days after Christmas so Mary could carry on with her planning, Charles's parents jumped at the chance, and immediately said yes, then Charles Father said, "Have you told them yet? Mary answered, "No not yet, I'll tell them after Christmas", "Better you than me, I don't envy you", Charles Senior said. Mary knew the task wouldn't be easy, but it had to be done.

Everyone arrived, the house looked wonderful, Mary was looking as beautiful as ever, there was a certain glow now, for everyone to see, Kathy was the first to greet Mary warmly, Joe nudged Maggie, to Maggie's annoyance, then finally went over to her, "Sorry about the misunderstanding Mary, I was totally in the wrong, sorry", Mary was magnanimous as ever, no need to apologise Maggie, it was as much my fault as yours I should have explained it better.

Suddenly Cynthia burst in laden as usual, "What on earth have you got there? Everyone asked, "Presents of course" in the tone everyone knew, the girls fell about laughing, "Where's Jeff" everyone asked, "He'll be here later he has called into the office" replied Cynthia. It was well into mid-afternoon when Jeff arrived, the twins where playing in the back yard with Joe and Pete, Jeff said, his hello to everyone and went out to see Joe and Pete they all shook hands, Charles Jr said, Uncle Jeff's on my side, Joe said, "I thought I was on your side" "Not now I want uncle Jeff" replied Charles Jr, so Jeff and Charles, played cricket against, Joe, Pete and Grace, Jeff was impressed with Charles prowess with a cricket bat, nobody could get him out, Grace was fed up and went inside.

An hour later dinner was ready, Cynthia could see Mary had things on her mind, "What are you up to now Mary Connor? You'll see replied Mary, the dinner was cordial it was mainly about how Maggie's children were up too, for Joe it was about the vineyard, Cynthia was getting bored, she butted in. "What about you Kathy", Cynthia said, Kathy looked at Pete, she then started to tell them, how in the New Year they were to adopt a boy and a little girl, aged four and five, whose parents, were junkies and died of an overdose, Kathy went onto say that she was really upset about this, as the authorities wanted to put them in a different orphanage, meaning they would be separated, everyone was listening intently, even the twins.

Had it not been for Joe, it may have never happened, but he vouched for us along with Maggie, the people who run the halfway house also put in a good word, and there you have it, everyone clapped Mary went over and kissed her on her cheek, and whispered I'm so happy for you, you deserve it, and thanks to you Mary as well as Joe and Maggie, the farm is ours, Mary just smiled, and said, don't forget Charles it was his idea, Kathy blushed. Cynthia also was very happy for Kathy she wished her and Pete the best of luck, Jeff shook hands with Pete and congratulated him, Jeff then went over to Kathy and whispered you keep in touch do you hear me, Kathy nodded at him. Mary said it was time for the twins to go to bed, they wanted Auntie Cynthia to put them to bed, which she did, they both said thank you for their lovely presents, Grace was the chatterbox, Charles was really pleased with his cricket bat and ball, they hugged Cynthia so hard, it took her by surprise, "What's all this" she said, Grace blurted, "We are going away to England with Mummy", Charles said, Mummy doesn't know we know, it's supposed to be a secret, Cynthia was speechless, "Then let it be our secret now", and kissed them goodnight.

By the time Cynthia had composed herself, everyone was waiting patiently for her, "Hurry up Cynth", Mary's got something to tell us, Cynthia looked at Mary, Mary knew instantly that she knew, and nodded to her, Mary made her announcement, and everyone was either stunned or shocked.

Mary then looked at Cynthia she came up to her and said to her in a whisper, "Did you know Grace and Charles know", Mary looked at her, "How do they know I was going to tell them tomorrow. "Will you excuse me I have to see the twins", Mary went to their rooms, I need to talk to you both, Charles piped in, "We know Mummy, and "How do you know? Because we've seen books and papers about England and heard you talking to Grandma and Grandad, replied Charles. What do you both think about going to England" asked Mary, the twins thought about it, Charles piped in, it depends where we live", "Why is that" asked Mary, "Grace said I want to live near Oxford so I can go to the University there," I want go to Cambridge said Charles because I want to play cricket at Lords Cricket Ground when I am old enough". Mary got hold of them both and hugged them so tight they could hardy breath, "Thank you", "I love you so much", tears were now trickling down her face, don't cry mummy, the twins said.

Mary told them to come downstairs with her, she didn't need to ask them twice they were off, they bounced into the dining room, Charles announced with great gusto, "We are going to England and I'm going to play at Lord's, "Strewth Charles if you play cricket for anyone it will be at the MCG", everyone laughed, Cynthia then said and what about you Grace, she thought a moment, "I'm going to be a great scholar at Oxford University". Wow! Cynthia said, "Well there's no arguing with that answer", Cynthia was most impressed, Mary had indeed come a long way since she married Charles there was an air about her. Even though everyone was shocked as, they listened to Mary's plans about leaving Australia and living in the Cotswolds in Oxfordshire. Joe was the first to speak, "Well I for one Mary wish you a safe journey and every happiness", Mary smiled at him, Kathy was next crying at the same time, "I'm going to miss you not being here", Mary answered, you have Pete now and this little boy and girl, you have your own life to lead with them", I know said Kathy but somehow it doesn't help.

Maggie was next, she was genuinely upset that Mary returning to England and feared for her, she feared for the twins also, she had read so many stories about how hard it was since the war over there with food shortages, "But Maggie, I have more money than I know what do with, if it doesn't work out I can always come back here, so don't worry about me, said Mary. Cynthia then looked around the table, and thought how well everyone had done, we did ok to think we travelled to the other side of the world each wondering what our destiny would be, well I think we found out one way or another, Jeff stood up "Raise your glasses everyone to Mary good luck and a safe journey, they all raised their glasses and wished, her every happiness.

It was a tearful farewell for all of them, things wouldn't be quite the same, now they all had different avenues to follow, Cynthia was the last to leave, "You better keep in touch Mary Connor, "I will I promise, and I want photos of the twins, "I will I promise," "Don't forget about my brothers in Oldham" said Cynthia, "I won't

I promise", Mary said. Now be off with you, Cynthia Boardman, don't make it any harder for me than it is already", said Mary tears falling from her face, Cynthia hugged her," This is Au-Revoir Mary Conner, Cynthia went out the door deliberately not looking back end of an era, Cynthia said to herself. Mary just closed the door. The only thing left for Mary was to thank Cook and Sara, Nanny Williams had already left Mary's employment as the children were now much older, Mary shouted both Cook and Sara into the lounge, "I just want to say, that I have been very happy with you both over the years, I truly am going to miss you both, then Mary gave them an envelope, and said with my love, by this time Cook and Sara were crying uncontrollably.

CHAPTER THIRTY-TWO

With all the necessary paperwork rubber stamped Mary and her children eventually set sail for England. After six weeks, they finally arrived at Southampton, it wasn't exactly what Mary was expecting, and the twins were very upset. Everything look grim and dirty to them and it was raining and cold, there was also a funny smell, Charles and Grace just looked at each other. Mary could see this, she reassured them that everything would be ok, by the time they reached Oxford, Mary booked a Hotel for a couple of nights to get her bearings, the children seemed happier now. After a couple of days, they eventually came to the village they would live, immediately Charles face lit up he smiled, they had the biggest green he had ever seen, there was even a cricket match going on, I think I'm going to like it here Mummy, Grace never said a word, the jury was out for her, Mary smiled to herself.

Meanwhile at the winery Yardy's wine was developing a reputation for good wine, so good in fact Joe named one of his unique wines after Charles Winfield, a Shiraz, which was Charles's favourite tipple, he called it Winfield's Shiraz. Joe and Maggie were now seeing the vineyard come to fruition after the hard sweat and toll over the years the winery was growing from strength to strength exports of Yardy's wine had now started to sell in England the quantity was small to begin with but Joe was hoping for more to follow, his home market was strong, his Company was in a good position, so he could afford to gamble a little, to be the first grower to export his wine over to England was a feather in his cap, Joe was looking his age Maggie thought, it was all the hard graft over the years. Maggie and Joe's twins, were now nineteen years of age, Mollie was off to teacher training college after the Christmas Holidays, Christine was training to be a nurse at Royal Perth and lived in, Jack was being taught everything about the wine growing business by Joe.

Their youngest Joseph, now sixteen, was the black sheep of the family always in trouble, Joe blamed Maggie, for being too soft with him, they rowed constantly about it, truth was Maggie didn't like the fact that her kids didn't need her as much, they were growing up too fast but now they had their own paths and dreams to follow which Maggie couldn't understand.

It was a Sunday, one of those lovely sunny days, when everyone just lazes around doing nothing, the wine shop was closed as it was early evening, Joe was taking stock with Jack, Mollie was lying on a hammock reading, and Joseph hadn't been seen all day, the Freemantle doctor was drifting lovely warm air through the slight breeze capturing the flowers, and roses, swaying to and fro as if they were dancing. Maggie was in the kitchen, preparing dinner which was almost ready, Mollie went into the kitchen, "That smells good", "Ring the bell Mollie", Mollie rang the bell, and helped mum to put dinner out, Joe and Jack entered, they were as hungry as horses, "No Joseph I see" said Joe, oh' don't go on so Joe, he'll be in he never misses dinner", said Maggie. Time was moving on by this time it was well turned 9.00pm, Joe and Jack had already retired to bed, as they had an early start, so did Maggie for that matter, Mollie suggested she went to bed, but Maggie refused, Mollie then suggested they should ring around to see if Joseph was stopping over with friends.

Maggie thought what a good idea, why didn't I think of that, so Mollie started to ring around, she had only made a couple of telephone calls, when suddenly the door opened, Joe entered staggering, his speech slurring, he was as drunk as a newt. Maggie couldn't believe it, she started to rollick him, he was laughing at her, saying all sorts of nasty things to his Mother, Maggie was upset and crying, Joe suddenly appeared, he caught hold of Joseph and gave him the biggest hiding of his life, Maggie tried to stop Joe. Stay out of this Maggie, this all your fault for being so darn soft with him., Joseph laid motionless on the floor, Joe looked at Maggie, and said, "From tomorrow Joseph will work on the estate like everyone else, and learn the business, do I make myself clear Maggie! He yelled, Maggie nodded, and she was trying to stifle back the tears.

The next day when Joseph woke up, he couldn't move, it felt like a horse had kicked him, he ached from head to toe, he managed to glance at his watch, it was 5.30am, he was just about to turn over best way he could, when wham, he was wrenched out bed by his Father, Joseph wondered what the hell was going on, Joe said, "Get dressed you're working on the estate today with me!" in an aggressive tone, "Joseph said, "Over my dead body", and made his way to the bed, Joe in temper lifted the bed, and yanked Joseph outside, and threw him outside onto the floor, "No work no lodgings take it or leave it!! And shut the door.

Maggie came in from the bathroom, "What's all the commotion", "You might well ask" said Joe, and turned away, Maggie looked at Jack, "It's our Joe, he is refusing to work, so dads tuft him out", "What", screeched Maggie" and headed straight to see were Joseph was, he was cowing as he only had his shorts on, the sun was only just rising, Maggie was about to take him inside, when Joe appeared with clothes for him, and tossed them to Joseph. It took young Joseph a couple of months to finally accept his fate, and work on the estate with his Father and Jack, even Mollie had to help out at the shop and coffee house, when she wasn't studying, eventually the Yardy household returned to normality, Maggie had to accept Joe's wishes, and left the decision making to Joe regarding his sons, Maggie could still be in charge of everything else, plus the shop which was Maggie's pet project she liked meeting people to have a chat it was refreshing to talk to other people on holiday, or from abroad visiting relatives.

The harvest for the grapes was unusually early this year, Joe starts to take on casual labour to help with the bumper harvest young Joseph is to help with the picking, along with Jack and his dad, more provisions for Maggie with more staff to help in the kitchens, Mollie helps out with getting the on the Yardy estate, many of the pickers have been coming for years it's like home from home for many of them. Maggie catches up with all the old timers, they tell her about their families how they are doing some even bring their wives with them, some even have their own trailers, Sunday is a day of rest, then there the usual shindig and of course wine.

Meanwhile in Toodyay Kathy and Pete after various meeting and interviews, were finally able to adopt a little boy called, Tom and a little girl called Jody, it had been quite traumatic for all of them, Tom and Jody especially have found it difficult to settle, they miss their Mum and Dad, Kathy understands this quite well, Pete on the other hand finds it difficult to understand, Kathy explains, it seems the more a parent is distant or unloving the more the child is dependent on them for some reason. If you come from a loving faming like you Pete, you just take everything for granted, if like Tom and Jody they trust no-one except themselves, so they build a barrier around them and the whole world, we have to try and break that barrier down and gain their trust it's not going to be easy, but we have all the time in the world, said Kathy.

Saturday arrived Pete and Kathy were in an excitable mood for his Mum had offered to babysit so they could go to the local dance that night, Pete made it an unwritten law that he would not work on Saturday, unless it was an emergency, so he and Kathy could spend as much time together with the children. The dance didn't start till 9.00pm most of the lads would be in the pub before they eventually drifted over to the dance hall, for their dates, or just looking, the girls would be waiting patiently, like flowers all blooming and waiting eagerly for them to arrive. Kathy thought this was very parochial, Pete of course went into the pub with Kathy, which bemused the lads no end, the ribbing he got made no difference, Pete just ignored them.

While Pete and Kathy were at this particular dance, Kathy learned something about Pete, which he had never spoken to her about or his family for that matter, one of the girls let it slip, the others just glared at her, Kathy was fearing the worst, then one of the girls said,

"I think we should tell Kathy what happened", another said. but if Pete's not mentioned it we shouldn't, another pipped in, "Well I think Kathy should know". Kathy at this point was in a state of trepidation, then Kathy suddenly said, I don't want to know if Pete hasn't told me it is for a good reason, I don't want to hear another word about it", the girls went quite for a while, the ice was broken when the lads arrived. Kathy was distant which Pete noticed, she didn't mean to be, her logic was that she had secrets of her own, she had no intention of asking him, "What's up babe? Asked Pete, "Nothing I was just thinking about the children, "Oh they'll be alright with Ma" replied Pete, Kathy didn't say another word except to make conversation with everyone, she really had come out of her shell.

One of the girls told her boyfriend about the slip up, "Bloody Hell what did she say", "Nothing" she just changed the subject, "Gee what'll a girl", "Why does Pete not want her to know what happened" the girl asked, "I guess he doesn't want it to rear its ugly head again, it was an awful time for him and his family the vendetta by her family was terrible, he probably just wants to forget about the whole episode, now come on let's dance, as he whirled her onto the dance floor.

Sunday was the day his other brothers came over to see Ma and of course Pete and Kathy and now the children, it was always a cordial get together, catching up on what each one was up, for the men it was mainly work, for the women it was mainly about the kids, Kathy never grew tired of Sundays she loved every minute of it, this time though she was going to ask one of her sisters in law to tell her about Pete, she was hoping she would be more forthcoming than his Mum.

Kathy had toyed with the idea to ask Anne, and now it seemed a great opportunity, "Fancy a stroll Anne" asked Kathy, "Good idea let the lads talk amongst themselves," Sylvia are you coming, "No I'll help Ma, said Sylvia, Anne thought it odd as Kathy never did walk unless she had too, "What's up" asked Anne, "Is so obvious" said Kathy, "A little", replied Anne, "I wanted to ask you about Pete and this other girl in his life Elizabeth, Kathy said in an enquiring way, Anne just stared at her. Why don't you ask Pete it would be better coming from him"," I promise on my Mother's grave I won't tell a soul if you tell me" begged Kathy. Anne began to tell Kathy all about it, Pete and Elizabeth were childhood sweethearts, everyone knew that one day they would marry, it was a natural assumption, when they reached the age of consent, they married, both families were delighted, twelve months later Elizabeth was pregnant Pete was overjoyed so was Elizabeth. They made plans to leave Toodyay, to live in the city, as Pete at that time had a good job that paid well, it was a wrench for Elizabeth to leave Toodyay and her family.

Elizabeth eventually agreed to go with Pete to Perth ways, but it only made matters worse, he was worried about the baby and sought advice. The doctor gave her mediation to help then suggested a trip home might just do the trick, so at the weekend Pete drove Elizabeth down to Toodyay to stay with her Mum and Dad for a couple of weeks, this lifted Elizabeth, but her family notice a change in her and were of course worried about their daughter and the baby. Her Mum decided to take Elizabeth to the local Doctor who examined her, that's when they noticed scratches and bruising on her arms and legs, the Doctor was alarmed at this, and asked Elizabeth who had done this to her, she immediately said Pete, (now bearing in mind that she had been staying with her parents for two weeks), her parents immediately jumped to conclusions and thought Pete was a wife beater, this got around the community, it was living hell for Pete and his family.

The families fell out big time, her Mother gradually began to realise that Elizabeth was becoming more aggressive, that in fact she was self-harming herself, Elizabeth's Father would hear none of it, a couple of months later the baby was born, a boy, Pete was over the moon, her Father refused to let Pete see the baby, he was so angry, even the towns folk were beginning to talk and realised it wasn't Pete who had done the things her family were saying.

Then one fateful day Elizabeth's Mother went into her room to check on her and the baby, what she saw was disbelieve, there was Elizabeth holding scissors in her hand stabbing the baby again and again, her Mother went to stop her, Elizabeth stabbed her Mother too, her Father hearing the screams went towards the bedroom and saw Elizabeth standing there covered in blood just staring at her mother. Of course the police came took Elizabeth away, she was diagnosed with schizophrenia, she was put into a mental institution where she remains to this day, "What of her Mother" asked Kathy, "Never got over it", she died three years later, some say of a broken heart, "Now come on they'll wonder where we've got too".

Sylvia greeted them, "Where the hell have you two been Tim Buk Tu", Kathy smiled to herself, it made her think of Cynthia, Kathy never said a word to anyone about what she had heard, in a way, she was really sorry that she had pressed Anne to tell her, "I'll wash up Sylvia" said Kathy, "I'll help too" chipped Anne, they both smiled at one another, Kathy looked across at Pete, their eyes caught each other, Pete just smiled at her, he was happy now with his family.

As they waved goodbye to his brothers and their families, it was time to put their own two children to bed, Pete read them a story, soon they were asleep, Kathy decided to write to Maggie and Cynthia, Pete's Mum had now returned to her own rooms.

Pete went in to see her. "What is it Son" "Nothing I just wanted to see if you were ok, I'm surprised Kathy went that walk with Anne instead of helping you like she usually does", "Now don't go reading into something that is not there Pete Wilson, she's not Elizabeth" his Mother scolded him, "Do not say another word do you hear", Pete nodded and kissed her, then said goodnight. Kathy pondered on what Anne had told her about Pete, she wondered if she should mention it to him, mainly because she wanted to get the monkey off her back with the Edwina episode, lay everything out in the open, she was in quandary. Kathy thought long and hard, then decided she would wait for the time being, and wait for the right time to tell him.

Movement was afoot to change the constitution for Singapore, Jeff was very busy with various consultations, the first Legislative Assembly General Election was to be held, it was known as the Rendel Constitution, the framework of a committee headed by Sir George Rendel. Jeff knew it was only a matter of time before full independence would come, Singapore wanted to break away from Malaysia, Jeff's concern was the communists, there was constant talk of insurgents creating havoc in other parts of Asia, it was a powder keg ready to go off, his concern was for Cynthia, he was forever pestering her to visit Mary and her brothers, Cynthia said she would only visit when Mary was ready to invite her, she wasn't going ad hoc so to speak, this exasperated Jeff.

CHAPTER THIRTY-THREE

The fact was that Cynthia was totally in love with Singapore with all its facets, it inspired her, she had two totally different cultures at hand, she loved to browse her time away in China town, this time in peace, she also loved the English culture, her favourite places being that of Raffles and the Singapore Recreational Club, not forgetting the clubhouse for members only. Little India was another favourite, the riverside with its restaurants and nightlife, their apartment was quite close to Raffles, at night she would just sit out on the veranda with inevitable glass of wine and just while the night away. So saw no reason to uplift herself and travel halfway around the world, when in her eyes she had everything on her doorstep. Mary in fact hadn't written for ages, Cynthia didn't even know if she even went to Oxford, and was waiting for news, Kathy was the only one keeping in touch with Cynthia, even Maggie had not written for ages at this moment in time Maggie too couldn't be bothered to put pen to paper she was in a rut, and still feeling extremely tired. Maggie still couldn't understand why she felt so tired all the time she was beginning to feel her age.

This particular night when Jeff arrived home, Cynthia was jolted out of her melancholy, she could see from Jeff's face that something was up, "What is it" she asked Jeff, "You'll never guess who I've just seen in Raffles as large as life" Who! Cynthia was irritated, "Only bloody Edwina Aston, her real name is Gertrude Steinberg to be precise, Jeff replied, Cynthia got up. "What the hell are you doing" asked Jeff, "Going to Raffles" a row ensued, Jeff was adamant that they wait till he sussed things out, then make their move, Cynthia relented, her vendetta was now greater than ever, Cynthia sat a while and never twigged the fact that Edwina was in fact Aunt Becky's niece. Jeff did his homework, it turned out Edwina was with a Trade Delegate sent by the German Government to look for potential International Markets to export their products, Singapore was an open door to the Eastern Asian Markets in Germany's eyes, the delegates where here on a fact finding tour for a month taking in Malaysia, Burma, Indonesia, as well as other Countries in that region. Time was of the essence, Cynthia was to follow Edwina's movements when not working, Jeff managed to get hold of the itinerary, which helped them in their planning, Jeff too had his motives to see the demise of Edwina Aston, alias Gertrude Steinburg.

Jeff knew it was Edwina Aston who ordered her henchmen to shoot to kill, for Jeff had the proof that he obtained from one of the notebooks, but instead of shooting him they made the mistake and shoot Cynthia instead, Jeff always knew the bullets' were really meant for him, after that Edwina went underground and disappeared completely only for her to resurface now As usual their planning was meticulous, they decided the ideal time was when the delegates had a seven day break in Bangkok Thailand, Jeff saw this as a golden opportunity, he arranged to take a month's leave which was due to him in Phuket, on the Panwa Cape with Cynthia, which is on the east coast of Phuket, at any other time the resort would have been perfect for them both, to just relax and enjoy the beautiful scenery and soak in the local atmosphere, from there they would fly up to Bangkok which would take a couple of hours, then staying as close as possible near to the delegates hotel.

For Jeff having the itinerary helped him enormously to mastermind his plan, during the days sightseeing was in order at night it was free and easy, with Cynthia speaking German, she would be able to pin-point exactly were the delegates would be going to do a spot of sightseeing. The plan was ready, to put into practise. Jeff in disguise, went to the Hotel said he was with the Trade Delegates he wanted to check their security to make sure everything was safe for the delegates to be able to completely relax after a gruelling ten days of no stop meetings, no need for them to worry that's my job Jeff said.

The next move was for Jeff was to visit an old friend for a favour, "Jeff your old scoundrel where have you been? Jeff replied, "Hi Rusty need a favour", "Anything for you mate" said Rusty, Jeff beckoned Rusty outside, Rusty followed him, the sun hit his eyes, "Gee's Jeff it's bloody hot out here", Jeff just laughed, "You're getting soft in your old age", Rusty put his arm around Jeff, "Come on mate what is it? Jeff outlined his plan to Rusty, "No problem mate, I can fix you up with the dope, and the girl anything else," I might need you to get me and Cynth out of Thailand no questions asked, any ideas, Rusty pondered a little, how about letting one of my mates use your tickets back to Singapore, I'll need three hundred for bribes that should fix it, "That's a bit steep Rusty even for you" Jeff said, "Take it or leave it Jeff times are hard", Rusty said he would get in touch in the next 24 hours.

Twenty-four hours had passed when Rusty got in touch with Jeff, Rusty shook Jeff's hand," Look me up if you ever get back to Aus." said Jeff "Rusty then laid out his plan, from here you will go to Vietnam, then onto Hong Kong. When you and Cynthia arrive in Hong Kong go to the Casino, everyone minds their own business in those sort of places, I'll drop you off near the border of Vietnam, a car will be waiting, I've arranged a buddy of mine to fly you to Hong Kong from Vietnam, again incognito, this will cost you another 150 notes, Jeff looked at him, things don't come cheap anymore Jeff, it's dog eat dog out there, the rest is up to you Jeff make it count", Rusty said, "Thanks Rusty I owe you big time", said Jeff, "See you tomorrow then", Jeff waved, his head was now full of what he had to do to settle his score with Edwina Aston once and for all.

Cynthia was patiently waiting for him, Jeff told her of the plan, we need to have everything ready to move out in the morning, he had given their tickets too Rusty, to give to a mate to take their place, no questions asked, when it's over, we will meet up with Rusty, Jeff said, Rusty would find a girl to distract Edwina. Rusty would get us through the borders with no questions asked he had greased

266

their palms, once we reach Hong Kong through the back door so to speak we will dump our disguise's. It was a long and arduous journey, there was a lot of activity in Vietnam with the eminent rise of Communism, in the region as a whole, Jeff and Cynthia had to be extremely careful, by the time they reached Hong Kong they were absolutely exhausted, the journey had taken its toll on them, I'm getting too old for this cloak and dagger stuff now, Cynthia said, Jeff just looked at her. Then Jeff said, I'm running out of cash Cynth, how are you fixed, Cynthia looked into her bag took out her wallet gave Jeff all the cash she had.

They stayed four nights at the Peninsular Hotel to recuperate, Cynthia just loved it there, this is what she was made for a life like this, she said to herself, Jeff was too busy he just scoured the papers, he couldn't see any news about Edwina, he was on edge. Cynthia calmed him down, just be patient Jeff, the plan was perfect. One night they went into the Captains' Bar, and mixed with other guess, then onto the Casino as Rusty had suggested, Cynthia bought clothes with her America Express card, which was more suitable for their surroundings, she looked stunning Jeff thought, to Cynthia it was fascinating just meeting different people from other parts of world, it was funny to Cynthia, but people still detected a slight English accent in her voice, which of course bemused Cynthia, Jeff just smiled, they wanted to be remembered for their charm.

After a few days when they were moving out, Jeff noticed the Times London edition, it was dated yesterday news, he took it with him to peruse while on the plane, Jeff used his diplomatic status again, so they were able to go straight to the departure lounge. Jeff scrutinised the paper, nothing, he was getting agitated about this once more, Cynthia then said to him, "Think about if Jeff, they are not really going to tell the whole world that one of their diplomats, was found dead with an overdose of heroin, and a girl prostitute being seen going into her bedroom late at night, are they". "I suppose you are right Cynth", said Jeff.

They arrived back mid-afternoon, Jeff decided to go into work, he was still inquisitive to find at least something out, he was met with, "Glad your back Jeff, all hell has broken lose here one of the German Delegates, a Gertrude Steinburg, has only topped herself, taking too much heroin, apparently she had a woman friend in her room, known to be a prostitute to boot, the Police are looking for the girl, some hopes of finding her in Bangkok, then he smirked. The boss was pleased to see him, "Blimey Jeff I thought you were going to take things easy, you look shocking", I've just heard about the Delegate overdosing. Yes, sad business that" said his Boss, comes out that she has always had a problem with drugs stems from the war they say, and always had a liking for female company", "How have the Trade Delegate reacted," asked Jeff, "Surprisingly well.

An acquaintance of mine rang me up right out of blue, he's retired now, he was really interested on how you manged to pull it off, and he grinned, "This friend wouldn't be by any chance General Howard would it? Said Jeff, His boss just smiled, by the way Jeff you have been recalled to Sydney," But I like it here can't you fix for me to stay," Jeff pleaded, "It's out my hands Jeff", his boss replied.

When Jeff arrived home, Cynthia was waiting to see if he fancied going out for dinner, then popping in at the recreational club for a night cap, I have been ordered back to Sydney Cynth, Jeff said in a quizzing sort of way, "Do you think they suspect something Jeff, "I don't know that's just it", "When do we leave? Asked Cynthia," Next week", Jeff replied. A week later they were back in Sydney, Jeff left Cynthia to go to headquarters, to see what was cooking, he was to report to a Roger Blake, he was in charge of Counter Intelligence for the Australian Government, Jeff was to take over Counter Intelligence in Perth, to be precise, your orders are in here, Jeff just stood there speechless, he couldn't believe it, he had a week to sort his personal things out, Roger Blake shook hands with Jeff. Well done Jeff you've earned this promotion, you came highly recommended for the job, Jeff just knew that somehow General Howard, had a hand in his promotion and posting. The week went by so quickly, Cynthia stayed in Sydney for another month to settle everything, as there was no saying when they would return to Sydney, the house belonged to the department, it was just a matter of utilities, banks and so on, and of course Cynthia's job. In a way she was pleased about being in Perth, it meant she could keep in touch with girls again, she immediately telephoned Kathy, to tell her the news that she had read in a newspaper in Thailand, about Edwina, she made up a story about her being found dead in a whore house in Thailand.

Kathy was overjoyed to hear this news, Pete came to her, "What is it Kathy? Oh' it's Cynthia she coming over to Perth to live, Cynthia said, "I presume you haven't told Pete about anything, "Nothing" replied Kathy, "Good keep it like that", then Cynthia asked Kathy had she heard from Mary, Kathy replied briefly, just to let us know where she is living, it sounds lovely Cynthia.

"Has Mary been in touch with Maggie? Asked Cynthia, "Just to give her the new address, don't know if Maggie has written back yet" Kathy replied. Kathy then gave Cynthia Mary's address in the Cotswolds, "Does she have a telephone number" asked Cynthia, "I think she does, just a minuet I'll have a look, here it is, Kathy read out the number to Cynthia, "Thanks Kathy, how is the family are Tom and Jody, settling in better now? "Oh much better now Cynthia, in fact they have done well and getting on with the other kids, "I can never repay you Cynthia for what you had done for me over the years, "Cynthia said think nothing of it that's what friends are there for. I'll ring off now Kathy, be in touch when I'm over there", Cynthia then rung off, the next phone call was to Maggie, Cynthia didn't think to look at the time, and the phone rang and rang, then "Hello who is it? "It's me Maggie, Cynthia". "Do you know what time it is over here" yelled Maggie in a grumpy voice, Cynthia replied, I've just spoken with Kathy and she never mentioned anything about time she was just pleased to hear from me!" Cynthia yelled, I'll ring when you're in a better frame of mind Maggie Hughes! Then put the phone down on her. Cynthia was fuming with Maggie, somethings going on over there I can feel it, she never used to be like this she is really grumpy now, she was always the placid one Cynthia said to herself, she made a coffee, looked at the time and tried to workout, the time difference, it was just 12 hours.

Good that makes the timing ok, Cynthia decided to ring, it took ages to get through, finally, a voice said, "Hello", "It's me Mary, Mary yelled is it really you", "Well who would it be, do you know anybody else named Cynthia", Mary laughed, "It's you alright". Cynthia had a really long chat with Mary, they had a lot of catching up to do, Mary warned Cynthia that the phone might just go off without warning, "Still on rations are we? In her cynical voice," Mary ignored her, "It's about time you came over here, take sabbatical stay with us, we'll do Oldham together, we could ask the others if they would like to come over travel is so much easier now so I'm told," Said Mary, "It's tempting Mary I'll think about it" replied Cynthia. Before Cynthia went over to Perth, she flew to Melbourne, to see her Bank Manager, Solicitor, and old man Barstow, she needed to close her account at the bank, and have her assets, sent over to the Commonwealth Bank in Perth, she called into the Solicitors, to see if there had any outstanding debt to pay them.

Her next call was Barstow's, to tell him that she was moving to Perth permanently, when she arrived, she was sorry to hear that old Mr Barstow had died, his son then said, "So you're the mysterious Cynthia Boardman", We all thought you were a figure of my Fathers imagination", and laughed, Cynthia wasn't at all amused, "Well if you manage to run the business like your Father, you will only be half the man he was" Cynthia was seething. "Do I have any outstanding debt!" she said in that withering tone of hers. In fact, her account was clear, said Barstow JR, Cynthia asked him to sell all her properties and to keep in touch with her Solicitor, which he reluctantly said he would do.

Mary had asked Cynthia to pop in to see Eleanor Winfield, to see if she was ok, Charles Father had passed away, her niece and nephew kept a close eye on her, they had been very good with Eleanor over the years. Cynthia did just that and went to see her, Eleanor was delighted to see Cynthia, of all Mary's friends, Cynthia was Eleanor's favourite, she thought the others too dull, Cynthia told her about living in Singapore, they both reminisced about their favourite places to dine, Cynthia said she would keep in touch once she had settled in Perth, Eleanor told her the best places to go once she was in situ.

Cynthia was now flying over to Perth, Jeff would be there to meet her, at the moment he was renting, he was relying on Cynthia to find them a suitable accommodation, he knew Cynthia had high standards in that quarter. Jeff was so pleased to see Cynthia, they drove to Freemantle, Cynthia wasn't that impressed with what she saw on the way to Freemantle, "Your quiet" Jeff said, "Just taking in the scenery Cynthia said in her usual sarcastic way, Jeff just smiled to himself. They reached the flat, Cynthia wasn't impressed with the flat either, Jeff said "No worries Cynthia, I've arranged a week off so we can look for a place here in Freemantle or in Perth, it makes no difference to me, it's up to you, "I just use this flat when I have to stay over, my headquarters are actually in Perth, Cynthia was pleased to hear what Jeff had said, "Well we can see what Freemantle has to offer first", said Cynthia.

CHAPTER THIRTY-FOUR

It took less than a week for them to find the perfect place, Cynthia choose, a lovey four bedroomed house, facing Freemantle Sailing Club, the outlook was perfect, the view was breathtakingly beautiful, especially when the yachts were out sailing on the deep blue water of the sea bobbing up and down like corks floating away, the sunsets, at times were spectacular at dusk, she loved to watch the sun edge away into the abyss. Cynthia also talked Jeff into buying a small apartment on the riverside in Perth, which meant they had the best of both worlds, as Cynthia said, they might as well use the money, and after all they've earned it, and really never had time to spend any.

Having the apartment in Perth was the perfect springboard for Cynthia, she loved Perth it was an up and coming a City of the 1960s, the shopping was great, with many of the big named stores in situ, she loved St George's Terrace, her and Jeff would spend many a night in Northbridge, Jeff sometimes would while his day away at the WACA, to watch his favourite sport cricket, dreaming one day he might see Charles Winfield Jr playing there.

They were content, and finally able to relax, even though Jeff had to work his job it wasn't too taxing for him, the bonus was it was nine to five, unless there was some activity going on such as insurgent's trying to infiltrate into Australia illegitimately which then needed his full attention, otherwise he was able to have time off, they would drive over to freo (Freemantle) most weekends. Again Cynthia just loved to browse, the atmosphere was totally different, it was a kind of an Avant-Garde place so to speak, she loved the local stalls, and the history of the place also the pubs where something else, for Jeff it was the fishing harbour, he could fish all day if Cynthia let him, all in all they were very happy.

Kathy had sent a letter to Mary, telling her about Cynthia, and that Cynthia was going to write to Mary, or telephone her, Kathy also mentioned that Maggie was still in the dumps, and didn't know why, obviously Mary knew about Cynthia being back in Perth. Mary decided to give Maggie a ring, she checked her watch, still time, the phone started to ring, gosh that was quick sometimes I wait ages, Mary said to herself, Joe here, It's Mary Joe, is Maggie there, "I'm afraid she's not Mary she is in Perth Royal with pneumonia, in a bad way I'm afraid, "Sorry to hear that Joe, tell her I rung and hopes she improves keep me in the loop Joe, tell Maggie I was thinking of asking her to come over and stay with me a couple of months, now the children are older," "That sounds a great idea Mary, I'll tell her," when I see her, said Joe, Mary then said "Goodbye."

It was a shock to learn that Maggie was in Royal Perth, and decided to ring Cynthia, the phone rang for ages, at last a voice said "Hello", it was Jeff, Mary here Jeff, just heard about Maggie," Cynthia's at Royal Perth with Kathy, so Joe can have a day off, he looks exhausted Mary" said Jeff, "Is it worth coming over Jeff, Mary asked, Jeff took a while to answer, "She is really in a bad way Mary, but it's up to you, the doctors have said there is nothing more they can do".

"If I decide Jeff to bring the kids, could you look after them, I don't want then to see their Aunt Maggie if it's that bad," Sure, nothing would please me more", Jeff replied, "I'll try to book a flight today," Mary said, "Don't forget Mary it's winter over here, Perth is much warmer than Melbourne, but it gets very cold at night", "If I manage to get a flight Jeff I'll telephone the details to you will you meet us at the airport," asked Mary, Jeff replied, "I certainly will". Mary shouted the children and told them the situation, and asked them if they would like to fly over with her to Perth then later on go to see Grandma in Melbourne, the twins jumped at the chance to return home their eyes lit up like diamonds, Mary hurriedly made plans with cook and her daily, said she would be away for couple of months or so, Grace looked at her, Mummy I need to come back sooner than that, Charles said the same, they were waiting on their results.

"Do you both want to stay here then, I trust you", No! Was the emphatic answer, they said at the same time," We just want a month there that's all". Said Grace. Mary booked an open ended ticket for Grace and Charles, it was no time before they were soaring into the clouds having taken off from Heath Row, Grace and Charles were really excited. Mary realised then that they had missed Australia, "Are you sorry I brought you back to England", Charles said sometimes, we don't like the winters here, and all that snow it's so cold", "You can go back anytime you want, just let me know" Mary said. "Not just yet Mummy I want go to Oxford University, said Grace," And you Charles what do you want to do? Charles studded for some time, "I don't know yet" was Charles answer.

It took the better part of 48 hours to reach Sydney, then they had to catch a flight to Perth, the journey seemed endless, Mary told them it took her seven weeks when she sailed over to Melbourne in 1937, so things have improved, by comparison the trip over to Perth didn't seem to take too long, of course it helps when you travel first class. Jeff was there to meet them, both Grace and Charles were tall for their age, nearly as tall as Jeff, Mary greeted Jeff, "No time to lose Mary she's sinking fast, I just hope you make it", said Jeff, Mary's eyes began to well up, Grace wiped her Mothers tears with her hankie, then put her arms around her. Mary was fighting back the tears as Jeff dropped her off at Royal Perth, she made her way to the ward and entered the room, she saw Joe, acknowledged him, then over to Maggie, took Maggie's hand, "I'm here Maggie", Mary whispered, "Is that really you Mary, Maggie smiled and said, "I'm so sorry Mary", then said "Is Joe here, and the children, "Yes Joe's here and the children" and the four musketeer's, tears were now falling from Mary face, Joe and the children moved closer, Maggie smiled at them and said, look after my babies Joe, then closed her eyes, Maggie never woke up again.

The funeral was a week later, Mary, Cynthia, and Kathy, along with the immediate family, went to the private burial after the service. Joe and his children were absolutely distraught, Joe knew, he now had to take care of his family and the Yardy Estate. Kathy and Pete were the first to leave, said they would keep in touch with Joe and the family, most of the people attending the funeral had quietly left, a few good neighbours stayed on for Joe's sake, soon it was time for Cynthia and Mary and Jeff to leave, it was heart-breaking for the three of them, Cynthia and Jeff said they would keep in touch as much as possible, Mary promised to keep in touch. Cynthia was just relieved it was over for Maggie," She suffered in the end Mary it was for the best", said Cynthia, "I know" replied Mary," It doesn't make it any easier".

They reached Freemantle, well after midnight, Charles and Grace were waiting for them, "You've been gone hours" said Grace, "I know" said Mary, "But we are here now". "How's Uncle Joe" asked Grace, "He's very sad Grace", her mother replied. Charles and Grace left to see their Grandma in Melbourne, Mary gave Charles a letter to give to Eleanor, "Remember Charles I need an answer, don't forget what we talked about, "I won't Mother" Charles was so indignant that his Mother thought he might forget. Mary stayed on, before she too had to leave, she thanked Cynthia and Jeff, for a wonderful time she loved the house in Freemantle, and the apartment in Perth on the Swan River, Mary hadn't realised how much she missed Cynthia, it was just like old times, she wished them every happiness.

I do hope you'll come over sooner rather than later, don't wait too long Cynthia, none of us know just how long we've got. "I promise I won't leave it too long", replied Cynthia, "I'll hold her to that" said Jeff, he kissed Mary goodbye, Cynthia took her to the airport, again it was tears and farewells, each not wanting to let the other go, finally Mary said "I have to leave now Cynthia" and made a dash to the departure lounge, not daring to look back, tears flowing like a waterfall again, "I hate goodbyes" Mary said to herself.

Finally, Mary reached home exhausted, I could sleep for a week, she said to herself, it was mid-afternoon, the twins were out, Mrs brown was pleased to see her, where's Daisy? Mary asked, "She's at the butchers", said Mrs Brown. Mary went upstairs, to rest for a while, she woke up to, "Mummy, Mummy, wake up, Mary slowly opened her eyes, it was Grace, Mary embraced her, gosh I've' missed you both, "So have we" said Grace, "We've lots to tell you", Mary gathered her thoughts, Grace started to tell her everything that had gone on, Mary listened intently, suddenly Charles appeared, Mother it so good to see you. Eventually Mary came downstairs, she had a chat with cook and Daisy, gave them an envelope thanked them for being there for the children, Mary said she would be forever in their debt Mrs Brown said, think nothing of it we have loved every minute.

Dinner was ready, by this time Mary was feeling quite hungry, the conversation turned to Grandma, Charles was eager to tell, Grace butted in, "Don't you think you should ask us about our results, "I'm sorry Grace I plum forgot", Grace gave her a dirty look, Mary thought she's Charles daughter alright. It transpired that Grace and Charles had both been offered a place at Oxford University, but Charles choose Cambridge instead, because they had a better cricket team, Mary laughed, "Well that's a first I'm sure, "Now tell me what Grandma had to say.", "Well?" his mother asked, Charles looked at her, "The answer is yes", Mary let out Yippee! cook came running in whatever's the matter, "It's alright cook, just some good news that's all". Grace looked at her mother, "Oh' its good news Grace, said Mary, Charles is to work for Grandma in the Company when he finishes his studies. Mary looked at her two children she was so proud of them how they had turned out, Charles too would have been so proud of them, Mary then started to reminisce, how did I manage to get here, from my humble beginnings. Mary, was saddened at the loss of Maggie, but she too had left a legacy for her children.

Cynthia was missing Mary so much since she returned to England, and with Maggie gone was feeling rather isolated, with her and Jeff being abroad so long, she really had no friends to call on except Kathy and Pete who she saw on regular basis, but all Kathy talked about was the kids, which wasn't exhilarating at all to Cynthia, but Cynthia loved Kathy dearly, so they kept in touch as often as possible, Kathy had learnt to drive, so that made things a lot easier for Kathy to travel up to Perth. Jeff and Cynthia had the occasional invite to Embassy Balls which Cynthia just loved, Jeff could take it or leave it.

Jeff and Cynthia went to see Joe as often as they could, he was still melancholy at losing Maggie, that's all he talked about, it was beginning to get on Cynthia's nerves, she looked at the kids, they just shrugged their shoulders, as if to say what can we do, Catherine their Aunt was very supportive, but she too was tiring of it all. Suddenly an eruption inside Cynthia got the better of her, "Oh' for goodness sake pull yourself together Joe, think of the kids, Maggie gone and is never coming back, you have a duty to your children now, Maggie will be turning in her grave, seeing you wallowing in self-pity, Jeff interrupted her, "I think you've, said enough Cynth." She carried on "You promised Maggie you would look after them Joe".

CHAPTER THIRTY-FIVE

Joe was furious, he just stared at Cynthia, "I think you should leave" in a very angry voice, "Fine, I will, but it needed to be said," Cynthia too was angry, Catherine then butted in she's right Dad, Grandma just got on with it when Uncle Jack died, and when Grandad died, you have neglected us Dad, we have lost our Mother as well! By this time Catherine was yelling at him and crying at the same time, then Mollie, Jack, and young Joe, even Joe's sister Catherine agreed with the children.

He got up and stormed out of the house, he went towards the family grave, "This is what he does all the time" said Jack, the Estate needs his attention, the workmen are very good, but they need guidance from Dad, Aunt Catherine can't do all the work, it's not fair. Cynthia put her arm around him, "It's hard I know, and if you need us for anything at all just ring us we'll come down right away", with that Cynthia and Jeff left, "Come and stay a while with us, Catherine and you Mollie if you can get away," yelled Cynthia.

Jeff was fuming with Cynthia, they had a spat all the way home, "How could you Cynthia, you don't know how he feels, I have never been so embarrassed in my entire life," Jeff went on and on, Cynthia didn't say a word she just looked out of the window, by the time they reached home, Jeff had cooled down somewhat, he parked the car up and stated to walk, "Where are you going? "For a Bloody drink!! Where do you think I'm going" Jeff retorted? Cynthia went inside sulking, and feeling sorry for herself, you and your big mouth can't keep it shut can you Cynthia bloody Owen. Jeff made his way over to the sailing club to have a quiet drink and to calm down, "Whisky and Dry please" Jeff said, "Let me get that" a voice said, Jeff looked around it was General Peter Howard.

Jeff shook his hand, they chattered away reminiscing about the good old days, which weren't really, it was just a terminology that everyone used, by the way Sir, "Less of the Sir, I'm on civvies street now, bought myself, Condo further down the coast, I come up now and again for the weekend, I love Freemantle it is a fascinating place," said Howard. Jeff said. "I always wanted to ask you a couple of things", "What did you want to know Jeff? Jeff looked at Peter Andrews, "Do you remember Julie Harris? "Of course I remember Julie", "Something always puzzled me with what you said" Jeff said," Howard burst out laughing and said, "I know what you want ask me, I shipped her off of too Moreton in Brisbane", she was well known for getting her hooks into fellas she went out with", and I always knew you were smitten with Cynthia and that she was the right one for you.

Jeff carried on the next question is, "You gave my boss a message in Singapore for me, "It was how did you manage to pull it off". "Jeff, I also knew, that you and Cynthia must have had a hand in Edwina Aston alias Gertrude Steinberg death, I just don't' know how you managed to get away with it, but you did", then he laughed out loud, Jeff just smiled at him, with no explanation whatsoever. They both left to go back to Jeff's house, Jeff stumbled in, "Steady on old chap" said Howard, Jeff put his fingers to his mouth and said shush" it was too late, he had woken Cynthia up, she came downstairs, saying "What the bloody hell are you doing at this time of night", Cynthia was in no mood, Jeff said, "This is General Peter Howard, he saved me from a fate worse than death" It took Jeff all his time to get his words out, "I think it is bed for you" Cynthia said.

Howard apologised to her, "It's my fault, I forgot Jeff is not a drinker", "Pleased to meet Mr Howard," Cynthia said, "Please call me Peter, I think I had better get going now", "You'll do no such thing, I'll make the bed up, you must stay the night, besides Jeff would never forgive me, replied Cynthia. The next morning sure enough Jeff was in no fit state, Howard was bemused by this, "I hope

I haven't caused all this", Cynthia replied, "No we had a terrible row last night he stormed out to the Sailing Club in a temper. "I do hope you'll stay for dinner", Jeff talked about you so much after the war when he worked for you", Howard replied, "He was always my favourite", after that Peter Howard became a regular visitor.

Meanwhile, back in Toodyay, Kathy was in a jubilant mood her and Pete where in Freemantle with the kids, when she suddenly saw someone who resembled her brother Christopher, he looked at lot older than she remembered, but she was sure it was him. At this time the Australian Government along with the blessing of the British Government, introduced the £10 assisted passage to migrate to Australia, which allowed people to stay for two years. Kathy was absolutely sure it was him. Pete said, "Do you really think it is your brother? Kathy said, "I certainly do he might be looking older, and more beef on him, but I would know Christopher anywhere. Pete was about to ask Kathy what was she going to do, when like whippet she was off, Pete couldn't see her anywhere," Where the hell is she? he said to himself, it was always crowded in Freo, (Freemantle) especially at weekends, Pete just hung around not knowing what to do, "Where's Mummy "Jody asked, she just gone shopping, "Can we have an ice cream Daddy", asked Tom, of course you can.

Kathy was scouring the market stalls, she was sure it was him, then she saw him, she hesitated, well here goes, she said to herself, and walked up to him, "Is that you Christopher? he looked and just stared, then said "I can't believe it! Is it really you," Kathy just kept nodding "Yes, it is really me", they hugged one other so tight, everyone started clapping, thinking they were courting and he had just proposed to her, they didn't care, Kathy said, "Come on I want you to meet my family".

Christopher had spent ten years in the Navy, then decided to emigrate to Australia, he was a qualified electrician which held him in good stead, he also mentioned that he had a sister already in Australia, but didn't know where, because they had lost touch with one another during the war, I gave them your details, they eventually told me you lived in Western Australia, a place call Toodyay, which is a funny name, Kathy said, "Well I never, to think they know about me living here", "Talk about big brother sis, it's here", Christopher said. Pete suddenly catches a glimpse of Kathy, over here Tom, Jody, "Well you took some time finding", Pete was not amused by it at all, "Sorry Pete, I would like you to meet my brother Christopher" Pete shook his hand, Kathy said it was you, she was adamant it was you and just took off, left me and the kids high and dry". Kathy and Pete took him back to their place till he found somewhere suitable to live, and more importantly a job.

After many months Christopher ended up staying in Toodyay, he had met a girl called Debbie, they got married, Christopher opened his own business as an electrician, they rented a cottage off an Uncle of Debbie's, he had no children, and looked on Debbie as his daughter, Debbie's family were delighted with the marriage, Kathy was overjoyed, her family was now complete, twelve months later Christopher announced they were to have a child, which was cause for great celebration to both families. Kathy and Pete kept the tea rooms, they rented them out for extra revenue, her brother Christopher replaced all the electrics for her, Pete made some more working units for the kitchen. They still keep in touch with Joe and family, and sometimes keep in touch with Cynthia and Jeff when up in Freemantle, Cynthia is always pleased to see Kathy, they just reminisce about the old days, and absent friends. Mary was so pleased Eleanor could come over to England, despite her age, she looked well, the trip seemed to rejuvenate her, Eleanor had a very long with the twins and what the future might hold for them, they both expressed their opinion's to their Grandma, Eleanor was very upset when she had to leave. (Wondering if she would ever see the twins again).

The twins finally graduated with honours, and now working, Mary knew in her heart that it wouldn't be too long before they would want to return to Australia, she was hoping it would be much later rather than sooner, Mary loved her children dearly, she had a very tight bond with them, and deep down she was heartbroken at the thought.

Cynthia and Jeff finally visited Mary for nine months, it was a belated honeymoon so to speak, Jeff and Cynthia had got hitched, Kathy and Pete stood for them, Catherine and Mollie attended, the others couldn't make it because of work commitments. Jeff and Cynthia had a wonderful time with Mary and the twins, Mary took then all over the place, Jeff, was surprised at the beautiful country side, and how lush and green grass looked, he was amazed by the large oak trees, they were enormous. Jeff thought that large trees only grew in Australia for some reason.

Jeff was awestruck by the two Universities, Oxford and Cambridge, and of course London, (This was nothing new to Cynthia going down to London or the other places they visited for that matter). Jeff's one passion was cricket, Charles arranged for him to watch a Varsity match between Oxford and Cambridge, on this occasion Cambridge won, Charles was man of the match, they also went to Lords Cricket Ground, Jeff was cock- a- hoop. Jeff also thought Scotland was awesome, also the Lake District and the countryside as a whole he didn't realise there was so much open spaces, Cynthia took Jeff to see her brothers, Mary and Grace travelled with them to visit the village of Dob Cross in Oldham, the brothers were overjoyed to see Cynthia they stayed for a for a month, before returning to Oxford, "Try to come over if you can" said Cynthia, they both said they would.

Grace was enthralled with the places she had visited in Oldham where her mother used to live but so much had changed for Mary and Cynthia, they were so disappointed in what they saw, they hardly recognised the place. All too soon it was time for Cynthia and Jeff to leave, Charles and Grace said their goodbyes, and promised to visit them when they are over in Aus., Mary said her Goodbyes, she hugged Cynthia and whispered, "Look after the children for me Cynthia", she looked into Mary's eyes, and a tear trickled down Cynthia face.

"Mary said the children don't know yet". Cynthia just hugged her back," Thank you for being my friend Mary, how long"? Asked Cynthia," Twelve to eighteen months at the most" deep down inside Cynthia was distraught, I promise you I will guard them with my life", tears now flowing, Grace and Charles couldn't understand why, they just looked at one another, and shrugged their shoulders. My turn said Jeff, thanks for a great time Mary, don't leave it too long to come over, I will always remember this holiday, it has opened my eyes, I thought England was just full of little houses and cobbled streets," Mary laughed you've been watching too much Coronation Street, then they set off with Charles and Grace waving and running after them as they drove away. Mary was philosophical about her illness, she was happy and content for first time in her life and was glad she had brought the twins over to England to see their heritage, she was proud of what she had achieved to give the twins the best education they could, indeed the twins had not disappointed her.

Mary died of cancer in 1972, the twins were devastated by their mother's death, Eleanor Winfield sent her most senior advisor over to England to help Charles and Grace manage their estate and affairs. Everyone was so upset to hear of Mary's death, especially Cynthia, Kathy, Jeff, Eleanor was also worried about her grandchildren she knew her dearest friend and advisor would make sure everything would be in order, she was only too pleased to help them any way she could, she was now looking forward to them returning to Australia as soon as possible.

Kathy, was extremely upset, and felt very guilty she hadn't visited Mary in England, but her and Pete were now fostering children, she really didn't have the time, Kathy and Pete's marriage was as strong as ever. Joe gradually pulled himself together and immersed himself into getting the vineyard back on track, Molly got married to a teacher they both teach in Mandurah, Catherine works as a nurse at Royal Perth, and lives in Perth with her partner Matt, the girls visit Jeff and Cynthia as often as they can, Jack got married and lives on the estate to help his father run the vineyards, young Joe went off to flight in Vietnam, happily returning home safely, he really wasn't interested in the vineyard but helped out, he planned something better, the war had opened his eyes to another world.

Kathy had a lengthy conversation with Joe about Cynthia, it took a lot of convincing for him to finally accept that Cynthia was only trying to help him and his family It was Joe who Broke the ice, he rang Jeff, Jeff answered the phone, Joe had a long chat with him, after a lot of persuasion from Jeff, Cynthia gave in and agreed to spend the weekend with Joe and his family again, they now visit as often as they can. It was never quite the same for Cynthia after Mary's death, a part of her died with her, Jeff was worried, he suggested she took up painting again, it was something she had always loved to do. Cynthia just yearned for the twins to return, as they were very special to her, they were the children she never had.

Charles and Grace finally returned to Australia, Grace now teaches at Perth University, Charles went to work for the Winfield Group as he promised his Grandma he would do, when the twins visited her in Melbourne after Auntie Maggie had died, Charles lived with his Grandma till her death, she left everything to the twins, both Charles and Grace were very upset about their Grandma dying, they too had had their fair share of heartbreak. Charles settled in well into his role as chairman, he had a good mentor that Eleanor Winfield had arranged, Charles was always pestering Grace to come over and live in Melbourne, much to Grace's annoyance, for the time being she was quite happy in Perth, she was also very fond of Cynthia and Jeff, so it suited her for the time being, she had also met a fellow professor James Kinsley, that she was quite smitten with.

Jeff and Cynthia were delighted of course, that the twins had returned to live in Australia, the only disappointment for Jeff, was, that Charles never ended up playing cricket, he and Charles would occasionally, meet up to watch the cricket at the WACA, or MCG especially if the Ashes Tests were taking place. As well as cricket, Jeff's other love was fishing when he could, he also liked to do a bit of sailing, sometimes Peter Howard went with him, Cynthia and Grace would meet up regularly, and Grace frequently travelled over to Melbourne to see Charles, in the summer month, Cynthia would sometimes travel over to Melbourne with her to see Charles.

Jeff and Cynthia got an invite to Charles wedding, which was a big affair, he married a girl called Joanna, her family were very wealthy, Charles was tinged with sadness that his, Father and

Mother, and his beloved Grandma Eleanor couldn't share his big day, of course Grace, James and Aunt Kathy attended. Pete of course couldn't make it as usual he always felt awkward around wealthy people especially the Winfield's, Kathy could never understand it, but never chastised Pete about it. Joe and the boys couldn't get away, but Molly and her husband William also Catherine and Matt, Charles was very disappointed that His Uncle Joe couldn't come over with work commitments. It was lovely for Cynthia and Jeff to see everyone there, Maggie and Mary will be looking down on them and smiling, thought Cynthia, the kids had done them proud, and the love they showed Aunt Cynthia, was just too much for her at times.

CHAPTER THIRTY-SIX

Tears started to trickle from her eyes, "What is it Aunt? Grace said, "It's nothing I'm just so happy for you all, Grace just hugged her tightly, we all love you so much. Cynthia was now at peace with herself at last, and took up painting again, she quite often sits on the veranda watching the sunsets, with the inevitable glass of wine and reminiscing, she had only her memories left now in her life, since Jeff passed away peacefully in 1983.

Cynthia missed Jeff terribly, the only consolation for Cynthia was Grace and Catherine visited her as often as they could, also Molly when up in Perth, and of course Kathy, her thoughts used to wonder if it was really worth all the effort, everything seemed so infinitesimal to her now.

After the death of Cynthia, Grace was so upset she decided to move over to Melbourne, to be with her brother, Charles and his family, Charles was absolutely delighted, Grace kept in touch with Aunt Kathy as much as she could, Kathy was never quite the same when Cynthia died, in fact she missed them all. Kathy outlived them all and was extremely happy with her lot, Kathy never questioned Pete on his past, nor did he, she was tempted once or twice. Kathy died peacefully in 2003 aged ninety. Grace and James finally got married, Grace now works with Charles at Winfield's, James got a teaching post as head of the science department at Melbourne University, Grace has a different emphasis on her life now and is really happy, Graces' is the flagship of the Company it also reminds Grace of their past, times were changing and Charles wondered about selling the store as it was running at a loss, but Grace was adamant that they keep the store no matter what, their Mother's and Eleanor's dream was that one day they would work together to forge the company ahead to become a Multi-National Company to leave a legacy for generations to come.

Charles eventually bought out Yardy Wines, as Jack and particularly Joe really didn't want the responsibility that their father had, they thought it put him into an early grave with all the worry of owning a vineyard, Jack still works on the estate, Joe decided to travel and see the world, hopefully to return one day, together with his brother and sister's share a 25% stake in the business, which was a very generous offer from Charles and Grace.

Mary would have been so proud of them. Grace and Charles keep in touch as much as possible with the Yardy's also Jody and Tom, they try to meet as often as they can for old time's sake, they often recall the stories their mother's used to tell them, were also amazed at the stories Aunt Cynthia use to tell them, tales about her and Jeff and the scrapes they got into, to the children it was fascinating listening to her, they were all very proud of what their mother's and Aunt Cynthia had achieved and the life they had led. On one occasion Grace produced a photo album that she patiently had put into chronological order, their cousins were fascinated, seeing their mothers from an early age posing for the photos in funny bathers, sometimes they would fall about laughing at the old photos, each tinged with sadness that they were no longer with them, but knew in their hearts that they were looking down on them and the photo album was something Grace and Charles would keep for posterity.

THE END

Printed in the United States
By Bookmasters